TIMELESS DECISIONS

To: Patricia, my SOROR

Thank you for your

love & support.

Enjoy!!!

Cathy Lynn Estes Davis

7-29-18

TIMELESS DECISIONS

Two Bites Out of an Apple

A woman embarks on a journey through life's circumstances, making decisions that impact her life and the people who love her.

by
Cathy Lynn Estes Davis

LOWBAR
PUBLISHING COMPANY

905 South Douglas Avenue • Nashville, Tennessee 37204
Phone: 615-972-2842
E-mail: Lowbarpublishingcompany@gmail.com
Web site: www.Lowbarbookstore.com

Lowbar Publishing Company
905 S. Douglas Ave.
Nashville, Tennessee 37204
615-972-2842
Lowbarpublishingcompany@gmail.com; www.Lowbarbook-store.com

Editor: Honey B. Higgins
Graphic and Cover Design Artist: Norah S. Branch

Printed in the United States of America
ISBN: 978-0-9969432-5-3

For additional information or to contact the author for work-shops or seminars, please e-mail the author at *cathydavis640@gmail.com*; or the publisher at *Lowbarpublishingcompany@gmail.com*

This book is dedicated to MY family, so that each generation will know the story of their existence and be REMINDED of why you are what you have become. In writing this book, I REFLECT-ED on the journeys of the past and the decisions that led to a family's healing of open wounds.

TABLE OF CONTENTS

Prelude: CELEBRATION OF LIFE ix

Chapters

1   PUSH 1

2   SWEET MILK 9

3   DADDY FREEMAN 19

4   LOVING DEEDS, REFLECTION, AND PLANNING 28

5   VALUABLE MINDS 34

6   FLESH 42

7   GO ON 59

8   WHEELS 63

9   ROOM AND BOARD . . . AND BEAUTY SCHOOL 73

10   THE ART OF SECRECY 97

11   WHAT I DO KNOW 110

12   ANYTHING ELSE? 116

13   THREE BITES OUT OF AN APPLE 120

14   A READY MIND 127

15   CLEAR IN THE MATTER 132

16   TEARS AND FEARS 143

17   WITH YOU 147

18 NO WATER IN THE CLOUDS 162

19 PRUNING THE WINDS 173

20 SECOND AND THIRD 183

21 SWING 190

22 THE MOVE 198

23 WHAT NEXT? 215

Celebration of Life

This day is not just any day. And unlike many, I choose not to celebrate this day with an egg received from a rabbit. (Such an animal does not produce an egg.) Rather, I choose to remember this day as the commemoration of the death, burial, and resurrection of Jesus Christ. Some call this day Easter Sunday. I, however, always call this day Resurrection Sunday. It is the day when Christians celebrate the resurrection of Jesus Christ.

On this particular day, the sun is shining. The weather is mild and beautiful for April. There appears to be one cloud in the sky that is hovering over our church. It is as though my God sent His angels to witness our earthly celebration and to remind us that we, as a family, are covered with His grace, mercy, and love.

Yes, it is now time! As I stand waiting in line to enter our church, Holy Grace Missionary Baptist Church, in Ripley, Tennessee, I see my appointed family members pulling out the casket from the hearse. I see them struggling under the weight of the brown, wooden casket of steel that is housing the body. Our entire family is sullen, waiting for the carriers to bring the casket to the front of the line. We then line up behind the casket, from the closest members of the deceased to the extended family.

The church music starts. It sounds so beautiful. The pastor of the church starts reading Scripture passages from the Bible. We all walk slowly through the church foyer, behind the casket. I notice many of our friends and loved ones in the church sanctuary. This makes me very happy, but I am shedding tears . . . no, I am *sobbing*. I am grateful for all the people who have come from out of town and for those from the area who left their church services early in order to be with my family.

As the congregation stands, we begin to walk down the aisle, finally stopping and passing by the now-open casket. After viewing the body, we move to our seats and sit down—one by one. After all the members of the family are seated, all the other people in the church take their seats. I find myself thinking, "Oh my goodness! Our family is here in front of a casket with one of our own!" The pastor stops reading the Scripture verses. The music stops, I hear the pastor read the order of the "Celebration Service" from the program, and then the "Celebration of Life" service designed to honor our loved one commences.

At this point I am in a daze, partly due to how the past four months have been for me. No one knows just how the events of the previous months have affected me. This death, in particular, made me stop and reflect on the lives of my family members. I start to reminisce on my childhood and think about what I witnessed and heard about our family. I come to realize that this is how we got here, to this place and time in each of our lives.

Chapter One

PUSH

It is the year 1950. I am Ruby—a twenty-five-year-old woman who was born on April 20, 1925, at the County Hospital. I am a graduate of Lauderdale County School, class of 1943. I find myself single and having my first baby on Monday, August 21, 1950. It is about three o'clock in the evening. My pain is not intense like the older folks had said would be the case. I believe God had shown me His mercy and deemed that the child would be a special child.

I am the only one here in the birthing room at the time. The cold air is flowing through my blue gown. I call out for someone to please bring me a warm blanket. No one answers me. I am hungry, weak, and feel like I want to faint. *Why is there no one in here with me?* Finally, the doctor comes in to see me. His name is Old Doc Jones. Colored folks have said that he is about sixty years old. He approaches the foot of my bed, wearing a yellow gown, large glasses, a face mask, and white gloves. A white nurse, approximately forty years old, comes into the room and stands beside Old Doc Jones. She is wearing a yellow gown and white gloves. A young colored girl in blue hospital clothes is at the door, holding a small baby blanket. She looks recognizable, like I know her, but I am too weak and can't clearly visualize her face or recall her name.

The white nurse who is standing beside Old Doc Jones says, "Ruby, the doctor is here and ready. You better push that colored baby out. Push hard, right now." I start to push as hard as I can, but my baby will not come out. I push each time the nurse prompts me to do so, but the baby feels stuck in my belly.

After my several attempts at delivering, Old Doc Jones tells the nurse, "She is not ready to deliver this baby and I will check on her in about two hours." By now, I am not just weak and cold but am feeling like I am going to die as well. I ask the white nurse, "May I have a blanket?" She tells the young colored girl standing at the door, "Get her a blanket and put it on her." The young girl goes and gets a blanket and puts the blanket on me. I begin to feel the warmth of the blanket and try to get comfortable. I think to myself, "I got to be awake when my baby is born!"

While waiting to birth my baby, I begin thinking about my mama, Cheri, and my daddy, Harvey. I wished at least one of them was here with me. In having no one there to help me through this, I stop and think back on my life, wondering how the decisions I have made up until now have led me to this moment.

*****

I think back to when I was five years old. Here is a little background history on my family: My mother was a Cherokee Indian and my daddy a colored man. I look like Momma; we have a similar complexion and similar facial features. My brother, Robert, who was eight years old at the time, is dark like our daddy and has Momma's Native-American hair and facial features. Our momma worked at home, ironing the rich white folks' clothes. The only person they wanted ironing their clothes was OUR mother; they paid her well. Momma and Daddy seemed to be happy together. They didn't argue or fight like what seemed to happen in other families. Momma would say, "Your daddy and I don't fight each other. We get along because we understand each other very well."

Harvey, our daddy, worked at night in the cotton factory. During the day, he worked as a lumberjack, cutting down trees to build homes. He worked on his night job starting at ten o'clock, so he would leave early before nightfall. He walked five miles to get to the factory. He and his colored friends, who worked at the same place, walked together because they did not want to be walking on the road when it was pitch dark outside.

Whenever Daddy left to go to work, Momma finished her chores and then got dressed for her fun night out. I always started to cry—tears running down my face—when Momma began to get dressed. I would say, "Momma, don't leave Robert and me at home.

Please take us with you." Momma would then kiss us both on the cheek and say, "I will be back shortly. Put your sleeping clothes on and go to bed. Don't say anything to your daddy about me leaving you alone at home. If you say anything to him, I will whip you until your skin comes off!"

But Daddy never asked us anything about Momma. Robert and I promised each other that if he did ask us about Momma, we would say, "We don't know." Every night, we would go to bed and talk about what we heard the colored folks say about our momma—how "Cheri" enjoys drinking and going to nightclubs. We heard them talk, but we didn't really understand what they meant.

One morning, after Robert and I woke up, we heard someone crying in the front room. We got up out of our beds and walked to the living room. There, we saw Daddy sitting in his big chair. He looked at us and told us to approach him. When we obeyed his wishes, he told us, "Your momma did not come home last night. Your momma is not ever coming back home again. Someone put poison in her drink. She did not know that the poison was in her drink and she drank it. She died last night."

It was not long after that that we had family and friends coming to our house, bringing us food to eat. A few days after our momma died, we went to church. Robert and I saw her in a box. "Momma, Momma," I said, "Wake up." But, she did not move or say anything back to me. She just slept in that box. We soon left the church and went to another place. Some of the men lifted the box with Momma in it and then placed it down on the ground. The next thing I know, someone was speaking words while standing over the box. Then a lot of men picked up the box with Momma in it and put the box in a huge hole in the ground. They put dirt over the box that Momma lay in.

When all that was done, we went back home and ate the food that was at the house. Robert and I were quiet while we ate. Daddy was quiet, too. When we finished eating, we got ready for bed.

Robert and I got up early the next morning. We got dressed for school. Daddy was already up and dressed for work. I prepared us all some breakfast. There we were, sitting at the dinner table and eating the biscuits and molasses. No one said a word. When Daddy finished eating, he said, "I love you two. Remember to do *your homework and chores when you get home from school." When we got home from school and did as Daddy requested, at 5:30 in the evening he left for work, leaving us home alone.*

After Momma died, the white boss at the cotton factory said, "Harvey, you have children. I'm going to put you on day shift, so you can be at home with your children during the night. I've talked to the white men. They say they like you and won't cause you any problems." Daddy was so happy; he said to his boss, "Yes, sir. Thank you, sir."

When Daddy got home, he told Robert and me the good news. He also said, "I believe the white boss favors me. I do what he tells me without complaining like the other colored folks do behind his back. I hear the boss tell the white men at work, 'All the colored boys, except Harvey, talk about me behind my back and complain about the work I need them to do. I am going to fire all of them, except Harvey. I'll hire other folks to work their shift.'"

One day, a year after Momma had been gone, Robert and I walked home after the school building closed. When we walked into the house, our Drum Mom (others call this certain type of relative their grandmother or something of this kind) was sitting in Daddy's big chair. She was wearing her best dress and shoes. She had a beautiful, fancy hat atop her head, and she was wearing gloves that matched her dress. She said, "Robert and Ruby, come over here." We walked over to the big chair. Next, she said, "Your daddy was chopping down a tree. The tree fell on him. He died right there with the tree on top of him." "Died," I said. "That's the word we heard about our momma. That is not a good word, Drum Mom."

Drum Mom got silent. I let the word "died" sink into my brain. I started screaming. I said, "Momma died. Daddy died!" I began crying, screaming, and running around the room. Robert was silent; he just stood in front of Drum Mom. Drum Mom then said, "Ruby, stop crying. You come here!" I obeyed Drum Mom's commands. She continued, "You two are going to live with me. Your clothes are in those two big, brown bags on the couch. Everything is there, except for the clothes you are going to put on today when you leave this house with me." I looked over and saw the big, brown bags and clothes on the couch. The clothes were our dress-up Sunday clothes. Drum Mom smiled and said to Robert and me, "We are leaving this house in style!"

After Robert and I put on our Sunday clothes, Drum Mom called us to the living room and again said, "We are leaving this house dressed in our best. We will not be coming back here again. Robert, take the bags with your clothes in it. You two go out on the porch and wait for me." Robert and I walked out to the porch and saw a white man standing on the grass in front of the porch. I took a step back and looked inside the house through the screen door. I saw Drum Mom looking around the house. She saw me observing her and then came out of our house. I walked toward Robert. Robert was standing closer to the steps on the porch, facing the white man. Robert, having noticed that Drum Mom was now on the porch, moved to the side so that she had a view of the white man.

When Drum Mom saw the white man, she closed the door to our house and walked over to Robert and me. She said, "Hold your head up and hold hands." She slung her Sunday purse over her left shoulder and grabbed hold of my left hand, and I grasped Robert's left hand. We walked hand in hand down the steps of the porch with our heads held up. We stopped walking when we neared the white man. Drum Mom reached out her left hand and gave him the house key. We then walked away from the house.

Drum Mom said to us, "Remember this day and everything I say. Always walk out of a problem with your head up high so no one thinks they can pull you down. You will slip, but you will not fall. When trouble comes your way, remember someone is always there to hold your hands. Reach out for their hands because one hand is the hand of God, and the other is the hand of your family. You come from a strong family, and nothing will tear this family apart. Remember, you look and wear your best so when the white man or anyone else doesn't see you for who you are, you see you as the best! Watch the road you travel, so at the end of that road, there'll be a highway of plenty opportunities for you to move forward. Most of all, never look back, unless it is for your own good."

Drum Mom started singing a church song. She sang "The Solid Rock." I looked at her happy face while she was singing a song. Robert and I sang with her when she began to sing these lyrics: "On Christ, the solid Rock, I stand: All other ground is sinking sand. All other ground is sinking sand." Drum Mom continued singing the song. Robert and I continued to sing along to the parts we knew. After singing the song, Drum Mom started praying and thanking God for all the many blessings He had bestowed upon our family.

We kept walking as Drum Mom continued to pray and shout. When she stopped praying and shouting, Robert said, "I feel the wind blowing on my back and I hear the wind blowing through the trees. It sounds like an owl. Look, I see a white owl! People say if you see a white owl or hear an owl during daylight, it means you are going to have some good luck." To this, I said, "Well, we already have good luck with our Drum Mom!" Drum Mom said strongly, "That's no owl. What you see is the Spirit of the Lord! What you hear is not the voice of an owl. It is the voice of the Lord! What you feel on your back is not the wind. That's the Lord breathing on us! He is giving us a new life together!"

We finally arrived at Drum Mom's house. Her daughter, known as "Sister," lived with her. Sister met us at the door. She was not married but had a daughter, Lizzie, who was younger than Robert. Sister said, "Come on in. We are so glad you and Robert are here!"

Then, before we knew it, Lizzie and Robert were graduating from the County School. They both got married and left Ripley: Robert and his wife moved to Indiana; Lizzie and her husband moved to Ohio. Sister later left and moved to Ohio with Lizzie.

*****

I stop thinking about the past and start feeling all alone. I hear the door open. Then I see Old Doc Jones and the white nurse walking toward my bed, both wearing a yellow gown and white gloves. They approach the foot of my bed. Old Doc Jones kneels down and says, "Open those legs and push. It's time for you to have this baby." I hear the white nurse who is standing beside him say, "Push, nigger girl, push." I push hard when I hear the white nurse say, "nigger girl." Nothing happens! I push and push so I won't hear her call me "nigger girl" again. Still, nothing happens. Then I push with all the strength I have in me—this time yielding the baby!

I can't see Old Doc Jones holding my baby, but I hear him slap my baby. I don't hear my baby crying. My heart starts to beat fast. Old Doc Jones slaps my baby harder, and, still, I don't hear my baby cry. My heart starts to beat faster, and I feel weak. I try to get out of the bed, but I can't move. I try to talk, but I can't say a word! I try to see my baby, but I can't see my baby!

I hear a third slap, harder than were the other two. My baby is still not crying! I say in my mind, "Lord! Help me. Don't let my baby be dead!" Then, I hear Old Doc Jones say to the white nurse, "This baby won't cry. This baby is looking at me like it wants to hit me back!" They laugh! I calm down. I know my baby is alive! I know I hear Old Doc Jones say that my baby won't cry—that my baby is looking at him and looks like it wants to hit him. My body then begins to relax. My heartbeat slows down, and I feel stronger.

Old Doc Jones then gives my baby to the white nurse. She says from the foot of my bed, "Girl, you got a strong, cotton-picking colored baby." But, she doesn't give me my baby. Instead, she walks toward the door saying, "I'll bring your baby to you after you get settled in your room." Next, Old Doc Jones walks to the door and tells the colored girl, who is standing in the doorway, to get me washed and cleaned. He takes off his yellow gown and white gloves and throws them into the trash can. As he is leaving, he looks at me and says, "Charlie will be coming to take you to your room."

The colored girl comes over to my bed, and I ask her, "What is your name?" She says softly, "My name is Mary Elizabeth. Miss Ruby, you know me. I am Sarah's daughter." To this, I respond, "Oh! Mary Elizabeth, I am so glad you are here . . . somebody I know. Did I have a boy or girl? Old Doc Jones and the white nurse didn't tell me what I had."

Mary Elizabeth says, "I don't have permission from the doctor to talk to you about anything. I know you wouldn't tell anyone on me if I did say something to you, but I still can't say anything to you. The nurse is with your baby. Miss Ruby, I need you to rest while I wash you and put a clean gown on you. Charlie will be here soon to take you to your room."

So, I wait for Charlie to come and get me out of this cold room. I have on a clean blue gown and a blue blanket is covering me. The room is getting colder and colder; the colder it gets, the more restless I become. I start screaming and crying, crying and screaming for my baby, whom they did not let me see. I begin to think, "I know my baby is a boy or a girl, but I don't know which one." I don't know if my baby has ten fingers, ten toes, arms and legs, or if my baby is healthy. That white nurse did not let me see my baby! Is she going to give my baby away? Maybe she isn't going to give my baby away. Maybe she is going to kill my baby! What other reason is there for why she would not let me see and hold my baby?" I begin to scream louder and louder, crying out with every inch of my soul.

Finally, someone comes into my room and rushes over to my bed. It is a colored man in a blue gown; he says, "Ruby, stop crying and screaming. It's Charlie, your cousin. I just saw your son. He is fine, and I'm here to take you to your room. The nurse will bring him to you shortly." Immediately, my mind is at ease—I am calm and at peace because Charlie is with me. He says again, "You have a son. Your son is fine! Don't tell anyone I said anything to you or they will fire me!" I stop crying and screaming and start thanking God for allowing me to have a healthy son.

Charlie then proceeds to push my bed out of the cold room. As we make our way out the door, I raise my head off the bed, look back at the door, and see a sign above the door that reads, "Colored Only." I sigh and think about the words above the door. I think about the words the white nurse says to me: "Nigger girl" and "a strong, cotton-picking colored baby." I begin thinking about the words and names that come out of my mouth for colored folks and white folks. Then I think, "Maybe the white nurse and I are no different, except she's allowed to say things directly to me, but me not to her!"

Charlie pushes my bed down a long hallway that has only a few lights working. We finally reach my room, which is in the basement of the hospital and seems to have a room temperature set to extremely hot. I think to myself, "I have just left a cold room and now I am in a room that feels like a furnace." I see five empty beds; there is a blue curtain that is pulled back, separating each bed. I ask Charlie, "Why am I in the basement of the hospital? Why is it so hot down here?"—to which Charlie replies, "There is another patient next to you. She is in the bed by the door. The white patients and babies stay on the first floor, where it is cool and comfortable. Ruby, don't ask a lot of questions. Don't tell nobody what I said or that I talked to you. I'll get in trouble. Just rest."

When Charlie finishes talking, he gently transfers me to my bed. He says, "The nurse will come here in a little while," then he leaves the room.

Chapter Two

SWEET MILK

A fter Charlie's departure, I fling the thin, blue blanket off my body. It's so hot in this room! I lay my head on the bed and place the pillow over my head and face; I do not want the lady in the next bed to see or hear me cry. I am so tired, weak, and hungry. I am alone without my son's daddy and thinking about the things that had gone wrong between us.

My son's daddy, Dexter, an educated, good-looking, brown-skinned, tall man, hails from a well-known and highly respectable family in this town. Dexter, whom I dated for five years, doesn't want to have anything to do with me and his baby. When I was pregnant, he would say that my baby isn't his baby. How could he treat me that way, and how could he deny his own child? How could he treat me like trash—never saying a word and refusing to see me after I told him that I was having his baby?

After my brief flashback, I hear someone walking down the long hallway. I take the pillow off my face and wipe my tears with the pillowcase. The person opens the door, stops at the bed next to the door, and pulls the blue curtain back. I can see a colored woman's feet in the bed next to mine. I hear noises, but I can't see anyone or anything because the blue curtain is between us. The person then leaves the colored woman's bed and walks out of the room.

A few minutes later, I hear someone walking down the hallway. Someone opens the door and closes it. This time, the person walks toward *my* bed. The person stops walking and my blue curtain is pulled back. I see the white nurse who had assisted Old Doc Jones earlier in my delivery room. She is carrying a small fan. She plugs the fan into the wall outlet and turns it on. The air from the fan feels so good and cool. The white nurse looks at me and says, "I'm bringing the baby to you, so you can feed him. Here is a washcloth. Wash your right breast really good so that the baby won't get sick from you." She stands there, beside my bed, until she knows that my right breast is washed clean. She tells me to put the white cloth in the brown bag she is holding in her hand. Then she says, "Don't touch or breathe on that right breast!"

She then leaves the room and the door closes. I start smiling because, finally, I am going to see my son, hold him, and count his fingers, toes, arms, hands, and feet. I am getting ready to feed my son! I relish in the thought that for the first time in my life, I am truly happy. I just want to shout out loud—shout it to the world! But, I know I can't do that in this place. So, I just keep smiling and, in my thoughts, giving thanks to GOD.

Suddenly, the woman in the next bed pulls the blue curtain all the way back. I see her beautiful face. She is a heavy-set woman with a pretty smile. Like me, she also has her right breast hanging out of her blue gown.

"What's your name?" she asks.

"My name is Ruby," I reply. "Who are you?"

To this, she responds, "Maggie. This is my seventh child. I have four boys and three girls. This last one is a boy. I had him four days ago. Took me only one hour to have him!"

I tell Maggie that I had just given birth to a boy, but the white nurse did not let me see him. I relay that Old Doc Jones slapped him three times, but the baby did not cry; and, that the nurse took my baby and told Mary to take care of me. Maggie asks, "If you didn't see the baby, how do you know it's a boy?" I answer, "Charlie told me." Maggie rises from the bed and looks at me as if she were going to kill me. Her facial expression changes from one belonging to a gentle soul to that of a person who is ready to fight.

With a harsh tone, she says to me, "If you want you and your son to get out of this hospital so you can take him home and let him grow up to be a man, you better not ever mention any colored people's names who work around here! They help us. If the white folks know that, they would kill them and you, too. So, you never call their name even when they take care of you. And as for me and you, we have never talked about this. Do you understand, Ruby?" "Maggie, I understand," I say in a soft voice.

Maggie then continues, "Do what I do and don't ask me why. Then, when you have your next baby, you teach that mother what I am teaching you. Somebody else had to teach me what to do and what not to say! Ruby, pull back your curtain. Here comes Mary Elizabeth. Listen to her footsteps and how she walks down the hallway!"

Mary Elizabeth, the colored girl who cleaned me up, comes into the room and stops at Maggie's bed. Then she comes to my bed and pulls back the curtain. She walks toward the head of my bed and says, "Here is some water, Miss Ruby." She places the cup of water on the table beside my bed. She leaves my bedside, opens and walks through the door, and then shuts it behind her. I hear the sound of Mary's footsteps trail off as she walks down the hallway. Maggie's blue curtain is pulled closed so I no longer can see her. She is quiet, so I know not to say anything else to her. I pull my curtain shut. I lay back on my bed with my head on the thin pillow. The fan is still blowing cool air, so I am very comfortable.

Soon, I hear a noise coming from the hallway. The door to our room opens. Someone enters the room, pushing something. The person pulls back the curtain that is concealing Maggie's area. I hear the person pushing something and hitting their body against the curtain. I can't see anything or tell from the body's hitting the curtain who the person is. The person comes to a halt at the head of Maggie's bed. No one is saying anything. "It is Maggie's husband visiting her," I think to myself. Then I hear a loud voice. "Maggie, wake up!"

I notice that the voice is not that of a man but of a woman. Maggie wakes up because the woman says, "Take this baby and feed her." "*Her,*" I thought. Maggie had told me that she had a boy five days ago, and now here she is, feeding her daughter. Oh my goodness! No one, not Old Doc Jones, not the white nurse, nor any of the colored workers, was able to convince Maggie that she had birthed a girl and not a boy. Wow! Maggie claims to have had a boy because she must want a boy!

When the nurse leaves, I don't hear her pushing anything out of the room. Maggie is not talking, but I can hear her moving around in her bed. I start smiling and grinning from ear to ear thinking about me and my son. *"The nurse is going to bring my baby to me! I am going to see my son, my very own son, for the first time. I will get to hold and feed him. I will hold him so tightly and by this, he will know how much his momma loves him."*

The door opens again, and I can tell that the nurse is pushing something small. I am so excited that I am beside myself! Then my curtain is pulled back. The white nurse has the baby in a beautiful little bed. I can't see his face, but I see he has a tiny white cap on his head. He is covered in a multicolored blanket. I see the blue, pink, white, green, and yellow in the blanket. The white nurse picks up the baby from out of his little bed. I still can't see his face! The nurse then hands me my baby.

I pull the blanket off his face, and when I look at him I start shaking. I look at the white nurse and say to her, "This is not my baby! This baby is white!"

She says to me," It's a white baby boy, and don't you open his blanket to see his body. Doc Jones wants you to feed this boy. He says you will have strong colored babies, and he wants this white baby boy to be strong, too. Your boy didn't cry when Doc Jones slapped him three times. Doc Jones looked at your boy's eyes and your boy's eyes looked like he wanted to hit Doc Jones. Now, you feed this precious white boy on your right breast. That's the breast you cleaned. Don't feed this boy with your left breast. That left breast is only for your colored boy. When you finish feeding this baby, I will bring your boy to you. You won't see your boy until this white baby boy is full. Let me see you put the boy to your right breast and feed him."

I put the white baby boy to my right breast. He starts suckling on my breast. After the white nurse sees the white baby boy sucking my right breast, she pulls the curtain back and leaves the room. After the door closes, Maggie pulls back her curtain. I see her face and a white baby suckling at *her* right breast. She says to me, "Ruby, let me know when your breast is half-full. I hear someone walking down the hall. Don't say anything." Maggie quickly pulls the curtain closed, so that I can't see her or the baby sucking her breast.

I can hear someone walking down the hallway yet again. It sounds like Mary Elizabeth. She opens the door. She pulls back the curtain to Maggie's bed and walks to the head of her bed. I hear her put something down onto Maggie's table. She leaves Maggie's bedside, pulls the curtain shut, and then walks to the foot of my bed. Mary Elizabeth pulls open the curtain and walks to the head of my bed. She says, "Here is your sugar." She places the sugar on the small table beside my bed. She gives me an angry look and then walks away from me. She pulls the blue curtain all around my area and leaves.

I hear the sound of Mary Elizabeth's footsteps get faint as she walks down the hallway. After the footsteps trail off completely, Maggie pulls back her blue curtain. I pull back my curtain to see Maggie sitting up in bed while the baby girl is sucking on her right breast.

Maggie says, "Feed that boy. Your breast is not in his mouth. Put your breast in his mouth! The nurse will know if you didn't feed that boy. Let me know when your breast is half-full. Listen, Ruby, I teach you so that you will teach other colored girls." I nod my head to let Maggie know that I understand what she is telling me.

When I feel like my breast is half-full, I say, "Maggie, my breast is half-full." Maggie pulls back her curtain, and I do the same. Maggie says, "So is mine. Lay the baby down on the bed like me. Put a little sugar in that cup of water that Mary Elizabeth brought you. Just a little. Stir that sugar in the cup of water good. Now, take that cup, just like me, and dip your nipple in the sugar water. Get your nipple real wet. Pick up the boy up off the bed and put your breast in his mouth." I do as Maggie instructs me to do.

Maggie says, "Girl! Look how he sucks your breast. White babies love to suck on a colored woman's breast! Now, in the hospital, the white nurse brings us the white babies, so they can suck the milk from our breasts before our own babies suck our milk. The white woman feels she is too beautiful to feed her own child. She wants to keep her breasts looking young for her husband. So, she doesn't let her own baby suck from them. That's why colored girls' breasts are long, and some have them hanging down their chests. But we give their baby life, the milk made from our own bodies.

"See how that boy already looks at you. He is happy and when he sees your breast, he wants your milk! Love him! Love feeding him! You are the only one keeping him alive. Without you and your milk, he may not live. Now, when he leaves the hospital and grows up, he will not remember you as the colored woman whose breast gave him his milk to live. He will not remember you as a human being, a person, nor will he speak to you when he passes you on the streets. His own mother will not want to remember or know anything about you. They will remember you no more.

"The white woman wants the colored girl's right breast to feed her baby. Your own child can't suck on the same breast that their baby sucks. But, oh! That left breast is for your child. That's where the heart is. When you hold your child to your left breast, he hears and feels your heart beating. His heart beats because your heart beats. Everything you have in your heart, and all that blood going through your body from your heart, is life. Yes, let the white woman have the right breast. They say if you white, you are right. I say if you are colored, you want to go to your momma's left breast so that you will be strong and know your momma's heart.

"See, this girl and that boy you are holding are full. You still have milk in your right breast. Those babies will sleep through the night. Try to make him burp up that air. Put him over your shoulder like this and gently tap his back." Maggie proceeds to demonstrate her instructions to me. "Keep doing this until he burps," she says, burping the baby. "Good, he burps. Put him back in his bed on this right side. Now, drink the rest of the water and sugar before the white nurse comes back in here!"

I do exactly what Maggie says to do. And though I am sleepy and want to fall asleep, I can't. Soon, as before, I hear footsteps coming down the hall. Maggie also hears the footsteps. She says to me through the closed curtain, "Here comes the nurse! She is coming to get the white babies. Don't say anything."

The door opens, and the white nurse says, "I am here to get these precious babies. Have you fed them? Are they full?" Maggie says, "Yes, they are full." I hear some noise and movement made by Maggie and the nurse. Then the nurse puts the baby girl into her beautiful little bed.

The nurse draws back my curtain and walks to the head of my bed. She looks at the baby boy, picks him up, and says, "He looks well fed and sleepy. Colored girls know how to feed babies!" Then the nurse pulls my gown from my chest. She puts my right breast in her hand and squeezes my breast. She says, "You still got some milk in that breast! Doc Jones is right about you. He says you're going to have strong babies!" She puts the white baby boy in his beautiful baby bed as well and says, "I will bring your baby to you in a few minutes." She pushes both baby beds to the door and leaves the room, with the babies in tow. Maggie and I hear the nurse and the beds travel halfway down the long hallway, then the sounds of movement stop.

Although I am hungry at this point, I am excited and start to smile because I am FINALLY going to see my son! Maggie and I aren't saying anything to each other now. I know we are both anxious to hold our sons. I hear Mary Elizabeth's footsteps in the hallway, so I sit up in my bed—but I don't hear Maggie moving. Then the door opens. It is Mary Elizabeth. She goes to Maggie's bed and pulls back her curtain. I hear a noise, but I don't know what she is doing. She pulls Maggie's curtain back into place. She pulls back my curtain. I see her with a fan in her hands. She puts the fan on the floor beside my bed, stands up, and then unplugs my fan from the electricity. She says, "The nurse is on her way." She picks up the other fan from the floor. With both fans in hand, she closes my curtain and leaves our room. I hear her walk down the hallway.

It is hot in our room; I can feel the heat. I hear Maggie moving in her bed. I don't say a word to Maggie. Sweat starts rolling down my face. I ponder to myself, "Why did Mary Elizabeth take our fans away from us? Why does my baby have to be fed in a hot room? I am sweating all over my body, and my breast is wet." I start frowning and getting angry. I look on top of the stand beside my bed. Mary Elizabeth has left me with a washcloth and a cup of cold water. First, I wash the sweat off my left breast. Next, I wash my face, leaving the cold water on it so that the white nurse will see that I am sweating. I put the wet cloth in my pillowcase and turn the pillow over.

Almost instinctively, I hear the nurse's footsteps in the hallway. I hear her pushing an object with wheels. I hear three wheels rolling and squeaking. The other wheel sounds like it is scratching the floor as the object is moving. I hear Maggie sit up in the bed. She says, "It's time to feed *our* babies!"

The nurse opens the door, pulls the object on wheels in first, and then follows behind it. The object stops at the foot of Maggie's bed. The nurse pulls back Maggie's curtain and gets something off of it. She starts coughing and clearing her throat with something in her hand. She moves toward the head of Maggie's bed. I hear a noise at

Maggie's bed, but I don't know what the noise is. Oh! I think she is giving Maggie her baby boy. She leaves Maggie's bedside, closing her curtain.

The white nurse then pulls back my curtain. What I see in that moment makes me want to cry! I do not see a beautiful baby bed with a thin mattress. Instead, I see an old, ragged, dirty cart! On top of this raggedy old cart is a brown drawer in which to store clothes. The white nurse picks up the brown drawer and starts coughing and clearing her throat. She brings the brown drawer toward me. She puts the brown drawer on top of the stand next to my bed, then says, "Get up out of bed, get your son, and feed him. I will be back soon." The next thing I know, the nurse is departing once more.

I sit up in bed and move my body toward the stand now situated beside my bed. I make it over to my son, who is on the brown drawer with a thin blue sheet under him. There is no mattress in the drawer, and my son is not wrapped in a blanket. He is not wearing anything except a white cloth diaper that is inside of his blue plastic baby panties. The diaper is held together with two huge pins, one on each side. He is hot and sweating.

I hold back my tears because I don't want my son to remember that his mother cried when she first looked at, held, and fed him. I take my son out of the brown drawer and hold him in my arms. I look at my son's body; he has dark hair and his eyes are closed. I count his arms, legs, fingers, and toes. I see no missing parts on his body. I look at him for a long time, and he doesn't cry! I hold him close to my chest and say, "Momma loves you! Momma loves you!" He opens his eyes and begins to smile. His eyes are dark brown.

I say, "My son, please cry or say something to your momma. I need to know that you can make a sound from your mouth." He starts crying. The cry from his mouth is sweet music to my ears! I say, "You're crying because you are hungry. Momma's going to feed her precious baby." I put my left breast into his mouth and my son starts suckling my left breast. I feel and hear his heart beating against my chest. His heartbeats are faster than mine. I can hear us making a song with our hearts. It is beautiful music! I say to my son, "Suck all the milk you want. My milk gives life and all the strong blood you need to grow and become a strong man."

After nursing him until he is full of my milk, I place my son over my left shoulder and pat his back; he burps. I put him on my chest and rock him to sleep. I hear the nurse walking and pushing that old, ragged, dirty cart up the hallway. The door opens yet again, with the cart pushed in first. The nurse says, "I'm here to pick up your boys and take them back to the colored nursery." Maggie gets up from the bed and puts her son into the drawer.

I get up and put my son down at the foot of the bed. I get my pillow and pull my sheet off my bed, wrapping the sheet around my pillow. Then I put it down into the drawer. I pick up my son from the foot of the bed and place him on top of the wrapped pillow in the drawer. The white nurse shouts, "What are you doing?"

I calmly say, "Doc Jones says I have a strong son and he wants me to feed the white baby boy, so he'll be strong. This boy carries my seed and his wife will be strong to help the other white boys born in their day. What are we going to tell Doc Jones if this boy hurts his back and gets weak from being on a hard drawer?" The white nurse says, "Okay. We'll keep him strong for Doc Jones, but you'll have to sleep without a pillow and sheet." The nurse walks to the foot of my bed, picks up the drawer with my son in it, and carefully puts the drawer on the cart. She opens the door and leaves our room with that old raggedy cart. We hear her footsteps and the cart moving down the hallway.

Maggie says, "Ruby, you handled that situation really good. I like the answers you gave her." I say, "My son deserves better than an empty drawer! I only use what they say to me so that I get what I want for my son." Maggie says, "You're good. I'll have to try that if I have another baby in this hospital."

The next morning, the white nurse wakes up Maggie and myself from our sleep. She says, "It is time to feed the precious white baby girl and boy." Maggie and I then proceed to wash our right breasts. Maggie breastfeeds the white baby girl. I breastfeed the white baby boy. We do the same sweet-milk feeding that we did yesterday. The white babies leave us, and the nurse brings our sons to us. We feed our sons and they leave us. Mary Elizabeth brings us something to eat. We eat and sleep, and then engage in the same routine all over again.

Each day, the nurse draws our blood for different tests. We breastfeed the white babies with sweet milk three times a day. We feed our sons from the left breast four times a day. One time, having brought our sons to us, the white nurse asks, "Why is it that the colored babies have feedings more times than the white babies?" Maggie says, "We have to feed our babies more times because the white babies suck out a lot of our milk before we can feed our own."

On my third day in the hospital, we feed the white babies and our sons in the morning. The white nurse says, "This precious baby girl and boy are going home with their mother after you feed them. There are no more white babies in the hospital. Maggie, you are going home today. Doc Jones will come by and check you before you leave." As expected, the white nurse leaves the room.

"Who feeds the white baby when the white woman goes home?" I ask. Maggie says, "She has a wet nurse." "What is a wet nurse?" I inquire of Maggie, to which she replies, "A wet nurse is a colored girl who has a baby and is still breastfeeding her child. She hires the colored woman because she is cheaper to hire than a house cleaner. The colored woman lives in their house, feeds the baby, and if there are other children, she takes care of them. She also cleans the house. The white folks pay her little money because they let her live in their home and because they feed her."

After our talk, Old Doc Jones comes to see Maggie. He asks, "Are you ready to go home?" Maggie says, "Yes, sir." He then says, "You can go home." Then Old Doc Jones leaves the room.

Mary Elizabeth comes to our room with Maggie's son. She gives the baby to Maggie. Mary Elizabeth says, "Maggie, I sent Charlie to get your husband and tell him you're ready to go home. Get your things ready to leave. Charlie said it will take him about two hours to get back to the hospital with your husband." Mary Elizabeth exits our presence. Then Maggie promptly puts her son on the bed and starts getting ready to go home.

Soon, Maggie's husband comes and is ready to take her and the baby home. It is about four o'clock in the evening. Maggie and I say goodbye to each other. I am happy for Maggie. She has a husband and children. She has a real family, and the children have a momma *and* a daddy.

I am also happy for me! I don't have to feed any more of the white folks' babies. I am just hoping that for the next four days, no white women come here with babies that I have to feed. For now, it's me and my son; this is our moment and our time together!

Chapter Three

DADDY FREEMAN

It is now my fifth day in the hospital. On this day, someone comes into my room and tries to wake me from my slumber. I open my eyes and look up at her. She is not Mary Elizabeth; she is someone I haven't seen before today. She is a very young, colored girl who is about sixteen years old. She says, "Breakfast is here." The young girl then puts my breakfast on the table and starts to leave. I say, "Who are you? What is your name?" "I'm sorry. My name is Sue," she replies. I say, "Well, Sue, my name is Miss Ruby. I'm in this room all by myself. If you have time when you come to my room, it's all right for you to speak and talk to me. I won't say anything to anyone about you talking to me." Sue smiles and says, "Yes, Miss Ruby," then she leaves the room.

As I start to eat my breakfast in bed, I hear a knock at the door. I say, "You can come in." A man walks into the room. I say, "Mr. Freeman, I am so glad to see you! Please sit in this chair beside my bed." He sits down in the chair and says, "I am happy to see you, Ruby. Go on and eat your breakfast." I unwrap the plastic from my plate. For my dining pleasure, I have eggs, two slices of toast, and a carton of milk. I am so hungry. Just before I take a bite of food, Mr. Freeman says in his deep voice, "Are you going to pray over your food?" To this, I say, "Yes, sir." I pray over the food and start eating. While I am eating, Mr. Freeman is silent and keeps looking at me. After I am done, he says, "Do you need more to eat? If you do, I will go and get more food for you." I say, "No. I am fine, thank you."

Mr. Freeman then says, "I have a fan for you." He takes the fan out of a new, sealed box and plugs the cord into the electrical outlet. He turns the fan on and asks, "Ruby, are you getting cool?" I say, "Yes, sir. Thank you. The fan feels so good in here." "I want you and your son to be comfortable while you are in this hospital," Mr. Freeman comments.

"I just saw the boy. He is a happy, good-looking boy," he continues. "He smiles a lot. What is his name?" "His name is Winston," I respond. "That's a good, strong name," he replies, then asks, "On Winston's birth certificate, whose name are you going to write down as his father?" As I ponder this question, I can feel Mr. Freeman looking at me. I say," I am not going to write down a name for Winston's father."

Mr. Freeman says, "Ruby, for Winston's sake, write my son's name as his father on his birth certificate. I know my son (Dexter) says for you to not write his name on the birth certificate because he believes your child isn't his child. But this boy is very special! This boy is fatherless, and he needs an identity. As for you, you are a single mother with a child. If you don't put a name down, you are saying you are a fast woman or that you don't want anyone to know that the father may be a white man. We all know you and Dexter were together for years. You don't have to tell Dexter that you put his name as the father on Winston's birth certificate. When the time is right for Dexter, I will tell him what I told you to do. People think that Dexter is the father, even if he says differently. This is just the proper thing to do.

"Ruby, you know Dexter is living in Denver. Yesterday, I talked with him on the telephone and told him that he is the father of a son. Dexter said he won't have anything to do with this boy. However, I will. I will love him and help you take care of him like he is my own. I am his Daddy Freeman and he will not ever have to need for anything. In this town, people, both colored and white, respect me and my name. We are a safe family because of this respect. Your son, Winston, has something that's special from me, and that is my blood. For that reason alone, Winston shall call me 'Daddy Freeman.'"

*****

Mr. Freeman owns his house, paid in full. He lives beside Drum Mom on Barbee Street, which is in one of the best colored neighborhoods. His house has a big living room, a dining room, three large bedrooms, one toilet room with a bathtub, a kitchen, and a quiet room. The house has running water and its own electricity. Mr. Freeman also has a driveway for his 1950 black Ford Sedan. And at a time when hardly anyone owns his or her own telephone, he owns a telephone with a hand piece you hold up to your ear. Mr. Freeman is proud to have two telephones—one at his house and one at the place where he runs his own business.

Mr. Freeman is a very quiet man, and people in the community respect him. He is an educated, good-looking man who is more than fifty years old. He stands over six feet tall. His first wife, Alice, died from pneumonia. She bore him five children. After Alice died, he took another wife, named Lydia. (She was a teacher who ended up leaving him. They had no children together.)

Whenever Mr. Freeman ventures out in public, he always wears a matching suit and tie, except for when he is at work. He is a barber and is the only colored person in downtown Ripley who has his own building. His building is on the corner of Main Street. He rents out about ten rooms on the second floor of his building. The first floor is where he has his own barber shop and rents out spaces for other colored barbers. When he cuts colored men's hair, he wears black pants and a nice shirt. This is the only time you don't see him in a suit and tie.

The building that Mr. Freeman owns and works in is located in the town square. Now, to put this in context, the courthouse is in the middle of the square. Inside the courthouse are county offices and a jail. People who are in jail or who receive notice to appear before a white judge go to the courthouse. Most of the people who are in jail and go before the judge are colored people. They usually end up staying locked up at the courthouse.

Across from the courthouse, on the other side of the street, are a repair shop, a pharmacy store, a grocery store, women's and men's clothing stores, two banks, a tire store, a church that white folks attend, an insurance company building, a jewelry store, an ice cream and sandwich shop, furniture stores, and a movie theater. (Here is an interesting aside: Inside the movie theater, white people sit on the main floor and colored people sit in the balcony. Colored people have the best seats! We look down at the white folks sitting on the main floor and spit saliva on them as they walk out of the movie theater.)

*****

Soon after Mr. Freeman got ownership of his building, several white people became so angry that a colored man owned property—especially in the town square—that they began talking among themselves about how they were going to take the building away from him. The week that the town's sheriff, Mr. Taylor, heard about their conversations, he sent word for the men to meet him in the courthouse that Sunday after the worship service.

Those same white men went to the courthouse after church service to meet with Sheriff Taylor. "Men, I know what you have been saying and are planning on doing to Freeman's building," Sheriff Taylor said. "So, I must meet with you to tell you what I know about this situation.

"We all know Mr. Knowles, the richest lawyer, from Tipton County. One day, he comes to Ripley and I see him talking to Freeman in one of our stores. They are talking and smiling at each other. Freeman looks directly in his eyes when he is talking to him. They leave the store and I follow behind them. Mr. Knowles gets in his car and leaves. Freeman starts walking and I stop him. I ask, 'Freeman, what were you and Mr. Knowles talking about?' Freeman says, 'Mr. Knowles just needs someone to talk to.' I said, 'okay.'

"What happens next with shock the hell out of you!" Sheriff Taylor continued. "I heard after Mr. Knowles gets home, he starts thinking about Freeman. He decides that he wants to do something nice for him and sends word, by a white man, for him to go and visit him in his home. A few days later, Freeman drives to Tipton County and visits with Mr. Knowles in his home. They talk, and finally, Mr. Knowles tells Freeman why he wanted him to come to this house.

"He says to Freeman, 'A man is more respected when he is protected and owns land and his home. I am selling my building in downtown Ripley. I want to help you and let you buy that building from me for five dollars.' Freeman shouts, 'You want me to buy that building in downtown Ripley from you for just five dollars!' Mr. Knowles says, 'Yes, five dollars. Do you have that kind of money on you today?' Freeman says, 'Yes, sir, I do.'

"Freeman puts one hand in his pocket and pulls out his wallet. He counts out five dollars and hands it to Mr. Knowles. Mr. Knowles puts the money on the table and walks to another room in the house.

He returns with papers in his hands and sits down beside Freeman. He hands Freeman some papers and says, 'These papers will give you ownership of the building that you paid to own. I know there is a silent law in Ripley that white people go by where[as] no colored person is to own any real estate, especially downtown. But you now own a building, a building in downtown Ripley. These are the papers that show you are the sole owner of that building. You must keep this paper in a safe place. Here is the insurance paper on the building. Just in case any of the white people try to burn down your building, this insurance will cover the building and make you a richer man. I need you to sign your name on these papers and I will take care of everything else for you.' Freeman signs the papers."

Sheriff Taylor continued his spiel: "About a month later, Mr. Knowles and Freeman meet again. He gives Freeman some papers to give to his family. The papers include the deed, the stamp for payment in full, a notary signature, and Freeman's relatives' names. Freeman's relatives' names are on the deed. In case there is damage or fire to his building, or if Freeman dies unexpectedly or by natural causes, his kinfolks will get the insurance money to rebuild on that lot.

"The papers also include the name of a federal judge in Nashville who has copies of the papers from Mr. Knowles, the notary date, a signature, and the court filing number. There are many kinfolks' names written down on the papers ensuring that Freeman and his family will always own that two-story building. Men, be reasonable. This is a battle that you will not win if you do harm to Freeman, his kinfolks, or that building." After Sheriff Taylor finished talking, the men left the courthouse.

*****

Shortly after Mr. Freeman started his business, colored folks started renting buildings for their business off downtown Main Street, a location called "The Hole." In "The Hole," there are about twenty buildings attached to each other—forming a "U" shape from the entrance to the exit of the street. Folks rent their buildings from a white man. On the first of the month, the white man makes his way down "The Hole," from building to building, and collects his rent money from the colored business owners and from the folks who live upstairs in his living quarters. Colored people, like Cousin John, who rent space at the entrance of "The Hole," cook and sell good food, allow dancing, and allow folks to play cards and buy liquor. On the upper level, where people rent rooms, is a barber shop and a beauty salon business. After you pass by all the businesses and before you exit "The Hole," there is a white folks' church facing Main Street, with the back of the church facing "The Hole."

"The Hole" is an important place for colored folks living in the town. On special holidays, it is the one place where people go to see family and friends.

On Labor Day Weekend, those who were born in the county yet departed to live in the city come back home to visit their families. At night, they go to "The Hole," dressed in their finest clothes. They show us how well they are doing in the city. For colored folks still living in Ripley, these days are the few days when we really feel free. We own the town! White folks living in town don't shop or aren't seen in town. They are nowhere to be found. Only white store owners are seen, making as much money as they can from us. I often wonder where the other white folks go when hundreds of colored people are in town!

And no matter how late colored folks stay out on Saturday night of the Labor Day Weekend, they are in church on Sunday mornings. One by one, each person states his or her name, where he or she lives, what church he or she attends, and who his or her relatives are that attend the church. While this is a long process, it is fine because people want to know who has come back home.

On Labor Day Monday, we have our Labor Day Parade. The parade starts at Lauderdale County School on Spring Street. Leading the parade is the red fire truck. Someone in the truck blows the horn to let everyone know to get in line—because the parade is on the move! Behind the red fire truck is a car toting the Grand Marshall of the parade. That person is always someone who is from Ripley and either is currently living in or has left Ripley and is contributing to the community. Behind the Grand Marshall are colored girls in beautiful outfits, all of whom are twirling a baton. The Lauderdale County School colored bands are next in line, followed by paper flower floats, cars, and trucks. Bringing up the rear of the parade are the beautiful, high-stepping horses.

The people in the parade start moving and arrive at the entrance of Main Street. Hundreds of colored people stand in front of

Freeman's building, around the square, on the sidewalks, and on the yard of the courthouse. The red fire truck and parade pass by Free- man's place and move slowly around the square. In front of several stores around the square, the parade stops. The baton-twirling col- ored girls dance, while the bands play music. When they finish, the parade moves on to its next stop around the square, where colored girls dance and the bands perform again.

After the parade leaves from the town square, people follow the parade until they arrive at Rice Park. At the park, people sell and buy food, and children play on the seesaw, swing, slide, and merry- go-round. In the middle of the park, the men play baseball. People cheer for their team. Labor Day Weekend and Labor Day are the happiest days for colored people in Ripley. Friday, Saturday, Sunday, and Monday are our days!

On Monday, after having enjoyed the parade and spending time at the park, kinfolks leave to return home. They leave behind joy, love, and happiness. For those of us left behind, on Tuesday (the next day), everything will be back to how it always is in Ripley. White folks will be seen in their places of honor, and we, the colored folks, will "know our place."

*****

After thinking on those things, I realize I am still in the hos- pital, in bed and holding my son, Winston. I look up to find that Mr. Freeman is still here in my hospital room. He is looking at Winston. Then, he looks at me. He says, "Ruby, I need to talk to you before you leave the hospital." I say, "Yes, Mr. Freeman." He says, "Ruby, call me 'Daddy Freeman' and not 'Mr. Freeman.' That is what I want Winston to call me, and you are to call me 'Daddy Freeman,' too." I say, "Yes, Daddy Freeman." He smiles.

He then proceeds to ask, "Ruby, what do you plan on doing to support you and Winston?" I look at him and think to myself, "Why is he asking me that question?" Daddy Freeman sees this look on my face, so he continues to talk. He says, "I know you work in 'The Hole,' fixing women's hair. So, I can imagine that you will continue to fix hair. Tell me this: How much money does Miss Johnson earn a day, and how much money do you earn a day?" I say, "I don't know how much money Miss Johnson earns in a day. After I pay her for rent space to fix hair, I have some money left over. I earn—" He interrupts me to say, "So, what you are saying is that you earn less money than Miss Johnson and you have to pay her rent money." I just continue to look at him.

Daddy Freeman continues: "You also don't have a license to fix hair like Miss Johnson. Because you don't have a certificate, you can't earn the same amount of money as she earns. Ruby, you have a high school diploma and Miss Johnson does not have a high school diploma. What she does have is a license to do what she likes to do, and you do not. You must become somebody like Miss Johnson if you want to continue to fix women's hair. I am going to give you money whenever Winston needs something that you can't buy, but you must help both of you get ahead."

Daddy Freeman looks at his watch and says, "Ruby, I have to go now. I will leave my telephone number to my barber shop for the nurse to call me when it's time for you and Winston to leave the hospital. I'll come back here at that time to pick the two of you up and take you to your Drum Mom's house." When he is done talking, Daddy Freeman begins to smile at Winston. Then he looks at me and says, "Ruby, have a good day, and I will see you when you are ready to leave from here." Daddy Freeman looks and smiles at Winston again. He looks at me again, smiles, and leaves my room. I look at my son and say, "Winston, don't you worry, we are going to be just fine . . . just fine. Your Daddy Freeman likes to talk a lot. It's just his ways."

I hear someone walking up the hallway. The steps sound like those of the white nurse. She opens the door and walks to the head of my bed. I notice that she has some papers in her hand. She says, "Can you read and write, girl?" "Yes, I can read and write," I reply. The white nurse gives me the paper. It is for information for Winston's birth certificate. I write my name as the mother. I write my son's name. I also write the father's full name, just as Daddy Freeman told me to do. When I finish, I give the nurse the papers back with my written information on it. She looks at the papers and then leaves my room.

On the seventh day, my last day at the hospital, Old Doc Jones and the white nurse come to my room. They walk over to my bed. I stare at Old Doc Jones because I haven't seen him since Winston was born. Old Doc Jones does not look at me. He looks hard at my son, who is by my side. I look at Winston. He is not smiling anymore. I can't understand why Winston isn't smiling. Old Doc Jones continues to look at my son and says to me, "Do you feel like going home today?" I say, "Yes, I do." He says to the nurse, "They can go home." Old Doc Jones says to my son, "You are a strong boy. We will have to keep an eye on you." Old Doc Jones then exits the room.

The white nurse says, "Get up from the bed and get yourself ready to go home." "Are you going to make a telephone call to Daddy Freeman and tell him to come and pick me up?" I inquire. To this, she responds, "I know he has his own telephone and car! I am going to call him right now." She turns away from me and leaves my room. I then get myself and Winston ready to leave the hospital.

When Daddy Freeman arrives at the hospital in his car, he parks and walks into the hospital through the "Coloreds Only" door. He tells the white woman at the front desk, "I am here to pick up Miss Ruby and her son." She says, "Wait in the colored section for Ruby and her boy."

At this time, I am in my room with Winston, anxiously awaiting Daddy Freeman's arrival so that we can go home. I soon hear some-one walking up the long hallway. I know it is not the white nurse or anyone who has previously come to my room. Having been in this environment for a while now, I had gotten a sense of how people walk and how their footsteps sound. Next, someone knocks on the door. "Who is it?" I ask. "It's Charlie!" he says. "I'm here to take you to Mr. Freeman. He is in the colored section, waiting on you and your son. Let me know when you are ready, and I'll bring the wheelchair in for you." I then reply, "I am ready to leave. Come on in, Charlie, and take us out of this room."

Charlie comes into my room. He helps me get into the wheel-chair and then hands me my son. He asks, "What is his name?" I say, "His name is Winston." Charlie then takes me to the colored waiting section. I see Daddy Freeman smiling and happy to see us. Charlie transports me and Winston in the wheelchair to Daddy Freeman's car. Daddy Freeman walks beside us, then unlocks and opens his car door when we get to it. He comes over to me and takes Winston from my arms. Daddy Freeman smiles as he holds Winston in his arms. "Look how Winston smiles back at me," he beams. Charlie helps me get into the car and then says, "Goodbye, Ruby." Daddy Freeman gives Winston back to me, walks over to the driver's side of the car, unlocks the door, and gets into the car. He smiles, prays, and thanks God for us. He starts the car and says, "Ruby and Winston, let us go home!"

Chapter Four

LOVING DEEDS, REFLECTION, AND PLANNING

W inston and I leave the hospital in Daddy Freeman's car. This is Winston's first car ride. He smiles at Daddy Freeman and me. Daddy Freeman drives slowly through the streets of Ripley. As he passes a landmark, he shares with Winston the rich history of that place. Winston is only a week old, but he looks at Daddy Freeman as though he understands every word coming out of his mouth.

When he arrives downtown, Daddy Freeman drives slowly and talks about the history of all the buildings around the town square. After he drives around the town square, he approaches his building on the corner of Main Street—parking his car in the front of it. He gets out of his car and walks over to the door on the side where Winston and I are sitting. After opening my door, he takes Winston from my arms and holds him tightly in his.

With Winston in his arms, Daddy Freeman walks over to the front window of his building. I hear him say to Winston, "When I go to be with my Father in heaven, this building I own will be yours. This will forever seal my love for you." He then totes Winston back to the car, gives Winston back to me, and closes the door. As he gets back into the car behind the wheel, he turns to Winston and me and smiles, then faces forward. He backs out of his parking spot toward Main Street. Daddy Freeman then points to the place called "The Hole"—but he does not drive down there. Instead, he says to

Winston, "Your mother will take you down there. You will see where she works and what she does to buy things you'll need."

Soon, we arrive at Drum Mom's house. When the car comes to a stop, Daddy Freeman gets out of the car and proceeds to take Winston from me so that I can walk up the porch steps. I walk slowly ahead of Daddy Freeman and Winston. When I successfully clear the steps to reach the top of the porch, I take a moment to catch my breath. After the three of us are on the porch, the door opens, and we see Drum Mom, standing there with a huge smile on her face. She says, "Come on in here. Freeman, bring that boy to me!"

Inside the house, Daddy Freeman waits for Drum Mom to sit on a chair and for me to sit down on the couch. He gives my son to Drum Mom and sits down beside me. Drum Mom says, "Ruby, this is a fine-looking boy! What's this boy's name?" I say, "His name is Winston." "I don't know anybody in the family with that name," she responds. "Do you know of anyone, Freeman?" Daddy Freeman replies, "No, I don't, but it's a fine, strong name. I'm going back to work and I'll see you all later." I say, "Thank you, Daddy Freeman, for everything you have done for me and Winston." "Freeman, thank you," Drum Mom adds to the sentiment. At this, Daddy Freeman says, "I'll be back tonight and check to see how everybody's doing. Ruby, when you go back to work, you can ride with me." I then reply, "Thank you, Daddy Freeman"—to which he nods and leaves the house.

Drum Mom looks at me and asks, "You call Freeman, 'Daddy Freeman'?" I say, "Yes, he asked me to call him 'Daddy Freeman' because he wants Winston to call him Daddy Freeman." "I see," Drum Mom responds. "Ruby, I'll keep Winston while you go get yourself clean, dressed, eat, and get in bed. I have food on the stove. Eat something before you go to bed. I'll bring Winston to you after you finish doing those things." "Yes, Drum Mom. Thank you," I say in appreciation.

As I leave the living room, I look back and see Drum Mom smiling at Winston. She looks at me but doesn't smile. I know she's disappointed in me because I have a son and not a husband or a father for my son. I understand her feelings and know that her disappointment in me is because she wants better for me. She wants to teach me to not bring another child into this world without my having a husband. Without a doubt, I know that whatever Drum Mom does or says to me is done or said out of her love for me.

I look at Drum Mom again and leave the front room, headed to my room. When I enter my room, I start to look things over. I quickly notice how Drum Mom has done a thorough cleaning of my room. It is so clean that I could drop food on the floor, pick it up, and eat it without hesitation! The room smells clean, unlike how my hospital room smelled. I think, "All this for me and Winston! I know Drum Mom did this because she loves me and doesn't want Winston to get sick from living in a dirty house." I continue to survey my room. I notice something round in a sock that is nailed to the wood over my door. *What in the world is that? Oh! I know. It is a clean sock.* After reaching for the sock, I grab it and look inside. It's an egg in the sock! "Wow! Drum Mom has an egg in a sock," I comment. "She doesn't want Winston to have pain and get a fever when he starts teething."

After reveling in my grandmother's thoughtfulness, I walk to the toilet room, wash up, and put on a clean gown and panties. I then make my way to the big kitchen, where I see that Drum Mom has cooked her delicious chicken soup. I eat the soup and then wash it down with some water. Afterwards, I walk to the front room and say to Drum Mom, "I'm ready to go to bed. You can bring Winston to me." As I climb into bed, I hear the sound of Drum Mom standing up from the chair in the front room, and her footsteps as she walks down the hallway. She comes into my room and hands me my son. "Drum Mom, thank you for keeping Winston, cleaning my room, and cooking that delicious chicken soup," I gush. "I love you, Drum Mom." Drum Mom smiles at me and then says, "Feed Winston. Then you and Winston can get some sleep." I heed her words.

For the next several weeks, I would find myself continuing the same routine: sit in the living room, keep us clean, feed Winston, eat, and sleep.

*****

I am now at the close of my time with Winston on maternity leave, so now it is time for me to go back to work at Miss Johnson's salon. I am so happy about going back to work because I love what I do for a living. I love to work my magic on women's hair. On the other hand, I am so sad that I must leave Winston with Drum Mom. I know she will take very good care of him, but leaving him is hard. He is only two months old.

On my first day back to work, I get up early in the morning, get dressed, and then wait for Daddy Freeman (who lives next door to

Drum Mom) to pick me up and take me to work. He pulls up in front of the house and lightly toots the horn of his car. At this prompt, I go and kiss Winston while he is asleep, walk to the kitchen, and say, "Love you, Drum Mom. I'll see you after work."

When I walk out of the house and get into the car, I greet him with a "Good morning, Daddy Freeman." He replies, "Good morning, Ruby. What has Winston been doing since last night?" Ever since I arrived at home with Winston after he was born, Daddy Freeman has made it routine to come over to Drum Mom's house every evening after he gets off from work and gets himself clean. He always gets comfortable in a chair and never misses out on asking me that very same question. But this time, upon asking, "What has Winston been doing since last night?" I say, "Winston slept through the entire night without waking me up for his feeding. It's as though he knows I need my sleep, so I can work." Daddy Freeman smiles at my response and says, "He's a smart boy!"

He drives to the front of the building that houses Miss Johnson's Beauty Shop, which is situated in "The Hole." When the car stops, I thank Daddy Freeman for giving me a ride to work. Daddy Freeman says, "I'll be here at 5:30 to pick you up and drive you back home. Remember, the white folks close their stores at six o'clock and they want us colored folks off the streets at that same time. On Saturdays, we have longer to work since the stores don't close until nine. So, Ruby, be ready to leave the salon when I come to pick you up." "Yes, sir," I reply to his advice.

I then exit the car and walk upstairs to the beauty salon. When I open the door, I see that Miss Johnson is present and already working. She is working on three women's heads of hair. One woman is at the shampoo bowl, one under the dryer, and one in the chair, getting ready to have her hair pressed and curled. I see Miss Johnson finishing the lady at the shampoo bowl and moving her to be under the other dryer. She goes to the woman in the chair and realizes that I am in her salon, ready to work.

"Hello, Ruby," Miss Johnson says. "Welcome back." I reply, "Hello, Miss Johnson and everybody. I'm glad to be back!" After our greetings, Miss Johnson continues working and starts pressing and curling the hair of the woman who is currently in her chair. Since there was no one waiting for me to fix their hair, I start cleaning around my area and setting my beauty tools in place. Then, I sit down in my beauty chair. I look at Miss Johnson, who is going from one woman to another, and begin to think about what Daddy Freeman asked me while I was in the hospital: *"Ruby, how much money does Miss Johnson earn a day? How much do you earn a day?"* Now, I know how much *I* earn in a day, but I don't know the amount of money that Miss Johnson makes in a day. What I do know is that if I want to figure out Miss Johnson's daily earnings, I need to devise a plan to find out!

The next thing I know, I am on a mission. That very day, I start writing down the number of customers she has in a day, every day, and how much money she makes, using the price list on the wall as a gauge. I do not let anyone know what I am doing.

I write down 0.75 on a small piece of paper—this is for the woman in the chair who is getting a shampoo, press, and curl. Every time Miss Johnson finishes up with a customer and receives money from the person, I write down on my paper the amount of money that it costs to do her hair.

Soon, it is noontime, and finally I have a customer. She is a customer looking to get a shampoo, press, and curl. When I finish up with her, I get 0.75 cents and put it in my pocket. Three more women then walk into the beauty salon at the same time. Miss Johnson takes two of the women, and she gives me one woman to beautify.

I smile at my customer and ask, "What is your name?" "Linda," she responds. I say, "Miss Linda, what would you like done to your hair today?" Linda says, "I need my hair fixed. I need a shampoo, press, and curl." To this, I reply, "Yes, Miss Linda. Please have a seat in my chair. You are beautiful now, and when I finish, I will have to pull you out of my chair because you will want to keep looking at yourself in the mirror." Miss Linda and I start laughing.

While I am fixing Miss Linda's hair, I realize how Miss Johnson controls this business, her customers, and the money she earns. She knows that I am in need of money, but *she* decides how much money I will earn each day. Daddy Freeman is right! I got a high school diploma, but I don't have a license to fix hair. Miss Johnson does not have a high school diploma, but she has a license to fix hair. This is *her* business! I pay her out of the money I earn from working here. She makes her money and then takes *my* money! I quickly realize that something is off about this system! "I've got to have a plan to make more money," I think to myself.

I carefully watch and study Miss Johnson and come to know what I must do to get ahead. I need more women coming to the beauty salon and fixing their hair. The more customers I have, the more money I'll earn. The more money I earn, the better off I'll be to attend beauty school and get my license to fix hair. When I get my license, I can have my own beauty salon. I plan on being the only one working in my own place, and no one will know how much money I am earning.

Miss Johnson earns $7.50 today. I understand now. I have a plan. In two years, when Winston is two years old, I will have enough money for beauty school. I then tell myself that I will start working my plan now, and I will never let go of it—a plan for a better me and a better life for my son!

It is about 5:30 p.m. when Daddy Freeman comes and picks me up from work. I say, "Goodbye, Miss Johnson. I will see you tomorrow." I walk down the stairs and get into Daddy Freeman's car, and greet him. "Good evening, Ruby," he responds. "How was your day?" I say, "Daddy Freeman, it was a good day. This was a good day! I had time to come up with a plan from the talk you had with me in the hospital. I know what I need to do to get ahead. I want to thank you, Daddy Freeman, for allowing me to see through your eyes. I understand everything now!" Daddy Freeman smiles at my comment and drives us home.

Chapter Five

VALUABLE MINDS

The number of customers I have in the beauty salon is steadily growing. I work from the time I arrive in the morning until Daddy Freeman picks me up. I am earning and saving a lot of money—enough to prompt Miss Johnson to say to me, "I am proud of you, Ruby. You are making a lot of money in my place." I reply, "Thank you, Miss Johnson. I couldn't do this without you and your help. You are so kind to me."

"Ruby, when are you going to start beauty school?" she then asks me. At this point, all the customers have left for the day, and I did not expect Miss Johnson to ask me about beauty school. Miss Johnson, Daddy Freeman, my friend Lucille, and Drum Mom are the only ones who know about my plans to go to beauty school. I told Miss Johnson so that I could keep things good between us, partly because I know that I will need some help from her when I finish school. "We are going to make a lot of money together after you finish school," she continues her thought, though I have not answered her initial question.

I listen to her, smile, and don't say anything about our not working together for very long and how my plans don't include our making money together. My plan is to have my own beauty salon. She knows only what I tell her—only what I want her to know. I am heeding the advice of Drum Mom, who always says, "Don't let your left hand know what your right hand is doing."

"I will be starting beauty school in the fall of this year. School starts in August," I reply to Miss Johnson, to which she says, "That's about nine months from now!" "Yeah, it is," I promptly respond.

Miss Johnson then says, "Your son will be two years old when you start school. This is how we're going to do this thing! The last week that you work in this salon, you will tell your customers that you are leaving for a few months to take care of your brother, Robert. We are not telling them you are going to beauty school. If your customers know you don't have a license to fix hair, they might give us trouble. A week is enough time for your customers to know you are leaving.

"If they know before then, they might start leaving you and looking for someone else to fix their hair. You will lose money and I will lose money. Tell them you will be back as soon as possible. I will do everything I can do to keep your customers coming here. When you get back, your customers will still be your customers. This place will still be a place for you to come back to and fix hair. When you come back here, you will put your license on the wall by your work station. Ruby, I am so happy for you!"

After Miss Johnson's spiel, she answers the ringing telephone; someone has called, asking to speak to me. Miss Johnson calls me over and hands me the telephone. "Hello, this is Ruby," I say. "Hello, Ruby. I am on my way to pick you up from work," I hear Daddy Freeman respond to my greeting. I tell him I am ready to go.

On the ride home, I say to Daddy Freeman, "Please come over to Drum Mom's tonight. I would like to talk to you and Drum Mom about beauty school." Daddy Freeman smiles at me and says, "I'll come by, Ruby. I can also spend time with my grandson, Winston." Then he bursts out laughing and says, "I haven't seen him since last night."

Soon, we are pulling up in front of Drum Mom's house. I get out of the car, and Daddy Freeman waits until I walk up the steps to the porch and go inside the house before he drives away. Once inside the house, I see that Winston is waiting for me. He laughs and runs to me. When he reaches my long legs, I pick him up. He kisses his "momma" all over my face. He smiles and laughs with me, hugging me with all his strength. When we sit down on the couch, we hug each other again. Winston is now fifteen months old. In this moment, I begin to think about how happy I was having given birth to Winston. Then, all of a sudden, I start recalling the time when my happiness started fading away—the day when I started crying and could not stop.

*****

I had stopped breastfeeding Winston when he was five months old. One morning, I went to the toilet room, wiped myself, and saw blood on the toilet paper. I had started my period. I had forgotten what it was like to have one. I sat there for a long time, crying and crying. Drum Mom heard me crying and walked into the toilet room. She said, "Child, what's wrong!" I said, "Drum Mom, I'm on my period." She started laughing and said, "Ruby, what did you think was going to happen? If you didn't come on your period, I would have thought you were carrying a child again and so soon. Thank God for your problem." She left the room, but I stayed on the toilet until I had the strength to get up and get what I needed.

I finally got up off the toilet and went to my room. I got a clean gown and panties, and then walked back to the toilet room. Everything else that I needed was already in the toilet room. I turned on the water and filled the sink half full. I washed, dried myself, and opened the large closet door. I would find the scraps of fabric in the brown grocery bag. Drum Mom sewed fine clothes for white folks; and if any fabric was left over from her sewing, they would let her keep the scraps and she would bring them home. She cut them into different sizes and then put them in the brown bag in the toilet room.

I took one long piece and two medium pieces of cut fabric from the brown bag. I folded the two medium pieces together until they were like a loose ball. I put the fabric ball in the middle of the long one and folded the long one, lengthwise, over and over, layering it on the fabric ball. I put on my clean sanitary holster belt and put the fabric between my legs. I took each end of the fabric and put them through the holes on the belt. I made sure everything was tight and firm so that if I bled, my bleeding would not spoil my clothes or my bed. I put my panties and gown on, cleaned the sink, washed my hands, and then went to bed.

While I was bleeding, Drum Mom would not let me take a bath or wash my hair. I had to wash up in the sink. "Bathing while you're bleeding will contaminate the water in the house, and cause you to have severe monthly and childbirth pains. Washing your hair will make your hair come out," she would say.

The day I stopped bleeding, I was so happy because I could finally take a bath! Drum Mom saw two boys playing in front of the house. She said, "You boys come here." The boys came over to Drum Mom. "Here is a nickel," she said. "Bring my steel tub in the house and put it on the floor." "It's not Saturday, it's Tuesday!" one of the boys said. To this, Drum Mom responded, "Hush, and do what I say!"

The boys carried the steel tub into the house and set it on the living room floor. Drum Mom gave each boy a nickel and said, "If you two are around when I finish with the tub, I'll give you each another nickel to take it back outside and pour the water out of the tub." "Yes, ma'am," they said in unison. "We'll be around outside."

I sat and bathed in the steel tub until the water got cold. When I finished taking my bath, Drum Mom went outside and called the boys to come into the house. The boys came into the house, picked up the tub, took it outside, poured the water out of it, and then came back to get a nickel apiece.

*****

At seven months old, Winston started walking. He walked before he crawled. One day, while sitting down in the front room as Winston played, I said, "Winston, come to Momma." He looked at me and sat there for a moment. Then suddenly, Winston walked to his momma! He fell on the wood floor, got right back up, looked at me, and started walking again. Finally, he made his way to me. I picked up my baby and hugged him tightly. "Winston, I am so proud of you for walking over here to your momma," I gushed. "I am also proud that you keep going even when you fall. You fall, but you get back up. You are a very smart son. I am so happy that I'm here with Drum Mom to see you take your first steps. Momma loves you."

After Winston started walking, Drum Mom and I told him to walk to the toilet room and use the toilet. Drum Mom and I had to put in a lot of time and patience for Winston to correctly do what we wanted him to do. After a week, Winston finally walked by himself to the toilet room, used the toilet, and cleaned himself. Every time he did this right, we rewarded him. We would give him a wooden spoon and a pot, and let him hit and bang the pot with the wooden spoon until we couldn't take it anymore.

Now that Winston knew how to use the toilet by himself, there were no more dirty cloth diapers that we had to empty into the toilet. We no longer had to take diapers (that we should wash and scrub *clean) from the toilet to the washboard. There were no more diapers to hang outside on the clothesline. We no longer had to deal with diapers!*

*****

When Winston turned one year old, we threw him the biggest birthday party at our house. All my co-workers and everyone in town were coming. Drum Mom baked a birthday cake, two chocolate cakes with chocolate icing, two chess pies, two apple pies, and one pecan pie. She made homemade vanilla ice cream. I made sandwiches for the small children. And I cooked fried chicken, ham, greens, sweet potatoes, fresh green beans, okra, cornbread, and homemade rolls for the adults.

So many people attended Winston's birthday party. The children played a lot of games; some played dodgeball in the street. Some of the girls jumped rope; some of the boys played marbles. There were some adults who watched over the younger children that were Winston's age. The other adults talked, laughed, and had a great time. After we ate and the children played some more, we called everyone to the front yard to sing "Happy Birthday" to Winston. After the "Happy Birthday" song, everyone said, "Winston, blow out the candle." I held a cake that had one lit candle on it. Winston blew out the candle. Everybody then started screaming and laughing.

Next, we brought Winston's birthday gifts to him. One by one, we gave him a present. He tore all the newspaper off each one, smiled, and loved every present he received. He had apples, oranges, pecans, different kinds of candies, handmade clothes, and a big, round ball. After the gifts from our friends were opened, Drum Mom and I gave Winston more clothes. Daddy Freeman gave Winston a red wagon and a red tricycle. When Winston received Daddy Freeman's gifts, he screamed, fell to the ground, and rolled over in the grass in excitement.

At twelve months, Winston was speaking well for a child his age. Everyone who talked with him said, "Winston is years ahead of his time." I always felt pride when people said this to me about my son. I knew he inherited his intelligence from his mother and from his Daddy Freeman's bloodline.

*****

I finally stop thinking about the past, loosening my embrace on Winston enough to put him back on the floor. I come to realize that Drum Mom has been sitting in her chair all this time. "Hello, Drum Mom. How are you doing today?" I ask. "I am just fine. How was your day?" she inquires. "It was a good day," I respond. "Daddy Freeman is coming over tonight. I want to talk to both of you about my plans. I hope this is okay to ask Daddy Freeman to come by tonight." Drum Mom replies, "Freeman's coming tonight? That's not news, child. Freeman comes here every night. Now you wanting to talk to both of us is news. I hope I can take whatever news you tell us." "Yes, Drum Mom," I respond.

Drum Mom finishes cooking dinner and sits down at the kitchen table. The food smells so good. I notice her taking a seat; "Drum Mom, is dinner ready?" I ask. "Yes, child," she replies. "I'm waiting for you and Winston to come and eat." Winston and I wash our hands and then walk into the kitchen. Drum Mom believes that family should eat together. If I have any place to go after work, I must be home by dinnertime. And if I don't come home when it is time for dinner, Drum Mom will not eat until I am home.

Before we eat, I put pillows in Winston's chair so that he is tall enough to feed himself. After I sit down at the table, Drum Mom and I bow our heads and say grace. When we finish saying grace, we look up to see Winston with his head still bowed and his hands clasped together in front of his face. He then says, "Amen." Drum Mom and I say, "Amen," and the two of us laugh and then smile quietly at Winston.

After dinner, I put the leftover food in jars that go in the icebox. When I see that the ice in the ice box has melted and that we need more ice, I am glad to know that the ice man is coming by tomorrow to sell us a block of ice! I proceed to wash the dishes and sweep and mop the floor. When I am done with those tasks, I go to my bedroom and get Winston's clothes out to get him ready for bed. I soon hear a knock at the door. "Come on in, Freeman," I hear Drum Mom say. Next thing I know, I hear Daddy Freeman come inside the house and say, "Hello, how are you today?" Drum Mom responds, "I am fine. Do you want anything to eat?" To this offer, Daddy Freeman says, "No, thanks, I have already eaten dinner. Where's my grandson?" "He's over here playing on the floor," Drum Mom replies. Daddy Freeman says, "Come over here, Winston." I hear Daddy Freeman talking to

Winston; I take deep breaths and get myself ready to have my talk with Drum Mom and Daddy Freeman.

I move to the front room, where I see Daddy Freeman seated and playing with Winston. Drum Mom is sitting down and laughing at Winston and Daddy Freeman's playtime. Drum Mom sees me enter the room and asks, "What do you have to say to Freeman and me?" Daddy Freeman takes Winston off his lap and puts him back on the wooden floor. "Good evening, Daddy Freeman," I say to greet him. "Hello, Ruby," he responds. I say, "Winston, go to your room and get ready for bed." Winston hugs Daddy Freeman and kisses Drum Mom and me. He says, "Good night," and leaves the front room.

"Daddy Freeman," I begin, "I specifically asked you to come here tonight so that I can talk to you and Drum Mom. You both know that I need to attend a beauty school so that I can get my license to fix hair. I want to become a licensed hairdresser and have my own beauty salon." Drum Mom, who seems to be nervous while rocking back and forth in her chair, says, "Ruby, we know this. Get to the point! You see how nervous I am, waiting for you to make your point."

"Well, Drum Mom," I continue, "the point is, I am going to beauty school this August in New York. I am taking Winston with me." "Why do you have to go to New York?" Drum Mom asks. "Why are you going so far away from home? Why are you taking Winston so far away from us?" I look at Daddy Freeman sitting quietly and looking at me. I say, "Drum Mom, the beauty school in New York is one of the best. I want to go to the best beauty school so that I will become the best person for what I love to do. This may be the only chance I have, and I don't see giving up on what I need to do for me and Winston. I'll take Winston with me. We'll be back home after I finish school."

"What are you going to do with Winston while you are in school?" Drum Mom asks, to which I respond, "Daddy Freeman, this is where I need your help." He calmly says, "Yes, Ruby." With excitement, I say, "I need you to talk to your sister, Beatrice. I need you to ask her if Winston and I can live with her for nine months while I'm in school. I have enough money for school and enough to pay her for rent. Ask her how much money she wants for me and Winston to stay in one of her bedrooms. Ask her if she knows someone who can take care of Winston during the day while I'm in school. I plan to go to school during the day and work some nights to help pay for someone to take care of him."

"Ruby, wait a minute!" Daddy Freeman urges. "You want me to ask my sister for a lot of things. You need to slow down for a minute." Drum Mom quickly chimes in with "That's right, Freeman!" Daddy Freeman then calmly continues: "Ruby, my sister owns a boarding house in New York for women who are trying to do better for themselves. I will contact her and let her know you need to rent a room in August. If she does, you will pay her for renting a room. Now, we need to talk about Winston going to New York with you and for someone having to take care of him while you are in school." "That's right. I agree, Freeman," Drum Mom again concurs with his words.

Daddy Freeman says, "Winston will be almost two years old when beauty school starts in New York. He will be in a place where he has never been or seen before. He will be around people that he does not know. New York is a fast city. It can be a violent place. Some people can make it in a place like New York. Some people try, but can't. Winston, I don't know. I think he will be one who will do some traveling, but will never feel free outside his hometown. He will always find happiness being at home. Let Winston stay here so you can focus on your studies. We'll take care of him."

"Yes, Freeman and I will take care of Winston," Drum Mom assures. "After you finish school, you will come back home and finish raising your son." Daddy Freeman then asks, "Ruby, are you in agreement with us?" I reply, "Yes, Daddy Freeman. Yes, Drum Mom. I'm in agreement with the two of you. Thank you for helping me follow my dreams. I promise I will not disappoint you!"

Chapter Six

FLESH

Currently, I work downtown at the beauty salon. I am continuing to earn and save my money for school. Every week, when I pay Miss Johnson for space to fix hair, I know that is lost money—money that I work for, and money that I freely give away. I end up losing money before I even start working! But now, I thank my God that I have a plan to make more money and two people who are willing to help me get ahead!

Today, at work, I am feeling particularly good about my life and my future! I begin to think about going out tonight to celebrate with my girlfriend, Lucille. I can't remember the last time we had fun together, seeing as though both of us are just too busy! I have a son and Lucille has a man. I know that Lucille will be here to get her hair fixed in about twenty minutes—and anytime she wants her hair fixed, I make her my last customer so that we have time to catch up on things.

While working, I look up to see Lucille walking into the salon. She is just twisting away. She knows how to let everyone know that Lucille is "here in this place." "Hello, everybody. Lucille is here!" she says loudly upon her entrance. She is a very beautiful colored woman. We have the same body dimensions. We call ourselves "Slim and Trim"—I am "Slim," and Lucille is "Trim." After making her presence known, Lucille walks and sits down in one of the empty chairs. She starts talking and laughing about her day at work. "Girls," she says, "How do you get a man to whistle at you?" No one says anything. Finally, one of Miss Johnson's customers asks, "Lucille, how do you get a man to whistle at you?" With a quick retort, Lucille says,

"You let out gas." Everyone in the salon starts laughing and then saying things about her answer and her bad mouth—followed by more laughter.

When I am ready to fix Lucille's hair, I call her to come and sit in my chair. We talk and laugh, and laugh and talk. She tells me everything that is going on with everybody in town. When she finishes talking, I say, "I feel like celebrating tonight! It's Saturday night and I feel like having fun! I feel like dancing!" "You sure do have a lot of good feelings," Lucille comments. "You're dangerous!"

"Lucille, let's go out tonight after I put Winston to sleep," I respond. "Okay, where do you want to go?" Lucille inquires. "Let's go to Covington," I reply. Lucille says, "Okay, I'll tell my boyfriend, Fred, we want to go out tonight. He just bought an old car. We'll pick you up about 9:00 tonight." "That's great," I say. "I'll be ready at 9:00."

Upon finishing Lucille's hair, she leaves the salon, laughing and telling everybody that she looks like Lena Horne. Afterwards, I proceed to clean my workstation. Shortly thereafter, Daddy Freeman calls the salon, asking to speak to me. When I reach the phone, I hear him say, "I'm on my way to pick you up from work." "Yes, sir," is my response to this information. As it nears the time for his arrival, I get my things and go to the front window of the salon to try to spot Daddy Freeman's car. Seeing his car in front of the salon, I say good night to everyone who is left at the salon, and depart.

I get into the car, speak to Daddy Freeman, and then think about going out tonight. Daddy Freeman can tell I am acting differently and that I have something on my mind. He says, "Young lady, desires of the flesh are not always a good thing." I look at him and ask, "What do you mean by that?" "You think about it. The desires of the flesh are not always a good thing," Daddy Freeman comments as he continues to drive to Drum Mom's house. "Good night, and thank you," I say when we arrive at our destination. "You are highly welcome," he responds.

He waits until I get in the house before he drives next door to his house. I open the front door and am greeted by Winston, who is running to me in excitement. I pick him up into my arms. Though I talk and laugh with him, I am in a hurry to get cleaned up, eat dinner, put him to sleep, get dressed, and get ready to go out. I put him back down onto the floor and hear, "What's your hurry?" from Drum Mom.

To this, I say, "I'm going out with Lucille tonight after I put Winston to sleep." Drum Mom responds with "I see."

When it is time, we sit down together to eat at the dinner table. After dinner, I get everything done and put Winston to sleep. I put on my slim, blue dress with matching gloves, and my black leather shoes; and I find my black leather bag. I proceed to put on red lipstick that I had bought from the Ben Franklin Store.

When Lucille and Fred finally arrive to pick me up, I go to Drum Mom's room and say, "Good night, Drum Mom. Winston is asleep. I'll be back later." "Good night, Ruby," she replies.

I get in the back seat of Fred's car. Fred is driving and has the music turned up loud. Lucille has on a red dress with matching gloves. She is singing and dancing to the music playing on the radio. Some of the songs playing on the radio are our favorite songs— songs from the Platters, the Drifters, Little Richard, Nat King Cole, and Fats Domino. I sing and dance in the back seat of Fred's car, displaying the same moves as Lucille. We know we are ready to have fun and bring life up in the place!

Fred turns off the radio and says, "Lucille, you and Ruby are getting crazy!" Lucille says, "Fred, turn your music off. Ruby and I are going to get our slang on for tonight. You dig, Fred." Fred and I laugh at Lucille. Lucille starts by saying the "slang word." I say the meaning of the "slang word" and Fred uses the "slang word" in a sentence. Lucille starts the game and says the "slang words." I follow Lucille, and Fred follows me. Here we go!

- Lucille says, "Hip." I say, "A person who is cool, knows about things." Fred says, "Fred is hip."

- Bread = money. Fred has bread. Lucille says, "Fred's going to spend his bread tonight!"

- Pad = home. Fred has his own pad. We laugh because Fred doesn't have his own pad. He lives with his sick grandmother and takes care of her.

- Big Daddy = an older man. Fred is not a Big Daddy. Lucille says, "I think you are big!" She looks down at him sitting on the car seat. She continues, "I wouldn't have it any other way." Lucille and I laugh. We continue playing our game.

- Horn = telephone

- Rod = car

- Sound = music

- Rock = diamond

- Split = leave

- Tight = good friends

- Weed = cigarette

- What's buzzing? = what's new?

- What's your tale, nightingale? = what's your story?

- Rap = to tattle on someone

- Fast = someone sexually active

- Later, later gator = goodbye. (See you later, alligator)

- Pound = beat up

- Make the scene = attend an event

- Heat = police

- Get with it = understand

Lucille and I laugh every time Fred utters a sentence using a "slang word." Upon our last burst of laughter, we arrive at the club in Covington. "You got the bread for me and Ruby to get in this place?" Lucille asks Fred, who responds with, "Yes, I said earlier that I have the bread."

We get out of the car and walk into the club. Fred gives the man at the door the bread for all of us. Fred leaves Lucille and me and finds a table where we can sit down and drink. He calls us over to the table, and when we go sit down, the sound is blasting! "Do the two of you want a drink?" Fred asks. Lucille says, "Yes, please." But, "No, thank you," is my reply. "Who wants some weed?" Fred then inquires. "I do," Lucille and I say in unison. Fred pulls out a pack of weed and gives one to Lucille and one to me. He lights it up for us. When I finish smoking my weed at the table, I say, "Got to split! I am here to dance to the sound."

I get up from my seat and I move on to the dance floor. I know that if I get onto the dance floor, someone is going to come and dance with me. Next thing I know, here comes "Big Daddy" moving toward me. After he reaches me, he starts moving and dancing to my rhythm. We dance together for two songs, and soon he starts sweating. "Big Daddy, you move real fine," I comment. "I'm going to go and dance on the other side of the room."

Having moved to the other side of the room, I once again start dancing to the sound. While getting my groove on, I see a man behind the bar, filling the liquor glasses for people with bread. My feet stop. I stop dancing. I can't move. People notice that I'm not dancing—I am just standing in one spot on the dance floor. They politely walk around me. I stand in that spot and just keep looking at this man. He is so good-looking, tall, and slender. He has a lovely wide nose and a "V" hairline. He finally looks up from the bar and sees me looking at him. We smile at each other. I feel his look and his smile all over my body. My body had never felt so warm. I am sweating, and I still can't move.

Someone pushes me, and that push propels me toward the bar. I walk closer to this man and see he is selling liquor to people at the bar. Our eyes meet again. I sit down right in front of him.

He says, "Hello, my name is Phillip. What is your name?" "Hello," I begin, "my name is Ruby." "Can I pour you a drink?" Phillip asks me. I say, "No, but I would like a beer. Please don't open it for me. I'll do that myself." Phillip says, "Okay, a beer, unopened, for the beautiful lady." He puts the unopened beer on the bar and continues to smile at me. I am smiling at him while I open the beer container. I take a small sip, pat my wet lips together, and put the beer back on the bar.

Phillip is still smiling at me. He talks to me like he is a nice person. I should have let him pour me a drink, but I couldn't. After my momma died from someone putting poison in her liquor, Drum Mom made my brother, Robert, and I promise never to let anyone give us an open bottle or glass of liquor. Drum Mom says, "You have to open your own liquor and pour it in the glass yourself. You are to never leave your open liquor with anyone or go anywhere without always having your eyes on your liquor. If you must leave, take your liquor with you. If you can't take it with you or finish drinking it, leave it be."

Phillip continues to work at the bar by filling every customer's order for liquor and taking their bread for the liquor. He comes over to where I am sitting at the bar and talks to me whenever he gets the chance to do so. I am still smiling and have been loving to look at this handsome colored man. When he gets his latest break, he comes over and talks to me. "Where do you live?" Phillip asks. "I live in Ripley," I say to him, then ask, "Why are you working so hard in this place?" Phillip responds, "This place is *my* place. I own this building and this business. I work hard for me. The more I work, the more money I make. Ruby, do you think that's a bad thing?"

"No, Phillip, I don't think that's a bad thing," I reply. "In fact, I think that's a good thing. I'm going to beauty school in New York this August. I am going to get my beauty license to fix hair and have my own salon." Phillip responds, "That's a good thing for you to do for yourself. I can tell you are more than just a beautiful lady. Yes, you are beautiful! You are also a smart, colored businesswoman. I like that! Did you come here by yourself?" "No. I am here with my friend Lucille and her friend Fred," I reply. "Will you need a ride home?" Phillip inquires. "No. Fred and Lucille will take me home," I answer.

Phillip says, "I'd like to get to know you better. You are the first woman I have met with class, smarts, beauty, and a money plan. I don't see the person who you are in the other women who are trying to chase after me. You are different. This time, for me, is different. I feel like we will be good for each other. Can we see each other next week at this place?" "Yes," I quickly respond.

"After next week, I am coming to your place to see you," Phillip says. To this, I comment, "Phillip, I live with my Drum Mom and have a fifteen-month-old son." Phillip smiles and then says, "Well, I am somebody's son. I bet he is handsome and smart like you. I'd like to meet your Drum Mom and son. What is your son's name?" "Winston," I answer him.

After our exchange, Fred and Lucille come to the bar. "Who's your friend?" Lucille asks. I say, "Phillip, these are my friends, Lucille and Fred." Phillip says, "Hello, Lucille and Fred." "Hello, Phillip," Lucille replies. "Ruby, it's time for us to split." I answer her, saying, "Okay." I proceed to pick up my purse from my lap, stand up, and say, "Phillip, I have to split. I will see you next week." "May I hold and kiss your hand?" Phillip asks me. I give him my hand, and he kisses it, then says, "We will see each other again, next week, here at my place." We smile at each other and I walk away.

We get in the rod to go home. Lucille is too drunk to talk and laugh; she is leaning on her car door. And Fred is driving well. He usually drinks very little or not at all when he is driving, which makes him a safe driver. As I ride in the back seat, I am thinking about Phillip; I am yearning for him. I can't wait to see him next week. That kiss on my hand was so gentle, yet powerful. My body heats up as I think about his touch.

Fred arrives at Drum Mom's house and parks, I get out of the rod. Lucille is asleep from drinking and is leaning against the door. "Thank you, Fred, for driving me to the place of paradise!" I comment. "Tell Lucille that I will talk to her later." Fred says, "You are welcome, and I will."

I creep into the house, careful not to wake Winston. I know Drum Mom is pretending to be asleep. I know she can't go to sleep until everybody is home and safe. When I peep into my room, I see Winston sleeping in the bed. I put my night clothes on. I then get into bed and think about Phillip, his kiss, and his place of business. All of these pleasant thoughts make me feel happy.

*****

It is now Friday, almost a whole week since I have seen Phillip. I can't help myself. I have been thinking about him every day—every hour of the day, every minute of the day, and every second of the day. Thoughts of Phillip get interrupted when Lucille arrives at the beauty salon for her weekly appointment. "Hello, everybody. Lucille's here!" Lucille greets everyone in the salon. Everyone then replies, "Hello, Lucille." She goes and sits in an empty chair and starts talking to the lady sitting next to her. Our eyes finally meet. We start laughing. "Lucille, what are you and Ruby laughing about?" Lisa, one of Miss Johnson's customers, asks. "Lisa, you should have been there!" Lucille retorts. "I should have been where?" Lisa inquires. Lucille says, "Lisa, you should have been there. *There*, Lisa, there." Everyone laughs softly at Lucille.

Upon finishing up with my customer who is currently sitting at my workstation, she pays me for fixing her hair. She then rounds up her things and gets up from my chair. "Thank you, and I will see you in two weeks," I say to her. "Yes, Ruby. I will see you in two weeks," she affirms. Once my chair is empty, I tell Lucille to come and sit at my workstation. She walks slowly over to the chair, her hips swaying from side to side. We both start laughing. "Lucille, I hope you can make it to my chair before Saturday night," I kid with her. We start laughing at each other again.

When Lucille finally sits in my chair, I ask, "Who do you want to look like this week?" "You know what?" Lucille begins, "I think Lena Horne looks like me this week. Fix it up!" I say, "Right! Lena Horne has your looks!" We smile at each other, then I say, "Lucille, ask Fred if he can drive us back to Covington tomorrow night. I really want to see Phillip." "I most certainly will ask Fred," Lucille responds. "We had such a good time, didn't we, girl!" "Yes, we did," I reply with excitement.

That night, Lucille says to Fred, "We had so much fun together last Saturday night. I would like to go back to Covington this Saturday night." "I'll drive you back there," Fred assures. "But this time, I will not buy you a lot of liquor. I don't like you drinking so much, and seeing you drunk like that." Lucille replies, "You are right, Fred. I had too many drinks. I don't like you seeing me that way, either. I don't like how being drunk makes me feel. I promise you I will have only one drink." Fred says, "Then I will just have the money for only one drink."

"Yes, that is all the money you will need," Lucille concurs, then she asks, "Can Ruby go with us?" "Lucille, this sounds like I need more money for Saturday night. I mean, more bread for your one drink and for all three of us to get into the place. Yes, Ruby can ride with us," Fred consents. "Fred, thank you so much," Lucille graciously says. "I love you, Fred." Fred smiles and says, "I love you too, Lucille."

*****

Lucille sends her nephew to the salon on Saturday morning. "Be ready by 9:00 tonight" is the message that he relays to me from his Aunt Lucille.

When I finish up with my last customer at four o'clock in the evening, I tell Miss Johnson that I need to leave early today. I am so excited about seeing Phillip. I leave the salon and stop by Daddy Freeman's barber shop. It is full of colored boys and men. Some wait to get their hair cut, some listen to the radio, and others are talking to each other. I look around for Daddy Freeman, but I don't see him anywhere. "Who are you looking for?" one of the men asks. "Daddy Freeman," I reply. "He's in the back," the man responds, then continues, "He will be back here in a minute."

Daddy Freeman hears me talking and comes to the front of the shop. "Hello, Ruby," he greets me. "Daddy Freeman, I am leaving early from work. You don't have to pick me up from work today. I am walking home," I say, wanting to be brief so that I can get out of the barber shop and get things done for tonight. "That's fine, Ruby," Daddy Freeman says. "Be careful and safe walking home." "Yes, sir. Thank you," I say in response to his well wishes.

It takes me about twenty minutes to walk and run home. When I finally reach the house, I am out of breath. I then rush into the house to find Drum Mom sitting in the chair, and Winston in the front room, taking a nap in the baby crib. The side rails are down on the crib, so when Winston hears me come into the house, he wakes up, jumps out of the crib, and runs to me. Regarding my hasty entrance, Drum Mom says, "Child, what's going on with you? Have you been 'touched,' rushing into this house like a crazy woman? You scared me."

"I'm sorry, Drum Mom," I say. "How are you doing?" "Fine, since I know you are not touched," she retorts. "I finished early at the salon and came home. Can you take care of Winston tonight?" I ask. "I'm going out tonight after I finish my chores." Drum Mom replies, "I'm here every night with you and Winston. Yes, I'll see after him, so you can go out tonight." "Thank you, Drum Mom," I respond in gratitude.

I soon work to get everything done. I put Winston to bed right after night falls; I then get dressed. As soon as the clock strikes nine o'clock in the evening, Fred and Lucille appear in the driveway. They are punctual. I get into the car, and then Fred drives us to Covington.

He gives the man at the door to the club the bread for himself, Lucille, and me for our admittance. Fred finds us a table at which we can sit down, and Fred and Lucille proceed to sit down at the table. I give my purse to Lucille and then make my way to the dance floor. Soon, I dance my way to the bar, and Phillip spots me—and I spot him! We talk; he hands me an unopened beer, and then I pour my beer into the liquor glass. As I sip my beer, he watches me and sees my red, wet lips press together after I sip the beer. After I put the liquor glass down, I gently pat my lips with my handkerchief. "Can we get together tonight after I close this place?" Phillip inquires. "I would like that," I reply.

I continue to sit at the bar. While there, I can see that Phillip is making a lot of bread tonight. On his breaks from bartending, Phillip comes over and talks to me. He wants to know my business plans and wants to talk about me, him, Winston, and beauty school. As I am telling Phillip about my only having two months left before I leave for beauty school, Fred and Lucille, who are standing behind me at the bar, start talking to Phillip. Lucille finally says to me, "Ruby, it's eleven o'clock. We are ready to split." Before I could say anything to Lucille, Phillip says, "Fred and Lucille, I'll drive Ruby home tonight." "Ruby, is this all right with you?" Lucille asks. "Yes, Lucille. It's all right with me," I confirm. Lucille and Fred then tell me good-bye and to be safe, then they leave the club.

As the club is getting ready to close, Phillip starts cleaning around the bar. He has another man cleaning the tables and taking the liquor glasses off the table. The music stops, then Phillip shouts, "Five minutes till closing." People put their glasses down and start leaving the club. I watch people leave as couples and some leave in groups. I begin to smile, knowing it won't be long before Phillip and I are alone.

When everyone leaves, and the club is clean, Phillip says, "Ruby, we can leave." He holds my hand as we walk out of the club, closing and locking the door behind us. He walks me to his parked rod, which is a 1949 black, two-door Ford Tudor! I know how much this rod costs because Daddy Freeman talked to me about buying Winston a car like this.

To this suggestion, I said, "Daddy Freeman, Winston is a child and the thought of him having a car is simply laughable." "This car only costs around $1,650," Daddy Freeman explained. "Winston is worth all of that, wouldn't you say so, Ruby?" "Daddy Freeman, who is going to pay for the gas for this car?" I inquired. Daddy Freeman responded, "I'll buy the car. You will pay for the gas. It's only $0.26 cents a gallon."

Upon our arrival at his car, Phillip takes out his key and unlocks the car door. He opens the door and lets me into his rod. He closes the door behind me, walks over to the driver's side, and then gets into his fine rod. "Phillip this rod is nice and classy," I comment, admiring his car. "I must learn how to drive." He replies, "I will teach you when you come back from beauty school. Now, let me take you to my pad."

Phillip drives and soon comes to a stop in a colored neighborhood. We sit in his rod with the engine running. It is dark, so I can't really see much of anything. I make mention of my visual impairment. Phillip turns on the brighter lights to his rod. The lights shine on the front of his pad. He says, "This is my pad, my house. I live here all by myself." I can now see the exterior of his pad. His house is beautiful on the outside, and I can see that one light is on in the front room. "Phillip, this is a nice pad," I say. He says, "Let me see where you live. It's time for me to take you back home to your pad."

Phillip starts driving me home. When we get to the main road in Covington, I tell Philip how to get to my pad. While travelling, we talk and laugh. Suddenly, a rod from out of nowhere starts following us. The rod's siren starts blaring. The rod's front lights start flashing on and off. This is a signal for Phillip to pull over and come to a stop.

Phillip pulls his car over to the side of the road. He keeps the rod's engine running. It is the heat (the police)! My heart is beating fast and pounding in my chest. I just know that Phillip can hear my heart pounding. Phillip looks at me and sees that I am very afraid. The heat gets out of his patrol car. He has a flashlight in his hand, which he is using to shine a light into Phillip's rod. "Ruby, we are okay," Phillip assures. "Let me talk to the heat."

The heat comes to the side of the rod where Phillip is sitting. He is an old white man dressed in a police uniform. He has a gun in his holster belt. He proceeds to shine the light into Phillip's face. He says, "Boy, roll down your window." Phillip rolls down the window. "Boy, whose car did you steal?" the heat inquires. "Sir, may I show you the papers to this car?" Phillip asks, offering up proof of ownership. "Yeah," the heat responds. "What's your name, boy?" Phillip replies, "My name is Phillip Browne."

Phillip opens the glove compartment in his rod and pulls out some papers. He holds the papers in his hand to give to the heat. The old man snatches the papers from Phillip's hand and looks over them. He then throws the papers back to Phillip, saying, "You, boy, and that girl, get on your way." "Thank you, sir," Phillip responds. The heat walks back to his rod. He gets in his rod and sits, waiting for us to pull off and drive away.

Phillip pulls off the side of the road and we continue our drive to my pad. Phillip looks at me, turns his head back to the road, and says, "Ruby, you are safe with me. Those papers come from an important, well-known white man who lives in this county. White folks know from these papers that I own this car. The papers also say for no white man to do any harm to me or mine. If they do, the federal agents with come and do an investigation to find out who harmed me or mine. This man I am talking about likes me and helped me buy his car. He also let me buy the building from him so that I have my own business. His name is Mr. Knowles. Again, Ruby, you are safe with me."

After Phillip says this, I feel safe being with him. *Mr. Knowles*, I think to myself: "Haven't I heard Daddy Freeman speak about a Mr. Knowles who helped him start his business? I'm sure this can't be the same white man Phillip is talking about. The same white man helping colored people! No way possible can this be—or can it?"

I don't see the heat following us anymore. My heart stops pounding, my heartbeats returning to a normal, steady rhythm. "This is 1952! Daddy Freeman and Phillip must have their freedom papers with them to show to the white man that they are worthy of having things like they have," I say to myself. "Things that were given to them by their own kind. These freedom papers have the same meaning today as they did for slaves who were freed by their own masters. Things have not changed. Only time has changed."

Phillip keeps driving toward my home. We then stop in front of Drum Mom's house. "It's too late for me to meet your Drum Mom and Winston," he says. "I will walk you to the door and see you go in your house." He gets out of the car, comes around to my side, and opens my door for me so that I can get out of the car. We walk to the porch together, holding hands. I take my key out of my purse and use it to unlock the house door. Phillip kisses my hand and says, "Good night, Ruby." "Good night, Phillip," I reply. "Can I come and see you Tuesday night?" he asks. "Dinner starts at six in the evening," I say with enthusiasm. He smiles, and I walk into the house and close the door behind me. I lean against the closed door and listen as Phillip walks down the steps of the porch, get into his car, and drive off.

*****

On Tuesday, Phillip arrives at our house before dinnertime. Drum Mom and Daddy Freeman are sitting in the front room; Winston is playing on the floor. I introduce Drum Mom and Daddy Freeman to Phillip. They all greet each other as I go and pick up Winston from the floor and then introduce Phillip to my son. When Winston sees Phillip, he immediately reaches out to Phillip. Phillip takes him from my arms and says, "See, Ruby, Winston knows a good man when he sees one."

Phillip sits down on the couch with Winston, and I sit down beside Winston. Drum Mom and Daddy Freeman start talking and asking Phillip about himself. While Phillip is talking to them, I notice how gentle and playful he is with Winston. He makes Winston smile and laugh out loud. This makes me happy. I also notice how Drum Mom and Daddy Freeman seem happy with Phillip getting along with a child that isn't his own.

I soon get up from the couch and walk to the kitchen to check on dinner. Once it is ready, I turn off the stove and put dinner on the kitchen table. When I walk back to the front room to tell everyone that dinner is ready, Winston smiles and says, "Amen." We all laugh at Winston's comment. Drum Mom and Daddy Freeman get up and head to the kitchen. Phillip stands up from the couch and puts Winston down on the floor. Then he says to Winston, "We need to wash our hands before we go to the dinner table." Winston understands what Phillip is saying. He grasps Phillip's hand and leads him to the toilet room so that they can wash their hands. I stand outside the door and watch them wash their hands.

When they finish and come out of the room, I then go in and wash my hands. Drum Mom and Daddy Freeman wash their hands in the kitchen. Once all hands are washed, Winston holds Phillip's hand again and leads him to the kitchen. He shows Phillip where to sit, and then we all sit down at the kitchen table. Winston sits between Phillip and me. There is silence. No one is saying a word. Drum Mom and Daddy Freeman look at the food on the table, while I look at everybody at the table. Finally, Phillip breaks the silence: "May I say grace and bless this food?" he asks. Drum Mom and Daddy Freeman look at Phillip at the same time. Then they look at each other and smile. Drum Mom says, "Yes, you may." Phillip says grace and blesses the food. When he finishes, we all say, "Amen." Winston says, "Amen."

When we finish eating dinner, we all walk to the front room to sit down and talk further. Winston plays on the floor and smiles at Phillip. Suddenly, Phillip says, "Please forgive my manners. I must go to my car. I left something in my car." I look at Phillip, puzzled. I think to myself, "He is going back to his car! He didn't leave anything in his car! He is leaving for the night!" I look at Drum Mom and Daddy Freeman, and they look at me. Phillip opens the front door and rushes out of it. The rest of us continue to look at each other in amazement that he is leaving in such a hurry.

After a moment, the front door once again opens, with Phillip reentering the house. I'm happy that he has come back! He has one small bag and two large bags in his arms. He sets them down on the couch, opens the small bag, and says, "Ruby's Drum Mom, this is for you." Phillip then proceeds to pull out a pink rose from the small bag. He hands the pink rose to Drum Mom. Amid her happiness, Drum Mom says, "Thank you, Phillip. I haven't had something so beautiful like this pink rose in a long time."

He reaches into the same small bag and pulls out a red rose. He hands the red rose to me. With the same happiness as Drum Mom's, I smile at Phillip and say, "This is beautiful. Thank you." "Beautiful roses for beautiful ladies," Phillip charmingly responds. "That is nice, Phillip," Daddy Freeman comments. "Thank you, Mr. Freeman," Phillip responds. "I didn't know you were going to be over here for dinner tonight. I don't have anything here for you." To this, Daddy Freeman says, "That's all right, Phillip, that you have nothing in the bags for me. However, for me, you have given me a greater gift! One that you can't pull out of a bag. Your gift to me is to be in the presence of a good man." "Thank you, Mr. Freeman," Phillip replies.

Phillip then reaches into one of the large bags and pulls out a red fireman's hat. He says, "Winston, come here. I have something for you." Phillip shows Winston the red fireman's hat; Winston starts jumping up and down with excitement. Winston runs to Phillip and Phillip places the hat on Winston's head. Winston turns around and lets us see him with his red fireman's hat on his head. "Look, everybody! I'm a fireman!" he says with excitement.

Phillip reaches into the other large bag, saying, "Winston, what good is a red fireman's hat without a red fire truck?" He proceeds to pull the red fire truck out of the large bag, and puts it on the floor. He makes the siren blare when he pushes the red fire truck. Winston starts screaming, "Look, Momma, I have a fire truck, too! Watch me and my truck go to a fire." Winston pushes the truck, while wearing his fireman's hat, and goes all around the house looking for a fire.

"Freeman," Drum Mom begins, "you say Phillip is a good man. I say he is a good man who gives Winston a red fireman's hat and a red fire truck with a siren that is going to take me to my grave." We all laugh at Drum Mom's comment; then I say, "Phillip, thank you for making all of us feel special and making us so happy. This is a good day." "You are welcome," Phillip replies. "It is my pleasure."

Phillip sits back on the couch beside me. While we continue to talk to each other, I watch Winston play with the red fire truck and with the red fireman's hat on his head. I look at Drum Mom swaying her pink rose from side to side and taking every opportunity to smell the pink rose. I hold my red rose close to my heart. Like Drum Mom, I take every opportunity to smell my rose. I see Daddy Freeman smiling as though this is one of the happiest days of his life since Winston was born.

"It's getting late," Phillip comments. "I want to get home before dark." I agree with Phillip's logic. He gets up from the couch, walks to the front door, then says, "Good night, everybody. Good night, Winston." Winston stops playing and runs to Phillip. He hugs Phillip's legs. Phillip picks Winston up from the floor and hugs him. "Good night, sleep tight. Don't let the bed bugs bite. Thank you," Winston says. We smile at Winston. "Good night, Phillip," Drum Mom and Daddy Freeman say in unison.

Phillip walks Winston over to where I am sitting on the couch. Winston and I go out the front door with Phillip. "I want to see you as often as I can before you leave in two months for beauty school," Phillip notes. "I can pick you up after work and take you to my place. Ask your friends, Fred and Lucille, if they can bring you to my club on Saturday nights. You may have to leave the club with them. I get off work so late and don't want to drive you home late at night. The heat may stop us again for being out so late. Tell Fred and Lucille that when they bring you to my club, they can get in at no charge and their liquor is free."

"Okay, Phillip," I say in agreement. Phillip kisses my hand and we say "Good night" to each other. "Good night," Winston chimes in.

I watch Phillip walk to and then get into his car, and drive off. Winston and I go inside the house and see Daddy Freeman standing by his seat. "I enjoyed myself tonight," Daddy Freeman says. "It's been wonderful. Ruby, I like Phillip. Good night, all. Good night, Winston." Drum Mom and I say, "Good night." I follow Daddy Freeman to the front door. When he leaves, I lock the door behind him. Drum Mom and I smile at each other, then head off to get ready for bed.

*****

For the next two months, except on Saturdays, I'm with Phillip. He picks me up from work and then we go to his pad and keep each other company. He has been telling me how much he loves me. He says, "Ruby, write me a letter every day while you are away in beauty school. I will write back. Inside my letter, I will have one red rose petal. This will be a symbol to remind you of my love for you. Always look for that one red rose petal." To his words, I respond, "Phillip, I love you back. I will write you a letter every day. I'll look forward to getting a letter from you. I will open it and will not stop until I find one red rose petal inside your letter. When I find the one red rose petal, I'll know that you love me and that you are still my lover."

Every night after we talk, we go to his bedroom. I know I am a fast woman. Phillip also knows that I am a fast woman, because I have a son. He touches me, and my body feels the heat from his body. He kisses me, and his kiss is sweeter than maple syrup. I want him badly. And I know he wants me, too. I can't stop this feeling. I can't stop myself. After we spend time in the bedroom, Phillip takes me back to my pad.

*****

This particular night is the last night that I will spend time with Phillip before I leave to go to beauty school. We are at his pad, sitting on the couch, after having just finished eating. Phillip looks at me and asks, "Ruby, are you all right? Your face looks a little pale. By the way, dinner was delicious." "Yes, Phillip, I am fine," I reply. "Well, I do feel a little different." After that profession, I vomit on him and on the couch. "Phillip, I am ready to go home. I feel really bad," I say. "Okay. Let me change clothes and get my keys," Phillip responds. He changes clothes, finds his keys, and gets a large brown bag for me to hold on the way home, just in case.

On the ride home, I put the bag to my mouth and proceed to vomit into the bag. Shortly thereafter, I vomit once again into the bag. "Ruby, you are sick," Phillip comments. "Do you need to stop at the hospital?" I say, "No, Phillip! Just get me home." I vomit again. I get mad at myself for getting sick in his car. Phillip looks at me. I look at Phillip. I then turn my head, facing the window on my side of the rod. I rest my head against the window, then start crying to myself. I think about Daddy Freeman. I think about what Daddy Freeman told me. Daddy Freeman is right! *The desires of the flesh are not always good.*

Chapter Seven
GO ON

Very early the next morning, I am in my bed at Drum Mom's house. She and Winston are still asleep. Still feeling sick, I get up from my bed, put on my house robe, and exit the front door of the house. Once outside, I run down the steps of the porch, but then have to stop running so that I can vomit. When I finish vomiting, I look toward Daddy Freeman's house. I see Daddy Freeman looking at me. He is looking out of his bedroom window that faces Drum Mom's front porch. I stand there in the midst of my vomit, unable to move. I say to myself, "Daddy Freeman just saw me vomit." He keeps looking at me until he thinks I'm okay. I then see him close the curtains to his bedroom window. I wipe my mouth with my hand and then head back into the house. Noticing that Drum Mom and Winston are still asleep, I go to the toilet room and clean myself up.

After cleaning up and putting on my work clothes, I hear Drum Mom get up from her bed and walk to the toilet room. I proceed to walk to the kitchen, and Drum Mom enters soon after. "Ruby, how are you this morning? You're up pretty early," she observes. "I am fine," I reply. "How are you?" "Fine," she responds.

"Drum Mom, I have to go to work early this morning, so I can talk to Miss Johnson," I say. "I have to remind her I'm leaving town and will not be back for several months." Drum Mom says, "That's right. You need to talk to Miss Johnson about going to beauty school." I then hear Daddy Freeman blowing the horn on his car. "Drum Mom, that's Daddy Freeman outside waiting on me," I note. "I should go. I'll be home early today."

I leave the house and go outside onto the porch. As I walk down the steps and approach Daddy Freeman's car, I see him looking at me. He is still looking at me when I get into the car. "Good morning, Daddy Freeman," I greet him. "How are you this morning?" Daddy Freeman says, "Good morning, Ruby. I am fine. How are you doing?" "Never better," I say. He smiles at me, never mentioning that he saw me vomiting outside Drum Mom's house this morning. I say, "Daddy Freeman, I am going to work today to fix one customer's hair and talk with Miss Johnson. This will be my last day working in her salon. I'll walk home. You don't have to pick me up from work today." Daddy Freeman responds with "Okay."

The engine of the car is still running. He puts it in gear and drives. While he is driving, he says, "I got everything finally taken care of with Beatrice. You can stay with her in her house. Instead of you paying her for rent, I will pay her the rent if you are in school. What you will have to pay for are your ticket to ride the bus to New York, money for you to attend beauty school, and any other expenses you have." I reply, "Thank you, Daddy Freeman. You are so good to me and Winston. I promise you that I will do everything you say." He continues driving until we are in front of the salon.

When I enter the salon, I see that Miss Johnson is there by herself. We speak to each other. I then proceed to say, "Miss Johnson, today is my last day at work. I will not be working here at the salon for several months. You know that I am going to beauty school to get my license to fix hair. I'll be coming back to work here when I have my license." She replies, "Ruby, I am proud of you. For a long time, we have been waiting for this day to come! Remember, I will do everything to keep your customers coming to this salon. I'll give your customers back to you when you come back to work." When Miss Johnson finishes talking, my customer for the day walks into the salon. It is Lucille!

Lucille greets Miss Johnson and me. We speak back to her. When I look at Lucille, I realize that this is the first time I have ever seen Lucille looking so sad. She doesn't look happy at all. "Lucille, what's wrong?" I ask. "Ruby, we promised not to talk about it. I am your only customer that knows you are leaving. I am going to miss you," she professes. I say, "I am going to miss you, too. Ruby will be back!" Lucille nods when I say this.

Miss Johnson's customer walks into the salon and Lucille walks over to my chair. Lucille and I don't say anything to each other. I continuously look up while I'm fixing her hair and our eyes meet in the mirror. Our eyes talk; they say what our mouths don't say. They say how our hearts feel about one another. They say how much we love each other.

Upon finishing Lucille's hair, we get our belongings and say goodbye to Miss Johnson and her customer. We then leave the salon together. Fred has arrived to pick up Lucille. I smile at Fred as he sits in his rod, then Lucille and I hug each other tightly. "Girl, you're putting on a little weight," Lucille comments. "Phillip must be feeding you well." We then loosen our embrace, and Lucille gets into Fred's rod. I smile at Lucille, and she smiles back at me. They drive away, and I walk home.

When I get home, Drum Mom is playing with Winston. Winston sees me and runs to me, and I then scoop him up and hug him. I am going to leave in a few days, so I don't want to let go of my baby! Drum Mom sees this and says, "Ruby, put Winston back down on the floor. I want you to wash up. Then, go to the kitchen and bake Winston a birthday cake. While you're in beauty school, Winston will turn two years old. We need to celebrate his birthday every day before you leave." I respond to her words, in total agreement to celebrate every day until my departure.

*****

For the next few days we celebrate, singing "Happy Birthday!" to Winston. Daddy Freeman and Phillip come over to the house every night with a gift for Winston. They buy him clothes, a rubber ball and bat, a ball cap, play dough, coloring books, and coloring pencils. And each of us eats a slice of the birthday cake.

We then sit in the front room, watching Winston play with his new toys. One day, Daddy Freeman says, "Ruby, I have another sister. Her name is Pearl-Lee. She lives further north of Beatrice. She is younger than Beatrice. I haven't seen or talked to her in years. When she left home, she never returned. Ask Beatrice about her well-being. If you see her or talk to her, let her know that her big brother wants to hear from her." I say, "Daddy Freeman, I didn't know you have a sister other than Beatrice. Beatrice is the only one you talk about."

"My momma and daddy have one boy and three girls," Daddy Freeman began to explain. They named us Freeman, Annie-Mary, Beatrice, and Pearl-Lee. Annie-Mary lives in Memphis. I drive to Memphis to see her whenever she calls for me to come down." I comment, "Daddy Freeman, I would love to meet all your sisters." To this, he responds, "My child, maybe you will someday."

"Ruby, this is our last night together for a while," Phillip says, joining the conversation. "Can I have your permission to come and spend some time with Winston while you are in school?" I smile and say, "Yes, Phillip. That's all right with me." I look at Drum Mom and ask, "Drum Mom, will this be all right with you?" Drum Mom says yes. Then she looks at Phillip and says, "Just send word or tell Freeman when you want to come by the house. Freeman will tell me what you say."

*****

When the week is over, I know Drum Mom, Daddy Freeman, Winston, and Phillip hate to see me leave. We've had so much fun celebrating Winston's early birthday. I hope my son will always re-member me and these last few days we have spent together.

When Daddy Freeman and Phillip arrive at the house—very early in the morning—I am packed and ready for Daddy Freeman to drive me to the bus station. I hug Drum Mom and say, "I love you so much. Thank you for taking care of Winston for me. Thank you for letting me better myself. I promise that I will do well and get my license from beauty school. I will write to you." I then hug Phillip, saying, "Phillip, I love you. I will miss you." "Ruby, I love you," Phillip responds. "Don't forget to look for the one red rose petal!" We smile at each other upon his words.

I said my goodbyes to Winston the night before. It is too early in the morning for him to get up and see his momma go off to school. Daddy Freeman says, "Ruby, it's time for us to leave." Phillip takes my suitcase to the car, and Daddy Freeman follows behind Phillip. And I take up the rear in the line. As I walk away from the house, I begin to reflect on the time when Drum Mom came to get Robert and me to live with her. I remember her saying to us, *"Walk and don't look back, unless it is for your own good."* I walk, but I can't help myself. I stop, look back, and see Drum Mom on the porch, standing in front of the door. "Ruby, go on. It's for your own good," she says.

Chapter Eight

WHEELS

It is still quite early in the morning when we arrive at the bus station. "Ruby, do you have your bus ticket and money?" Daddy Freeman inquires. "Yes, I have my bus ticket in my purse. I also have five dollars in my purse," I note. Drum Mom had put the rest of my money in a handkerchief that she pinned to my bra, so that no one would take it. "How long will you have to ride the bus to get to New York?" he asks. "The trip to New York will take about three days," I respond. Phillip, who has trailed us, gets out of his car and walks to Daddy Freeman's car. He says, "Ruby, here comes the bus!" Daddy Freeman gets out of the car and retrieves my suitcase from out of his car, and we then proceed to stand on the side of the road so that the bus driver knows to stop because someone is at this stop, waiting to ride the bus.

As the bus approaches the spot where we are standing, I kiss Daddy Freeman and say, "Goodbye, Daddy Freeman. I love you." Then I turn and kiss Phillip, saying, "Goodbye Phillip, my love." He says, "Goodbye, Ruby. Look for the one red rose petal in my letters!"

When the bus comes to a stop, Daddy Freeman hands my suitcase to the bus driver when he exits the bus. The driver then puts it in the colored section under the bus. I give the bus driver my ticket and get on the bus with my two large, folded blankets and a large bag of food that Drum Mom prepared for the trip. Upon entering the bus, even though I see empty seats in the front of the bus, I must walk to the back of the bus where colored folks are only allowed to sit. As I walk down the aisle to the back of the bus, I walk past some white people and some empty seats, and hope there is an empty seat on which I can sit down. I get to the back of the bus and, lucky for me, there is one empty seat on the left side of the bus—and it is a window seat! I sit down and look out of the window to see Daddy Freeman and Phillip smiling at me. I know they are happy to see that I have a seat on the bus.

The bus driver gets back on the bus; he proceeds to count the number of people on it. "Our next stop will be Nashville, Tennessee," he says. "We will be there in five hours. Enjoy your ride." As the bus starts moving, I wave goodbye to Daddy Freeman and Phillip; I see them wave back. I then turn away from them and don't look back, because I must go and do what I must do!

When we get to the county line, I realize how cold it is on the bus! I hear the little boy who is sitting behind me say, "Momma, I am so cold." "I know, child," his momma responds. "Hush now, you are on a bus!" I look back and see a little boy (who is about seven years old) with his momma's arms wrapped around him. He is wearing jeans and a white T-shirt. I know he is cold, so I give the mom one of my blankets. "Thank you. This is my first time riding a bus. I didn't know it would be so cold," she responds to my gesture. I watch her put the blanket over her son; I then hear him say, "Momma, thank you. Look, this is a long blanket! It's room for you, too, Momma." She moves the boy to the middle of his seat and puts the blanket around him, and then drapes the rest of the blanket over herself. I put my other blanket around me. I soon notice that everyone, except the bus driver, is asleep on the bus. I go to sleep as well.

The next thing I know, the bus comes to a stop, and I hear the bus driver say, "We are in Nashville, Tennessee. The bus stops here. Everyone get off the bus. White people first. Get all your things you brought inside the bus and take them off this bus. The baggage boy will give back your suitcase from under the bus. Take it and keep it with you. Look on the board or ask the ticket clerk what time your bus leaves to get to your next designation. Have a great day. Thank you for riding this bus."

Colored people wait for the white people to get off the bus before they can depart the bus. "I wish they would hurry and get off the bus. I have to use the toilet!" I say to myself. Finally, when there are no more white folks on the bus, the bus driver says, "Colored folks off the bus." The mother who has been sitting behind me gives me back my blanket, saying, "Thank you for letting us use your blanket to keep warm. Nashville is our home. We won't be riding any farther." I gather up my blankets and the large brown bag in my arms and get off the bus. I get my suitcase from the baggage boy.

I walk fast to get inside the bus station, and then ask the first colored person I see where the toilet room is. "You must be from down south," the man says with a laugh. "There is no toilet room here. There is a colored restroom for women down the hall and to your left." I thank the man and then proceed to walk quickly down the hallway, where I see a line about a mile long. "If I don't get to the toilet room, I mean *restroom*, I am going to wet myself," I think to myself.

A white woman standing outside the long line says, "If you got a nickel, you can come and use the restroom." I reach into my purse and get my nickel, though I don't understand why I need a nickel to use the restroom. "I have a nickel," I say to the white woman. Everyone in line looks back at me! The white woman says, "Come up here." She sees my nickel and tells me, "You can go and use the restroom."

Nickel in hand, I hold on tightly to my purse and belongings. There is another white woman in the colored women's restroom, which is dirty. She says, "Put your nickel in the slot on the door. The door will open for you to go in and use the restroom." "That's why the line is so long. Those women don't have a nickel to use the restroom. I am so blessed to have Daddy Freeman and Drum Mom. They made sure I have coins and enough money for my trip," I think as I relieve myself. I wait and stay a while on the toilet seat, because I don't want to spend another nickel to use the restroom. I soon finish my business, wash my hands, and leave the restroom.

Once outside the restroom, I notice that the line is now shorter. I reach into my purse and pull out some nickels; I give the nickels to the colored women who are still standing in line. They smile and say either "Thank you" or "God bless you." I find a seat in the bus station and count my coins inside my purse. I had given ten nickels to the colored women in line to use the restroom—and I still have plenty left for my trip. "I just need to make sure I don't drink a lot of water," I tell myself.

After assessing my financial situation, I walk to the board on the wall to see when the next bus is leaving for New York. I know how to read the board because Daddy Freeman went over this with me. I see that the next bus to New York leaves at 3:00 p.m. That is four hours from now. Standing beside me is an older white woman. She looks like she is having trouble reading the board. "Miss, are you having trouble reading the board?" I ask the woman. "I can help you." To this, she says, "I can read! I don't need no help from no colored girl!" She then walks away.

I go back to my seat and sit down. I stay awake and notice the same old white woman getting up and going back and forth to the board. She walks to the desk, looks around, and says nothing to the colored man working behind the desk. A white woman finally goes around behind the desk. The old white woman promptly gets up, and so do several other white people. They get in line to talk to the white woman behind the desk. When the old white woman is finally at the front of the line, she talks to the white lady who is behind the desk. She starts crying, leaves the line, picks up her suitcase, and walks out of the station. I think she missed her bus!

My bus soon arrives, bound for Kentucky and New York. The bus driver calls for people going to New York to board the bus. After the white people get on the bus, I give my suitcase to the baggage boy, get on the bus, and then walk to the back to get my seat. I find a seat on the left side of the bus, which happens to be a window seat. We soon pull out of the Nashville bus station and head to Kentucky.

The bus driver says, "It will take us four hours to get to our next stop in Kentucky." I stay awake so I won't miss any historical landmarks on my way to Kentucky. I am excited because I have never been out of the state of Tennessee—but now, I can tell people back home that I've been to Kentucky!

The bus pulls up to the station in Kentucky. "We are in the state of Kentucky," the bus driver announces. "This bus will be leaving Kentucky in six hours headed for New York. Those going to New York will come back to this bus in six hours. If you are not traveling to New York, look at the board or ask the ticket clerk how to get to your destination. The baggage boy will get your suitcase for you. Everyone, get off the bus. White folks board the bus first. Have a nice day. Thank you for riding this bus."

I get off the bus, get my suitcase, and walk toward the colored restroom for women. There is no line outside the restroom and no white woman to ask me if I have a nickel to use the restroom. I then wonder if the restroom is open or if I should go somewhere else to relieve myself. I open the door and find that the restroom is clean and smells good. There is no white woman in the restroom to tell me to put my nickel in the slot of the door. I go to the door and see the coin slot on the door, then I put my nickel in the slot, go in, and relieve myself.

Next, I go check out the board to make sure that my bus is going to New York. *I have come too far to miss the bus!* The board shows that the bus driver is correct: I am going back on the same bus to get to New York.

Another white bus driver is taking over. He says, "This bus is heading to New York. I need everyone to get their ticket for me to look at when you get on the bus. All white people get on the bus." So, they get on the bus. The bus driver then states, "Colored folks who came to Kentucky on this bus, get on the bus now." I get on the bus and go to my same seat. Lastly, the bus driver says, "All you other colored folks riding to New York, get on the bus now."

While sitting on the bus, I look up and see an old colored woman slowly walking and leaning on a walking stick, trying to make it to the back of the bus. She is wearing a green polyester suit, and gloves, a hat, and shoes that are black. The hat covers the top of her shiny gray hair that flows down to her shoulders. She is wearing pretty earrings and a necklace to accent her dress. "Lord, have mercy. Is she going to make it back here?" I wonder to myself. She finally makes it to the back and sits down beside me. I see that she is old in the face; she is about sixty years old. We say "hello" to each other.

The bus leaves the station headed toward New York. It is so quiet on this cold bus! Soon, everyone has fallen asleep except for me, the old woman sitting next to me, the bus driver, and some colored people sitting on the right side of the bus. The old colored woman notices that, too. She looks at me and smiles. She then reaches into her purse and pulls out a can of snuff. She puts a handful of snuff between her bottom lip and gum and does this until her chin is filled with it. She turns to me and asks, "Girl, you want some?" "No!" I respond emphatically, turning my body completely away from her and pulling my blanket over my head. I say to myself, "How awful! This old colored woman is riding a public bus and putting snuff in her mouth. I know she has something to spit that snuff into." She reaches back into her purse, pulls out a sealed jar, unscrews the jar, and spits that snuff into the jar. "Oh, my goodness! She's doing this again!" I think to myself. "I don't want to see this!" I turn my back to her and go to sleep. I don't want the colored people to think that the old woman is with me. "There she goes again!" I think, once again hearing her put that snuff into her mouth and spit it out in that spit jar.

After the bus ride, we finally arrive at our next stop. "We are in Philadelphia, Pennsylvania," the bus driver announces. "The next stop on this bus is New York. Those who are going on to New York will come back to this bus. Inside is a board with information to help those of you who are not going to New York. Those not going to New York, take all your things off this bus. The baggage man will give you your luggage. Everyone exit the bus now."

I hear the bus driver's words. His words sound different here compared to the words he speaks in Kentucky and back home. Back there, the bus driver calls us black people "colored folks." Here, he calls us "those" and "everyone." Back there, the bus driver says, "the baggage boy." Here, he says, "the baggage man." Back there in the South, he says, "suitcase. Here, he calls it "luggage." Back there, he says, "Get off the bus after the white folks." Here, he says, "everybody exit the bus."

I get off the bus and wait to get my suitcase. I finally get all my belongings and walk to the restroom, where there is a beautiful, young colored woman adjusting her green dress and looking in the mirror, washing her face. I go to the toilet with my things. Once done with my business, I come out and find the same colored woman at the mirror, putting makeup on her face. I wash my hands and notice her looking in the mirror at me. "How are you?" she asks. "Fine," I respond, then ask, "How are you doing today?" She says, "I am fine, too. What is your name and where are you from?" I say, "My name is Ruby. I am from Tennessee." I then ask, "What is your name and where are you from?" "My name is Beth Eden Finch," she replies. "They call me Beth Eden, and I am from Mississippi."

She keeps looking at me by way of the mirror, and I begin to feel a little uncomfortable. "Beth Eden, why do you keep looking at me?" I inquire. "Ruby, don't you know me?" she asks. "We have met before." "I don't know you!" I exclaim angrily. "I have never met you! I am asking you for the last time, why do you keep looking at me!?"

She says, "Now, wait a minute, Ruby. You met me on the bus! I am the old woman with the walking stick that sat next to you!" "Old woman!" I say snappily. "You are not an old woman!" "Yes, I am," Beth Eden assures. "I dress like an old woman to make sure I get a seat on the bus. Dressing like an old woman always works for me when I am riding the bus. The colored men will get up and let an old woman sit down before they will anyone else. People don't talk much to an old woman. This time, there just happened to be an empty seat on the bus—an empty seat on the bus next to you.

"Ruby, what was I going to do? Pull my clothes and gray wig off in front of everybody on the bus because I found a seat next to you! That would have been a sight to see. The bus driver and white people would have thrown me off the bus! I took those clothes and wig off in this restroom and threw them in the garbage. I am on my way to New York and, girl, I got to look good with my pretty self!"

We both laugh. I laugh until I cry. Then I stop laughing and look at her. I say, "Beth Eden, I need to ask you something. Did you dip snuff, and how do you have the nerve to ask me if *I* want some snuff?" "Ruby, that wasn't snuff!" Beth Eden replies. "That was cocoa and sugar mixed together to look like snuff. Some I swallow and some I spit in the spit jar." I respond, "Oh, my goodness. I thought that was snuff in your mouth!" We laugh together again and again.

After our conversation ends, we walk to the bus lobby and sit down. "How did you make yourself look like an old woman?" I ask Beth Eden. She replies, "Two days ago, the white woman in Mississippi who hired me fixed my face up so that I looked like an old woman. She does this for me when I need to ride the bus so that I can get a seat. She puts chimney ashes, clay, and some of her makeup on my face. She is very good at changing women's faces and enjoys every minute of it. She likes me a lot!" We laugh. Chimney ashes, clay, and makeup! "Beth Eden, you are something to behold!" I comment.

Soon, we hear the bus driver calling for everyone who rode the bus from Kentucky to Philadelphia—and who are headed to New York—to board the bus first. I notice that Beth Eden is getting in line with the new riders. "Beth Eden, why are you not boarding the bus first?" I ask. She says, "Ruby, I will. You just go on and get on the bus." I proceed to board the bus and sit in my same seat. Everyone who was on the bus when we stopped in Philadelphia boards the bus, except for Beth Eden. The bus driver then calls for everyone else going to New York to board the bus. When I look up, I see Beth Eden, walking and leading the colored people to the back of the bus. I smile as Beth Eden makes her way to the seat beside me. I say, "Beth Eden, what was that about?" "I don't want anyone from the Kentucky bus station to think that I am that old woman who dips snuff in her mouth and spits in a spit jar!" she replies. We laugh.

Once everyone is aboard and settled, the bus starts moving— bound for New York. The colored folks in the back of the bus begin to talk. "I am so glad that old woman is not back on this bus," one person comments. The colored folks start laughing. Someone else says, "She was sitting in that seat where the pretty woman is seating. You need to check that seat, lady." Colored folks, including me, laugh as Beth Eden is looking around her seat. "I know that's right!" someone else chimes in. "Did you see how she was dipping that snuff, putting it in her mouth, and spitting it in that dirty jar?" Once again, the colored folks, including Beth Eden and me, laugh!

While everyone is laughing, I notice a young colored man, around mine and Beth Eden's age, sitting across from us. He is not laughing, and he looks so sad. He is a fine colored man, with a baby face, who is dressed in a black suit. When we stop laughing, I ask him, "What is your name?" He says, "London Rhodes." I say, "I am Ruby, and this is my new friend, Beth Eden. Where are you going, London?" "New York," he responds. "We are going to New York, too," Beth Eden and I say in unison.

"That's good. Maybe we can be friends," he replies. I don't know anyone there. I am having to leave Philly because my family turned their back on me. They said for me to get out of their life. 'We don't know you anymore and we wish you weren't born!' So, here I am, on the bus to New York forced to start a new life." "Well, London Rhodes, you got new friends now," Beth Eden says to him. "Ruby and I will be your true friends! So be happy and smile!" Beth Eden starts singing. London and I laugh and smile when Beth Eden sings:

"The wheels on the bus go around and round,

Around and around, around and round;

The wheels on the bus go around and around,

All day long!"

After the bus crosses the New York state line, the bus driver says, "We will be arriving at the bus station in New York in one hour. If your stop ends in New York, please prepare yourself and get all your things together to take off this bus. Any of your things left on the bus will be transferred to our next stop in New Jersey, or will be thrown off the bus in New York. If you are going on to New Jersey, you should return to this bus. If you are going someplace else, check the information board or ask someone to help you get to your next destination. Thank you for traveling this bus line."

Beth Eden, London, and I are getting so excited! We are here in New York! "What are your plans in New York?" I ask my two new friends. "Where will the two of you be living?"

"I plan to attend beauty school with you, Ruby," Beth Eden informs me. "I must find a job and a place to live. I am like London—I don't know anyone in New York."

London says, "I have no plans, except to be me. I know that I will find a place to live once I learn myself around New York."

"I am going to live with my Daddy Freeman's sister, Beatrice," I begin explaining. "She owns a house and lets women who are trying to go to school and have a career rent from her. Beth Eden, maybe she has an extra room you can rent. We can go there together and find out if there is room in the inn for you." "Sure, I'll go with you, Ruby," Beth Eden says with a smile.

I add, "Beatrice told Daddy Freeman that she would have someone pick me up at the bus station and take me to her place. There might be room in the car for all of us to ride there. That way, we can all know where at least one of us lives."

"Ruby, that sounds good to me," Beth Eden comments. Then London asks, "Ruby, are you rich?! Girl, does your family have money?" I reply, "I just know someone who knows someone."

When the bus arrives at the bus station, the three of us stay together. We get all our things we carried onto the bus, exit the bus, retrieve our suitcases, and then walk into the bus station. "Ruby, a colored man is holding up a sign with your name on it," London points out. "Girl, you are too hip . . . you got your own chauffeur!"

"You two stay with me," I instruct them. We walk to the man carrying the sign with my name on it. When we reach him, I say, "I am Ruby. Beatrice said someone would be here to pick me up and take me to her place." "Yes, I am Marty, Beatrice's friend. She sent me here," the man said. "Marty, do you have room in your car for my friends?" I ask. "Yes, if they are going to Beatrice's place," he responds. My friends and I then get into the car, knowing that we are starting a new life together.

Chapter Nine
ROOM AND BOARD . . . AND BEAUTY SCHOOL

After the car ride from the bus station, we arrive at Beatrice's house. I knock on the door, and a woman who I presume is Beatrice comes and opens the door. She is a beautiful, dark-skinned woman with a huge smile on her face. She is wearing a plain brown dress with an apron around her waist. Her smile makes me feel welcome. "Ruby, I have been waiting for you!" Beatrice says, greeting me. "I am glad you're here. Come on in!"

All three of us go into Beatrice's house. It is beautiful! The living room is huge, containing many antique chairs in which people can sit, congregate, and enjoy her company. Down the hall from the living room, there appears to be a large kitchen and eating room. To the right of the living room, I notice a closed door. "That room must be Beatrice's bedroom," I say to myself. There is a large stairway to the left of her living room. I see three doors. "Upstairs must be the bedrooms for people who live here," I think to myself.

"Come and sit down," Beatrice encourages. We each go to an antique chair and sit down. "Ruby, who are these people with you?" she asks. I say, "This is my friend, Beth Eden. She is going to beauty school with me. She doesn't know anyone in New York and needs a place to live. I wonder if you might have an extra room that you can rent to Beth Eden."

"Ruby, you are very quick in asking me something like that," Beatrice swiftly retorts. "I only rent to people I know, or people I know who send women to live with me. I have an extra room, but Beth

Eden and I will need to talk before I rent her that room." I say, "Yes, I am sorry, and I understand." "Hello, Miss Beatrice," Beth Eden interjects. "How are you doing today?" Beatrice says, "Hello, Beth Eden. I am doing well today."

Beatrice then asks, "Ruby, who is the young man?" I reply, "This is London Rhodes. He is a friend whom we met on the bus in Philadelphia. He is here to live in New York. The three of us have become close friends while riding on a bus."

"Hello, Miss Beatrice," London says. "How are you today?" Beatrice stares at London, smiles, and nods her head. "Do you know a safe place where a young man can lay down his head?" London then asks her. "No, I don't," Beatrice replies. "You can call Marty and see if he knows of someone. Let me write down his telephone number for you."

Beatrice writes down Marty's phone number on a piece of paper and hands it to London. London says, "Thank you, and I will follow up with Mr. Marty. I'm going to leave so I can find a place before dark. Ruby and Beth Eden, I will see you two later. Don't forget, we are true friends." London proceeds to leave the house with the only thing he owns—the clothes on his back.

Beatrice says, "Ruby, follow me upstairs and I will show you to your room. At dinnertime, around five in the evening, come down to the living room and we will talk about your living situation and beauty school. Beth Eden and I need to be alone so that we can talk." I say, "Beth Eden, I will see you later." I follow Beatrice upstairs to my room and look back, noticing the sadness on my new friend's face. Beth Eden sees the sadness on my face. We don't smile at each other. We look like our thoughts are in the clouds. I hope Beatrice will find favor in Beth Eden and let her stay in that empty room.

At a quarter to five, I go downstairs to the living room. Beth Eden is still here. I see a big smile on her face. She runs to me and says, "Miss Beatrice is going to let me stay at her house!" We smile and jump up and down just like little children who are happy to get some candy from their momma. When we finally stop celebrating, we sit down in a chair. The two of us want to be ready at five o'clock, just like Beatrice asked of us. At 5:00 p.m., Beatrice comes into the living room and sits down.

"Ruby, I am sure by now that you know Beth Eden can stay," Beatrice says. "Yes, Beatrice, I know! Thank you," I reply. "Ladies," Beatrice continues, "you must understand that I have rules in my house and you must follow my rules." She then proceeds to lay out the rules:

- "Men may only visit during the hours of 7:00 p.m. to 9:00 p.m.

- Men may visit you only in the living room, and not in any other rooms of the house.

- Under no condition will you have a male friend stay overnight.

- At 9:30 in the evening, the door is locked, and all will be quiet for the night.

- You will clean your room every day before you leave the house.

- Dinnertime is at 5:30 p.m. You will be at the dinner table unless you are working.

- Rent is due the first day of the month. If you don't have the rent money by the fifth of the month, I will put you out of the house. Rent money pays for food, water, and electricity.

- You will pay me five cents each time you use the telephone.

- You must find work. When you leave beauty school for the day, you go to your job and work. This will keep you busy and help you stay out of trouble. Men look to take advantage of beautiful, young women like you. Don't be their prey!"

After explaining her rules, Beatrice looks at the two of us, then asks, "Do you have any questions about my rules?" "No," Beth Eden and I say in unison. "Then it shall be as I have said," Beatrice concludes.

Beatrice smiles and appears to be satisfied with Beth Eden and me. "Ruby, call Freeman later and let him know you're here in New York with me," Beatrice instructs me. "Leave your five cents on the table by the telephone. As for beauty school, the school is only two blocks from this house. It's good you're here a week before school starts so you'll know ahead of time how to get there. Tomorrow, the two of you will have to walk to the beauty school.

"Always stay together! Find work! You'll need extra money to make it in New York. In this house, you will only bring home God's righteous money. There is no place in my house for the devil's money! Do you two understand?" We say, "Yes." Beatrice notes, "Well, then, I have added you both to my family. It's 5:30. Let's eat dinner!"

*****

On our second day in New York, Beth Eden and I leave the house and walk down the street to find the beauty school.

"Beatrice told us the beauty school is only two blocks from the house," I remind Beth Eden. As we walk, we immediately see colored women in their fine dresses and colored men in their fine suits walking the streets. The colored men read the newspaper as they walk. And when we pass by them, they stop reading the newspaper, tilt their hats, and say, "Good morning, ladies." Beth Eden and I smile every time we hear one of them say this to us. We continue on our mission.

A block and a half from Beatrice's house, we see colored people begging for food, people sleeping on the sidewalks, people selling things in packages, and women dressed in tight, short skirts and dresses. I say, "Beth Eden, I have never seen anything like this before! These people are poor and have no food to eat, no nice clothes to wear, and no place to sleep. Let's stop and ask them what we can do to help them." "Ruby, you can help by praying for them," Beth Eden replies. "Let's keep walking. We don't need to stop in these places! Come on, Ruby. We got to stay together."

When we finally reach the beauty school, we enter the building and proceed to meet our instructor. We sit down and talk to Mrs. Foxx. She is happy to talk with us, saying, "The two of you have made a good first impression. Most students don't take the time to talk to their instructor before class begins. That doesn't mean you will pass my class; that only means that I have met you and I see potential in you." We leave Miss Foxx's office, knowing that our walking to the beauty school and meeting Mrs. Foxx was worth our time.

After leaving the school, we hop on the city bus and ride to the other side of town. When the bus stops, Beth Eden and I walk over to and enter the diner. Beth Eden goes over to the counter and asks, "May we see the manager?" The lady at the counter calls out to the manager, and he comes out to the front. "My name is Mr. Schapiro," he says. "I am the manager and owner of this diner. May I help you?"

We introduce ourselves to Mr. Schapiro and begin talking to him. When one of us says something, the other finishes with a strong statement. We talk like we are one in spirit—as though we have rehearsed the whole conversation. "Mr. Schapiro, sir, we are looking for a job," I explain. "We are going to beauty school and we need your help."

"We will work hard, and you'll find that you can trust us," Beth Eden adds. "We are from the South. We know and don't mind hard work. You can help us, and we can help you make a profit and expand your business. We will not let you down!" Mr. Schapiro looks at us and says, "When can the two of you start to work?" "Today," we promptly reply.

We start working at the diner that very night. We end up working the rest of the week before school starts. When Mr. Schapiro notices how hard we work at his diner, he says, "Come to work when school is out and work as many hours that you can work. You two are from the South and have proven that you don't mind the hard work it takes to run a diner. I like the fact that the two of you are going to school and trying to better yourself. I want to help you as much as I can. I promise you, if you continue to help me, I will help you."

*****

The day that beauty school starts, Beth Eden and I arrive at the classroom thirty minutes before class is scheduled to begin. At that time, we are the only students in the classroom. We sit beside each other in front of the instructor's desk. Ten minutes before class starts, other students come into the classroom. We count eight other students. That makes ten of us in beauty school.

At 7:00 a.m., Mrs. Foxx enters the classroom. She doesn't say anything but goes to the board and writes this on the board: "My name is Mrs. Foxx." She turns to the class and says, "My name is Mrs. Foxx, and I will be your instructor. Before I talk about the subjects and rules for this class, I would like each one of you to stand, give your name, where you are from, and tell the class why you have chosen to enroll in beauty school. We will start with those sitting in the front row to my right."

I stand up and say, "My name is Ruby. I am from Ripley, Tennessee. I work in a beauty salon back home. I have chosen beauty school to get a diploma that will help me get a license to do hair. I love helping women look beautiful and want to learn the proper techniques to improve my skills. My diploma will also help to define me and allow me to open my own licensed beauty salon. Thank you." As I sit down, the students start clapping. Mrs. Foxx ignores the clapping and says, "Next."

"I am Beth Eden. My last residence was in Mississippi. I met Ruby in Kentucky. I have chosen beauty school for the same reasons as my friend Ruby."

"I am Lydia Streets from Ohio. I am here for the same reasons as Ruby."

"I am Doris Ann Jones from Alabama. I, too, am here for the same reasons as Ruby."

"I am Lisa Lee from New York. I, too, am here for the same reasons as Ruby."

"I am Carla Whitfield from New York. I, too, am here for the same reasons as Ruby."

"I am Linda Clayborn from New York. I, too, am here for the same reasons as Ruby."

"I am Rochelle Davis from New Jersey. I, too, am here for the same reasons."

"I am Shirley Faye Jenkins from Mississippi. I, too, am here for the same reasons."

"I am London Rhodes. I do not spell my last name *r-o-s-e* or *r-o-a-d-s*. *Rhodes* is spelled R-h-o-d-e-s." (Beth Eden and I look at each other in amazement, then look at the student standing up to see if—*no, this can't be the London Rhodes we know. This class is for women only.*) "I am from Philly," London continues. "Hi, Ruby and Beth Eden. Remember me? I met you all in Philly. It's London—your true friend, London. I am here because of Ruby and Beth Eden."

After his introduction, London sits down and looks at us. Beth and I look at London, who is dressed up like a woman—with heels and makeup on, and wearing a woman's wig on the top of his head.

London is beautiful! Beth Eden and I are totally in shock and are trying to refrain from drawing attention to our facial expressions. But the man we know as London Rhodes—who rode the bus with us to New York, who sat in Beatrice's house with us, and whom we call our true friend—is in this class saying he is a woman. How did he—I mean *she*—get away with this?

Mrs. Foxx says, "I have reviewed and approved London's application. She meets all requirements to be in this class. You do not deserve to know why there will be exceptions for London, but she has asked that I acknowledge why our rules change for her:

- "London has problems with her own hair. She was in a fire when she was seven years old. The fire left scars on her head and she has not been able to grow her hair back. She prefers to wear a beautiful wig. For this reason, no one will wash her head or style her wig or pull the wig off her head to be styled.

- "London is fine. Her hands do not prevent her from washing and styling your hair. She has no scars on her hands.

- "The fire also left scars on her body. For that reason, London feels more comfortable using the ladies' restroom when there are no other ladies in the restroom. Please respect her wishes and immediately adhere to my rules for her. After all, you are now a family and must learn to work together under different circumstances. The only way you will pass my class is to work together."

Mrs. Foxx looks at the ladies in the class, and then at London. "London, is there anything you would like to say?" she asks. "No, Mrs. Foxx. Thank you," London says in a mild, teary voice.

"Then let us move on!" Mrs. Foxx exclaims. "The next thirty minutes, I want all of you to get to know each other. Take your restroom break during this time. Class will start back in thirty minutes." After her announcement, Mrs. Foxx leaves the classroom.

Everyone stands up from their desks and begins talking to one another. Beth Eden and I run to talk to London, who is still standing at his desk. I say in a whisper, "London, what in the world is going on here?" "How are you doing, Ruby? Good to see you, too," London replies. Beth Eden is laughing so hard that she starts crying. "How are you doing, Beth Eden?" London asks her. Beth Eden continues to laugh so hard that she can't answer London's question.

"I am the same London that you know as a man, but this London wants to be a woman," London says in a whisper. "That's why my folks have nothing to do with me. While in New York, I thought about the two of you going to beauty school together. I thought, 'I have no plans, but I do have friends, and I want to be with my new friends.' So, I came to this school dressed as a woman and talked to Mrs. Foxx about attending beauty school. We talked, and she said that she was very impressed with me. My brain said to me, 'I'm sitting right in front of this woman and she doesn't see that the person she's talking to is a man.' For the first time, I feel free and good about who I really am—a woman!"

London looks away and then turns back to look at us. "Since Mrs. Foxx sees me as a woman," London continues, "I tell her the story about the fire, so I wouldn't have to take my wig off my head in front of the class. That excuse worked. Then I realized I needed a plan to use the ladies' restroom with no one in there but me. So, I used the fire story again and told her about my back. I did everything I could to keep from laughing about what I was saying to Mrs. Foxx. She believed everything I said! So, here I am in beauty school, with my true friends!"

The three of us start laughing. Beth Eden says, "London, you are remarkable! Your secret will stay between me and Ruby. You are a beautiful woman. Ruby will need to keep you from any man she wants to date in New York!"

"Girlfriends, let's go to the restroom," London suggests. "When I go in, I need you both to stand outside the door and make sure no one comes in." "Don't forget to let the toilet seat down when you finish!" Beth Eden quips. We all laugh!

Soon, Mrs. Foxx returns to the classroom and goes over the rules and requirements for graduation and for getting a beauty school diploma. After she finishes with the rules and regulations, she says, "You must pass the subjects and skills I will cover in class. You must make a passing grade of an A, B, or C on the written exams and on the skill exams. If you find that you are failing to meet the passing grades, I am here to help you succeed. Failure to complete the requirements is your choice, not mine!"

"Take notes," Mrs. Foxx continues. "If you need a notebook and pencil, come up front and get what you need." Some of the students walk to the front of the class and get a notebook and pencil. After they all sit down, Mrs. Foxx explains, "On our first day, we will discuss the anatomy of hair and the different types and textures of hair. After my lecture, you are to run your hands through everyone's hair and define the texture of their hair. You will write down the student's name and the texture of their hair in your notebook. There are several mannequins in the back of the class that have names. Do the same with them. We will discuss this when everyone has finished. Now, let us begin!"

As Mrs. Foxx lectures the class, all of us focus on every word coming out of her mouth. The room is so quiet that you can hear a strand of straw drop onto the floor! "I can't believe I have been doing hair for years and know so little about hair!" I think to myself. Soon, Mrs. Foxx is finishing up her lectures for the day. We are silent and taking the time to absorb all the information we have been given. This has truly been an exciting moment for me! I am glad that I'm here in beauty school and Mrs. Foxx is my instructor.

Mrs. Foxx says, "You may begin identifying the texture of each other's hair and the hair on the mannequins. When you finish, we will discuss your observations. After that, the class will be dismissed for today and I will see you tomorrow. Tomorrow morning, you will have an exam on the information you learned today."

After the class is dismissed, Beth Eden, London, and I walk toward the city bus line. Beth Eden and I are going to work at the diner. "What are you going to do the rest of the day?" I ask London. "I'm going home," he responds. "I have to have dinner ready by six o'clock." "London, that's great," Beth Eden comments. "You've found a place to live. Where is home?"

"I live with Marty!" London reveals. "What? You live with Marty? The man who picked us up at the bus station?" Beth Eden and I both inquire. "Yes!" London replies. "Remember, Beatrice said to call Marty. She gave me his telephone number when I was over her house. I called him, and he picked me up at a neighborhood store. He said I could live with him if I could pay him rent and cook for him. I have his dinner ready every day when he comes home from work, and I keep his house clean. He buys me anything I need. I'm in beauty school because of Marty paying the fees."

"London, are you and Marty a couple?" I ask. "Ruby, a lady never tells," London responds. Beth Eden and I are silent. "I'm going to invite the two of you for dinner at the house," London continues. "I hope you will come. I am a great cook."

We break the silence, agreeing to have dinner at Marty's house whenever he invites us. Beth Eden then says, "Ruby, from what I know today, you have an average of 100,000 strands of hair on your head." I say, "Beth Eden, from what I know today, you've lost an average of 100 strands of hair today." "From what I know today, I am not average!" London jokes. We all laugh. We soon make it to the bus line and say goodbye to London. "Goodbye, ladies, and remember: *'Don't buy where you cannot work!'*" London says.

When Beth Eden and I arrive at the diner, the place is full, so Mr. Schapiro is glad to see us. We start our shift and work hard to wait on our customers. After a while, there is only a small group of people left. Mr. Schapiro asks me to wait on table 7. "Yes, sir," I comply. I walk over to table 7 and see a handsome, well-dressed colored man. He is sitting by himself and reading the newspaper. "Sir, my name is Ruby," I say. "I will be your waitress. What can I get for you today?" He says, "Ruby, I would like a cup of hot coffee, no cream or sugar, and today's special. I like my hot coffee before my meal, please. That will be all." "Yes, sir," I respond. "I'll place the order for your meal and bring your hot coffee to you right now. I'll bring your meal to you as soon as it is ready."

While I am getting table 7's coffee, Beth Eden walks up to me and says, "Why do you get the good-looking ones to wait on?" I say, "Beth Eden, it's my beauty and brains. Men see you for your looks before they know your brain. With me, they see both!" Beth Eden says, "Ruby, did you just give me a compliment?"

I get the hot coffee out to table 7 and take his meal to him when it is ready. After about ten minutes into his meal, I go to his table and ask him, "Sir, how is your meal? Would you like to order anything else on the menu?" He replies, "The meal is great, and I will not be ordering anything else." When he finishes his meal, he leaves the diner. I go clean table 7 and see that he has eaten everything on his plate. Then I pick up his dirty plate and find two dollars left for tip money. I take a moment to relish the generous tip; I then put the money in my pocket and take the dirty dishes to the back. When I turn around, Beth Eden is standing behind me. "Ruby, did he leave you a tip?" she asks. I say, "Yes, his last two dollars." Beth Eden says, "You know, Ruby, that's a good title for a song: 'His last two dollars!'"

We work hard during our shift, and I reflect on how great school is. When we get home to Beatrice's house, it is about 8:30 in the evening. We go to our respective rooms, wash up, and then go downstairs to eat dinner. Beatrice has left us a feast. We eat and clean up the kitchen afterwards, trying to finish before quiet time.

While cleaning, I say, "Beth Eden, when I go back to my room, I'm going to write a letter to my son, Drum Mom, Daddy Freeman, Phillip, and my best friend, Lucille, and ask Beatrice to mail them tomorrow. I miss my son, my family, my friends, and my boyfriend." "Ruby, that's nice," Beth Eden comments. "I am glad you have a special family, friend, and a boyfriend. I wish someone would love me like you are loved."

"Beth Eden, I love you as only a friend could," I reply. "I am your family and my family are your family. I am serious, Beth Eden. I am also serious that this includes everyone except my man, Phillip." Beth Eden smiles and hugs me. I hug her back because I want her to know what love feels like between friends.

We go upstairs to our rooms. I sit at the table and write a letter each to Drum Mom and Winston, Daddy Freeman, Lucille, and Phillip. To Phillip, I write this:

My Beloved Phillip,

I have arrived in New York and have started beauty school. I am living with Beatrice, Daddy Freeman's sister. I also have found a job as a waitress at a diner in a neighborhood on the other side of town. School and work are keeping me very busy. I met two people on my bus ride to New York. We have become friends and the three of us go to beauty school.

I hope you are well. I deeply miss you and can't wait for us to be together again. I miss your thoughts, your sweet breath, your hug, your smell, your compassionate kiss, and spending time with you. I miss my man! The thought of knowing that I will see you soon keeps me motivated to quickly finish my business so that I can come to you.

I thank you for agreeing with me in helping me to find my financial place in this world. The two of us will be better because of our sacrifices. Together, we will hold the world in our hands, and the world will no longer hide us from our dreams— for we are the new world!

Wait for me, my beloved, for I am yours for eternity! Places may separate us for a while, but LOVE will always find its way HOME… back to you.

Forever my love,

Ruby

The next morning, I place my letters in the mail basket by the telephone for Beatrice to mail. Beth Eden and I leave early for our walk to beauty school. We can't wait to get to school and hear Mrs. Foxx lecture the class. We try to guess what she will talk about today. Finally, we stop guessing and begin asking and answering questions that might be on our exam for this morning. We know we have got to pass the test!

We arrive at the classroom and find that everyone is here, except London. It's 6:30 in the morning; at this time, London has thirty more minutes to come to class. When it gets to be ten till 7:00, I say to Beth Eden, "Where is London? I hope London didn't drop the class." Suddenly, London enters the class. She says, "Hello, everybody, London is in the house." Everyone starts laughing. She takes her seat and Mrs. Foxx then enters the classroom.

"Good morning, class," Mrs. Foxx says. "Take everything off your desk and prepare yourself to take the exam. I remind you, you must pass this test!" She passes out the test and says, "You have thirty minutes to complete the test. You may begin." We take the test.

Thirty minutes later, Mrs. Foxx says, "Time is up. Give your test papers to me and take a break for thirty minutes. I will be grading your papers during that time. My lectures for today's class will commence in thirty minutes."

We give our papers to Mrs. Foxx and leave the classroom. As Beth Eden, London, and I stand together in the hallway, I say, "London, I was worried about you this morning when I did not see you in the class. You barely made it before seven o'clock. What happened?" "Ruby, don't be so slow! You know I have to be careful and I do have to make my grand entrance in the classroom," London confesses. We laugh.

When we return to the classroom, Mrs. Foxx says, "I thought my lectures yesterday were easy for you to learn and understand. I thought my lectures were clear and effective enough for you to have time to apply your knowledge with hands-on skills on each other and with the mannequins in the back. You all have shown me that there is still more work we must complete. You are one class and one people. I expect everyone to pass this class. With that said, everyone DID receive an 'A' on this test! Be proud of yourselves and each other!" London starts screaming and clapping, and everyone joins in with her.

Mrs. Foxx says, "Today, I will be lecturing on diseases of the head and medications that affect the growth of hair. After the lectures, you will be dismissed. These lectures will take time to cover and understand. Take good notes. Every day, you should study your notes. Don't wait to study until the night before the test, because you will not pass my test if you choose to do that. You will be tested when these lectures have been completed. Let us begin!" Mrs. Foxx starts her lecture.

When class is over, Beth Eden, London, and I walk to the bus line—with Beth Eden and I heading to work, and London going to Marty's house. Before we part ways with London, he says, "Have a great rest of the day. Remember, ladies, *'Don't buy where you cannot work!'*"

When we arrive at the diner for our shift, Mr. Schapiro says, "I need to see the two of you in my office now before you start to work." Mr. Schapiro walks away from us and goes to his office. Beth Eden and I look at each other, and I say, "Beth Eden, he is going to fire us! Let's go on into his office and get this over with. We can take the rest of the day to look for another job."

We then walk into Mr. Schapiro's office. This is the first time we have been in his office; it has a large desk with a lot of papers scattered on top of it, a chair behind the desk, a small filing cabinet against the wall, and two chairs in front of his desk. Mr. Schapiro says, "Ruby and Beth Eden, please sit down." We comply.

"Ruby and Beth Eden, you have been working here for a while," he starts. "I observe your work, your attendance, and how you treat me and my customers. You don't steal from me and you don't even eat here or take food out of the diner. This is like nothing I've ever seen before since taking over this business! I must say that the two of you are exceptional workers. I am highly pleased with you. Today is pay day. In addition to your weekly check, I am giving each of you an extra $10.00 dollars for school and for helping me grow my business. I hope that you will accept this as my appreciation for the fine work you're doing."

"Accept my check plus $10.00? I'll roll over dead in my grave if I don't take this!" Beth Eden remarks. Mr. Schapiro smiles. I say, "Mr. Schapiro, we thank you for your kindness toward us. We love working for you, and this extra money sure does help us. Thank you so much for thinking about us."

"I may not always be able to give you extra money," Mr. Schapiro continues. "When I can, I will be happy to share some of my wealth with you. That's all I have to say." "Thank you, Mr. Schapiro! Ruby, let's get to work!" Beth Eden responds.

We start working and finish our work at the diner when our shift is over. During the course of walking to the bus line and riding the bus home, we talk and talk about Mr. Schapiro. This is a man who is Jewish, having hired two colored women to work for him—letting us work when we are not in school, letting us leave work when we need to, and giving us extra money when he makes it. We reflect on how Mr. Schapiro is a good man, and how we are so glad that we had stopped by his diner that day and asked for work. Beatrice, Marty, Mrs. Foxx, and Mr. Schapiro live in New York—New York is a great place with great people!

*****

It takes Mrs. Foxx two weeks to finish her lectures on the diseases of the head and the medications that affect hair growth. On the day when we are tested on our knowledge of the information, she administers the exam, gives us time to take it, and then grades it.

After grading the tests, she says, "I have two students with a grade of 'B'; everyone else has an 'A.' Those whose grade is a 'B,' please see me after class." When Mrs. Foxx passes out the graded test papers, Beth Eden and I smile—we both got an "A." We then look to the back of the room at London; she is holding her test paper on her forehead, which also has an "A" on it. The three of us smile.

After all the test papers have been given back, Mrs. Foxx says, "We are now going to study hair products and changing the color of hair. This will take a while to finish. Take notes and go over your notes every day so that you will pass my test. After I finish my lecture, you will have a test. Do not wait until the day before the test to study. If you do, you will not pass the test. You must pass this test! After I finish lecturing on hair products and changing the color of hair, you will take a strand of your hair for each color and see if your hair type is compatible with that color. London, you can partner with someone for this project. After everyone finishes that project, you will take a strand of hair off the mannequins in the back and determine if the color works for that hair. Do you understand?" The class responds in unison, "Yes, Mrs. Foxx." Mrs. Foxx says, "Let's begin."

After we finish the class session for the day, the three of us walk to the bus line. London says, "See you two tomorrow. Remember, *don't buy where you cannot work!*" After parting ways, Beth Eden and I travel to the diner; when we arrive there, it is packed with customers. We go to the back area, put on our waitress uniforms, and go out front to start working. While we are working, Mr. Schapiro comes to me and says, "Ruby, I need you to take care of the customer sitting at table 7." So, I walk over to table 7 and see sitting there the same man who was here two weeks ago, at this very table. "Sir, my name is Ruby, and I will be your waitress for today," I introduce myself. "May I get you anything?" He looks up from his newspaper and says, "Yes, Ruby, I will like hot coffee with no cream or sugar, and today's special. Please bring my coffee before my meal." "Yes, sir. Your coffee is coming. Your meal will be here when the cook has it ready for you," I reply. "Thank you," he responds.

I get table 7's coffee ready and take it to him. I then wait on my next customers, get their orders, and give them to the cook. Beth Eden then comes over to me. "You got table 7 again and wouldn't you know it, he is the same guy that was here two weeks ago. Either the food here is good, or he sees someone in here that is good," she comments. "Hush, Beth Eden. Get to work!" I demand. To this, Beth Eden says, "Find out his name."

When table 7's food is ready, I immediately take it to him. I say, "Sir, your meal is here." I proceed to place his meal in front of him. He looks at me and smiles, then says, "Thank you, Ruby." I say, "Sir, I have been your waitress twice and I don't know your name. Do you have a name?" "Edmond," he says with a smile. "Well, Edmond, I will check back with you in a few minutes and see if you need anything else with your meal," I reply.

I leave table 7 and Beth Eden follows me to the beverage section. "What did he say? What is his name?" she asks. "I asked him his name," I explain. "He said his name is Edmond."

Edmond soon leaves the diner after finishing his meal. I then go and clean up after him. *He didn't leave a tip, but I have a name. I guess that's better than nothing.*

We finish up our shift and go home. When we arrive at home, Beatrice is sitting in the living room. "Beth Eden, my rent money is due today. Dinner is ready for the two of you to eat," she informs us. Beth Eden hands Beatrice money for rent. Then we both thank Beatrice for preparing dinner.

I say, "Beatrice, I need to call Daddy Freeman tonight. Tomorrow is my son, Winston's, birthday. I need him to have Winston and Drum Mom over to his house so that I can talk to them on the telephone. I'll leave a nickel on the table by the phone for tonight and one for tomorrow night." Beatrice replies, "That's fine. Tell Freeman I said hello." "Beatrice, thank you for everything," I say with gratitude.

Beth Eden and I eat our dinner and then clean the kitchen. "Ruby, you didn't give Beatrice your rent money," Beth Eden points out to me. "Beatrice has already gotten her money from me" is my response to her observation; I have said this because I don't want Beth Eden knowing that Daddy Freeman is paying my rent.

After I answer her question, Beth Eden goes upstairs to her room. When I call Daddy Freeman and he answers the telephone, I ask, "How are you doing, Daddy Freeman?" "I'm well, and so is Winston," he responds. He tells me everything that Winston is learning. I start to cry, and Daddy Freeman picks up on this. He knows that I miss Winston, but that I am glad that he is doing so well and he's happy.

"Daddy Freeman, tomorrow is Winston's birthday," I note. "I know," he replies. "Daddy Freeman, can you get Winston and Drum Mom to come over to your house by 8:00 tomorrow night? I want to call and talk to them. I want to talk to Winston and wish him a happy birthday," I explain. Daddy Freeman says, "Yes, I'll have them here tomorrow at 8:00 so that you can talk to them." "Thank you, Daddy Freeman," I reply. "I'll talk to all of you tomorrow night at 8:00. Oh, and Beatrice says hello. Goodbye, and thank you for everything. I love you." Daddy Freeman says, "Tell Beatrice I said hello. I love you too, Ruby." I hang up the phone, go upstairs to my room, and study my notes from school.

After I finish studying, I look over to my bed and see a letter lying on it. It's a letter from Phillip! I sit on my bed and open the letter. One red rose petal falls out of the envelope. I pick it up, smell it, and put it next to my heart. I start crying, remembering that Phillip had told me to always look for one red rose petal in his letter. "Phillip still loves me!" I say to myself. I hold the one red rose petal in my hands and read the letter:

My dear Ruby,

I am glad that you arrived safely in New York and are doing well. I am happy that you are doing well in school, living with Beatrice, and have found some good friends. Everything is well with me. I plan to see Winston on his birthday and give him a gift.

My love, I miss you. I yearn to have you near me. I miss having you here with me, talking to me and seeing your beautiful smile. I lay on my bed at night, smelling your sweet scent that you left on my pillow. Your scent is like the lilies of the valley. Who would destroy the lilies? Not me! For its beauty and smell are like no other.

Come to me quickly! For my arms are not too far to reach out to you. Nor are they too weak to hold you. We are one in mind, spirit, and soul. No one can destroy the love I have for you. I am yours today, tomorrow, and forever.

I send you one red rose petal, sealing my love for you. Hold it to your heart and let your heart beat against it. When you do this, I will hear your heart producing a love song. A love song that only we can sing together.

One red rose petal for my love,

Phillip

After reading Phillip's letter, I go to sleep dreaming about my beloved man.

*****

The next morning, Beth Eden and I start our routine. We go to school and then, after school, we head to work at the diner. I see Edmond at table 7, walk over to him, and proceed to take his order. "Edmond, your coffee and the special for today will be right up," I say with confidence. He smiles at me. I then go and get his coffee. While in her presence, Beth Eden says, "Ruby, find out where Edmond works. He always comes in here in a suit and tie and brings a news-paper to read while he waits for you to take his order. He always sits at table 7. I know this man has a good job in the city."

I take him his coffee. "Edmond, you are one of my best cus-tomers. Do you work or live close to the diner?" I ask him. "I live on the other side of the city; I work nearby," Edmond responds. "I am a teacher at one of the schools in this neighborhood." "That's good. We need good teachers for our children," I reply.

"Is this the only place that you work?" he asks. "Yes. I am at-tending beauty school and come here to work after school," I explain. "The other waitress in here is my friend Beth Eden. We both attend beauty school." He responds, "That's good. Women want their hair looking nice. Some of them will pay to get their hair done before they buy food to eat." We smile at his words. I then leave and walk over to get his meal.

After I have given him his meal, Edmond eats and then leaves the diner. As usual, I go and clean off the table. In doing so, I find a note that reads, "Ruby, I'd like to get to know you, Edmond." I smile and go to show the note to Beth Eden. I proceed to tell her that he is a teacher in the neighborhood and that he lives on the other side of the city.

Soon, Beth Eden and I are finishing up our shift and heading home. As discussed, at 8:00 in the evening, I call Daddy Freeman. He answers the telephone and hands it over to Drum Mom. I talk to her for several minutes; then she gives the telephone to Winston.

"Hello, Momma. I love you," Winston says when he is hold-ing the telephone. I say, "I love you, Winston. Happy birthday! You are two years old today. Momma is so sorry she can't be home with you to celebrate your birthday—" Winston interrupts me, saying, "Momma, I know you can't be here. You're in school! You must go to school, so you can work when you come home. Momma, when are you coming home? I miss you." As he talks, tears well up in my eyes; I miss Winston so much.

"Winston, Momma will be home as soon as she finishes school. It shouldn't be too much longer. When I finish school, Momma's coming home," I explain. "I'm in school, Momma," Winston tells me. "You are," I say. "Drum Mom and Daddy Freeman are my teachers," he notes. "They say I am very smart. I know my ABCs. I can count to ten. I can spell and write my name. Momma, my name is Winston—W-i-n-s-t-o-n. Drum Mom says she is going to help me write a letter to you. Write me back. I must go and get ready for bed. Daddy Freeman wants his telephone back. I love you, Momma."

"Winston, I love you more," I profess to him. Daddy Freeman comes back on the telephone. I say, "I want to thank you and Drum Mom for taking great care of Winston. I love both of you. Beatrice says hello. We will talk later." Daddy Freeman replies, "All right. We love you. Keep busy. Goodbye."

*****

On the day that Mrs. Foxx finishes the lectures on hair products and coloring hair, she tests us on the lectures and what we have learned in the skills lab. Upon grading the exams, it is found that everyone in the class has received an "A." Mrs. Foxx is extremely happy about her students' progress. She tells her students that this is the first time that all her students in one class fully understand the material she has presented.

"My lectures today will cover washing, rinsing and drying the hair, pressing and curling the hair, and applying cosmetic products," Mrs. Foxx announces to us. "You will learn how to use different tools for pressing and curling hair. These lectures will not take as long as the last two. You will apply your knowledge in using the correct hair products for washing and rinsing each other's hair. Then you will dry the hair, and press and curl each other's hair. I do not expect to see anyone losing any unusual strands of their hair because you fail to apply what you have learned. After curling the hair, you will apply the correct makeup to their face to help accent the hair."

Mrs. Foxx looks at the class. "Doris Ann, you will do my hair. London, you will wash, rinse, and dry the mannequin's hair. You will press and curl Doris Ann's hair," she continues. "Are there any questions?" "Doris Ann, since you are from Alabama, I am going to call you *Selma*. When I finish your hair and makeup, you will look like a model and have a new name for your new look," London says to Doris Ann, who smiles at what he has said.

"If there are no other questions or comments (Mrs. Foxx says while looking at London), please take out your notebooks and begin taking notes. You know what you have to do to pass my test, so let's begin!"

After sitting through the lectures and the class session ends, Beth Eden, London, and I walk to the bus line. "London, why did you say that you are going to make Doris Ann look like a model?" I ask. "And why did you call her 'Selma'?" "Doris Ann looks and dresses like a country girl," London notes. "She is from Alabama, and there is a city in Alabama called Selma. She needs a new look and a new name. She says she likes me because I say nice things about her. She says she likes the name *Selma*. With a new name, she needs a new look." I reply, "Well, London, you did something good for someone today."

When we reach our bus line, London leaves, saying, "Ladies, have a great rest of the day. Remember, *don't buy where you cannot work*!" After riding the bus over to the diner, Beth Eden and I arrive there and proceed to start our work shift. Then, when our shift ends, we go home. We eat dinner, clean the kitchen, and then retreat to our rooms to study.

The next day at school, Mrs. Foxx says, "We have finished this course." When she tells us who she wants each of us to partner with at the hair stations, she notes, "I am going to grade you on washing, rinsing, and drying hair, and the proper techniques for holding the pressing comb and the curling iron. I will also grade you on curling the hair with the curling iron and then styling the hair. Any questions? If not, go to your hair station." Upon her orders, we go to our respective stations, work, and complete the assigned tasks.

Once done, Mrs. Foxx says, "Start applying makeup on your partner. Meet me back in the classroom in thirty minutes. We will have a 'show and tell' session. The class will comment on what you have done and what you did not do, and recommend what you should have done. You will receive a grade from the comments of your peers, what I observe, and how well you discuss your skills to the class. Begin applying the makeup."

After we have done as Mrs. Foxx asked, we return to the classroom. Mrs. Foxx calls the partners to the front of the room. One by one, we discuss our skills and work. Mrs. Foxx appears to be pleased with everyone and everything. "London and Doris Ann, come to the front," she beckons. Everyone has been so busy showing off their skills that no one notices that London and Doris Ann are not in class. "Where are London and Doris Ann?" Mrs. Foxx asks. I look at Beth Eden, and she looks at me.

Suddenly, London enters the classroom and says, "Mrs. Foxx, we finished on time and I would like to present to you 'Selma, the beautiful model from Alabama.'" Doris Ann (aka, "Selma") enters the classroom and stands beside London. We are speechless! She is so beautiful. London has been successful in transitioning her into a model. London talks about how he styled Selma's hair to accent her face, and the makeup she applied to accent her beauty.

"I was not on time in class because I was next door finding a dress for Selma to wear during our 'show and tell' session," London confesses. "If we are going to present our skills and work, everything about the person that we put in front of an audience must be right. Otherwise, you can miss the true beauty of a person and you might be judged wrongly." Everyone in the class stands up and claps for London and Doris Ann. Someone shouts, "Doris Ann! Doris Ann! Doris Ann! Now, you're Selma! Selma! Selma!"

Mrs. Foxx ends the shouting. "Very nice, London and Doris Ann, but the two of you are late," Mrs. Foxx points out. "If you are going to present a client and your skills in front of an audience, then you must be on time. No one should have to wait for you because you are not prepared and because you must go shopping just before your expected presentation. London and Doris Ann, take your seat. Class, you may take a break for thirty minutes. I will have your grade when you return."

We leave the class and huddle around London and Selma. London begins to talk to Selma, who is crying about being late for class and possibly failing the course. "Selma, you better stop crying,"

London demands. "You will mess up your makeup. Even if we get a failing grade, we passed everything else, and that gives us a C average. We can bring that up with the other courses. Stop crying, right now!" Selma stops crying.

"London and Selma, the two of you will be okay," Beth Eden assures. "That woman, Mrs. Foxx, is as sly as a fox! I know I did a good job," London responds. "London, don't talk like that about Mrs. Foxx," I interject. "She is only preparing us for our future. It's not always about the grade, but being the best at what we do."

We go back and sit down at our desks. Mrs. Foxx then says, "Everyone did fine. Everyone but London and Doris Ann makes a grade of A-. An A- is considered a good grade for everything that you had to complete. London and Doris Ann, you heard my comments: *You must be on time.* Because you were late and did not participate in reviewing and discussing the skills of others with your peers, I took off a point from your grade. The two of you would have made an A+, but now it is a B. Excellent work." Everyone stands up and claps for London and Doris Ann. Everyone in class puts the name "Doris Ann" to death in its grave—for the name *Selma* now lives! Everyone chants, "Selma! Selma! Selma!"

"Everyone clean and sterilize your tools you used today," Mrs. Foxx chimes in. "After you finish, class is dismissed. I will see you tomorrow."

As is usual, when the class session is over, we walk to the bus line. As is also the norm, London says, "Goodbye, ladies. Remember, *don't buy where you cannot work*!" Today, however, I ask, "London, why do you tell us that every time you leave us? What do you mean by that?"

"Ruby, you need to learn colored people's history," London begins. "Not everybody was born privileged with a silver spoon in their mouth! In the thirties, colored people protested in the North because of hiring discrimination practices. They picketed white-owned businesses that refused to hire colored people. Colored people wanted more job opportunities and more economic power in the community. This was their slogan that they adopted for the colored movement. Even today, we don't have the basic things we need. That's why you see some sleeping on the streets, some selling their bodies and doing the unthinkable, and some selling drugs—so they can earn that money and live another day.

"They don't have jobs to get off these streets. Because our people live on the streets and have no jobs, they have no perseverance. Where there is no *perseverance*, there is no *hope*. Where there is no *hope*, there is no *character*. Where there is no *character*, they learn to *thrive* and *survive*. So, DON'T BUY WHERE YOU CANNOT WORK!"

I am overwhelmed by what London has said to me. He's right! I am privileged. I have a good family, I am attending beauty school, I have a place to live in New York, and I have a job. So many colored people don't have what I have or the opportunities I have. As I am reflecting on this, I look up and see the bus. Beth Eden and I part ways with London, then we get on the bus, endure the bus ride, and arrive at the diner. We start and complete our work shift, and then go home.

Upon arriving at home, Beth Eden goes upstairs to her room, and I make my way over to the living room, where I sit beside Beatrice. I say, "Beatrice, I am not feeling well. I need to see a doctor. Do you know one?"

Beatrice says, "I've noticed you're putting on some weight. There is a colored doctor on 123th street. His name is Dr. Battle. He is a very good doctor and all the colored people go to see him. I understand he graduated from a colored medical college in Nashville, Tennessee. I've been told that a colored woman graduated from that same medical college. Anyway, go by Dr. Battle's office after you finish school. You'll have to wait for a long time to see him. Tell your boss that you can't work the day you decide to see Dr. Battle."

*****

The next day at school, Mrs. Foxx says, "Today, I will be lecturing on washing, cutting, rolling, drying, and styling your partner's hair. You will learn how to braid hair. I will demonstrate these things on this mannequin. After my lecture, you will move to your hair station and perform what you learn in class. Do not start without me. I must be present at your hair station when you perform these things. I'll look at your final work and dismiss you from class after we finish. If there are no questions, let's begin." We perform our tasks, showing our results to Mrs. Foxx. She approves everyone's work. We all go home for the day.

When we return the next day, Mrs. Foxx says, "This is my final lecture! Today, I will discuss Business Management. This will include how to manage your own beauty salon, how to have and promote quality customer service, business advertisement, making money, paying taxes, buying products, scheduling your clients for their appointments, licensing, and dressing for success. After completing my final lecture, you will have your comprehensive final exam on everything.

"After Christmas and through the end of this class, which is in February, you will be working with real customers who will come here to have their hair done. They will pay you only thirty cents because you are still students and have not taken your state exam for your license. They will come here because it is much cheaper than going to a salon. So be prepared to work, apply what you know, and do everything to satisfy your client. A reminder: don't relax. Keep studying. Beauty school's graduation is in February. If there are no questions, let's begin!"

*****

Before dismissing for the holidays, we take our final exam at the beauty school. After Mrs. Foxx is finished with grading our tests, she says, "Everyone got an A on the final exam. Congratulations! You are the best class that I've had the pleasure of teaching. You have a few days off. You are to return to class on December 26 and be prepared to start doing hair on customers. Have a Merry Christmas, and I'll see you back on the twenty-sixth."

Upon exiting the classroom, I ask London, "What are you going to do for the holiday?" "Marty and I are going to spend Christmas together," he replies. "What about you and Beth Eden?" "We are going to work at the diner and have Christmas at Beatrice's house," I respond. "I must mail Winston's Christmas gifts in time for him to get them. I bought him a set of marbles, Legos®, a slinky, crayons, a coloring book, a paddle ball, a can of silly putty, and a toy soldier set. I'm also going to write him a letter."

"Wow, the privilege! All those toys for one child," London points out. "Anyway, ladies, have a great holiday and I'll see you in class after Christmas. Remember, *don't buy where you cannot work*!"

Chapter Ten

THE ART OF SECRECY

After Christmas, people start coming to beauty school to get their hair and makeup done by students in our class. One day, a colored woman in her late thirties comes to the school. She talks to Mrs. Foxx at the reception desk. Mrs. Foxx assigns Beth Eden to take care of the colored woman. She is a pretty lady with distinguished dimples on her face. Beth Eden goes out front and escorts the woman over to her hair station. "My name is Beth Eden. What is your name?" she asks. "People call me 'Dimples,'" the woman replies. "Well, Dimples, I am going to take very good care of you and your hair. I think you will be pleased with my work," she assures her. "I sure do hope so. Make sure you cut my kitchen," Dimples requests.

Beth Eden and Dimples talk and talk. They act like they've known each other for years! "Where do you live?" Beth Eden asks her. "Everywhere up North. I just come here to New York and don't officially have a place to live," Dimples responds. "Dimples, the lady in the next hair station is my friend Ruby," Beth Eden informs. "We live with her cousin who owns her own house and rents rooms for women trying to do better for themselves. She has an extra room for rent. Maybe, if you go home with us, and talk to her, she might rent that room to you. What do you think about that, Ruby?"

"Dimples, are you working or are you in school? Are you running away from trouble?" I inquire earnestly. "The reason I ask is because the lady we live with does not want any trouble, and no devil's money coming into her house." Dimples replies, "No, I'm not in any trouble. My parents gave me money before they passed away. I have been wise in spending my money. I can pay the rent if she allows me to live in her house." "Yes, Dimples. You can go home with us," I accept the suggestion.

Beth Eden does a marvelous job on Dimples's hair. Afterwards, Dimples stays at the shop and waits until Beth Eden and I finish work so that she can go to Beatrice's house and try to rent a room. When we get home, we find Beatrice sitting in the living room. I introduce Beatrice to Dimples and tell her why we have her in her home.

Beatrice says, "Ruby and Beth Eden, you should know me by now. I don't take in strangers unless someone I know recommends them. Well, I do know the two of you. Okay, the two of you leave the living room so I can talk to Dimples."

We leave the living room and return at 5:30 p.m. for dinner. Upon reentering the living room, Beatrice says, "Dinner is ready, and Dimples will be joining us for dinner. I'm going to rent her that extra bedroom. The four of us must get along. Sometimes, there's always trouble when two or more women live together. But that will not happen in this house! Do I make myself clear?" "Yes, we understand," we all respond in unison. We then proceed to walk to the kitchen and eat dinner. After dinner, Beth Eden and I go upstairs, but Dimples stays downstairs and talks to Beatrice. About 10:30 at night, I hear someone (who I assume to be Dimples) walk upstairs to the extra room, and shut the door.

*****

In the morning, Beth Eden and I get ready to leave the house and go to school. Dimples is still in her bedroom. Her door is closed. Beth Eden and I are now concerned about Dimples not getting up and staying in bed while we get ready to leave the house. Still, we leave and walk to the beauty school. When we arrive, the school is full of customers, and Mrs. Foxx assigns the student who will do each person's hair. We all do a great job and work quickly to finish doing the hair of all those who are waiting in the lobby.

London is the "Master of Art in Hair and Makeup." He is getting good tips from his customers. "What is your secret?" I ask him. "Help me make more tips." London comments, "Do a great job on your client's hair. Listen to what she wants done to her hair, and then recommend what she needs done to her hair. Let her know she is more important than those out in the lobby. Be her psychiatrist. Listen to her problems and try not to respond unless she asks you to respond. Apply what you have learned in our Business Management class and be compassionate!" "Thanks. London," I say. "You're right." After my talk with London, I take his advice, and this leads to customers starting to request for me to do their hair. His advice helps my tips to increase.

After the salon closes, we walk to the bus line. "London, we had a busy day," I begin. "What are you going to do for the rest of the day?" London says, "Ruby and Beth Eden, I am looking for a salon where I can work after graduation. I must stay a step ahead of everyone else. I'm interviewing for jobs. By the time I have my diploma, I will already have a place to work. I'll work at their salon and increase my clients. When I leave their salon, I hope my clients will follow me to my own place of business."

"London, you are so smart. That's a good plan," Beth Eden replies. "Yes, it is, London," I say in agreement. "I already have a place to work in my hometown. I, too, plan to work there for a while and then open my own salon. Beth Eden, what are your plans after graduation?"

"I haven't made any plans," Beth Eden admits. London and I look at Beth Eden. After reaching the bus line, London says, "Goodbye, ladies. Have a plan and make it happen. Remember, *don't buy where you cannot work*!"

Beth Eden and I get on the bus, headed to work. She is silent. For the first time, Beth Eden has nothing to say. I know it's because London and I have plans after graduation and she doesn't have any plans. We arrive at the diner and it is full of customers. I see that Edmond is at table 7, and someone else is sitting at the table with him. "Beth Eden, that's a fine man sitting at the table with Edmond," I point out. "I'm going to get his name so the four of us can go out together." Beth Eden says, "Ruby, I have no interest in meeting anyone, nor do I want to go on a date with anyone." I reply, "Okay, Beth Eden."

I approach table 7. "Hello, Edmond. Who's your friend?" I ask. "Ruby, this is Gatewood. He builds houses. He works for me. I have several houses I own and rent to colored people," he explains. "Hello, Ruby," Gatewood says. "James talks a lot about you." I smile and ask, "Who is James?"

"In the business community, people call me James," Edmond chimes in. "My friends call me Edmond." I say, "Edmond, I'll bring you your coffee and today's special." Edmond responds, "Ruby, that'll be fine." "Gatewood, what would you like to order?" I ask. "Just coffee. No sugar and no cream," Gatewood notes. "I have to get back to the construction site or this man is not going to be happy with me." I say, "I will bring you your coffee right now."

As I am getting the two cups of coffee, Beth Eden walks over to where I am standing. "Beth Eden, the man sitting at table 7 with Edmond is named Gatewood," I say. "He calls Edmond 'James,' and he builds houses for him. Are you sure you don't want to meet Gatewood?" "I'm sure," Beth Eden says.

I then take two cups of coffee to table 7. The two men are having a deep conversation. I place the cups of coffee on the table and walk away. A few minutes later, Gatewood leaves the diner and Edmond is alone at the table. When I take Edmond's food to him, he asks, "Can you go with me this Saturday and look at the houses I own?" I tell him yes. Then we make a plan to meet outside the beauty school around noon to go look at the houses.

When our shift is over, Beth Eden and I walk home. I tell Beth Eden that I'm going with Edmond on Saturday to look at the houses he owns. "That's good, Ruby. Be careful," she cautions. Upon arriving home, we find Dimples and Beatrice sitting in the living room.

Dimples says, "Beth Eden, I'll be at the school tomorrow for you to fix my hair and cut my kitchen." "Okay," Beth Eden says with a smile. Beth Eden and I then go upstairs and get ready for dinner. When we come back downstairs, the four of us eat at the dinner table. We talk and talk and talk—and when we finish talking, Beth Eden goes upstairs to her room, Dimples and Beatrice go back into the living room, and I make a telephone call to Daddy Freeman.

"Hello, Daddy Freeman. How are you doing?" I ask. "I'm doing fine. Winston is right here," he says, then hands the telephone to Winston. I say, "Hello, Winston. It's Momma. I love you."

"Hello, Momma," Winston responds. "How are you doing? I got all the Christmas gifts you sent me. I love all of them. Daddy Freeman gave me a lot of pencils. Drum Mom baked me a cake and gave me some candies. Santa Claus brought me some toy cars. This was a good Christmas! Did you write me back?"

"Yes, I answered your letter," I reply. "You will get it in a day or two. You can really write a letter. Daddy Freeman and Drum Mom are good teachers, and you are a good learner. Momma must say goodbye for now. I love you and I'll be home in a few months. Be good." Winston says, "Okay, Momma. I miss you and I love you." After ending the call, I leave my nickel for the telephone call on the table. I then go upstairs and read Winston's letter again:

Hello, Momma,

I love you and I miss you. Come home soon.

Winston, your son

After reading the letter, I get into bed and fall asleep. In the middle of the night, I hear someone quietly walking upstairs and going to Dimples's room. Her door opens and closes. *I can't believe that Dimples has a man in her room.* I put the pillow over my head; I don't want to hear what is going on in her room. I fall back asleep and wake up a few hours later. At that time, I hear someone leave Dimples's room and go downstairs. I hear a door close downstairs and I go back to sleep. The next morning, I don't say anything about what I heard the night before. I like Dimples, and I'm not going to start trouble in the house. This is something Beatrice should find out for herself!

Beth Eden and I go to the school. At some point, Dimples walks into the lobby and sits down. Beth Eden soon calls her to come to her work station. I don't say anything—I just stare at Dimples. I am so disappointed that she had a man in her room. Beth Eden is glad she's at her station and the two of them talk. I say nothing to them while Dimples is getting her hair done.

*****

On Saturday at noon, Edmond picks me up in front of the beauty school. He drives to the counties outside New York and shows me his houses. Gatewood is at one of the houses, and he lets us go in to see the place. The house has two bedrooms, a living room, a kitchen, and a bathroom. It is beautiful! "Edmond, you own this house?" I ask. He says yes. After touring the house, we leave, and Edmond drives back to the beauty school. "The house that Gatewood is working on now will be finished the last week in January," Edmond explains. "Maybe you can go there with me when it's finished." I reply, "Yes, that'll be fine."

When I get out of the car, Edmond drives away and I walk home. On the walk home, I think about the beautiful house that Edmond owns. This man has a lot of money and a lot of potential. I soon find myself beginning to like him as Edmond, instead of as the man at table 7.

Upon my arrival at home, I find that everyone is in the living room. I don't talk about my day with Edmond, because Beatrice knows about Phillip and me. We eat dinner together, and then Beth Eden and I go upstairs to bed. Later that night, I hear someone walking quietly upstairs to Dimples's bedroom. I am upset with Dimples; she knows that Beatrice does not approve of such a thing. I get out of the bed and walk to my door to make my way to her room. As I turn the knob on my door, I suddenly decide that I'm not going to Dimples's room. I just return to my bed, place the pillow over my head, and try to go to sleep. At some point in the night, I wake up when I hear someone walk downstairs and close the door. This has become a regular occurrence—so much so that at night, I try to sleep and just ignore the noise in the other room. After I hear the steps going down the stairs and the front door closes, that is when I fall asleep.

*****

Today is Monday, February 3, and while we are in class, Mrs. Foxx says, "This Friday, you will have your final written test on all my lectures and your performances at the hair station. I hope all of you have been studying and will pass the test. If you don't pass the test, you will not be able to take the state test that will be given on Friday, March 20. This week will be a classroom study week for the test. If you have any questions for me, I will be sitting at my desk to answer your questions. Class will be dismissed every day at noon. Begin studying." The class engages in a study session.

That night, Edmond and I meet and go to his house that Gatewood was fixing up for him. We arrive at the house, enter the house, and walk into the living room. I look around and see that the room is beautiful but doesn't have any furniture. There are two bedrooms, but only one has a bed. We walk to the kitchen, where Edmond opens a bottle of wine and pours some wine into two glasses. He gives me one glass of wine, and then we both drink our glasses of wine to celebrate his beautiful home.

When we finish drinking the entire bottle of wine, Edmond takes me to the bedroom. We fall onto the bed, and I let Edmond kiss me and take me in his arms—and then we make love. What he does to me while in the process of love making is like heaven! When we finish making love, he gets up from the bed and tells me, "Get yourself dressed. We need to leave." After we get dressed and leave the house, he drives me to the beauty school. As I walk home, I start crying, feeling bad about the things that Edmond and I had just done together. "What did I just do with Edmond, and what did I just do to my relationship with Phillip?" I ask myself.

*****

When Friday, February 7, rolls around, I and my fellow class-mates arrive in class that morning to take our final test. Prior to start-ing the test, Mrs. Foxx says, "You have four hours to complete the written test, and three hours to apply your skills at the hair stations." We get to work on our missions.

After four hours, Mrs. Foxx says, "Time is up. Please turn in your test papers." We turn in our test papers. "Please proceed to the hair stations," Mrs. Foxx instructs. "I will walk around the stations and grade you on your skills. There will be no talking during this time." We move to our hair stations and do our partner's hair. After the allotted three hours, Mrs. Foxx says, "Time is up. Clean and sterilize your tools. Then go to the classroom so I can fully examine your results."

We walk to the classroom, where Mrs. Foxx intensely reviews our work and takes a lot of notes. When she finishes, she says, "Monday, your grades will be ready. Good luck. Have a good week-end. Class is dismissed." We walk to the outside of the classroom. "I am collecting money for a graduation gift from our class for Mrs. Foxx," Beth Eden says. Everyone contributes to funding Mrs. Foxx's gift.

*****

On Monday, we return to the beauty school and await the re-sults of our efforts. "I have graded your written tests," Mrs. Foxx be-gins. "One student made an A, and everyone else made a B. At the hair stations, two students made an A, two made a B+, and all others made a B. Congratulations. You have all passed this class! School is over! Graduation will be here on Saturday, February 28, at 5:00 in the evening. Invite your family and friends." After this announcement, one by one, she looks at each of her students and pays a small compliment to each of us.

"For your graduation on the twenty-eighth, please wear a black dress and black shoes," Mrs. Foxx continues. "The test for your state license will be given on Friday, March 20, in your home state. Please write to me and let me know if you pass or fail the test. Good day, class. It has been my pleasure to teach you." Everyone stands and gives Mrs. Foxx applause, for which she smiles.

That night, I find lying on my bed a letter that is from Phillip. This time, when I open the letter, there is no one red rose petal falling out of the envelope or letter. I cry and read his letter. "*I love you,*" he has written. I stop reading; "How could you love me? There isn't one red rose petal in your letter!" I say to myself. "Oh no! Phillip knows I have been unfaithful to him." I continue crying and reading his letter. *"Look on the back of this page"* are the words I read at the end of the letter. When I look on the back of the page, I notice there is one red rose petal glued to the back of the page. Under the rose are these words:

> *I glue this one red rose petal to this letter to remind you that nothing or no one will ever separate me from you or the love that I have for you.*
>
> *Come quickly to me.*
>
> *One red rose petal I attach to my heart and no one will ever take that away.*
>
> *Phillip*

*****

In late February, I pay a visit to Dr. Battle. He exams me, runs tests, and takes my blood. After this process, he comes out of his lab and says, "Congratulations, Ruby. You haven't been feeling well because you have a common medical condition. You have an infection. These pills will get rid of that infection. By the way, I examined you, and your test showed you are pregnant."

I start crying in the examination room. "Dr. Battle, how many weeks have I been pregnant?" I ask. "About a month," he answers.

After my time with the doctor ends, I leave his office and get myself together to face everyone at the house. I can't let anyone at the house know that I am pregnant. When I arrive at the house, Beatrice asks, "What did Dr. Battle say?" "He says that I have an infection," I respond. "He gave me some pills that would get rid of it. I'm going upstairs to study for the state exam in March. I hope you can attend our graduation on the twenty-eighth of this month." "I'll be there," she says. I go upstairs and sit on my bed, wondering about what I am going to do—what are my plans now that I'm carrying another child?

Beth Eden and I still work at the diner and wait for graduation day. I soon realize that after being intimate with Edmond, he has not returned to the diner. One day, Gatewood comes to the diner. "Where is James, or, Edmond?" I inquire. "I haven't seen him since I finished his house," Gatewood replies.

"Gatewood," I begin, "tell him that I need to see him and talk to him. I'm graduating on February 28 and would like for him to be there. Tell him I'm pregnant with his child. I need to see him before I leave to go back home." "If I see him, I'll certainly tell him what you said," he responds.

*****

The next day, I try to find Edmond. I walk to every school in the neighborhood, asking if there is a teacher in their school named Edmond. The secretaries at two schools say no. Then I ask, "Is there a teacher here named James Edmond or Edmond James?"—to which they respond no.

When I journey to the last school in the neighborhood, I have my head down as I walk into the office; simultaneously, I notice a man (whose face I could not see) hide behind a wall at the end of the hallway when he sees me walking into the office. I ask the secretary, "Do you have a teacher named Edmond or James Edmond or Edmond James?" She says no. I then leave the office and the school, crying. I am carrying a man's baby and I don't know his real name, where he works, or if he is even a teacher as he had claimed to be.

After the man (who it turns out is Edmond) sees me leave the school and walk off campus, he goes to the office. "Why was that woman in the office?" he asks. "She was asking if we have a teacher here named Edmond, James Edmond, or Edmond James. She has no idea who she is looking for," the secretary comments. Edmond walks out of the office and says to himself, "I told Ruby my friends call me 'Edmond' and my business partners call me 'James.' My students call me Mr. Shaw. No one here knows my middle name, Edmond." (The real story is that Edmond's full name is James Edmond Shaw, and his coworkers call him "James.")

*****

Graduation day has finally arrived! Friends and family are seated, waiting for the graduation participants to walk into the lobby of the beauty school. As the music begins to play, everyone in the lobby stands. Our graduating class walks down the aisle to the front of the lobby. I see Beatrice, Dimples, Gatewood, Marty, and Mr. Schapiro in the group. But, there is no Edmond. "He is not here to help me celebrate this occasion," I think to myself. After we march in, we sit down on the front row.

Mrs. Foxx goes to the podium and says, "This is the graduating class of 1953." Everyone starts clapping. "I would like to present our achievement awards to the following students," she announces. "When I call your name, please walk to the podium and receive your award:

- "**Valedictorian** goes to Ruby. *(I stand, walk to the podium and receive a huge bag.)* For graduating with an A average, the school awards you all the products and supplies you need to start working as a beautician and cosmetic artist." I go back to my seat after receiving my award.

- "**Cum Laude** (grade from 3.5 to 3.69) goes to Beth Eden." *(Beth Eden stands, walks to the podium, and receives a certificate. She then returns to her seat.)*

- "**Certificate of Achievement** goes to Ruby." *(I receive my certificate and return to my seat.)*

- "**Most Talented** goes to London Rhodes." *(Everyone from our graduating class gives London a standing ovation. We stand until she receives her certificate and returns to her seat.)*

- "**Most Likely to Succeed** goes to Ruby and London Rhodes." *(London and I walk to the podium, receive our certificates, and then return to our seats.)*

- "**Most Congenial** goes to Beth Eden." *(Beth Eden walks to the podium, receives her certificate, and then returns to her seat.)*

- "**Most Improved Student** goes to Doris Ann Jones." *(Everyone from our class stands and shouts, "Selma! Selma! Selma!")*

"Beth Eden has an award to present," Mrs. Foxx announces. "Please come to the podium." Beth Eden walks to the podium and says, "Mrs. Foxx, will you please stand here beside me? On behalf of the graduating class of 1953, we present to you a necklace. On the necklace is a symbol of a pressing comb. On the pressing comb is engraved, 'The Class of 1953.'" Beth Eden puts the necklace around Mrs. Foxx's neck, and then our graduating class proceeds to give her a standing ovation for more than a minute; once it is over, Beth Eden returns to her seat.

"Will the Beauty School Graduation Class of 1953 please stand and come forward to receive your diplomas," Mrs. Foxx instructs. She calls each of our names, one by one. When we receive our diplomas, our family and friends shout out our names. After Mrs. Foxx finishes giving us our diplomas, she says, "Audience, I now present to you the Beauty School Graduation Class of 1953. Class, please stand and exit the lobby."

We walk down the hallway. After doing so, we hug each other and promise to keep in touch with each other. Our family and friends walk to the hallway and grab their loved ones. We leave the school and then walk to the house. Beatrice is so proud of me! As soon as we get in the house, she calls Daddy Freeman and tells him about the graduation ceremony. She also tells him about the awards I received. Then she hands me the telephone. I talk to Daddy Freeman and tell him that I have my beauty school diploma and will be coming home within a week.

*****

The next day, Beth Eden and I have dinner with London at Marty's house. We talk and laugh about the fact that London and Beth Eden are staying in New York. I know they will remain friends and take care of each other. Who would have known that a bus ride to New York would allow three strangers to come together and become best friends forever?

While with them, I let London and Beth Eden know Drum Mom's address so that I can be reached at any time. Though London and Beth Eden aren't sure at this moment about what their addresses will end up being, they promise to always write to me.

After our fellowship ends, I walk to the diner to see Mr. Schapiro and thank him for allowing me to work at his diner. I see Gatewood sitting at table 7. I walk over to his table. "Gatewood, thank you for coming to our graduation," I say. "Edmond wasn't there. I haven't seen him since I went to his new house."

"Ruby, I did see Edmond a while back and told him what you told me to tell him," Gatewood reports. "He said nothing and kept on about his business. You are a smart young lady. I advise you to go on with your life and with your child." After hearing what he has to say, I leave the diner.

*****

The day soon arrives for me to leave New York. I am finally going home—with my diploma and awards in hand.

When it is time, Marty takes my suitcase to the car. I hug Beth Eden, Dimples, and Beatrice, saying, "I'm going to miss all of you. Beatrice, I didn't meet Daddy Freeman's sister, Pearl-Lee. Please tell her I was here and wish so to meet her."

"Ruby, you've met Pearl-Lee!" Dimples exclaims. "Dimples, I haven't met Pearl-Lee," I reply. "I'm Pearl-Lee!" she announces. "What, who?" I say, confused. "Dimples is Pearl-Lee, Beatrice and Freeman's sister," Dimples explains. "Why did you not say anything?" I inquire. "You didn't ask," Dimples responds. "I come and live with Beatrice whenever I'm in New York."

I look at Beth Eden; "Did you know Pearl-Lee is Beatrice's sister?" I ask. "Yes, I did know that," Beth Eden replies.

Dimples, aka Pearl-Lee, says, "I'm leaving tomorrow morning. I'm on my way to Michigan." "Dimples, I hope you have a nice trip to Michigan," I say. "Beth Eden, all these surprises. Get your suitcase from the living room so we can ride to the bus station. It's time to leave."

"That's Dimples's suitcase in the living room," Beth Eden says. "Ruby, I'm staying here with Beatrice. I'm in love with Beatrice."

After all the bombshells are dropped on me, I soon find myself contemplating everything as I ride to the bus station in Marty's car. I am speechless; I am motionless. I think about all the juicy tidbits I am leaving behind in New York:

- London Rhodes is a man, but he prefers to be seen as a woman. "She" dates and lives with Marty. They love each other.

- Edmond does not answer to Edmond or James, or James Edmond, or Edmond James. However, he is the father of the child I'm carrying.

- The woman I had known as Dimples is Pearl-Lee, Beatrice and Daddy Freeman's sister.

- Beth Eden is my friend and she is in love with Beatrice. Beatrice was the one walking up and down the stairs to Dimples's bedroom. They used Dimples's room so that I wouldn't know it was Beatrice and Beth Eden sleeping together.

Now, I'm part of all of this, too. How am I going to tell my beloved Phillip that I am pregnant? How can I tell Phillip that I don't know the name of my unborn child's father? This is all a big mess. I am in this mess!

Chapter Eleven

WHAT I DO KNOW

I am now on the bus and headed home to see my family, my son, Winston, Lucille, Fred, and Phillip. Of all the people I have not seen in nine months, Winston and Phillip are the only ones I have missed seeing the most.

I know that everyone is proud of me for getting a diploma from the beauty school. I know that even Phillip is proud of me. But the thought of having to face him is just too overwhelming for me right now. I decide to use the time I have on my ride home to get myself together. The cards are against me, but I get to deal the winning hand! This is something that I've got to do for me and my children. I've got to think about what I am going to do before everyone finds out I'm pregnant. I have devised a plan and am sure that it will work. I'll just need some time alone with Phillip. He's a good man. I know I can work out this plan with him.

Soon, the bus pulls into the station. I am finally home in Ripley! Daddy Freeman and Winston meet me at the bus station. I can see them through the left window of the bus. Winston is waving his hands, smiling and standing beside Daddy Freeman. The last time I saw Winston, he was almost two years old. Now, he is two and a half years old, standing straight up and not falling to the floor. When he smiles at me, I see he has teeth in his mouth. I then look at Daddy Freeman, who is smiling and keeping Winston from running to the bus. I get off the bus and run to meet them.

Daddy Freeman and I make a trade; he takes the suitcase out of my hand and then gives Winston to me. Winston tries to jump into my arms; he wants me to pick him up and hold him. I know he needs me and wants to get close to me. But in my condition, I can't do what he wants his momma to do for him. I kneel on the ground and hug my son until we are both breathless.

Daddy Freeman carries my suitcase as we walk together to the car. Once in the car, Winston sits between Daddy Freeman and me, and he starts talking and talking. "Look, Momma, I have teeth in my mouth," he informs me. "Winston, you most certainly do," I reply. "How many teeth do you have now?" Winston says, "Eighteen. I have nine at the top and nine at the bottom. Nine plus nine equals eighteen." "Winston, you are so smart. Momma is so proud of you," I comment.

When we arrive at Drum Mom's house, she is standing and smiling on the front porch. I take Winston's hand and we walk to Drum Mom. We hug and say how happy we are to see each other. Daddy Freeman brings my suitcase into the house and takes it to my bedroom. After he returns to the front room, I show everybody my beauty school diploma and awards. "Ruby, those things are great!" Daddy Freeman says. "I'll be back here tomorrow night." "Thank you, Daddy Freeman, for everything," I respond. "We'll see you tomorrow." Daddy Freeman then leaves for the night.

Drum Mom, Winston, and I sit in the front room. Winston wants me to pick him up, but I say, "Winston, you've grown so much, Momma can't pick you up. But come and sit on Momma's lap." Winston follows my instructions, saying, "I know my ABCs, I can spell and write my name on paper, and I can count to thirty." "I want you to do all those things for Momma," I reply to what he has said.

He says his ABCs, spells his name, and writes his name on a sheet of paper. Then he counts to thirty. "Winston, that's excellent! Drum Mom and Daddy Freeman are excellent teachers. You've learned so many things since I've been away," I comment. "Momma, are you going to leave me again?" Winston asks.

"Winston, I will never leave you again!" I assure him. "I will always be here for you until God wants me to come home with HIM. Until that time, I think you'll grow up and continue to go to school until you're over twenty. In school, you will find you a beautiful woman, marry her, and leave me here to take care of Drum Mom."

"I'll never leave you, Momma! Will you leave me when you get married?" he asks. "No, I will not leave you when I get married," I respond. "Where I go, you will also go." Drum Mom then says, "Winston, it's time to brush your teeth and get ready for bed. Your momma will see you before you close your eyes and go to sleep." Winston leaves the room.

I noticed that the whole time I was talking to Winston, Drum Mom was looking at me and rocking back and forth in her chair. "Ruby, I am so proud of you getting that diploma and graduating first in your class," she says. "I wish we could have been there to celebrate with you. As you can see, Winston is doing a great job. I know you're proud of him. He is a learner, a happy child, loves his family, and is very obedient. God couldn't have given you a better son!"

Drum Mom takes a breath and then says, "How are you doing?" I say, "Drum Mom, I am doing just fine. Tomorrow, I must talk to Miss Johnson about starting back to work next week. Winston and I will need to stay here until I have enough money for us to move out on our own. I hope this will be fine with you." "Yes, that will be fine," Drum mom replies. "You can live here until you can get your own place."

"I plan to see Phillip this week," I add. "We need to talk and spend time with each other. Also, I hope to see Lucille and Fred this week. Other than that, I plan to spend time with you, Daddy Freeman, and Winston."

"Ruby, you are telling me a lot about what you plan to do this week, but very little about what I ask you," Drum Mom points out. "I want to know, how are you doing?" I look at Drum Mom and say, "I said I am fine. What else do you what me to say?"

"I want you to tell me if you are pregnant!" Drum Mom blurts out. My mouth opens widely. I stare at Drum Mom. "What are you talking about?" I ask, acting oblivious. "Last week, I had a dream about a fish swimming in my kitchen sink," Drum Mom explains. "A dream about a fish means someone is pregnant. And that someone isn't me!"

"Drum Mom, asking me if I am pregnant because you dream about a fish is nothing but an old wives' tale. That doesn't make it truthful!" I reply. "Well, what I know to be truthful is that you won't pick up and hold Winston," Drum Mom retorts. "You haven't seen him in nine months. You should let him sit on your lap. What I know to be truthful is when he lays his head on your breast, you act like he is hurting you. You move his head off your breast and put his head on your shoulder. What I do know to be truthful is that you have put on a little weight in your belly. What I do know is that you walk like a woman carrying a child. What I do know is that you are smart mouthing me and that stops right now! Wives' tale or not, I know what I see, and I see how you are acting."

I start crying. The cry happens so suddenly and so unexpectedly. Not only am I crying intensely, but also, my nose is flowing with snot. I start gasping for air and jerking back and forth as though I need to vomit. "When you stop all that mess, tell me . . . are you pregnant?" she asks.

"Drum Mom, yes, I am pregnant," I say in a tearful voice. I can see the tears in her eyes. She pulls some tissue from the pocket of her dress and wipes her eyes. She says in a tearful voice, "Ruby, tell me everything about this child you're carrying."

I say, "Last month, I was with a man named James Edmond." I wouldn't dare tell Drum Mom that I really don't know the man's real name. This would have been too much for her to accept and me to handle.

"I call him Edmond," I continue. "He would come and eat at the diner where I worked. I was always his waitress and we started talking. Edmond is a teacher in one of the public schools in New York. He also owns houses that he rents out to people in New York. Once, when he was at the diner, he had his friend Gatewood at the table with him. Edmond introduced me to Gatewood, who was working on one of his houses. Edmond asked me to go with him to that house so that he could see what Gatewood was doing and to see if the house would be finished on time. I told Edmond that I would go with him, and I did go with him to his rental house. Anyway, when Gatewood finished the house, Edmond and I went back to the house. We went to one of the bedrooms and that's when it happened."

Drum Mom says, "Does Edmond know you're carrying his child?" I knew I had not seen Edmond since that night in his house, but I knew Gatewood had told him that I was pregnant. I reply, "Yes, Drum Mom. Edmond knows I am carrying his child."

"Ruby, when is the child going to be born, and what is Edmond going to do about this? Is he going to marry you?" she asks. I say in a sad voice, "The baby is due in November. Edmond and I are not going to get married. I don't love him enough to marry him, and I refuse to move to New York. New York is not a place to raise children."

Drum Mom stares at me and finally says, "You are a woman with two children and two different fathers for your children. Not one of your children's fathers will marry you! Children are a blessing from God! This burden is yours alone." She stops speaking, wiping the tears from her eyes, then continues. "Your first child, your son, Winston, is your responsibility to make it right between you and God. This child that you are carrying is without excuse. You knew what you were doing when you went into his house and let him go into you. We are not talking about unwanted sex due to rape or slavery. We are talking about the desires of your flesh.

"This is the last time you will get pregnant as an unwed woman and live in my house. You are right. You must find a place to live. If you want to continue doing what you are doing, I won't continue raising your children. You are their mother. Your place is to raise your own children. My place is to help when you need help!" After she stops speaking, Drum Mom gets up from the chair; she is crying.

"Drum Mom, I am so sorry that I disappoint you," I say. "Ruby, there is no disappointment," she responds. "There is hurt! I am hurt! You are every bit like my own daughter, Cheri, your mother. She gave birth to two children. She and your daddy, Harvey, never married. Your daddy lived with your momma, but he would never marry her. Now, you are an unwed mother with one child and carrying another child. I pray to God that you don't end up like Cheri. She loved to drink and was poisoned. After that, she lost her mind and died from that drink of liquor! Ruby, you will reap what you sow! I'm tired and I'm going to bed."

After Drum Mom retires to her room, I sit in the living room for another hour, crying and hurting because Drum Mom just told me things that I didn't know about my momma and daddy. I know she is hurting, but she didn't have to hurt me back like that. I hurt, too, and I'm mad.

After I stop crying and being mad at Drum Mom, I understand how she wants me to have a better life than the life my mother lived. "Reap what I sow." Drum Mom is right. I'm sowing the same seeds my momma gave to me. The only difference is that my seeds are by two different men. I'll show Drum Mom that I will not be like my momma. I'll show her I am a better mother!

Finally, I get up off the couch and get ready for bed. When I get in bed, I hug my son with one arm. With my other arm, I hold my belly to keep Winston from getting too close to me. I get comfortable in bed and say, "Yes, I'll be a better mother. I have a plan and my plan starts with Phillip."

Chapter Twelve

ANYTHING ELSE?

The next morning, I am up early so that I can cook breakfast for Drum Mom and Winston. When I finish cooking, they come into the kitchen and eat breakfast. Drum Mom says nothing to me, but talks and plays with Winston.

"Drum Mom, can I leave Winston with you so that I can go and talk to Miss Johnson about working in her salon?" I ask her. Drum Mom moans in a yes tone. "I'll be back home after we finish talking, and I'll take care of Winston and do all the chores," I say—to which she replies, "Sure you will." We finish breakfast, and I get Winston dressed for the day. Then I get dressed, leave the house, and walk to the salon.

I soon arrive at the salon, where I see Miss Johnson and several of my customers who are waiting to have their hair done. Everyone greets me and asks if I am coming back to work. "Yes, if Miss Johnson will take me back" is my response. "Ruby, stop being foolish," Miss Johnson replies. "I need you back! Can you start working right now?"

"Not today," I answer. "I just got back in town and came up here to see if I can start working next week. I've been gone for a long time and I need to make sure everything at home is good." Miss Johnson smiles and says, "Then I'll see you next week."

"Ruby, how is your brother, Robert, doing?" one of my customers asks. For a moment, I forgot why she would ask me about Robert. Then I remember telling all my customers that Robert was sick, and I had to suddenly leave to help his wife. "Robert is doing great. His health has returned, and he is back at work," I respond.

"That's good," another customer chimes in. "It's great to have family help you when you need help. I know they all appreciate the sacrifices you made to help take care of him. But praise be to GOD that Robert is fine, and we are glad you're back!"

When I leave the salon, I see Lucille standing outside. We hug each other and talk about how good it is that we are back together. I say, "Lucille, a lot of things happened in New York and I'll have to tell you about everything later. I should make my way to Drum Mom's house, take care of Winston, and do my chores. I'll be back working here next week. In the meantime, will you ask Fred if he can take us to Covington this Friday so that I can see Phillip?"

"Yes, we can do that for you," she responds, adding, "Fred and I got married!" "You and Fred are married?" I ask. "Yes, we married six months ago. I didn't want to tell you in my letter I wrote to you," she replies.

"Lucille, I am so happy for you and Fred. He sure knows how to pick out a wedding ring. It's beautiful!" I comment. Lucille replies, "Thank you, and he sure knows how to put a ring on a woman's finger. I know you've got to go, Ruby. Fred and I will pick you up about 8:00 in the evening." I reply, "Thanks, Lucille. I'll see you Friday."

After we part ways, I walk home, thinking about the fact that Lucille and Fred got married. I wish that I was married, too. But the more I think about love and marriage, the more I think, realizing that I don't know what love is, or how to love like Lucille and Fred. My family, my friends, and Phillip truly love me. I once was in love with Winston's father, Dexter. After I got pregnant, the love I had for him wasn't the same love that came back to me. The love I had for Dexter was the love I lost.

Edmond was totally different. That was not love, but physical passion. Edmond was with me at the right time and in the right place. He got what he wanted, and I got what I needed. With Phillip, I feel the two of us as being one person. He wants nothing but the best for me. He treats Winston like his own son. Of the three relationships that I've had, I now understand that real love is about honesty, truthfulness, and believing in each other's dreams. I hope that those traits will be enough for Phillip to stay true to his love for me. I know he loves me. But he may not stay with me, considering the wrong that I've done to him, unless he follows his heart. I hope he follows his heart and not his emotions. If he follows his emotions, I know he will vanish like mist in the air.

I arrive at home, play with Winston, and give him some home-work to do. I then get all my chores done and cook dinner. Daddy Freeman comes to the house and sits in the living room with all of us. He asks me, "Ruby, how was your stay with Beatrice?" I see Drum Mom staring at me. I say, "My stay with Beatrice was great! On my ride to New York, I met a young woman named Beth Eden in Ken-tucky. We became close friends. Beatrice had her friend Marty pick me up from the bus station. I asked him if Beth Eden could ride with us.

"When we got to Beatrice's house, I asked Beatrice if she had an extra room to rent to Beth Eden. She sent me upstairs to my room, and then she and Beth Eden talked. When I walked back downstairs, Beatrice said she had an extra room to rent and Beth Eden could stay in that room. Beth Eden and I attended the same beauty school and worked at the same diner after school was dismissed. Beatrice treated us well. Thank you for making everything happen for me."

"I don't understand why Beatrice won't get married and have children of her own," Daddy Freeman says. "She tells me that she is too busy in her house to get married, and that the women who come and live there are like her children. I tell her that she's getting old and she and Marty need to marry. They've been friends forever!

"Beatrice tells me that she and Marty are just friends and that's why they can't get married. She jokes with me and tells me, 'There have been more people living in my house compared to the number of children raised in your house.' I laugh every time she says this to me. Is there anything else about Beatrice and Marty that you haven't told me?" "No," I answer slowly.

"Did you hear from or see my sister, Pearl-Lee?" he asks. I gasp and say, "Yes, Pearl-Lee, for a while, stayed at Beatrice's house. She has beautiful dimples! Because Beth Eden and I love her dimples, we called her 'Dimples.' She was leaving for Michigan the day after I left New York. She told me to tell you hello, and she is doing fine. She is still not coming back to Ripley. However, she prom-ises to write and call you more often." Daddy Freeman then asks, "Is there anything else about Pearl-Lee?" I say no.

"Ruby, now how are you doing?" he inquires. I look up at Drum Mom and notice that she is looking straight at my face. I say, "Daddy Freeman, I am fine. I'm home with my family, got my diploma, and start back to work next week. Things couldn't be better."

Drum Mom reaches for her Bible, opens it, and starts reading it to herself. When she does this, Daddy Freeman looks at her. I get Daddy Freeman's attention, saying, "Daddy Freeman, I need another favor from you." Drum Mom stops reading her Bible and looks at me. "Daddy Freeman," I continue, "I have my diploma from the beauty school. I must take the state test to be a licensed beautician in the state of Tennessee. That test is on Friday, March 20. The test is in Memphis. I must be there before 7:00 in the morning. I will be finished with the test at about 4:00 in the evening. Can you drive me to Memphis to take the state test?"

"Yes," Daddy Freeman responds. "That will give me time to spend with my sister, Annie-Mary, and her husband, Joseph." After a brief pause, Daddy Freeman asks, "Is there anything else that went on in New York that you haven't told me about?" I say no.

"I'd better leave; it's getting late," he says. "Winston, come hug Daddy Freeman and tell me good night. I'll see you all tomorrow."

After Daddy Freeman leaves, Drum Mom asks, "Ruby, why did you not tell Freeman about your condition?" "Drum Mom, I will tell him," I assure her. "Tonight wasn't a good night to tell him."

"Tonight wasn't a good night to tell Freeman about your condition, but tonight was a good night to ask him to drive you to Memphis so you can take your state test!" she replies. "I'm going to bed. Before I lay my head down to sleep, I'm going to pray for you, child!" She gets up from her chair and leaves Winston and me in the living room. I hear Drum Mom slam her bedroom door shut.

Chapter Thirteen

THREE BITES OUT OF AN APPLE

The next morning, Lucille sends her cousin over to Drum Mom's house. Her cousin says to me. "Cousin Lucille and Fred will come by Friday night around 8:00 in the evening to pick you up." "Tell Lucille and Fred that I'll be ready. Take this letter and give it to your cousin Lucille," I reply, handing him a letter. "Yes, Miss Ruby," he responds.

In the letter that I gave the boy, I ask Lucille and Fred to send word to Phillip that I will be at his house on Friday night. Soon afterwards, Phillip sends a letter back to me. I open it and one red rose petal falls out of the envelope. Tears come to my eyes. He writes,

> *My beloved,*
>
> *I miss you and can't wait to see you. Nine months were so long for us to be apart. I am proud of your achievements. See you on Friday. One red rose petal for my true love.*
>
> *Phillip*

"Yes, Phillip still loves me for now," I say to myself. But will he still love me when I talk to him about everything that happened to me in New York? This will be hard for him, but I hope that our relationship is truly deep-rooted.

Drum Mom wakes up, comes into the living room, and sits in her chair. "Drum Mom," I begin, "I'm going to see Phillip on Friday and tell him about everything. I'll take Winston with me so that we all can be together. I'll be back by Monday so that I can go back to work on Tuesday."

"No!" Drum Mom responds sharply. "You are not taking Winston! What you must tell Phillip is between you and him. Winston doesn't need to be there, and you will not use him to hide behind or guard you from your unfaithfulness. Phillip is a good man. But no one knows what a good man will do or say when he is hurt. You made your bed, and you will lie in it without Winston. Do you understand?" I say, "Yes, Drum Mom," ending the conversation.

*****

Lucille and Fred come by on Friday to take me to see Phillip. Before I leave, I put Winston to bed and then say goodbye to Drum Mom. She never looks at me or says a word. I leave the house and get in the car. "This is like old times—friends getting together to have a little fun," Lucille says. "Yes, this is nice, except that I'm hanging out with an old married couple," I joke. We all laugh.

"Fred, take me over to Phillip's house," I request. "He is waiting for me, and he will take me back home." Lucille says, "Nine months is a long time to be without the man you love. I don't know what I'd do if Fred left for that long. Come to think about it, I do know what I'd do: I'd wait for him to come back home."

After a while, we arrive at Phillip's house. He is standing on the front porch, waving and smiling at us. I get out of the car and run into his arms. He holds me tightly in his arms and kisses me. We wave at Lucille and Fred as they depart, and then go into his house.

"Ruby, my beloved, you look so beautiful!" Phillip comments. "I am so proud that you have your diploma and now you can work toward having your own business. Please sit down on the couch. Are you hungry? Do you want something to eat?" I say, "No, Phillip. I'm not hungry."

I sit down on the couch, with Phillip sitting down beside me. He holds me in his arms. I realize how I missed his scent, his sweet breath, and the way his hands touch me. I move one of his hands to my heart; then I place one of my hands on his heart. Our hearts begin to beat in the same rhythm. I know for sure that Phillip's heart and my heart beat as one heart!

"Ruby, I love the letters you wrote to me," Phillip says. "I read them every night before I go to sleep. I feel as though I know all your friends and Beatrice from New York. Your letters make me feel like

I've been to New York. Tell me more about your stay." All at once, my heart starts beating faster and faster. My heart is no longer in rhythm with Phillip's. I can hear the pounding of my heart against my chest. "Ruby, why is your heart beating faster? Are you all right?" Phillip asks.

"Phillip, yes, I'm all right," I reply. I start to feel light-headed. I can't breathe. When I try to breathe, very little air comes in or goes out. Then, the next thing I remember is Phillip shaking my body. He is calling my name: "Ruby, Ruby, Ruby, wake up!" I slowly open my eyes halfway. Phillip has my body stretched out on the couch. He sees my eyes trying to open. I feel something cool on my forehead. I hear Phillip calling my name again: "Ruby, Ruby, Ruby, please wake up!"

My eyes open wider; "Phillip, what happened to me?" I ask in a soft voice. He puts his head on my heart. Then he gets up and puts a pillow under my head. "Do you need some water or something to eat?" he asks. "Please give me some water," I respond. "I'm feeling better now." Phillip gets up off the couch, goes into the kitchen, and then brings me a glass of water. He sits me up on the couch and I drink the water. I give him back the cool cloth that has been on my forehead.

Phillip says, "Ruby, your heart started beating fast and I could hear it pounding against your chest. Your eyes rolled back, and you fell faint. I thought about running to my neighbor's house, but your heart started beating, and you were breathing. So, I waited here until you woke up. Thank God that you are alert and talking! What's wrong with you, Ruby?"

"Phillip, sit down beside me," I say. "I need to talk to you about what happened to me in New York." Phillip sits on the couch. He has a puzzled look on his face, and he rubs his head. "Tell me what happened," he says.

I say, "Phillip, you know every day I worked at a diner after beauty school. My friend Beth Eden also worked there. I met this man named Edmond. The owner of the diner, Mr. Schapiro, always wanted me to wait on him. One day, Edmond asked me to go with him and look at one of the houses he owns that he's renting out to a colored man. I went to that house with him. I let him come into me. I am pregnant with his child."

Phillip quickly stands up from the couch and starts pacing the floor. I am quiet. I know he is taking in what I just said to him. Finally, in a loud, angry voice, Phillip says, "Woman, you are pregnant and here in my house, carrying another man's child! You and I, the two of us, never had that kind of relationship. I've never gone into you!"

Phillip stops talking and continues pacing the floor, with one of his hands on his forehead. I know he's angry at me. The tone in his voice is different. He never calls me "woman"; he always calls me "my beloved."

Phillip sits down in the chair across from me. He continues to speak strongly, stares at me, and says, "Does Edmond know you are pregnant with his child? Who else knows you're pregnant?" I say, "Yes, Edmond knows I'm pregnant. I didn't immediately tell Drum Mom when I arrived home. But she knew, just by looking at me. She asked me to tell her the truth, and I told her everything. Winston is at the house with her tonight; this way, I could be alone with you and tell you the truth."

"Woman, this thing really hurts me," he admits. "Even being miles apart, I trusted you, that you would be faithful to me! I trusted you in your love for me! I trusted you to get your diploma! I trusted you to come back like you left me! But you have been unfaithful to me and this is something that's too hard to bear!"

Phillip stands up and asks, "Are you finished?" I say, "No, Phillip, I am not finished." He looks at me with hate in his eyes and sits back down. "Woman, finish what you have to say!" he exclaims.

I say, "Phillip, I love you, and for the wrong I've done to our relationship, I am so sorry. Most of all, I am sorry for hurting you. You are such a good man and don't deserve to be hurt like I hurt you. I love you, and only you do I love. You are the apple of my eye."

"You love me?" Phillip retorts in bewilderment. "I am the apple of your eye! Woman, stop your jiving! Are you finished?" I say no. "Tell me everything else you got to say. Let's get this over with," he says.

I say, "Phillip, I am just over a month pregnant. You loved me before we talked tonight. I am asking for you to love me again. I am asking you to marry me, take me as your wife, and take this baby as your own. You don't have any children, and your last name will die with you. No one will know that this child is not yours if we marry soon. I promise you that I will be a faithful wife and the best wife. We all can live as a family."

Phillip walks over to the kitchen counter and gets an apple out of the basket. (He loves apples; he always keeps them at his house.) He washes the apple and takes a huge bite out of it. He chews it up and says, "This is my commitment to Winston." He takes another large bite next to where he had taken the first bite. He chews it up and swallows it, saying, "This is my commitment to the child that you are carrying." He gives me the apple and tells me to take a bite. I turn the apple where it has not been bitten. I take a very tiny bite out of the apple and eat it. Then I give it back to Phillip.

Phillip says, "Woman, it's late. Get up from the couch. You can sleep in my bed. I'll sleep on the couch. I will answer you later." I get up from the couch and go to bed.

Phillip takes the bitten apple and throws it into the garbage can. He takes all the apples that are on the kitchen counter and throws them into the garbage can. He then looks around the kitchen, searching for apples to throw away.

He says to himself, "I take two large bites out of the apple, eat them, and make a commitment to Ruby's children. Ruby doesn't take a bite next to my bite; this means she will never be by my side. I take large bites from the apple, and Ruby takes a tiny bite. This means if I marry her, we will never be one. After each bite from the apple, I make a commitment to one of her children. Ruby doesn't commit to anything. This means she will not be faithful to me and she will do what her heart desires.

"When Ruby finishes eating her tiny bite from the apple, she gives it back to me. This means Ruby doesn't care about holding on to me or anything good about me. Ruby will do what she wants and then, in her time, let me go. She will deceive me like a serpent. Like the serpent did to Eve and Eve did to Adam, Ruby will do to me. Ruby is my Eve!"

He stops and thinks more and more. "On the other hand, I do love her and believe she loves me in her own way," he says to himself. "Ruby makes a point when she says I need to leave my last name for someone to carry on in life." Phillip continues to think, saying, "Ruby is right again. She is early in her pregnancy. If I marry her, no one will know the child is not really my child. I need to think about these things. I'm going to sleep."

*****

The next morning when I wake up, I get out of his bed, walk into the kitchen, and see that Phillip has breakfast ready for me. I fix my plate and sit at the kitchen table. Phillip says, "I'm leaving the house for a few hours. I'll be back later." He gets up from the table and then leaves the house.

After noontime, Phillip comes home. He says, "Ruby, come in here and sit on the couch." I do as he says. Phillip sits in a chair across from me. "I thought about a lot of things you said to me last night," he begins to explain. "I thought about things that I see in you that I never had seen before. Get up and open that blue box on the kitchen counter."

I get up from the couch and walk over to the kitchen counter. "I hope I find one red rose petal in it," I say to myself. When I open the blue box, instead of finding one red rose petal, I see a wedding ring. I take it out of the box and say, "Phillip, this is a wedding ring! Thank you. You're going to marry me!"

Phillip says, "Yes, I'm going to marry you, Ruby. I left this morning to get the ring. On Monday, we will go to the county clerk's office in Memphis and get married." I say, "Phillip, I love you so much. Will you put this ring on my finger?" "No!" Phillip exclaims. "You can do that yourself! I'm going to take a nap, so I can go to work tonight. I'll sleep on the couch." He then proceeds to lie down and take a nap.

When Phillip gets up from his nap, he says, "Winston will come and live with us. I have a cousin who will take care of him when I'm not at work. I'll give you two weeks to live with your Drum Mom in her house. Two weeks should give you enough time to make whatever preparations you should make to move here. Every other night, I'll be in Ripley to see my family. I know this one thing 'woman,' you'd better do right by me while we are apart. You can sleep in the bedroom. I'll sleep on the couch when I get home from work."

*****

On Monday morning, we get up early to go to Memphis and get married. When we finally reach the county clerk's office, we go into the building and wait our turn. Soon, a man calls our names. During the ceremony, Phillip puts my wedding ring on the wrong hand and the wrong finger. The man laughs and says, "Phillip, you put the ring on the wrong hand and finger. This is where the ring belongs." The man points to my correct hand and finger, then Phillip takes the ring off and puts it on the right finger. The ceremony is over in seconds.

The man says, "I now pronounce you man and wife. Phillip, you may kiss your wife." Phillip pecks a kiss on my forehead. I notice the man stare at Phillip and then at me. I then kiss Phillip's lips. Next, we obtain our wedding license, and then Phillip starts driving me home to Drum Mom's house.

Chapter Fourteen

A READY MIND

When we arrive at Drum Mom's house, she is sitting in her chair, and Winston is playing on the floor. Phillip and I speak to Winston and Drum Mom. Winston stops playing and runs and hugs my legs. I bend down and kiss him. "Phillip, how are you doing today?" Drum Mom asks him. Phillip responds, "I'm doing all right. How are you?" Drum Mom replies, "I'm doing all right." She does not say anything to me. She doesn't look at me; instead, she just keeps her eyes on Winston. She then looks up at Phillip.

"Ruby and I got married this morning in Memphis," Phillip says. Drum Mom quickly looks at me; she sees the wedding ring on my finger. "Ruby is here because she has to start working at the salon tomorrow morning," Phillip continues. "She is going to work for two weeks in Ripley. This will give her time to prepare to quit her job and move in with me. Winston is going to live with us. My cousin will take care of him when I'm not working. Ruby and I agreed to this."

Drum Mom continues to look at Phillip; she doesn't say anything. "Will you allow Ruby and Winston to live here for two more weeks and for me to come by here at night to spend time with my family?" Phillip asks.

Drum Mom says, "Phillip, yes, I most certainly will allow you to come here and spend time with your family. You are a good man. Not many men are like you. I will be happy to help you in any way I can." Drum Mom is smiling and appears to be happy about the marriage. I hadn't seen her this happy since my return from New York. She gets up from her chair and says, "I'm going to bed. Good night, everybody." She then walks down the hallway to her room, and closes the door behind her. "Drum Mom didn't slam her door. She is happy for me," I think to myself.

"I'm going to leave," Phillip announces. He picks up Winston and kisses him, saying, "Good night, Winston." He puts Winston back on the floor, then looks at me and says, "I'll see you later. He puts a kiss on my forehead and leaves.

*****

The next morning, I gather up my hair supplies and get ready to ride to work with Daddy Freeman. When Daddy Freeman is parked in front of the house, I walk to Drum Mom's bedroom and say, "I'm leaving for work. Winston is still sleeping. Thank you, Drum Mom. I love you." She replies, "I'll see you later. I love you, too."

When I arrive at the salon, I see that it is completely full of customers. I say, "Good morning, everybody." Everyone responds back. I walk over to my work station, take out my hair supplies, and put my diploma on the wall. One of the customers notices my wedding ring and asks, "Ruby, when did you get married?" Everyone is now looking at me. "Yesterday," I answer, then ask, "Who is going to be my first customer today?" Miss Johnson says, "Sadie was here first." I say, "Sadie, come and sit in my chair. You are beautiful now, and I'm going to have you looking more beautiful." She smiles at me and walks over to my chair.

I use all the techniques I learned at beauty school on Sadie's hair. When I finish, Sadie poses in front of my large mirror. Then she starts walking around in the salon like a model. "Ruby, I love what you done to my hair and how you cut my kitchen!" Sadie comments. Then she pays me and gives me a nickel tip. "Thank you, Sadie," I reply. "When do you want to come back and see me?" "In a month!" Sadie eagerly replies. "Write my name down in your appointment book right now!"

All the customers tell Sadie how beautiful she looks. I then turn to Miss Johnson. She doesn't look at Sadie, nor does she say a word to either of us.

I ask, "Who is next?" All the customers raise their hands. Miss Johnson sees this and points to the customer who is next in line. The customer sits at my work station. I look up frequently and observe Miss Johnson through my large mirror. She appears to be rolling her eyes and frowning at me. I continue my work until I finish with my customer. Like Sadie, she is in awe with all the things I have done to make her look more beautiful.

"Today has been a very good day!" I think to myself. My pockets are full of bills and coins. I received tips from all my customers. When I finish for the day, I sit in my chair and rest. I reflect on the way Miss Johnson looked at me, the way she controlled my customers, and the way she didn't talk to me. I know Miss Johnson sees my work and knows my skills are excellent! I think Miss Johnson has acted like this today because she realizes that my going to beauty school has given her some competition.

I stand up, clean my work station, and put my hair supplies and my diploma in my bag. Daddy Freeman is waiting outside for me to come to his car. When Miss Johnson's last customer walks out the door, I also walk to the door and say, "Goodbye, Miss Johnson." Miss Johnson says, "Ruby, we made a lot of money today. I'll see you tomorrow." I then open the door and leave.

When I get home, I play with Winston. Drum Mom still has a smile on her face as she looks at me. We eat dinner and go to bed by 8:00 in the evening.

The next day at the salon, I work harder. Miss Johnson gives me a lot of customers, and other customers wait for me to do their hair. I make a lot of money and get a lot of tips.

Phillip is in the living room, sitting in the chair, when I make it home today. I speak to everyone, kiss Winston, and then kiss Phillip. Next, I leave the room to wash up; afterwards, I go back to the front room and sit down on the couch next to Phillip. We talk, and then when dinner is ready, we go to the kitchen and sit at the table to eat dinner.

"I want to pray," Winston professes. We all say okay. Winston prays, "Thank You, God, for our food. Thank You for Drum Mom, Momma, and my new daddy. Amen." Phillip smiles and says, "That's right, I'm your new daddy. What name will you call me, Winston?"

Winston looks at Phillip, thinks about what he has asked him, and then says, "I have a Daddy Freeman. I'm going to call you 'New Daddy.'" We laugh. "'New Daddy' will be just fine," Phillip assures Winston. When we finish eating, Phillip leaves for the night.

At the end of two weeks, I earn more money than I have ever earned in a whole month. Business is booming. I am hopeful that some of my current customers will come to Covington to get their hair done. I walk to the door to leave and Miss Johnson says, "Ruby, you're always welcome to come back here. We will make a fortune together." "Thank you, Miss Johnson, for everything. I enjoyed working here," I respond.

The next day, Phillip comes to Drum Mom's house. He greets us, saying, "Ruby, where are your things? It's time to go home. I know how busy you've been, so I talked to Mrs. Williams. She has space available and you can work at her salon. We just need to let her know the day that you want to start. I also talked to my cousin; she will take care of Winston when I'm working." He then looks at Drum Mom and says, "Thank you for everything. We should leave right now. We need to get everything in our home."

Phillip and Winston take the bags to the car. I hug Drum Mom and say, "Thank you for everything. Thank you for taking care of Winston and me. Most of all, thank you for loving me." Drum Mom replies, "I'm proud of you. I love you very much. It's time for you to go with your husband. I'll see you and Winston later."

Phillip and Winston are now in the car, waiting for me. I walk out of the house, off the porch, and onto the front yard. I know Drum Mom always says, "Don't look back unless it's for your own good." But I stop, turn toward the house, and see Drum Mom on the porch. I think about leaving this house for good. This house is where my brother, Robert, my son, Winston, and I have lived. I think about all the family, friends, and memories I'm leaving behind in this house. Tears start flowing from my eyes. I look at Drum Mom on the porch, who is smiling and waving. I finally wave back, turn away from the house, and walk over to get in the car. "Let's go home," Phillip says.

When we reach Phillip's house, I get out of the car. I notice there are a lot of women sitting on the porch in front of Phillip's house. There are a lot of men talking in the yard. I say, "Good evening." The women and men wave at me. I hear one of the women say, "We're going to have to keep an eye on her. Look at her."

Another woman says, "You are so right! She's got frog legs, and you know what they say: Frog legs taste like chicken." I open my mouth to talk back to those women, but Phillip, who is standing beside me, says softly, "Ruby, go in the house. Right now."

As I'm walking to the house, I hear a man ask, "Phillip, do you need any help?" Phillip says, "No, I can take care of everything." I walk into the house, put the bag down on the table, and walk to the front window. I pull back the curtain. I see the women talking back and forth, laughing and pointing at the house. Phillip comes into the house with Winston. "Ruby, close that curtain and help get these things in order!" he says. "We need to eat and let Winston get used to this house. Then we need to go to bed." And that's what we do.

Chapter Fifteen
CLEAR IN THE MATTER

What I am doing during the first week of our living together in Phillip's house is getting mine and Winston's things put away, cleaning the house, and cooking. When I have free time, I study for the state test. I let Winston ride his tricycle in the driveway and on the sidewalk; whenever Winston is outside playing and riding his tricycle, the women living on the same street get together and sit on the porch in front of our house.

This one particular time, one of the women calls Winston over to the porch to talk to him. Winston stays on the sidewalk and says, "My momma tells me to stay on the sidewalk and the driveway, and not talk to strangers." I hear the same woman ask Winston, "Where is your momma? What is she doing?" Winston looks at the woman but doesn't answer her.

I come out the house and tell Winston, "Playtime is over. Go back in the house." I walk over to the house where the women are sitting on the porch and ask, "How are you ladies doing today?" "Fine, and you?" they all reply.

"I'm fine," I respond. "I noticed from looking out of the window that you *(I point to the woman who was talking to Winston)* are talking and asking my son about me. He doesn't talk to strangers. I am right here. Is there anything you'd like to know about me and my family?" The woman replies, "No, there's nothing I'll like to know." "Is there anyone here who would like to know anything about me and my family?" I then ask the women. "No!" they all say emphatically.

"I see," I respond. "It's best that we be good neighbors and not gossip or talk about each other. If you'd like to know anything about us, please feel free to ask me and not our son, Winston. However, if you see my son doing anything wrong, I want you to correct him and tell me about it. I hope you ladies have a good rest of the day." I leave the porch, go into our house, and look out the window. I notice that the women are not talking to each other but are, instead, looking at me as I'm looking at them.

Soon, when Phillip comes home, he says, "Ruby, I'm going to take you to see Mrs. Williams so you can talk to her about a job at her salon." I say, "Phillip, I need time this week to study for my test. After this week, I'll go and talk to Mrs. Williams. If I pass the test, I can show her both my diploma and license. Those papers will show I'm very qualified to work at her salon. Some salons won't let you work unless you show them your license." Phillip seems to nod his head in agreement with what I am saying.

*****

On Friday, Daddy Freeman comes to our house at 4:00 in the morning so that I can get to Memphis on time to take the state test. While we are riding in the car, he says, "I'm going to visit my sister, Annie-Mary, and her husband, Joseph. I usually visit them on Monday when my barber shop is closed. This visit will be a special one because I can stay longer. On Mondays, when I go and visit them, I'm always in a hurry to get back home before dark. Ruby, write down their telephone number. If you finish the test before four o'clock, call me at that number. Otherwise, I'll be back to get you at four."

It is 6:00 in the morning when we arrive at the building where the test is being administered. The building is open, and people are already walking through the front door, though the test doesn't start until 7:00. I walk in and sit in the lobby on the "colored people" side. There are two other colored women sitting and waiting to take the test. They are going over their notes, so I just sit down and remain quiet.

A white woman comes into the lobby and tells us to go to the classroom when our name is called. She calls the last names in alphabetical order. When she calls my name, I go to the classroom, where another white woman proceeds to tell me where to sit down to take the test. My seat is in the back of the room next to the two other colored women. I count twelve white women and three colored women taking the test.

The other white woman who was giving instructions in the lobby comes into the classroom. She goes over the instructions for taking the written test: "One of us will tell you when you have thirty more minutes to finish. When the time is up, you must put your pencil down. We will come by and pick up your test and grade it. You will stay in your seat until your name is called. When your name is called, you can come to the front and watch us grade your test paper. You must score 75 percent to pass the test to get your license today. If you fail the test, you'll have to take it over on the next date the test is given. Any questions before we pass out the test?" No one says anything.

The test papers are then passed out. One of the white women who is monitoring the test taking is sitting in a chair in the back, beside me and where the two other colored women are sitting. She looks at us the whole time we take the test. The other white woman from the lobby is sitting at the front desk, near where all the white people are taking their tests; she is reading a book while the test is being taken. "You have thirty more minutes to complete the test," the white woman sitting beside me says as a warning. We continue to take the test. Then, after the final thirty minutes, she says, "Time is over. Put your pens down and turn your papers over. Stay in your seat until we call your name."

The two white women start calling the last names in alphabetical order. One of the white test takers goes to the front when they call her name. She watches while they grade her test papers. Everyone looks at her when she starts crying—having failed the test. They ask her to leave the classroom and cry outside!

I am nervous. My heart starts beating fast. Everyone in class now looks scared. When my name is called, I walk up to the front desk. I watch them grade my papers. The white woman who was reading a book during test time grades my paper once, then twice. She then gives my test paper to the white woman who had been sitting in the back beside me, and has her grade my papers. I see that they both have the same score. I scored 98 percent on the test! I smile and throw my hands up in the air. The white woman who had been sitting beside me says, "Take your papers across the hallway and pay for your beauty license."

I walk across the hallway, go into the office, and then show my papers to the clerk. She looks up at me, stares at me, and then says, "Give me your money for the license." I give her my money for my license and go sit in the lobby.

After a while of waiting, I find myself still waiting at about 4:30 in the evening. As I sit in the lobby, I think about all the people who sacrificed everything so that I could go to the best beauty school. I think about Mrs. Foxx, who is the best instructor in the whole world! I can't wait to write to her and let her know that I passed the state test. I soon get up, call Daddy Freeman, and tell him that I passed the test and I'm ready to leave. I go back to my seat in the lobby and sit down. Soon, the two white women come out of the classroom and walk over to me. The white woman from the lobby says, "Your score is the highest in the class!"

As I revel in what I have been told, I see Daddy Freeman's car parked in front of the building. I walk out of the lobby and Daddy Freeman sees the huge smile on my face. He is also smiling. I get in the car and say, "Daddy Freeman, thank you for everything! I didn't quite understand you or listen to you when you talked to me in the hospital about getting a license. After I went back to work for Miss Johnson, it was at that point that I realized what you said to me and how you were correct in what you said. I need my license so that I can make my own money, take care of Winston, and own a salon. Things may never have changed if it weren't for you. Now I understand! Having your own land and owning your own business are things that give colored people a little power and a little control over their own life."

"Sometimes, people can't see the forest because of the trees," Daddy Freeman begins to explain. "In this family, we see the forest, the trees, the grass, the trenches, the rocks, and the dirty roads. We are not afraid to walk through all the good times and hard times to get through and out of that forest. When we work together and help each other, we all benefit from owning a part of that beautiful land beyond the forest. Teach this to Winston. He will eventually find what he loves to do and will go after what he loves, just as you."

*****

When I arrive home, I run into the house, shouting, "Phillip, I passed the test. My score was 98 percent—the highest score in the class!" "Ruby, I knew you would pass the test. You are on your way to having your own salon," Phillip responds with a hug. "Next week, I'll take you to Mrs. Williams's salon, so you can tell her when you can start to work."

"Okay, Phillip," I reply. "I'd also like to meet your cousin who is going to take care of Winston. I would like for Winston to be with her for a couple of days so that I'll know he'll be all right in the care of someone new. Winston and I don't know your cousin. I'll feel better knowing your cousin is a good, loving person." "Okay. I understand," Phillip responds.

That night before I go to sleep, I write a letter to Mrs. Foxx about my score on the test, and about getting my Tennessee license and working toward having my own salon. Out of everything that I write, the main reason for writing this letter is to thank her for being the best instructor in the world, preparing us to take the test, and giving us an opportunity to succeed in the business.

The next day, I mail the letter. Later on, Phillip drives me to meet Mrs. Williams at her salon. He pulls up to her place of business, and I get out of the car. Phillip stays in the car with Winston. I walk up to her salon and notice that she is working in a very old building. When I go inside, I see water dripping from the ceiling and a pot on the floor collecting the water. The wooden floors are rotten. She has one wash sink, one floor hair dryer, and two work stations. On the level above her salon, I hear a man and woman yelling and screaming at each other; then I hear a toilet flush.

"Mrs. Williams," I begin, "I am Ruby. Phillip talked to you about me." She says, "Yes, sit down on the couch." When we sit down on the couch, she says, "Let me see your state license." I show it to her; then she asks, "What beauty school did you go to?" I say, "The one in New York." "I hear that's a good beauty school," she comments. "Will you have your own customers coming here, or do you expect me to provide customers for you?"

"I don't have any customers at this moment," I reply. "I see you have only one wash sink and one floor hair dryer. How will the two of us work that out when we both have customers here at the same time?" Mrs. Williams says, "Your customers will have to wait their turn, or you will have to schedule them when I don't have a customer. If the two of us have customers here at the same time, when I finish washing a head, then you can wash a head. When I finish with the hair dryer, your customer can get under the hair dryer. This is how we will work together."

"I understand. How much will you charge for renting space?" I ask. "I'll charge you $5.00 a month, and you can start at any time," Mrs. Williams notes. "You can come to the salon and get any new customer that walks through those doors. Do you have any other questions?" I reply, "No, Mrs. Williams, and thank you for your time. I'll get back with you real soon." I leave the salon and get back into the car.

"How did the interview go?" Phillip asks. "Phillip, my interview was great. I'll tell you more later. I told Mrs. Williams I would get back with her real soon," I explain. Phillip smiles. Then I ask, "Phillip, do you think your cousin can take care of Winston tomorrow?" "Let's drive by her house and see if she can take care of Winston tomorrow. This will give you some time to get to know my cousin," he says. "Phillip, you've never told me your cousin's name. What is her name?" I inquire. "Cousin Eunice," he replies.

We arrive at her house and knock on the door. A woman comes to the door, sees Phillip, and lets us come inside her home. Eunice is a tall, beautiful colored woman in her late fifties. Phillip introduces us, and she tells us to sit down in the living room.

"Cousin Eunice, Phillip speaks highly of you," I begin. "I wanted to come by and meet you. You have a beautiful, clean home. There are so many antiques. I know you are proud of your home."

"Thank you, and yes, we are proud of our home," Cousin Eunice responds. "My husband, Raymond, works at night. He's in bed asleep right now." "Will he be bothered by Winston being here during the day when he is trying to sleep?" I ask. "No! It won't bother Raymond when I keep Winston during the day. I keep children over here all the time," she assures me. "How many children are you taking care of now?" I inquire. "None," she responds. "Winston will be the only one. The other children I keep start school this year."

"Can you keep Winston tomorrow and the day after that?" I then ask her—to which she replies, "Yes, of course." I say, "I will start work next week and need you on Tuesday through Friday." "I will keep Winston on Saturdays until Ruby comes home from work," Phillip chimes in. "Cousin Eunice, after this week, can you start taking care of Winston full time, beginning next Tuesday?" I ask. She responds yes, then Phillip says, "I'll bring him over here in the morning." Phillip and I then part ways with Cousin Eunice and head home.

That night, as I am getting Winston's things ready to go to Cousin Eunice's house, I sit down with him and say, "Your Cousin Eunice is going to take care of you for the next two days. Momma wants you to be a good son. Let me know if she is nice to you." Winston seems happy about the arrangement. "Winston, why are you so happy about going over to Cousin Eunice's house?" I ask him. "I've been in this house for a long time and I want to go somewhere else. Drum Mom and I always go out of the house," he responds.

"Do you miss your Drum Mom?" I inquire. "Yes, and I miss Daddy Freeman," he replies. I say, "It's time to go to sleep. Go to your room. Phillip and I will go to sleep in our bedroom."

After Winston goes off to his room, Phillip and I get ourselves ready for bed as well. But, when we are in bed, Phillip lays on his left side and I lay on my right side. Even though we are married, Phillip doesn't touch me or get intimate with me. He remembers that I am pregnant and am carrying another man's child.

*****

In the morning, Phillip takes Winston to Cousin Eunice's house. He returns home and asks me again about the interview with Mrs. Williams. I say, "Phillip, I am not happy with her place. The salon has water dripping from the ceiling and a pot on the floor collecting the water. You can hear the people upstairs arguing and flushing the toilet. She only has one sink to wash hair and only one floor hair dryer. I must work around her customers. They get the first choice at the hair sink and dryer. That is not fair to me or my customers who must wait for Mrs. Williams to finish with her customers.

"Mrs. Williams is going to charge me $5.00 a month to rent space that is not equipped for me to do my work. I paid Miss Johnson less than that and she has everything I need to make money. Plus, I have customers at Miss Johnson's salon. Here, I will have to start all over and find customers. Phillip, do you understand what I'm saying?"

"We are a family and we'll stay together as a family," Phillip replies to my words. "We live here, and you'll just have to do what you need to do to find your customers. You can start by talking to the women on the porch in front of our house. After that, you can go to the next two streets and tell those women that you fix hair. When you finish, come home and we'll talk some more."

After Phillip is done talking, I leave the house and walk over to talk to the women on the porch. I say, "Ladies, I am a licensed beautician and I do hair. I'll be working at Mrs. Williams's salon. If you don't have a beautician, I would love to have you as a customer."

One of the women says, "So that's what you do! You are a beautician. No, Mrs. Williams does my hair." The other women then take turns saying, "No. Mrs. Williams does my hair," or, "I do my hair myself," or, "My cousin does my hair." I say, "Thank you," and leave the porch.

Next, I walk from house to house, talking to the women who are at home. Their responses are the same as those of the women sitting on the porch. When I walk home, those same women are still sitting on the porch in front of our house. I walk into our house and sit down on the couch. I know that those women on the porch are talking about my going door to door trying to find work. I am embarrassed!

Soon, Phillip comes home with Winston, who looks happy and full of energy. "Winston, come sit by Momma and tell me what you did today," I request. "I sleep and eat. Cousin Eunice is very nice," he says. *Did I just hear Winston say that he only sleeps and eats at Cousin Eunice's house?* "Winston, go wash your hands and get ready for dinner," I instruct him. "How many customers did you get today?" Phillip asks. "None!" I exclaim. "Well, tomorrow will be another day and you can try again," he comments. I say nothing; I just stare at him. Then Winston comes into the kitchen, and we all say grace and eat.

During the night, Phillip and I try to sleep, but Winston keeps us up all night—playing with his toys, singing, counting, talking, and walking throughout the house.

The next morning, Phillip and I are restless from having not gotten any sleep. I get Winston ready to go to Cousin Eunice's house. After preparing for the day, we eat breakfast, and then Phillip takes Winston to stay with Cousin Eunice.

When Phillip returns home, I say, "I'm going through the neighborhood to find me some customers. I need you to take me somewhere around one o'clock. Will you be home to take me where I need to go?" "Yes, I'll be home," Phillip responds.

*****

After getting done with our missions, Phillip and I get back to the house at the same time. When I get into the car, Phillip asks, "Did you have any luck today?" I reply, "No, Phillip, I didn't have any luck today." "Where are we going?" Phillip inquires. "Are you going to try and find another salon, so you can go to work?" I say, "Take me over to your Cousin Eunice's house." "Why?" he asks. "You want to pick Winston up early today?" I respond, "No, I just want to see how they are doing."

When we arrive at Cousin Eunice's house, we walk up to the front door and Phillip knocks on the door. No one comes to the door to let us in the house. "They're not at home," Phillip says. My gut tells me that Winston is in the house, so I start knocking and knocking on the door. Finally, I hear Cousin Eunice say, "I'm coming. Stop all that loud knocking!" I stop knocking on the door and she finally opens the door. She is surprised to see us. I see that she still has on her pajamas and is wearing a stocking over her head.

"Hi, Eunice," Phillip says. "Where is my son?" I inquire loudly. She says, "Come in the house and be quiet. Winston is asleep in the bedroom." I say, "Show me the bedroom." She takes me and Phillip to the bedroom, where I find Winston asleep in the bed. I say, "Winston, wake up. It's Momma." Winston does not move. He is breathing like he is in a strange deep sleep. I shake him; he doesn't wake up. "Winston, Winston, wake up," I plead. He then opens his eyes and says, "Momma, I'm sleepy." I look over to the table and see a bottle. When I pick up the bottle and read the label, it reads, "Sleeping Syrup."

I put the bottle down and ask Cousin Eunice, "Did you give my son some of this 'Sleeping Syrup'?" "Yes," she answers in a scary voice. Raymond works at night. I don't sleep when he is at work, so we sleep during the day. I gave Winston only a teaspoon of the syrup, so he can go to sleep and let us sleep."

"Come pick up my son so you can take him to the car!" I command Phillip. "He's going home." I then turn toward Cousin Eunice.

"What kind of woman are you?" I say loudly and angrily. "You drug my child so you and your husband can sleep! I'm going to the police and tell them what you've done to my son." When we walk out of the bedroom to the living room, Raymond comes out of his bedroom and asks, "What's going on?"

After letting out a scream, I say, "Your wife tried to poison my son with some sleeping syrup so all of you can sleep. Winston won't fully wake up for me. 'Winston, Winston, wake up.' *(I am trying to wake him up.)* You see what I mean! He hardly wakes up. I should go to the police and tell them what she did to my son."

Raymond says, "Hold on now. You don't need to do that," Raymond retorts. Suddenly with all the loud talking, Winston wakes up and says, "Momma, Cousin Eunice whipped me for getting off the couch. I was just getting my toy off the floor so I could play with it on the couch. I sit back on the couch. She says she told me to not get off the couch, that's why she whipped me."

When Winston says this, I say, "Eunice, I'm going to beat your ass for drugging and whipping my son!" I charge at her, but Raymond gets between me and Eunice. Phillip puts Winston down on the floor and immediately pulls me away from Raymond. Phillip drags me out of the house, puts me in the car, and says, "You'd better stay in this car until I bring Winston to the car." He goes back into the house, gets Winston, and puts him in the back seat of the car. Phillip gets into the car and says, "We'll talk about this when we get home."

When we get home, though Winston wants to go to sleep, I don't let him. Instead, I look his body over and see whipping marks on his back. I show them to Phillip, then I tell Winston to go outside and ride his tricycle.

"Phillip, why did you stop me?" I ask. "You don't fight some-one in their own house. Ruby, you need to calm down!" he answers. "Calm down!" I exclaim. "That woman drugged my son so they could sleep, and then she whipped my son for no earthly reason!" Phillip says, "You have reason to be angry, but fighting won't make things better."

"It'll make me feel better," I retort. "I'll tell you this: I'd better not see that woman anywhere in town. If I do, I'm going to finish what I didn't get to start. I'll beat her so bad she won't be able to talk or walk!" I then try to calm down, but I can't.

"Phillip, Winston and I are going to Drum Mom's house," I inform him. Phillip says, "Wait a minute, Ruby. You're mad and not thinking clearly." "Phillip, I *am* thinking clearly," I reply. "I love you. I thank you for loving me and marrying me with my circumstances. But this town and these people in this town are not what's best for me. There's no work for me here, and I will not let anyone else but my family take care of my son. I'm also afraid of living in this town with all the gunshots we hear at night. I don't want to be here!"

Phillip says, "You don't want to be here! Does that include not wanting to be here with me?" "Yes. You can come visit me in Ripley through the week, and I'll come here on Sunday and Monday," I say. "How soon can you take me to Drum Mom's house?"

Phillip says, "You are perfectly clear in what you want to do and what you want *me* to do. I will take you back as soon as you are packed and ready." I reply, "Thank you. I'll go outside and get Winston." After I go outside to get Winston, he and I go back into the house. Then I fall asleep with Winston.

After Winston and I go to sleep, Phillip walks around in the kitchen and stands by the counter. He looks at the counter where he always had a basket of apples, then says, "Apples! I took two large bites out of the apple, and she took one very tiny bite out of the same apple. I said what that meant to me, but I just didn't want to believe that an apple could predict who a person truly is or what a person would really do. I didn't listen to myself. I love more. But now, I am clear in this matter of our love and our marriage."

Chapter Sixteen
TEARS AND FEARS

Over the course of the subsequent few days, Phillip watches me pack up all my things that I brought to our house.

"I love Ruby so much," he says to himself. "I love Winston and even the child she's carrying. I know this child is not mine, but I love it anyway. I only want the best for us. Now, they are leaving me. Even though I'll see them during the week and spend time with her when she's not working, I wonder if this will be enough for the both of us. Marriage is between a husband and wife. It is not between a wife's work and the gunshots we hear at night. I'm here to take care of Ruby, Winston, and the baby—to make them feel safe—and here to protect my family. I can do this! I *have* done this! But, Ruby has no valid reason to leave me, except for not loving me like I love her. We vowed before God that nothing will come between us, even through sickness and health, and only till death do we part. This is my own sickness and death, seeing them getting ready to leave me."

On the day that I finally have everything packed, I say, "Phillip, we can leave at nighttime when all the neighbors are asleep. I don't want them to know what is happening. You deserve the utmost amount of respect, and I don't want to change that by having people see us leave in daylight." "I appreciate that, Ruby," Phillip answers.

In the pitch dark of the night, we round up all the bags and the tricycle, put them into the car, and then drive away from the house. On the ride to Drum Mom's house, no one says anything. When we arrive, we take everything out of the car and put them on the porch. I know Drum Mom is asleep, so when I open the door with my key, I announce loudly, "Drum Mom, it is Ruby, Winston, and Phillip." I say this again, so she is not afraid that someone has come into her house at night. "Ruby, you're here. I'll be out there in a second," Drum Mom says.

Drum Mom comes out of her bedroom, wiping her sleepy eyes. She looks at us and says, "Winston, go to bed, so I can talk to your momma and your new daddy." When Winston goes to the bedroom, there is another knock at the door. "Who's there?" Drum Mom inquires. "Freeman," he says. "Can I come in?" Drum Mom says, "Yes, come on in, Freeman." After seeing Phillip and me standing there, he says, "I heard some noise outside and I looked out my bedroom window. I saw you all here in the house. I came over to see if everything is all right over here."

"I don't know, Freeman," Drum Mom professes. "They woke me up from my sleep, and I came in here to see what's going on with them. I sent Winston to bed so I can talk to them. Close the door and let all of us sit down in the living room."

Daddy Freeman shuts the door, then we all sit down. "Somebody better start talking!" Drum Mom demands. "Ruby decided she wants to come back here," Phillip begins. "She says that she can't find work and doesn't like hearing the gunshots at night. My cousin Eunice whipped Winston and gave him sleeping syrup so she and her husband could sleep during the day. Ruby was right in this matter. Having my cousin Eunice keep Winston was a disaster! Now Ruby doesn't trust anyone else to take care of him except for her family. She wants to come back here and live with you instead of living with me. I have Ruby and Winston's belongings on the porch."

"Ruby, is Phillip telling the truth?" Daddy Freeman asks. "Did Phillip hit or hurt you?" "No! Phillip is nothing but a good husband and father!" I reply. "Phillip is a good husband and father, and you want to leave him to come here?" Daddy Freeman questions. "You want to leave what you have for something that you want! What is wrong with you? Are you out of your mind?"

I say, "I tried to find work in Covington and walked throughout the neighborhood trying to find customers to do their hair. I didn't find any customers. I had an interview with Mrs. Williams to work at her salon. Her salon has water dripping from the ceiling and a pot on the floor collecting the water. She is not equipped to have two beauticians in her place. She says that her customers get first choice at the washing sink and the floor dryer. My customers wait behind her customers to use her equipment. She charges me more to rent her salon than Miss Johnson. You know Miss Johnson has a nice salon and equipment for me to do my job.

"We hear gunshots throughout the night. I know Phillip will keep us safe, but I'm still afraid when I hear the shooting. As for Winston, Phillip and I know the problems I have with his cousin Eunice taking care of him! Phillip and I agree that he will come to visit me here during the week, and I will go visit him on my days off. This is what we need to do for a while so that I can work. So, Daddy Freeman, sir, there's nothing wrong with me, and I am not out of my mind."

Daddy Freeman asks, "Phillip, is Ruby speaking the truth?" Phillip says, "Yes, Mr. Freeman, Ruby speaks the truth." "I've never heard of married people not living together except during slavery and war times," Drum mom interjects. "Those times are not these times. Ruby, if you let your husband bring those bags back in this house and leave this house without you, I think you are touched and out of your mind! I'll say this: for Winston's and your unborn child's sakes, if you don't leave with Phillip, I will allow you to stay here in my house. But the next time you go back with Phillip, don't come back here unless you make my house your home. You will not keep bringing your family matters in and out of this house. Phillip, if you leave Ruby here with me, the two of you will have to work hard to stay married. Circumstances should never keep married people apart."

Phillip looks at me and I look at him. I say, "We will work hard to make this work and stay together." Phillip says, "I will work hard to keep us married and keep our family together."

"We will see if what you say is what you two will do," Drum Mom comments; then she says to Phillip, "If you choose to, you can bring everything on the porch inside the house." Phillip hesitates, then gets up and brings everything into the house. When he finishes, he kisses me and says, "I'll be back here in a few days. I love you." "I'll see you then, and I love you, too," I respond. Phillip then leaves Drum Mom's house.

Daddy Freeman then tells us good night and leaves the house as well. Drum Mom looks at me and says, "I'm going back to bed.

Ruby, make sure the door is locked." She proceeds to walk to her bedroom, shutting the door behind her. I lock the door, find and put on my sleeping clothes, and then go to bed.

When Phillip gets home, he sits in the chair. He looks around the empty house and feels all alone. He thinks about everything Mr. Freeman and Ruby's Drum Mom said about marriage. He thinks again about Ruby's tiny bite out of the apple and says, "Ruby is not going to do right by me." He weeps; the weeping is so intense that the tears seem to gush from his eyes.

Chapter Seventeen

WITH YOU

O n Tuesday, I go and talk to Miss Johnson at the salon. It is full of customers, and Miss Johnson seems overwhelmed with work. I say, "Miss Johnson, we're going to live in Ripley. Will you allow me to come back and work here at your salon?" She says, "Yes, Ruby! Can you start right now?" I say, "Yes, Miss Johnson. Thank you."

I speak to all the customers and they speak back. Someone says, "Ruby, I'm glad you're back here to help Miss Johnson." I reply, "I'm glad to be back and to be here with Miss Johnson. She is a wonderful person to work for and I appreciate her so much." Miss Johnson smiles when she hears my comment.

I walk over to my work station, take my supplies out of my bag, and put them in place. I put my diploma and state license on the wall above my station. I then look at Miss Johnson. She nods and smiles at me and my license on the wall. She is the only one in the salon who knew when I first started working here that I did not have a diploma or license to do hair. Now I have both. "Miss Johnson, who is our next customer?" I ask. "Wilma is next," she responds. "Wilma, please come sit in my chair," I request of her.

Miss Johnson and I work hard all day. By the time we finish with all the customers, we have made a lot of money. As soon as the last customer leaves, Miss Johnson asks, "Ruby, are you still married?" I reply, "Oh yes, I'm still married. I didn't like the salon in Covington. Phillip and I agreed that I should see if I could come back and work here. Thank you so much for letting me come back. I don't plan to take any more time off from work until I have this baby." "Ruby, you're going to have a baby!" she asks excitedly. "Yes, I just found out. Phillip is very excited," I explain. "Ruby, you amaze me," Miss Johnson comments.

Meanwhile, when Phillip arrives at Drum Mom's house, she tells him that I am still at work. So, he drives over to the salon. When he arrives at and comes into the salon, Miss Johnson and I are talking. "Hello, Ruby and Miss Johnson," Phillip says, greeting us. "Ruby, I came by to take you home." "Okay, I'm ready to leave," I respond. "Hello, Phillip, and congratulations about the baby," Miss Johnson says. "Thank you, Miss Johnson," he replies.

After leaving the salon, we ride to Drum Mom's house. "Why did you tell Miss Johnson that you are having a baby?" Phillip asks. "It's the proper timing with our marriage and when the baby is born. Phillip, we talked about this before we married," I note to him. Phillip says slowly, "Yes, now I remember talking about that." I say, "Phillip, it's the right time to tell Daddy Freeman that I'm pregnant." "Yes, you've got to tell him now that Miss Johnson knows," Phillip answers.

When we walk into the house, Daddy Freeman is there talking to Drum Mom and watching Winston. We speak and then sit down on the couch. "Ruby, how was your workday?" Daddy Freeman asks. "Daddy Freeman, it was a good and busy day," I reply. "Miss Johnson was glad I came back to her salon to work." "That's good," he responds. "Phillip, how are you doing?" Phillip says, "I'm fine. Just miss my family."

"Daddy Freeman," I begin, "speaking of family, Phillip and I are having a baby. Drum Mom already knows." Drum Mom looks at me. Daddy Freeman then looks at Phillip and says, "Congratulations! That was mighty quick." Phillip replies, "Yes, this baby will have my name. That's something that makes me proud." Freeman turns to Drum Mom and says, "I didn't know that you could ever keep a secret." "Believe me, this one was hard to keep to myself!" Drum Mom answers.

"Does Winston know he's going to be a brother?" Daddy Freeman inquires. "No, but I'll tell him later," I reply. "Probably when I start showing or at his third birthday." Daddy Freeman says, "Well, it's time for me to leave." As he gets up from the chair, I ask, "Daddy Freeman, can I come over to your house tomorrow night and make a telephone call to Beth Eden? She lives with Beatrice. I would like to know how she's doing and if she passed the state test and has her beauty license." Daddy Freeman agrees to let me use the phone. "What time can we make the call?" Phillip then asks. "I would like to be there when Ruby tells her friends in New York about us." Daddy Freeman says, "Yes, of course. Come over about 7:00."

After Daddy Freeman leaves, Drum Mom says, "Phillip, it's good that you want to be there when she calls her friend in New York. It's never a problem when a good man wants to be with his wife when she makes such a telephone call. A good man keeps an eye on the woman he marries. Come on, Winston. Let's get ready for bed." Drum Mom and Winston then head upstairs to go to bed. Phillip stays for a short time after their departure and then leaves for the night. I go to bed as well.

*****

I wake up the next morning, get ready for the day, and then ride with Daddy Freeman to work. "Ruby, I'm so happy about your marriage and having a baby," Daddy Freeman says. "This time is different. Winston has a 'New Daddy,' and the baby will have the last name of the father." I reply, "Yes, that's right. Thank you for being proud of me."

After having a good workday, Daddy Freeman picks me up and proceeds to drive me home. On the ride home, I say, "Daddy Freeman, remember Phillip and I are coming to your house tonight around 7:00. I want to call Beth Eden." His response is, "I remember." When we pull up in front of the house, I exit the car and walk into the house, where I find a waiting Phillip. We all walk to the kitchen to eat dinner. Winston prays, and then we eat. After we finish eating, I get Winston ready for bed.

At seven o'clock, Phillip and I walk next door to Daddy Freeman's house. This will be the first time Phillip has been in his house. I knock on the door, and Daddy Freeman comes to the door and lets us in. We speak to each other; Phillip looks around the house and tells Daddy Freeman how beautiful his home is compared to the homes in Covington. When Phillip finishes looking around and talking to Daddy Freeman, I ask, "Daddy Freeman, may I use the telephone?" Daddy Freeman nods, points to the telephone in the hallway on the table, and then sits on the couch. I smile at Daddy

Freeman; he knows that I know where his telephone is in his house. I've been in this house with his son, Dexter, many times. Phillip follows me over to the phone.

When I make the call to Beatrice's house, she picks up her telephone and says, "Hello." I say in an excited voice, "Beatrice, this is Ruby. How are you doing?" "Hello, Ruby," she replies. "I'm just fine. How are you?" I respond, "I'm fine, too. I'm over Daddy Freeman's house. I'm calling to talk to Beth Eden. Is she there?" Beatrice says, "Yes. Beth Eden is right here. I'll give her the telephone. When you finish talking to her, let me speak to Freeman." I say okay.

When Beth Eden has the telephone, she says, "Ruby, hello, girl! I passed my state test. I got a score of 97 percent! Did you take the test?" "Yes, I passed, too," I reply. "I got a score of 98 percent." "How did London do on the test?" I then ask. "London passed the test. Her score was 97 percent. Mrs. Foxx is writing a letter to everyone and letting us know how our class performed on the state test," Beth Eden informs me.

"So, what are you doing now?" I inquire. "I'm still living with Beatrice. I'm working at London's salon," Beth Eden says. "London got his, I mean her, own salon?!" I ask with excitement. "Yes, girl!" Beth Eden exclaims. "She found an old building about a block from here. Marty paid cash for the building. They had Gatewood redo the outside and inside of the building. It is beautiful. She has room for five beauticians. Right now, it's just her, me, and Selma (Doris Ann from Alabama) from the beauty school working at the salon.

"London is interviewing someone right now for the fourth booth. She only wants the best beauticians to work at her salon. The salon is booming with high-class colored people and those who can afford to pay. She calls the place 'London Rose Salon.' That's 'Rose' spelled 'R-O-S-E.' She gives every customer a fresh rose when we finish their hair. You would think the rose was like a diamond the way those women act when she gives it to them! But, the rose works. It helps bring in the customers."

"So, London is still being the London that she was in beauty school," I remark. Beth Eden says, "Yes. Men don't do women's hair. If they do, they are called all kinds of names. Plus, a man wouldn't let another man do his woman's hair. What else is going on with you?"'

I say, "Phillip and I are married and expecting a child. He's here beside me right now." "Ruby, I'm so glad for you!" Beth Eden screams through the telephone. "You always talked about how much you love that man! Let me know when you have the baby. I'll talk to you later. Beatrice wants to talk to her brother." I say, "I'll write or call you soon." She says, "I'll be waiting to hear back from you."

I call out to Daddy Freeman, saying, "Beatrice wants to talk to you." He comes to the telephone and I say, "Phillip and I are leaving. I'll lock the door." After I hand Daddy Freeman the telephone, Phillip and I leave and walk over to Drum Mom's house. Phillip goes into the house with me, makes sure everything is all right, and then leaves. I go to bed.

After work the next day, Drum Mom hands me a letter that is addressed to me. "That's from New York, right? Why did you give out my address?" she asks in a mean voice. "Yes, the letter is from New York," I confirm. "It's from Mrs. Foxx, my instructor, at the beauty school. I gave your address to make sure her letter comes safely here and would not get lost in Covington." I notice Drum Mom get more relaxed; I think she was assuming the letter was from Edmond, the father of the child I am carrying.

I open the letter and read it out loud:

Dear Graduate,

It is my pleasure to correspond with you and to let you know how your class performed on their State Examination. All graduates passed with scores ranging from 92% to 98%. This is the highest achievement for our Beauty School! We are very proud of you and wish you success in your business in the beauty of hair.

Sincerely,

Mrs. Foxx

License Instructor for Beauty Schools
Licensed Beautician in the States of New York,
New Jersey, Ohio, and Georgia

*****

For a while now, my life has followed the same routine: I work, see Phillip at Drum Mom's house, talk to Drum Mom and Daddy Freeman, teach Winston, eat, and then go to bed. But one day, when everyone is at the house and we are eating dinner, Winston says, "Momma, your tummy is getting big. You eat a lot!"

We are all surprised by what Winston has said. Drum Mom and Phillip look at me, then I say, "Winston, Momma's tummy is getting big and it's not because I'm eating a lot. Momma has a baby in her tummy. You are going to have a little sister or brother. Your 'New Daddy' is going to be a father to you and your brother or sister."

"I'm going to have a sister or brother!" Winston replies. "Tell me which one you're having, a boy or girl." I say, "Winston, that will be a surprise to all of us! We all like surprises! Only God knows if it's a boy or girl, and He will tell us in His own time." "Well, I'm going to ask God for a little brother," Winston replies.

*****

On August 21, 1953, we celebrate Winston's third birthday. We have the birthday party at Drum Mom's house. I'm just as happy as Winston. Last year, we gave him a party, but it was not on his actual birthday. We celebrated it early because I left prior to his birthday to go to New York for beauty school. I'm here now, and so are his New Daddy, family, and friends, and other children. Everyone is having so much fun—there's plenty of food, children are playing, grown folks are talking and laughing, and there's lots of birthday presents and a cake with three candles on it.

When it is time, everyone comes into the kitchen and sings "Happy Birthday" to Winston. He makes a wish and blows out the three candles. "What'd you wish for, Winston?" someone asks. "I wished for a little brother," he replies. "You know, you're not to ask him what he wished for! I was going to do that later!" Drum Mom retorts jokingly. Everyone laughs. Then Winston opens all his presents and thanks everyone for a fun day.

*****

Nearly three months later, on Sunday, November 1, 1953, I wake up from my sleep and run into Drum Mom's bedroom. I wake her up, saying, "Drum Mom, my water broke. Go get Daddy Freeman now and tell him I need to go to the hospital."

Drum Mom quickly puts her gown on and then goes over to Daddy Freeman's house. They both come rushing back over to the house. When they see me on the bed and hear me groaning, Daddy Freeman gets me up and carries me to the car. "Daddy Freeman, put me down. I can walk," I say softly. He says, "No, you can't walk, Ruby. You're too weak. God is having mercy on me and giving this old man the strength I need to get you to the car. I'm fine!"

He gets me into the car. When the pain hits me, I scream. He drives fast to the County Hospital—so fast that we get there in three minutes. Daddy Freeman runs into the hospital and yells, "I need help! I have my Ruby in the car ready to have her baby!" The people working in the emergency room run out of the hospital, put me on a bed, and take me inside. "Is my Ruby going to be all right?" Daddy Freeman inquires loudly. Old Doc Jones says, "Freeman, she will be fine. We are taking her straight to the operating room. She's screaming like the baby is ready to come here."

Daddy Freeman goes and sits in the colored section of the hospital. He is the only colored person in the place. Soon, he gets nervous, gets up, and starts pacing the floor—then he remembers Phillip. He goes to the front desk and says to the white lady, "May I please use your telephone?" "We don't allow colored people to use the telephone!" she replies. "Miss, I am Mr. Freeman, and my Ruby is having a baby!" he says. "If I can't use your telephone, I ask that you call this telephone number and I'll tell you what to say."

While Freeman is saying this, a white woman from behind the emergency room door comes to the desk. She looks at Freeman and says to the white lady at the desk, "Give that telephone to Freeman and let him make his telephone call. I'm sorry, Freeman. This lady doesn't know you like we do in this town." He says, "Thank you, Mrs. McBride."

The white lady gives him the telephone and he calls Phillip. The telephone rings five times before Phillip picks it up and says, "Hello. Who's calling me this time of night?" "Phillip, this is Freeman," he answers. "I'm at the County Hospital. Ruby is having the baby. Get here quickly! I think the baby will be here soon." "I'm on my way!" Phillip responds excitedly. "Don't drive like you're crazy! Get here safely," Daddy Freeman instructs.

He then gives the telephone back to the white woman at the desk. He thanks her. "Freeman, I am sorry," she says. "I don't live in this town and I don't know you. If you need anything while you're waiting in the colored section, let me know." Freeman replies, "Please let me know when my Ruby's husband, Phillip, arrives here." She says, "Yes, Freeman."

Daddy Freeman goes back into the waiting section. His nerves have calmed down. He notices that he is sweating, so he takes his handkerchief and wipes his forehead. Phillip arrives twenty minutes after having received the telephone call. "Has Ruby had the baby yet?" he asks Daddy Freeman after arriving in the waiting room. "Phillip, you can calm down now," Daddy Freeman comments. "Old Doc Jones was in here and says Ruby is fine. She'll have the baby in about an hour. Old Doc Jones will come back in here and let us know when she has the baby. Phillip, do you need me to stay here?" Phillip says, "Please stay here with me."

Phillip calms down, then Freeman says, "Phillip, let me tell you what happened tonight. I get about ten knocks on my door. I get up from bed and go to the door. I open the door and see this woman in a gown with a stocking over her head. I think, 'Lord, who is this woman and what does she want with me?' She says, 'Freeman, Ruby needs to go to the hospital. She's having the baby.' I say, 'Come in and let me put some clothes on.' Now, if this woman hadn't called my name and said this about Ruby, I would have told her to go on her way and I would have locked my door. I didn't recognize this woman in a gown with a stocking on her head!" They both laugh.

"I go to my bedroom to get my clothes," he continues. "Well, you know how I dress. I put on a suit and tie, my good shoes, and find a handkerchief and belt for my pants." "How long did that take?" Phillip asks. "I do this quickly," Freeman replies. "I feel like I have plenty of time to dress because the woman at the door said Ruby is waiting for me to take her to the hospital and she is having the baby. So, if Ruby is waiting on me, I know I have time to dress like I always do." Phillip gets a puzzled look on his face.

"We leave my house and go next door to get Ruby and take her to the hospital," Freeman continues. "I am walking slow, and I hear someone say, 'Hurry, Freeman.' I start running to the house." Phillip says, "You run to the house!" I say, "Yes, I'm running faster than running water." They both laugh again. "I get in the house and find Ruby on the bed, screaming," Freeman explains. "Oh, she's screaming. Oh no, Ruby is having a hard time with this baby," Phillip comments. "Phillip, that's what a woman does when she is having a baby," Freeman says. "Anyway, I pick Ruby up from the bed and throw her over my shoulder."

"You pick Ruby up and throw her over your shoulder!" Phillip responds in amazement. "I never could pick her up. I *know* I couldn't pick her up with the baby inside her. But you picked her up and threw her on your shoulder!"

"Well, maybe I just picked her up and carried her in my arms," Freeman confesses. "See, Phillip, a woman is beautiful when she carries a baby. The baby grows, and there are two people instead of one. Anyway, Ruby is no different. My back is too weak, so I carried her in my arms." Phillip looks at Freeman and they burst into laughter.

"I have Ruby in my arms," Freeman continues. "I run to the front door and see the same woman in a robe with a stocking over her head." Phillip says, "You know that is Drum Mom!" Freeman retorts, "Thank you for telling me who that woman is!" They both laugh again.

Freeman continues, "I'm carrying Ruby in my arms. I dash out of the house, on the porch, down seven steps, on the grass, to the car, and put her in the car in two seconds. I run as fast as I could—faster than the second drop of rain that falls onto the ground during a rainy day. I know while I'm running to the car, I can't drop Ruby. If I do, I know this is going to be the end of me, and Ruby is having this baby in the front yard and on the grass!" They again laugh.

"We're in the car and I see someone driving a police car. He is driving very, very slowly. I blow my horn and shout, 'Move over!'" "You shouted at a policeman?" Phillip asks. "Yes, I shouted," Freeman confirms. "Anyway, the policeman starts driving slower. So, I decided to pick up speed in my car and I passed the policeman in his car." Phillip says, "What?"

Freeman replies, "Yes, I passed the police car. At the point when I am speeding, and we are side by side, the policeman looks at me and I look at him. I'm sure he recognizes me and my car, and I know he sees Ruby's head and face against the window. So, I pass him and then he speeds up and passes me. He beats me to the hospital!" They laugh at Freeman's words.

Freeman proceeds to say, "The policeman parks in his space and I park right on the sidewalk, in front of the emergency room. The policeman runs to my car and keeps an eye on Ruby. I run inside the hospital, screaming and telling them I need help with my Ruby. People from everywhere come running, get Ruby on the bed, and take her inside the hospital. Yes, Phillip, that's what happened tonight. And here we are, sitting and waiting for Ruby to have the baby."

"Mr. Freeman," Phillip begins, "it took you longer to tell me what happened than it did for you to carry Ruby to the car." They laugh. As they are laughing, Old Doc Jones comes walking into the waiting room. Freeman and Phillip stand up; they can hear their own hearts pounding against their chests. "Are Ruby and the baby all right?" Phillip asks loudly. Old Doc Jones walks to where they are standing. "Doc Jones, this is Phillip, Ruby's husband," Freeman says, introducing the doctor to Phillip.

"Ruby and the baby are doing fine," Old Doc Jones assures. "She has a girl. After we got Ruby in the room and on the bed, she pushed one time and the baby came out. Freeman, you got her here just in time. It took Ruby no time to have her baby."

"When can we see them?" Phillip asks. "You can go down to the basement in about thirty minutes," Old Doc Jones responds. "Doc Jones, can I stay with her?" Phillip then asks. "Yes, they are the only ones in the basement. As soon as there is another patient in the room, the nurse will ask you to leave," Old Doc Jones explains. "You'll have to do as she says. Ruby is tired. It was an easy delivery, but she is worn out. She may not be awake or may be too tired to talk. If you need anything else, let the nurse know and she will contact me. Good night." "Good night and thank you," Phillip and Freeman both say.

Freeman then says, "Ruby and the baby are in the basement. It's hot down there. Phillip, since we have thirty minutes before we can see them, I'm going to the house to get a fan. That will keep her and the baby comfortable. I'll be right back." When Freeman leaves, Phillip sits and waits for him to return. After a while, he finally sees Freeman returning to the waiting room with a fan.

They then proceed to walk down to the basement, where Phillip immediately notices the heat. They make their way over to the window of the nursery to see the new baby girl. "I can't see her face.

Why is she in a drawer and not in a baby bed?" Phillip asks. "Phillip, that's how things are done," Freeman notes. "A lot of things you will find that you don't agree with, but you'll have to accept. Don't make trouble here. Do as you're asked, and Ruby and the baby will be home soon."

"I see her face. She's beautiful!" Phillip comments. Freeman says, "Phillip, when Winston was in the nursery, he didn't move much. He just kept looking around and at everybody. I said back then, he is going to be someone who will be satisfied with being still. He is going to be smart and search for what he wants in life and he will get it."

Freeman looks at the girl again and says, "This girl here is beautiful! See how she keeps her eyes closed as if she is thinking about something. I believe she's going to be smarter than Winston. She's going to be so smart that white and colored people will try to keep her behind. But she will overcome the challenge. Phillip, look at that! She's stretching her arms out and moving those fingers in the air. I believe she's trying to talk to us. Now look! She puts both arms to her chest with one hand over the other hand. I believe she will always hold onto love and try to help others love. She also will be looking for love until she finds it.

"Look, Phillip! Now she is putting her hands together like she's praying! I believe she's asking God for mercy! Oh, my goodness! Look, Phillip! She's doing this again: eyes closed, stretching out her hands, moving her fingers in the air, crossing her hands over her chest, and putting her hands together like she's praying. This girl is something else! I believe she keeps doing this because she's going to live just long enough to enjoy her life. She's going to leave a great legacy her family will always remember. So, what I'm saying is that this girl is going to be very beautiful inside and out, very smart, love-able, helping others, wanting to be loved as she loves, and she will leave behind a great legacy."

"You can tell me what kind of girl she will grow up to be just by looking at her in that drawer and doing all those things?" Phillip inquires. "Yes, I believe this to be true," Freeman responds. "I'm leaving, and I'll drop by the house and tell them the baby girl is beautiful. Tell Ruby I'll see her later. This is your time to spend alone with your wife and baby girl."

Phillip then walks into my room. He notices that I am behind a blue curtain and am lying in the bed asleep. He observes that in the heat, my body is sweating all over. He puts the fan on the nearby table and turns it on; then he moves the chair closer to the bed and sits down. "Ruby, Ruby, Phillip is here. I'm right here with you," Phillip says. I say nothing—I just hold out my hand. Phillip reaches for my hand. I squeeze his hand and keep hold of it. "Ruby, we have a beautiful baby girl!" Phillip says. I smile. "Rest, Ruby. I'm going to be here with you all night. I'm not leaving you!" Phillip assures.

*****

The next morning, I wake up when someone brings me my breakfast. I see Phillip and say, "Phillip, you're still here with me!" "Yes, Ruby! I'm still here with you!" Phillip replies. "We have a beautiful baby girl!" I ask, "Phillip, is my baby girl all right?" Phillip responds, "Yes, she is fine! Mr. Freeman and I saw her last night while you were sleeping. Come now. Try to sit up in the bed so you can eat your breakfast. You need to eat to get your strength back." I sit up in the bed and ask Phillip to hand me a wet towel, so that I can wash my hands and eat.

A nurse then comes to my room. "Good morning, Miss Ruby. It's Mary Elizabeth. Remember me? I was here when you had your son," she says. "Yes, Mary Elizabeth, you know I remember you," I reply. "You were so helpful to me when I had my son. I'm so glad you are still working here. How is my baby girl?" "Your daughter is fine. Who is this person in the room with you?" she asks. I say, "This is my husband, Phillip. Phillip, this is Mary Elizabeth." They speak to each other.

Mary Elizabeth then says, "Mrs. Ruby, I need to help you wash up before the nurse brings the baby into the room. Mr. Phillip, would you like to stay in the room?" "No, I'll leave and get something to eat. Can I be in the room with Ruby and our baby?" he asks. Mary Elizabeth says, "Yes, sir." "Ruby, I'll leave you here with Mary Elizabeth and I'll be right back after I eat," Phillip says. "Okay, Phillip. I'll be here," I respond.

Phillip leaves the room. While he is driving to get something to eat, he thinks about why he doesn't want to stay in the room while Ruby is getting cleaned up. He thinks to himself, "I have never seen Ruby's body! The whole time we dated, we laid on top of the covers with our clothes on. After we married, Ruby would go and get ready to sleep in the bed, and I would get ready to sleep on the couch. When Winston and Ruby came to live at my house, Ruby would get in bed first, then I would get in bed. We slept back to back. I never touch her, go into her, or see her body because she carries another man's child.

"Where is that man now? That man is nowhere to be found! I'm the one here with Ruby when she needs someone and when the baby is born. I'm the one who married Ruby and takes care of her, her son, and his daughter. That man makes the baby, but this man, me, Phillip, gives Ruby and his baby a life they deserve. That makes me the husband, father, and daddy! Because of what I do for Ruby and her children, I have joy."

While Phillip is out, I ask Mary Elizabeth, "Are there any white babies in the hospital?" Mary Elizabeth smiles and says, "No! You're the only mother with a baby in the hospital now. You don't have to feed any other baby but your own!" I am so thankful to hear that news that I say, "Thank You, Jesus!"

When I am finished with my wash-up, Phillip knocks on my door. "Ruby, is it okay for me to come into the room?" he asks. "Yes. Come in, Phillip," I reply. He comes in and sits in the chair.

Phillip is quiet. I look at him. He looks happy, but I can tell he has something on his mind. I know I don't want to talk to him or hear him say what's on his mind, so I say, "Phillip, wash your hands so you can hold our baby. The nurse is bringing her in here soon. We'll look at her and decide what we want to name her." Phillip gets up smiling. I just got him to think about something else other than what he was thinking about before. I know I have him thinking about seeing the baby and naming her. I assume that, for now, we don't have to talk, meaning I don't have to hear what he has on his mind.

When Phillip comes back and sits down, I say, "Phillip, please don't say anything to the white nurse. If anything, I will say what needs to be said. The service is just what it is for colored people in this hospital. Things will be better after I leave the hospital." Phillip says okay.

"Get ready, Phillip!" I say with excitement. "The white nurse is bringing our baby here." The nurse opens the door and pushes in the dirty old cart with my baby girl in the drawer. I look at Phillip to remind him not to say anything. Phillip stands up and moves out of the nurse's way. She then picks up the drawer containing my baby girl and places the drawer on the table. She picks up my girl and gives her to me. She says, "Here is your little girl. She's hungry. She can stay with you until you want her to go back to the nursery. Tell Mary Elizabeth when you want me to come and get her." The white nurse then leaves the room.

I look at my baby girl, then say, "Phillip, look at her. She is beautiful!" "Yes, she is! Can I hold her?" he asks. "Yes, just for a little while. I have to feed her," I explain. I give the baby to Phillip. He holds her as if he has done this before. "She finally has opened her eyes," he remarks. "Last night, they were closed. Baby girl, this is your daddy. Your daddy loves you very much. You look just like your daddy."

"Let me have her back so I can feed her," I say. "I'll give her back to you after she is full. Do you want to stay in here while I feed her?" Phillip replies, "Yes, please, Ruby." I put her to my left breast and she starts suckling slowly. Then, she starts suckling faster to get my milk. I feel her heartbeat against mine. I smile and look at Phillip, who is looking at me. He sees my breast for the first time, then he focuses on the baby nursing my breast. "She sure is hungry," Phillip comments. "Yes, she is!" I say in confirmation. "This is the first time I've fed her since her birth. She'll be full in a little while. Phillip, this is momma and daughter's bonding time. We can talk after I finish feeding her."

Phillip is silent. The only noises in the room are the sucking noises and the noise from the fan. Every now and then, I say something very softly to my baby girl: "Hear my heartbeat. I love you. Daddy loves you. Winston, Drum Mom, and Daddy Freeman love you, too." I then sing the song "Jesus Loves Me." When I sing, she stops suckling at my breast and looks at my lips and smiles. When I stop singing, she goes back to my breast and gets my milk.

After she is full, I make her burp up the air from her stomach. Then I give her to Phillip. He holds her, smiles, and talks to her: "My baby girl. Daddy's little girl. Daddy's going to take care of you. Daddy loves you. Yes, baby girl. Keep smiling for your daddy."

"Ruby, her name is Joy Grace Browne," Phillip announces. "Phillip, how did you come up with a name like Joy Grace?" I ask.

Phillip says, "'Joy,' because I am complete. This baby girl brings me great happiness. My joy is full! 'Grace,' because it was God's amazing grace that softened my heart to love you again and to marry you when you were carrying this baby girl. *Grace* means beauty and kindness. It also means God's favor. When I call her name, I will forever remember how she makes me feel inside. Yes, her name is Joy Grace!"

Chapter Eighteen
NO WATER IN THE CLOUDS

When Phillip finishes holding Joy, he gives her back to me. I place her in the bed with me; she is lying on my chest. She is ready to take her nap. "Joy looks like she's ready to go to sleep, and so do you, Ruby," Phillip notes. "I think I'll leave the two of you alone and I will be back tomorrow morning. If you need me before I come back, tell Mr. Freeman to contact me." "Okay, Phillip. I'll see you tomorrow," I reply sleepily. Phillip smiles, kisses Joy and me, and then leaves.

The routine in the hospital is not quite the same as it was when I had Winston. The differences are these: I do not have to feed a white baby before feeding my own; Joy is the only baby in the hospital; I have the hospital room to myself; Joy stays in the room with me until she goes to the nursery to be monitored by the white nurse.

When the white nurse comes to get Joy, I sleep. When she brings Joy back to me, I am happy that we are together. I look at her toes, hands, fingers, face, eyes, hair, and ears. She has all her body parts, and everything is working. I thank God for a healthy baby!

Next, Mary Elizabeth knocks on the door and comes into the room. She says, "Mrs. Ruby, I have a cup of coffee, sugar, and milk for you to drink. Here is a spoon for you to mix your coffee. I know how you love to drink coffee." I lay Joy beside me on the bed, then Mary Elizabeth helps me sit up in bed. Afterwards, she leaves.

I look at the cup of black coffee, the sugar, the spoon, and the milk on the table. Before I pour the milk into my coffee, I stare at the folds of Joy's upper ears. I look at her face. The folds of her ears are much darker than her face. Colored people say you can tell what skin color your baby will be by looking at their ears. It's funny how I look at her ears and compare her skin color to a cup of black coffee.

I take the cup of black coffee and notice that when I add a little white milk to the coffee, the coffee becomes lighter. I say to myself, "Oh my goodness. I bet I can find Joy's skin color by adding white milk to my black coffee." The black coffee gets lighter when I add the milk. I keep adding milk until, finally, I match Joy's color with the milk in the cup of coffee. I say, "Joy is going to be a beautiful, dark-brown girl. She is the same color as Edmond."

I laugh and say, "A cup of black coffee with white milk added gives you beautiful colors you see in the colored race. Wow! I act like I have nothing else to do. Let me drink my coffee!"

After I finish my cup of coffee, I think to myself, "Phillip says Joy looks like him, but this is not true. She looks just like Edmond, her birth father. Edmond is someone in my past. He is dead. Joy will never know her real father. I must move forward. Phillip is Joy's father. He accepts her, loves her, and wants her. I am a very lucky woman to have someone like Phillip!"

*****

The next morning, Phillip comes to the hospital. The white nurse brings Joy to me and then leaves the room. Phillip is so happy to see Joy! She starts crying. Phillip becomes frightened and says, "Ruby, what's wrong with Joy? Call the nurse so she can come in here and tell me what's wrong with my Joy!"

"Phillip, Joy doesn't need a nurse," I respond. "She is crying because she is hungry or needs changing. Her cloth diaper is not wet, so she must be hungry." Phillip calms down after she starts feeding on my breast. When I finish feeding and burping Joy, I let Phillip hold her so he can try rocking her to sleep. I notice that the two of them are smiling at each other. Joy finally goes to sleep in Phillip's arms. I also go to sleep.

When Joy starts crying again, I wake up and Phillip hands her to me. Phillip says, "I checked her cloth diaper and it's wet." I say, "Joy, you're wet. Let Momma put a clean, dry diaper on you." I then proceed to put a clean, dry diaper on Joy; she continues to cry. I give her my breast and she stops crying.

After her feeding, the white nurse comes and gets Joy and takes her back to the nursery. When the nurse leaves, Phillip says, "Ruby, I want you, Winston, and Joy to come back home to my place." "Phillip, I just gave birth," I note. "I need to go back to Drum Mom's house. I need a woman to help take care of Winston, Joy, and me. Winston, like Joy, will need my help. This is not an easy thing for one woman to do alone."

"Ruby, I'm here to take care of my family," Phillip replies. I say, "Phillip, I know you are. The next few weeks, I just need Drum Mom's help. After a few weeks, we'll come home with you." Phillip says, "Okay, Ruby. All this is new for me. If this is what you and the children need, I'll go along with this. But after you're well, you and the children will come back home and all of us will live together." I nod in agreement. "Do you need anything?" he asks. "No. Phillip. I'm fine," I assure him. "I'm going to take a nap while Joy is in the nursery." Phillip says, "Okay. I'm leaving and I'll see you tomorrow." He kisses me and leaves.

Later that evening, Daddy Freeman comes to see us. Joy is in my bed, smiling and playing with her hands. "Daddy Freeman, you can pick her up and hold her if you want to," I suggest. "I can see her from here," Daddy Freeman says. "I don't think I can pick up another soul since I picked you up to get you to the hospital." I reply, "Well, I said I could walk." We laugh. Then he asks me what her name is. I tell him it is *Joy Grace Browne*. "I like that name. She's going to bring joy to all of us," he comments.

"How are Drum Mom and Winston doing?" I ask. "They're fine," he responds. Winston says, 'I just can't wait to see my baby sister. I'm a big brother. I'm going to take care of my little sister. I'm going to teach my little sister to be smart like me. My sister is beautiful. When is my sister coming home?'" Daddy Freeman and I smile at Winston's words.

Daddy Freeman continues, "Winston is something else. He's a handful!" I say, "Tell him I love him. Momma will be home in about five days with his baby sister, Joy." Daddy Freeman nods. He continues to look at Joy and how she is doing everything she did with her hands and fingers as when he first saw her in the nursery. "Ruby, she's going to be really smart," he remarks. "You will never have to worry about that. Let her have fun and enjoy life. There will come a time when she will know for herself what she should do to be happy.

Well, I'm leaving. Let me know if you need anything. I'll see you when you and Joy come to the house."

*****

Phillip has come to the hospital every day to see Joy and me. So, he is here when Old Doc Jones discharges me from the hospital. We soon get all my things packed. Phillip then reaches into a bag and pulls out a dress, socks, baby shoes, a cap, and a coat for Joy to wear home. Everything he has handed me for Joy is pink! "Do you think people will know we have a girl?" I ask. We laugh.

When we get Joy ready to leave, the same Charlie who was around during my previous hospital stay comes to set me and Joy in a wheelchair and wheel us to Phillip's car.

After our car ride, we arrive at Drum Mom's house. She and Winston are looking out the front door. Winston comes running and screaming toward the car, saying, "Momma's home! Momma's home! My baby sister, Joy, is home!" Drum Mom shouts, "Winston, get back in this house! Let them bring the baby in here. It's cold outside." Winston goes back into the house and stands beside Drum Mom at the front door. I can see him jumping up and down. Drum Mom is smiling.

When we make it into the house, I sit down on the couch. Phillip gives me the baby and stands beside me. I take off her coat and say, "Winston and Drum Mom, come see Joy." They walk over to the couch to see Joy. Winston says, "She's beautiful." Then when Winston tries to hold Joy, I say, "Winston, you can't hold Joy. She's too small. When she is bigger, I'll let you hold her. Your momma will need your help! You can help Momma when Joy is wet by getting me two clean, dry cloth diapers. When you bring me the diapers, you should leave the room, so I can put a clean diaper on her. Boys can't look at girls." "I don't like girls. I like you, Drum Mom, and my sister, Joy," he comments. We all laugh.

"Winston," I continue, "as I said before, Joy is small. Right now, all she wants to do is eat and sleep. When Joy is hungry, Momma must be with her by herself, so I can feed her. You are too little to see Momma feed Joy. When she is asleep, don't wake her up, because Momma may need to sleep when she sleeps. This will only be for a little while. After she grows up, you'll be able to do a lot of things with her." "Okay, Momma," Winston says.

Drum Mom says, "Winston, you can sleep in the other bedroom. Joy has to sleep with her mother and your New Daddy." Phillip and I look at each other. "Winston, go to your room and play. Drum Mom wants to talk to your momma and New Daddy," she requests. Winston leaves the room.

"What's going on here?" Drum Mom asks. "Drum Mom, Phillip is staying at his house and coming over every day to visit us," I explain. "When Ruby gets better and can take care of our children, we will be going back to our house in Covington," Phillip chimes in. "She says she needs your help for a few weeks before everybody moves in with me." Drum Mom says, "I see."

After our discussion, Phillip stays for Joy's feeding and then leaves when it is time for us to go to sleep.

*****

For the next few weeks, I take care of my children, clean diapers, cook food, and play with Winston. I sleep less and less each day. I thought Drum Mom was going to help me recover. But, Drum Mom only helps me when she sees I am exhausted. Daddy Freeman comes over for a few minutes every night to see how we are doing. I sleep through his visit.

After six weeks of being at Drum Mom's house, I think about going back to work at the beauty salon. I also think about my promise to Phillip. I think about me and the children going back to live with Phillip. I know Covington is still the same Covington. I don't have any work, nor do I know of anyone who will take care of my children while I'm at work. I wish there were homes for colored people in Ripley to buy or rent. If we had more homes for colored people, several families wouldn't have to live in the same house. Maybe Phillip will be happy to move here with Drum Mom and his family. I don't blame him if he doesn't want to move here. Why should he give up his home to live with someone else and someplace where he doesn't own a home? I think about how good Phillip has been to me. I conclude that I will have to try to live with him again and become the wife that he deserves.

*****

Twelve weeks after Joy's birth, we leave Drum Mom's house and move to Covington with Phillip. We move our things during the night so that no one witnesses it happen. Phillip has two bedrooms, so he lets Winston sleep in one, and Joy and I sleep in the other; Phillip sleeps on the couch. During the second night, twice, Joy wakes us up crying. I change her diaper and try feeding her—but she doesn't eat and continues to cry. After looking around the room, she cries louder. She doesn't know this place. When I sing to her and rock her in my arms, she calms down a little.

While this is happening, Phillip comes into the bedroom and asks, "What's wrong with Joy?" I say, "I change her and try to feed her, but she keeps on crying. She looks around this room and cries even louder. This room and this house are strange to her. Finally, I get her quiet by singing and holding her to let her know she's safe. She's still restless, but she was calming down until she heard a gunshot." Phillip replies, "Good. Joy slept all night last night. She'll get used to the room and this house."

*****

During the next night, Joy is a lot calmer and is sleeping through most of the night. When I hold her and sing to her, she remains calm.

*****

By the fifth night of our being at Phillip's house, I am restless, having not slept much over the past few days. But Joy is back on her nightly feeding and diaper-changing schedules—until the gunshots go off. We muddle our way through the night.

The next morning, I ask Phillip, "Do you have someone in mind who will take care of our children?" Phillip answers no, then I say, "Phillip, you know I need childcare to go back to work. We talked about this. Why haven't you been trying to find someone? You know I don't know these folks out here. What are we going to do for childcare?" Phillip says, "I'll keep looking and asking around. Most colored women I know work around here. Ruby, you don't have to go back to work. I'll take care of us."

"Phillip, I love the work I do," I reply. "I love fixing women's hair. This is what I went to school for and why I got my beautician's license. Remember, you were there with me through all of that. I plan to go back to work as soon as I get Joy weaned from my breast.

That's about three months, in May. We have three months to find childcare and for me to find work here."

"Ruby, are you a woman that's never satisfied?" Phillip asks. "I will take care of my family. I love my family. Think about *me* for once in your life!" "Phillip, I love you and I think a lot about you and everything you do for me. Let's just try to find childcare and work for me for the next three months. Three months is plenty of time to find out who can help us," I explain. After our conversation, we proceed with our day.

*****

Over the next two months, Phillip and I search for someone to take care of our children. We finally hear about a lady who moved to town. She is a teacher and has her own childcare business. Soon, I contact her.

"My name is Ruby Browne," I say. "I have two children. Can you take care of an infant and a three-year-old?" She replies, "My name is Elaine, owner of Elaine's Child Care. Yes, there are two vacancies and I can take good care of them." "May I come by your place tomorrow around one o'clock and see what you have to offer?" I ask. "Yes. That will be a good time," Elaine answers.

After our conversation is over, I tell Phillip about the discussion. I inform him that we are visiting her business tomorrow.

*****

Bright and early the next morning, I prepare breakfast and get the children ready to go by the childcare house. When I point out to Phillip that it is 9:00 in the morning, and that my plan is to be at the childcare place by 10:00, he says, "I thought you told her you were coming by at one o'clock?" "I did, but I want to show up early. Are you ready to leave?" I ask. "Yes, I'm ready" is his response to my question.

When we arrive at Elaine's Child Care, I say, "Phillip, please park the car in front of the building beside the childcare. We'll walk from here to Elaine's business. Please carry Joy and I'll take Winston by his hand." After Phillip parks the car, we walk from the side of the building to the front door. I open the front door and hear a lady screaming at three children who are about Winston's age. The children are sitting on the floor and crying. When she finishes screaming at them, she says, "You all better not tell your momma or daddy!" The lady then turns around and sees us standing in the doorway; she is surprised to see us here.

She turns back to the children and says in a loving voice, "Please, be quiet. We have visitors." Then she walks toward us and says, "Good morning, my name is Elaine. May I help you?" I say, "My name is Ruby Browne, and this is my family." "Oh! I was expecting you at one o'clock," Elaine retorts. "I know, but I decided to come early in the morning," I reply. "Why are you screaming at the children, and why are the children crying?" Elaine says that they are just sleepy. "Why are you telling them not to tell their momma or daddy?" I inquire. "Oh! I don't mean anything by that," she responds.

I walk over to the children, who are crying on the floor. There are two boys and one little girl—and they are all looking at the floor. "Children, has Mrs. Elaine hurt you?" I ask. "You can tell me, I'm your friend." None of the children say anything, but the little girl starts shaking when I ask the question. The children don't look at me at all. I then walk away from the children and toward Miss Elaine. "You are hurting these children. I should report you to the police," I say to Elaine.

"Mrs. Ruby, you and your family need to leave my place of business," Elaine retorts. "You are not welcome here. I should call the police on *you* for trespassing!" "Ruby, let's leave. This place is not worthy of our business," Phillip remarks. "I wish these children's parents would surprise you and come by this place. They may find what we just witnessed." We then proceed to walk off her property and get in the car to go home.

"Something isn't right in that place," Phillip comments. "I'm taking you all home, then I'm going to visit with Mr. Knowles. I'll tell him what we witnessed at the childcare and ask if he will talk to the police. The police will listen to Mr. Knowles before they'll listen to me. I know Mr. Knowles will have them keep an eye on Elaine and the colored children." Phillip takes us home, then he pays Mr. Knowles a visit.

*****

When Phillip returns from talking to Mr. Knowles, I say, "I am saddened by what we just saw. Can we go see Drum Mom tomorrow?" "Yes, Ruby," Phillip answers. "I understand how you can be upset by all of this. I'll take you to see your Drum Mom tomorrow. I need you to understand that this is just a visit. I'll be back tomorrow night to pick everyone up to come back home. We have one more month to look for childcare and for you to look for work. Elaine is not going to stop our plans."

*****

Around midday on the next day, Phillip takes us to visit Drum Mom. She is so happy to see us, and we are just as happy to see her! "Ruby and the children need to see you," Phillip comments. "This is just a visit. I'll be back to pick them up later tonight." After Phillip leaves, I tell Drum Mom about our experience with the daycare and how I am unable to find work. "Drum Mom," I begin, "I'm going downtown to Miss Johnson's beauty salon. I just want to visit and see the people. I am not here to ask for work but just to visit. I'll be back in time for Joy's feeding. She is almost weaned from my breast milk." "I see," she responds. I then head out toward Miss Johnson's salon.

When I arrive at Miss Johnson's salon, I speak to everybody, saying, "I'm in town and just want to visit. How is everyone doing?" Miss Johnson and everyone say "fine." The salon is still busy with customers. "Miss Johnson, you are as busy as ever! If I did not know you, I wouldn't know how you do what you do," I remark. "Ruby, how long are you going to be in town?" Miss Johnson asks. "I'll be here until tonight," I answer. Miss Johnson then replies," Oh! I sure could use the help. If you ever, ever decide to work in Ripley, you will always have a job here."

The customers start cheering after Miss Johnson's dialogue, with some of them saying, "Yes, Ruby, come back and help Miss Johnson out. Come back, Ruby, please." Miss Johnson says, "See, Ruby, I'm not alone when I say you can come back anytime." I say, "Thank you, Miss Johnson, and everybody. It's been good seeing everyone. I have to go back to Drum Mom's and feed my baby girl, Joy."

I then leave the salon and start walking back home, thinking about the grand welcome I received at the salon. That is a place where I can go back to work and build up my customers for my own business. I can't find this in Covington.

When I make it back to Drum Mom's house, Drum Mom asks, "Ruby, did you ask Miss Johnson if you can work at her salon?" "Drum

Mom, no I did not," I reply. "I just went to visit." After our brief exchange, I feed Joy and then proceed to do chores around the house and cook. In the evening, when 5:00 rolls around, we eat dinner.

After dinner, Daddy Freeman comes over and plays with Winston and Joy. When Phillip comes to pick us up, Daddy Freeman leaves when we leave. We go home, and I get the children ready for bed. Then soon, we all go to sleep.

*****

It is now one month later, and I say to Phillip, "We do not have childcare for the children and I truly want to do hair. I've tried. You tried. But Covington is not the right place for me and the children. I'm moving back to Ripley." "Ruby, I can take care of you and the children. You don't have to move back to Ripley," Phillip says in protest. I say, "Phillip, this place is not going to work for both of us. You deserve better than me. I want to work in Ripley and not Covington. I want to live in Ripley with our children. I know you will take care of us; it is your kind heart that makes me dearly appreciate you and love you forever and ever. I know many women would give up everything to be with you and to live this kind of lifestyle. But, I am not like many women."

"Ruby, if you leave me this time, I will not come after you," Phillip notes. "Phillip, I know this," I respond. "Again, you deserve better than me." "When do you want to leave?" Phillip asks. "As soon as possible. We can leave later tonight," I reply. "Ruby, I only ask that you let me see Joy and Winston. Please let me see Joy grow up. Please don't put her out of my life," he pleads. "Phillip, Joy will always be ours," I comment. "I will do nothing to keep her away from you, her father. On the heart of Drum Mom, Daddy Freeman, and Winston, I promise you, Joy will always know you as her father. Whenever you want to see her or spend time with her, no one will stop you from doing so." After I am done talking, I walk to the bedroom. Phillip watches me as I walk away from him.

Phillip then sits down and stares at the walls. As I am getting everything packed and ready to leave him for good, he gets up quickly and comes into the bedroom as well. He picks up Joy, and holds and kisses her. "My Joy," he utters. "I remember why I named you Joy Grace. I remember that special feeling I had for you when I first saw you. I still have that special feeling. I will always feel this way when I think about you or call your name. My Joy. I need you to feel my heartbeat." Phillip puts Joy's hand to his heart.

"Joy, that's Daddy's heartbeat," he continues. "Remember how my heart feels. This is what true joy feels like." He puts Joy back into her bed.

Phillip walks back to the kitchen, sits down, and thinks about me. He thinks about how people make choices for the things that they love or for the things that they hope to love. He says, "For Ruby, there was no love for me and no hope for true love. I am not me. I let Ruby destroy me. I will never marry again!"

Phillip thinks to himself, "I know someday soon there will be water back in my clouds. When it comes, I will have peace, and my water will flow again like a mighty stream. I will be watered, and I will become myself again."

Chapter Nineteen
PRUNING THE WINDS

When I get done with packing mine and the children's things, I then round up the children so that we can go back to live with Drum Mom. We, again, leave in the pit of darkness, so that the neighbors don't see our activity. As we make the journey, I hold Joy in my arms, and Winston is asleep in the back seat. While Phillip drives, he tries to look at Joy, but he can't see her face in the darkness.

"Ruby," he begins, "you have two months to change your mind and come back to me and come home. If you don't change your mind, I will file for divorce. This will give you freedom to live the life you want without me. Remember, we agreed that I can see Joy anytime I want." "I understand, and I agree that you can see Joy," I respond. After reiterating the terms of our agreement, there is no more talk on our ride to Drum Mom's house.

After we arrive at the house, I get out of the car with Joy, walk up the steps to the porch, and knock on the door. When the door opens, I go into the house. After being in the house for a minute or so, I put Joy down on the couch and walk back to the car. "Phillip, I'll get Winston while you bring our things in the house," I suggest.

I pick up Winston, take him inside the house, and put him in bed. Soon after, Phillip comes into the house with our bags and Winston's tricycle; he says to Drum Mom, "This is Ruby's decision and not my decision to come back here. I can't force Ruby to stay with me when she is grasping for the wind. I have given her two months to change her mind and come back and be with me forever. If Ruby doesn't come back, we will get a divorce. If this happens, we agree I can continue to see Joy."

Phillip then proceeds to walk to the couch and pick up Joy. He looks at Joy and kisses her face. "My Joy, Daddy loves you very much," Phillip says to her. "You will always be my child. I will always take care of you and will always be here for you." Phillip gives Joy to me and walks out the front door.

Drum Mom locks the door behind him and says, "Ruby, that man really loves you and his family. One day when it's too late, you will come to understand what I said to you." After saying what she said to me, Drum Mom leaves the front room and goes to bed. Joy and I go to bed as well.

When the sun rises the next morning, we all get out of bed and eat breakfast, and I feed my children. "Joy is almost weaned from my breast. Once she is weaned from my breast, I'm going back to work at Miss Johnson's beauty salon. That should be in about two weeks," I explain. "So, what you are saying to me is that you are not going back to your husband, Phillip?" Drum Mom inquires. "You and the children plan to stay here with me?"

"Yes, Drum Mom," I reply. "I just need to stay until I find a place for us to live. Since there are no homes for colored people in this town, you know this may take a while. But I will keep looking for a place to live."

Drum Mom says, "Since you have left a man with his own home and came back here to stay, I expect you to search and find a home as soon as you can. This is best for you and your children." Drum Mom is then done speaking her peace.

*****

Now that Joy is a little more than six months old, Winston has a great time playing with her. She is weaned from my breast and is able to sit up on her own; since this is the case, Winston teaches her to count and teaches her the alphabet. And when he talks to Joy, Joy repeats what he says in her baby voice.

One day, when Winston says, "Joy, it's time for school," Joy crawls, pulls herself up on her feet, and sits on the couch. "Let's count to ten," Winston then suggests. Joy starts counting the numbers with Winston. And when Winston says, "Let's say our ABCs," Joy says all of them with Winston.

"Drum Mom, did you hear that! Joy knows how to count to ten and say her alphabets!" I say excitedly. "Yes, I hear them! Winston is a great teacher, and Joy is very smart. She just needs to learn how to walk and use the toilet," Drum Mom comments.

Drum Mom and I look at Joy, and Joy looks at each of us. She then gets off the couch, starts walking, and goes to the toilet. I follow her to the toilet. I see her taking off her plastic panties and taking the safety pins off her cloth diaper. I then watch as she throws the plastic panties and diaper into the garbage can, and sits on the toilet and pees. After she is done, she gets down from the toilet, takes some toilet paper, and wipes herself.

Although Joy tries to reach for the sink to wash her hands, she is too small to reach the sink. However, she finds a wet cloth in the toilet room and wipes her hands. She looks at me and says, "Momma, panties. Momma, panties. No diaper. Joy don't want diaper."

"I don't have any little girls' panties!" I think to myself. I then walk to Winston's room, and Joy follows me. I reach into Winston's drawer, pull out a pair of boys' underwear, and hand the underwear to Joy. Joy looks at me; she then gets a confused look on her face and says, "Want my panties." I say, "Joy, Momma doesn't have any girls' panties. I have to go to the store and buy you your own panties."

Joy sits down on the floor and puts on Winston's underwear. Then she stands up, pulls the underwear up to her waist, and walks back into the front room. She resumes her play with Winston. "Drum Mom, Joy threw her panties and diaper in the garbage can," I explain. "She used the toilet by herself and put on some underwear." "Joy just did that? I'm not surprised!" Drum Mom comments. "I told you, this child is special. She is very smart!"

"Drum Mom, I need to leave and go downtown to buy her some girls' panties," I say. "Will that be okay with you? I'll be right back." Drum Mom responds, "Go on, Ruby. Joy is weaned from your breast. You can take your time coming back home. She will have dinner ready when you get back!" Drum Mom says, and then we share a laugh. Joy looks at us as if indeed to say to herself, "I will have dinner ready when Momma gets back."

I soon leave the house and walk downtown. After I buy some panties for Joy at the store, I stop by Miss Johnson's beauty salon. The place is busy, as usual. "Miss Johnson, I can start to work next

Tuesday. Will that be okay with you?" I ask her. Miss Johnson and all the customers say, "Yes, Ruby."

Satisfied with the outcome of my visit to the salon, I leave the establishment and proceed to walk home. When I reach my destination, Winston is playing on the floor and Joy is in the kitchen watching Drum Mom cook dinner. "Drum Mom, I'm back," I announce. "I can finish dinner." "No, I'll finish dinner. I love how Joy keeps watching me cook," she comments. "Drum Mom, I told Miss Johnson that I could start working on Tuesday," I note. Drum Mom points out that she already knew my plans.

*****

Soon, it is Tuesday—the day I start working at the salon again. When it is time, Daddy Freeman drives me to work.

I get my workday started, and Miss Johnson and I work hard all day. By the end of the day, I am tired but very happy—and we have earned a lot of money. I think about how I'm doing what I love and making money. I say to myself, "I'm able to make and save money to rent or buy a house. This is the town where I can own my own salon. I know my decision to leave Covington was right, even if it does mean I'll lose Phillip. I just have to do what I have to do for me and my children."

*****

Two months have now passed since I started working at Miss Johnson's salon again. One day, after I get home from work, Phillip comes by Drum Mom's house. "Ruby, can I see Joy and Winston?" he asks. I tell him yes. Phillip then proceeds to play with Winston and Joy. When he picks up Joy, he holds and kisses her—and when he puts her down on the floor, Joy says, "Daddy, Daddy, hold."

Phillip becomes amazed that Joy talks and calls him "Daddy." He then picks her up and throws her up and down in his arms. After he stops this play, he kisses her all over her face, saying, "My Joy, Daddy loves you so much." Joy starts smiling and laughing. "Phillip, Joy is special. She is very smart," I inform him. "She learns fast and understands what you say to her." Phillip kisses Joy and puts her down on the floor. Joy looks at Phillip and looks at me afterwards. She then walks over to Drum Mom and holds onto Drum Mom's knees.

"Ruby, I have the papers here for you to sign," Phillip announces. "Everything will be done in nine months," he goes on to say, while looking at Joy. "No! No!" Joy shouts in protest. I look at Joy and then turn and look at Phillip, then say, "I'll get a pen and sign these papers!"

I get up from the couch and leave the front room to get a pen. Phillip looks at Joy, who says, "Dad, Dad, no." Phillip feels his heart beginning to break; he says to her, "Yes, Joy, yes." Joy replies, "Okay, Dad, Dad." I come back with the papers signed and give them back to Phillip. He takes them from me and then leaves the house.

*****

Joy is thirteen months old when mine and Phillip's divorce is final.

I am at work at the beauty salon when, one day, I notice a colored man (who appears to be my age) working downtown at the repair shop across from the beauty salon. He looks like the man who lives five houses up the street from Drum Mom's house. He is a tall, lean, brown-skinned colored man. I notice how strong he is when he picks up and puts down the heavy equipment that is in need of repairs.

That same day, after Daddy Freeman picks me up from work, he drives by the fifth house from Drum Mom's house. I see the same man from the repair shop, sitting in the swing on his porch. I note how funny it is that I never noticed his sitting on his porch until now.

We soon pull up at Drum Mom's house. When I get out of the car, Daddy Freeman drives home. I then look up the street, see that man looking at me, and proceed to walk up the street. The man, noticing me approaching, gets up from the swing and walks to meet me halfway.

When we are face to face, I say, "My name is Ruby. I live here with my Drum Mom." "I know," he replies. "My name is Eddie. I live with my mother and father. It is such a pleasure to meet you, Ruby. I see you and your children when you come out of the house. In fact, I make sure I'm on the porch when you all come outside." "Really? You've been watching us?" I ask. "Yes," Eddie responds.

"Since you've been watching us, why haven't you come to the house to talk to us?" I inquire. "I really don't know," Eddie confesses. "But when I saw you coming this way, I didn't want to miss my chance to talk to you. I know you work at the beauty salon. When I'm at work at the repair shop, I always look through the side window to see if you're there at work. When I see you at work, I work hard hoping you see me, too! Sometimes you look my way, and sometimes you don't look. But, you never notice me. Sometimes, I wish you would catch me looking at you!"

"Well, Eddie," I begin, "I have to go home. I hope we talk again." "How about tomorrow?" Eddie suggests. I look at him and say, "That'll be fine. Tomorrow will be fine." We part ways and I walk home.

"Drum Mom, do you know Eddie who lives up the street?" I ask, once inside the house. "Yes. His momma and daddy go to the same church as me and Freeman," she explains. "His momma and I talk sometimes. She is a woman set in her ways. If she believes she is right, she'll hold on to that for life."

After her explanation, Drum Mom looks at me, then says, "Now, let me think. Eddie has a son. His momma didn't like it when his girlfriend had his son and she wouldn't marry Eddie. To this day, she never sees or talks about her grandson. Why do you ask me about Eddie?" "No reason, other than we just talked on the street for a little while," I comment. "I've lived in this house almost all my life and I have never been to her house. It's like you know you're not welcome in her house," Drum Mom notes. The conversation ends with those words.

*****

Over the course of a few months, mine and Eddie's spending time together has become a *very serious* thing. We have begun to like each other—so, we find ways to get closer to one another. And, we are always talking on Drum Mom's porch. When this happens, his momma always comes outside, sees us talking, and then goes back into her house. When I speak to and wave at her, she doesn't speak or wave back.

*****

In April, after my having been spending quite of bit of time with Eddie, there is a *very serious* talk I need to have with him.

So, one night, when Eddie comes over to talk and visit—which he does at his regular time—we talk. Over the course of our talking, I say, "Eddie, I am pregnant with your child. I can't be an unwed mother carrying your baby. You have to marry me!"

"I'm not surprised you're pregnant," Eddie comments. "These last few months, every chance we get, we do what married people do." He then gets up from the swing and gets down on one knee. "Ruby, will you marry me?" he asks. "Yes, Eddie, I'll marry you!" I say with excitement.

We then talk about our marrying. We agree that we will secretly get married on Monday, keep living the way we are currently living, and then look for a place in which to live together. We don't want to live with his parents or Drum Mom, unless we must. Then, the following month, we will tell everyone that we are married and having a baby. This will be close to eight months before the birth of our child; people in town will think that an eight-month baby means I wasn't pregnant when we rushed to get married. So, our plan was set.

*****

On Monday, Eddie and I go and get married. We spend the day together—and that night, Eddie goes home to his parents' house, and I go home to Drum Mom's house. But I do not wear my wedding ring at home; instead, I do everything the usual way and hide behind the secrets of my marriage and pregnancy.

*****

One day in May of 1955, Eddie takes me over to his parents' house. When I walk into the house, his momma looks at me in a strange way. "Eddie, why did you bring this woman here in my house?" his mother asks. "Momma and Daddy, Ruby and I got married last month. She is now Mrs. Ruby Morgan, my wife," Eddie announces.

"Eddie, no!" his mother shouts. "You did not marry that woman with two children. How could you do this to us and to yourself? She is not fit to become your wife!" "NOT FIT!" I exclaim. "Ruby, let me talk," Eddie interjects.

I take a deep breath so that I can hear what Eddie has to say. My heart starts beating fast. I think, "Eddie's momma calls me 'not fit.' Who does she think she is! She reminds me of the father of my first child. Dexter felt I was not fit to marry, but I was fit for him to come into me. Now, Eddie's momma is calling me 'not fit.' I took that from Dexter, but I'm not going to take it from this old woman!" I look at her sternly, then turn and look at Eddie.

"Momma, I love Ruby, and this time, you are not going to stop me from being happy and living my life!" Eddie says. "You stopped me from seeing my son, but you will not stop me again from what I want to do or cause me to lose another love. As for her two children, I love both. I love them just as I love my child she's now carrying. She is one month pregnant and expecting in December."

Eddie's momma says, "Well, Mrs. Ruby, you sure do know how to catch a man! Eddie, I feel sorry for you. This is not right! This is wrong! She is wrong! Eddie, your wife and those children will not live here with your daddy and me. The two of you go and find rest at her family's house down the street. You can come back to the house and visit your father and me." Eddie looks at his father and says, "We will do as you say. Daddy, I wish you well. Momma, you will not disrespect my wife."

Once the conversation is over, we leave Eddie's parents' house and talk in the street. "Eddie, why does she hate me so badly that she doesn't want me in her house?" I ask. "She is a bitter woman," he replies. "All you need to know is that I love you and we will make it through this."

After hearing his reassuring words, we walk to Drum Mom's house. We go in and Drum Mom looks at me and can tell by the expression on my face that I am upset. "What is going on with the two of you?" she inquires. "Ruby and I secretly got married a month ago," Eddie responds. "What!" she says, looking at me. "Ruby and I got married a month ago. We've been living separately since that time. Ruby is one month pregnant with my child. She is having my baby in December."

"Ruby, is Eddie telling the truth?" Drum Mom asks. "Yes, Drum Mom. The wedding ring is hidden in my bedroom," I confess. "I didn't want you to know until we were ready to tell you. We just left from over Eddie's parents' house, where we told them. His momma didn't take the news very well. In fact, she says I'm NOT FIT to marry Eddie. The children and I are not welcome in her house. She told us to leave." "Eddie's momma said that to you? I will certainly have a talk with her!" Drum Mom says sharply.

"A talk with my momma will not change her mind," Eddie says, chiming in. "Ruby is my wife and we need a place to stay. Can we stay here for a little while until we find us a home? I have a job that pays well, and I am saving money for a house. I just need a home to live and stay in with my wife and children."

"Ruby, now you will have three children and a husband living in my house," Drum Mom notes. "The two of you and the children can stay for a while. Now is the time for you to start looking for a home. This house is not big enough for all of us. Eddie, your parents' house is big enough for all of you, but so be it with that. A little while will not mean a long time. You two were so quick to marry. The two of you better be quick to find a home. Ruby, show Eddie the bedroom, and you come back in here and talk with me." We then leave the room to do as she has requested.

Drum Mom sits in her chair, waiting for me to come to the front room and talk with her. When I finally walk back into the front room, she says, "Sit down and hear me out. Ruby, just like Phillip says, you are a woman grasping for the wind. Understand me—understand what I say to you! When the wind blows, you might know the place where it starts, but you don't know how long it will blow, how long it will stay, or when and where it will stop. You, Ruby, are that wind, and you are chasing after it. Don't you know you can't outrun the wind? This wind that you're in may satisfy your body for a while, but it will surround you until it finally throws you down. It will hurt you, even to the point of your own death or destruction.

"What I also see is that you are a woman pruning the wind. You hold the wind in your hand. You take it, trim it, and shape it into something that you want it to become. All that time and work you spend pruning the wind, when you are finished with it, you release it and let it go. You let it go and it vanishes in the air. Into the air it goes, so that you see it no more. These are your pruning winds:

- "You look at the works of your hands and take pride in what your hands can do. With those skillful hands, you toil all day for your own pleasure, thinking that money answers everything.

- "You see, but are not satisfied with what you see.

- "You hear, but are not satisfied with what you hear.

- "You search to satisfy your flesh, but you are still empty.

- "You are love, but do not know how to love.

- "You walk in the ways of your heart, but your heart is like steel.

"These things that you do for yourself are worthless. Life is something that's real and short. Making the wrong choices in life could lead to a life of misery—where you could possibly die having never known true love and happiness. Stop pruning and start planting. Work at this marriage and family like you love working with your hands."

After Drum Mom finishes talking, she gets up from her chair and goes to bed. I sit in the front room alone. Then I get up and go to bed with my new husband, Eddie.

Chapter Twenty
SECOND AND THIRD

When Daddy Freeman picks me up to go to work the next morning, he sees Eddie coming out of the house and walking with me to his car. Eddie and I get in his car. I say, "Daddy Freeman, this here is Eddie Morgan. He lives up the street and needs a ride to work. He works downtown at the repair shop." "I see" is Daddy Freeman's response.

"Daddy Freeman," I begin, "can you come by Drum Mom's house tonight? Eddie and I need to talk to you." Daddy Freeman replies, "I'll be there tonight." I look at Daddy Freeman. I can tell by the look on his face that he does not like being in the middle of mine and Eddie's situation. He keeps driving and doesn't talk to us. He drops us off at the beauty salon and makes the circle around the "Hole" to get back to his barber shop and building. We all go to work.

Later that evening, as requested, Daddy Freeman comes over to hear what we must say to him. I say, "Daddy Freeman, please sit down. You see Drum Mom sitting in her chair, and the children are in the back room." He sits down and looks at Drum Mom. She doesn't look up at him; she just keeps her eyes and hands on the Bible that is on her lap.

Eddie and I sit down. "Daddy Freeman, Eddie and I got married last month!" I say excitedly. "I am one month pregnant with his child." Daddy Freeman looks shocked. "Ruby, when did you divorce Phillip?" he asks. "Our divorce was finalized about three months ago," I answer. "I see," he says. "So that is why Eddie came out of the house with you this morning, needing a ride to work." "Yes, sir," I reply.

"Eddie, what do you have to say about this?" Daddy Freeman asks. "Ruby and I are married, and she is pregnant. We are staying here because we have no other place to live," Eddie explains.

"What about your parents' house up the street? Can't all of you live there?" Daddy Freeman inquires. "No, sir," he answers. "We can't stay at my parents' house. Ruby and I are saving money and looking for our own place." "I see. Anything else you all need to tell me?" Daddy Freeman asks. "No, sir," I answer.

Daddy Freeman says, "Ruby, go get Winston and Joy so I can see them. Since there's a man in the house, I won't come over as often as I've been doing to check on everybody. I want you to bring the children over to my house, so I can spend some time with them." I say, "Daddy Freeman, I will certainly do that." I get up from the couch, go get Winston and Joy, and bring them in the front room to see Daddy Freeman. He enjoys his time of talking and playing with them, then he leaves.

*****

The next day, while Eddie and I are at work, Daddy Freeman goes to Drum Mom's house to talk to her. "What do you think about the conversation last night?" he asks her. "Freeman, there's nothing I can say about Eddie and Ruby marrying so quickly," Drum Mom responds. "Eddie treats the children well and acts like he loves Ruby. I've talked to them about finding their own place. They both work, and Ruby makes sure money is put aside for a home. My problem is with Eddie's parents. They aren't going to help them. His momma tells Ruby that she doesn't like her and her children, and doesn't want them in her house. That's why they stay here."

"Okay. I'll keep my ears open," Freeman assures. "When I hear of a place for them to buy or rent, I'll let everyone know. Don't let Eddie's momma be your problem. We know how strange that woman acts toward other people." Drum Mom nods at Freeman's words.

*****

On Thursday, December 29, 1955, eight months after our marriage, I give birth to a baby girl. The baby girl is born quickly, right there in the emergency room. The nurse lets me and Eddie see her. She lets me hold her until they move me to the basement. After I get settled in my room, the white nurse takes my baby and goes to the colored nursery. Everything that happened when I gave birth to Joy happens to this baby. There are no white people with babies in the hospital. My baby girl stays in my room until the white nurse comes to take her back to the nursery. Eddie and I name her Kathleen Morgan.

When it is time, Daddy Freeman picks us up from the hospital and takes us home. Drum Mom, Winston (who is five years old), and Joy (who is two years old) will finally see my baby girl for the first time.

When we arrive at Drum Mom's place, Daddy Freeman drops us off and then leaves. We walk inside the house, and I sit down on the couch with Kathleen.

"Winston and Joy, this is your little sister, Kathleen. Come and look at her," I say to them. Joy comes to see Kathleen, but Winston does not come and look at her. "Winston, what's wrong?" I ask. "Come and see your new sister."

"Momma, you were supposed to bring a boy home, not a girl," Winston says. "You have a boy, then a girl, then a boy, not a girl!" "Winston, it doesn't work out that way," I explain. "God gives us the boy or girl He wants us to have. This time, God gave us another girl. Who knows, you might be the only boy your momma has in this family! Kathleen is the second girl and the third child in the family. Now, come see your new sister. She needs to see her only brother." Winston smiles at his momma, then walks over to look at his little sister.

When Joy and Winston finish looking at Kathleen, I stand up from the couch and give Kathleen to Drum Mom. "Oh my! She's a pretty, little yellow thing," Drum Mom points out. "Except for her little fat nose, she looks like your momma, my dear daughter, Cheri. I think she'll be smart, too—not like Winston or Joy smartness, but they'll help her get there. Ruby, you can take her back. She reminds me too much of Cheri." Drum Mom gets up from her chair and proceeds to walk to her bedroom, saying, "Lord, she looks like Cheri! Please don't let that child live her life like Cheri." Drum Mom's bedroom door closes behind her.

"Kathleen not only looks like your family—she looks like my family, too! She has my momma's skin color and fat cheeks. She's both of us!" Eddie comments. I think to myself, "Did I just hear Eddie say Kathleen looks like his mother? She doesn't look like that woman!"

"Does it really matter who she looks like in our family?" I ask, looking at Eddie. "What matters is Kathleen is our daughter and she is a healthy baby." I then turn away from Eddie and look at Kathleen. I begin to wonder why Eddie made such a fuss about who looks like whom. I then think, "This is so petty. I think he is changing. No! What am I thinking? Eddie lives with my Drum Mom and under her house rules. He is getting impatient living here. He's a man. He just wants us to have our own home."

*****

We experience a cold winter soon after Kathleen's birth. Drum Mom, Eddie, and I work hard to keep the house warm. We work hard to make sure that none of us catch a cold. Three times a day, everyone in the house takes a spoonful of liquid medicine that Drum Mom cooks and puts in the ice box. I let the liquid medicine get to room temperature and put some on my breast for Kathleen. Eddie walks to work while I am home weaning Kathleen and taking care of Winston and Joy. He walks to work in the cold because he doesn't want to ask Daddy Freeman for a ride.

*****

As springtime is nearing, Drum Mom asks Eddie to build a swing on her porch facing up the street. Eddie builds the large swing with his own hands—taking some large screws and attaching the swing tightly to the roof over the porch. When he finishes, he calls out to Drum Mom: "Drum Mom, can you come out to the porch and sit down on the swing?" he requests.

Drum Mom goes outside, sits down on the swing, and starts swinging. "Eddie, this is fine. Really fine. I can see all the way up the street. When the children come outside and play, I can sit here and watch them from my swing," she notes.

*****

When summertime arrives, I go back to work at the beauty salon. My first day back, Lucille arrives and sits in my chair, saying, "Ruby, you better stop having those babies. Look at my hair and my kitchen! They are a mess!"

"Girl, hush up! When I finish with you, I'll have you looking like Lena Horne," I boast. "You'd better, because Fred needs to see his wife looking beautiful again. How are you and Eddie doing?" she asks.

"Eddie and I are fine; we just need our own place," I respond. "Have you seen Phillip lately?" she asks. "No, I haven't. Have you?" I inquire. "Yes, Fred and I go to his club every now and then," she replies. "He looks fine. He doesn't ask us or say anything about you." When I hold my head down in thinking about Phillip, Lucille notices and says, "Well, you do have a husband and a baby by Eddie." I raise my head. I know that Lucille is right. Phillip doesn't have to ask her about me. I have a husband. But though Eddie is the person I should be thinking about, Phillip is on my mind.

*****

On Monday morning, the day when both Eddie and I are off from work, Phillip comes knocking on the front door. Since Drum Mom is in the kitchen and I'm in the bedroom, Eddie is the one who goes to answer the door. When he opens the door and sees Phillip, the two of them are shocked to see each other.

"What do you want?" Eddie inquires loudly. Drum Mom hears Eddie and rushes to the door. And when I see her on the move, I also rush over to the door. Drum Mom sees Phillip and says, "Eddie, go and sit down on the couch." Eddie looks at Phillip, then at Drum Mom, and finally at me. Eddie then sits down on the couch, and I sit down beside Eddie. I can tell that he is upset.

"Phillip, come on in this house!" Drum Mom insists. Phillip comes into the house and stands by Drum Mom, then says, "I'm sorry to disturb everyone. I was in town and came by to see Winston and Joy." "Well, Ruby is married to me, Eddie Morgan!" he says with an angry tone. "Winston, Joy, and Kathleen are my children now! You have no right to be here!"

Phillip is shocked to hear Eddie say that he is married to "his" Ruby. "And there's a child? Who is this child, Kathleen? Kathleen is Ruby and Eddie's daughter!" Phillip thinks to himself. I observe the shock on Phillip's face and say, "Phillip, I'm married to Eddie. We have a daughter together. Her name is Kathleen." Phillip then looks at Eddie and says, "I honestly didn't know this, Eddie. I never would have come to another's man house if I had known this beforehand."

"Phillip, this is my house!" Drum Mom chimes in. "You wait right here, and I'll bring Joy to you." Drum Mom proceeds to walk back to the bedroom, then hears Eddie say, "You come by today, on a Monday. The day that Ruby is off from work. Man, do you think I'm a fool?"

When Phillip is about to speak, Drum Mom walks back into the front room with Joy, saying, "Phillip, here she is!" Phillip looks at Joy and smiles. "Joy, my, you've grown. How are you today?" he asks her.

"Hello. I'm two years old," Joy says, holding up two fingers to show Phillip. Joy continues, "I'm fine, thank you, sir." "Sir!" Phillip utters in a strong voice, without thinking. He quickly realizes how strongly he is talking to Joy, then wonders what other name he would expect her to call him. "I haven't seen Joy in a long time. There is no other name she can call me except 'sir,'" he thinks to himself.

"Well, you are a very pretty and nice little girl," Phillip says to her in a soft and loving voice. Then he touches the top of Joy's head. She smiles, looks at him, and says, "I remember you. You came here before to Drum Mom's house when I was real little like Kathleen. You sit with Momma on the couch where Daddy is sitting. You talk and play with me. See, I'm smart. I remember."

"You are smart," he says with a smile. He looks at Joy as though he is looking at her for the last time, then says, "I guess I'll leave. Goodbye, Joy. You all have a good day." As Phillip is leaving the house, he thinks about how Joy remembers him. "My Joy! You still remember me after all this time being away from you. I named you right. You bring nothing but joy to my life," he thinks to himself.

"Joy, go to your room," Drum Mom directs her. When Joy leaves the room, Drum Mom walks over to Eddie and me. She knows that Eddie is still upset about Phillip coming to her house to see Joy.

"Eddie," Drum Mom begins, "Joy is Phillip's child. No matter how much you love Joy, no matter that you take good care of Joy, and no matter how you accept Joy as your child, Phillip will always be Joy's father. Nothing you can do, feel, or say will ever change that.

"Did you hear that child? Joy remembers! Eddie, Phillip will respect you and not come back around here again. But when the time comes, and Joy starts asking why her last name is not your last name, somebody here is going to have to answer to that. Eddie, lastly, you love Ruby. You married Ruby knowing about all four of them." After she speaks her peace, Drum Mom leaves the front room and goes in the back where the children are playing.

I look at Eddie. Soon, he gets up from the couch and leaves the house. I get up, lock the front door behind him, and then go in the back with Drum Mom and my children.

Chapter Twenty-one

SWING

At the start of summer, Kathleen is six months old. She is not walking like Winston and Joy did at six months of age. They try to teach her to walk, count, and say her alphabets, but she can't quite get it. I tell them that Kathleen is still young and will catch up with them soon.

*****

Every day, Eddie and I walk to and from work. We love this time together. In fact, it is the only time we have together. People see us laughing, holding hands, and running after each other. We act like little children. And when people tell us that we need to stop acting like children and act our age, we ignore them and keep having fun together.

Then, one day, Eddie says, "I'm going up the street to visit my parents. Can I take the children with me?" I hesitate, but I know that the children need to know Eddie's parents. I know I don't need to stop my children from seeing their grandparents. I know what it's like not to have parents in your life. I want more for my children. Parents, grandparents, family, and friends should be in a child's life—as just one big circle of love!

"Yes, you can take the children with you," I say in a soft voice. I get the children cleaned and nicely dressed for their visit to see their grandparents. When I finish, Eddie takes the children and walks up the street. Winston and Joy hold hands, and Eddie carries Kathleen in his arms. I watch them walk away; then I see Eddie knocking on the door and someone comes and lets them in. When they disappear into the house, I go back inside the place where I live.

When Eddie and the children walk into the house, they stand by the front door. His father and mother are sitting down in the front room, looking at them. "Who are these children that you bring inside my house?" his mother asks. Eddie says, "Momma and Daddy, these are Ruby's and my children. This is Winston and Joy, and I'm holding Kathleen." Winston and Joy say, "Good evening, everybody." Eddie's mother then says, "All of you find a seat and sit down." They all sit down on the couch.

Eddie and his mother look at each other for a long time. Neither one says anything. Winston and Joy are looking around the big front room. Finally, Eddie's father, Arthur, asks, "How you been doing, Son?"

"Daddy, I'm just fine," Eddie answers. "Ruby, her Drum Mom, and the children are all fine. How are you all doing?" "Your momma and I are fine. Your children are very obedient. They are sitting quietly on the couch and keep looking around this room," his father remarks.

"Winston and Joy, come over here to me," Eddie's mother then requests. Winston and Joy then proceed to get up from the couch and go stand in front of the chair where she is sitting. "Winston and Joy, I want you to call Eddie's daddy, Granddaddy. You can call me Big Momma." Winston and Joy say, "Hello, Granddaddy. Hello, Big Momma."

"Now go and sit back down on the couch," Eddie's mother says. The children go back and sit down on the couch. "Eddie, turn that child around you are holding so I can see her face." Eddie turns Kathleen around so that his mother can see her.

She looks at Kathleen, then Arthur, and lastly, Eddie. "Is there anything else you want, Eddie?" she inquires. Eddie says no; he then looks at Winston and Joy and says, "Winston and Joy, get up. We must leave this place and go back home. Say goodbye." "Goodbye, Granddaddy and Big Momma," they say in unison. Eddie and the children then proceed to leave Eddie's parents' house and walk down the street, headed back home.

When Eddie and the children walk into the house, Eddie says, "Ruby, I'm going to the corner store and will be right back. Do you need anything?" "Eddie, I need some sugar!" Drum Mom yells from the kitchen. "I don't need anything," I say. Eddie then leaves the house. Drum Mom knows that I'm going to grill the children to find out what happened over at the other house, so she comes from the kitchen and sits down in her chair.

"Winston and Joy, tell Momma about Eddie's parents," I say in an upbeat voice. "She keeps her house clean," Joy responds. Winston knows that what Joy is saying is not what Momma wants to hear, so he says, "Momma, we sit down on the couch. We are very quiet. Daddy's momma tells us to call her 'Big Momma,' and to call her husband 'Granddaddy.' They look at Kathleen and ask us to leave. We leave their house and walk home." "Winston and Joy, take Kathleen, go in your room, and put the clothes back on that you wore earlier," I reply. They leave the front room to do as they are told.

Drum Mom says, "Eddie's momma just showed us that she doesn't want anything to do with you and your children. I think she also has a problem with her own son! That woman has a hard heart. She is going to miss out on the love these children can give her. When it comes to you, Ruby, I might understand why she is so angry. But the children, it is good they don't understand. When they get older, they will look back and know they didn't deserve to be treated the way that woman treated them."

*****

When it is summertime, it is cooler outside than in the house!

Drum Mom and the children go outside several times a day to get some cool air. Winston and Joy play all kinds of games. They know not to play in the street and to only play in the front yard and in the yard between Drum Mom's and Daddy Freeman's houses.

Drum Mom sits on her swing, with Kathleen in her arms. She has put a small cap on Kathleen's head, so that she won't catch a cold in the hot and breezy wind. As Drum Mom is moving back and forth in her swing, she looks up the street and sees the children's Big Momma on her swing. Big Momma's swing faces Drum Mom's swing. From their respective swings, Big Momma can see down the street, and Drum Mom can see up the street.

Every day, Drum Mom looks out the front window, waiting to see the children's Big Momma go outside, sit down, and get comfortable in her swing. As soon as this happens, Drum Mom and the children go outside; Drum Mom and Kathleen sit in the swing, and

Winston and Joy play in the yard. Big Momma sees them and then starts screaming for Arthur. "Arthur, come help me get up off this swing!" she yells. The street is so quiet that you can hear her crying out from all the way down the street. (Arthur helps their Big Momma because she can't get up by herself. She is a big woman.)

"Arthur, Arthur, you hear me! Come help me right now!" she calls out again. Arthur finally comes outside. "I just put you in this swing. Why you want to come back in the house?" Drum Mom hears him say to her. "Help me get up!" she demands. Arthur helps her get up from the swing. Then they slowly walk back into the house.

Since Drum Mom knows that Eddie's mother doesn't like me and the children, she makes the children go outside when their Big Momma goes outside. This causes their Big Momma to not be able to enjoy being outside.

"I ask her own son, Eddie, to build me a swing facing up the street," Drum Mom says with a laugh. "He builds it and puts it facing up the street, where his own momma lives. His momma likes to come outside and sit on her swing. Now, she can't enjoy herself outside. What a pity! She looks at me and makes a point to go right back in the house as soon as the children come outside. If she doesn't watch herself, she's going to miss being outside in the summertime."

As Drum Mom causes the swing to move back and forth, she feels the cool breeze and enjoys being outside. She looks up and down the quiet street where she lives. She lives on the east side of town, on Barbee Street. She knows everyone who lives on Barbee Street. A few white people live at one end of the street. But the rest of the street is full of colored people who are buying or already possess their own home. The colored people on this street are teachers, labor workers, Cousin John (who has his own restaurant in the "Hole"), Cousin Samuel (who owns Watkins' funeral home that is attached to his house), domestic workers, an electrician and a plumber, an equipment repairman, a licensed beautician, and Daddy Freeman (who owns his business and a building in town). There are children who live on Barbee Street who are the same age as my children; they all play together in my front yard.

Barbee Street changes into Scott Drive, where other colored folks live. On Scott Drive, there is the colored cemetery. The colored people who live on this street are a preacher, businessmen, and labor workers. Barbee Street and Scott Drive—one street with two different names. This street is a beautiful place to live because everybody knows everybody, everybody helps everybody, and everybody is trying to help the colored community.

*****

In August of 1956, Winston is six years old and starts elementary school. The colored school educates children from grades 1 to 8. The school is only about two streets from the house, so he and the other children on our street walk to school together.

Winston does well in school. He already knows how to count, knows the alphabet, and can read and write. He does so well in school that the teacher asks him to help teach the other students.

Whenever school lets out, the colored children walk home together. Then Winston does his homework and teaches Joy all the things he has learned that day.

One day, on a Saturday, Daddy Freeman brings Winston to the beauty shop while I am working there. Winston walks in, speaks to everyone, and then runs over and kisses me. He is smiling and talking because he is so happy. When he finishes talking to me, Daddy Freeman takes him out of the salon.

When they leave, the customer in my chair asks, "Mrs. Ruby, who is that boy?" "Gloria, that's my son, Winston," I reply. "Why do you ask?" "I just wanted to know," she responds. Gloria is twelve years old; she notices how Winston loves his momma and how polite he is to everyone. "He is so handsome. I'm going to marry him when he's older," Gloria says to herself.

From then on, any time she would be at the beauty salon—getting her hair done—and see Winston when he comes to visit me at work, Gloria would smile at Winston and promise herself that she will marry him someday.

*****

In September of 1956, nine months after having given birth to Kathleen, I get pregnant again. Winston is six, Joy is almost three, and Kathleen will be one in December. This baby is scheduled to be born in June 1957. We all hope this time that the baby is a boy.

One September evening, I say, "Eddie, I'm taking Winston over to see Daddy Freeman. We'll be back in about ten minutes." Winston and I then head over to Daddy Freeman's house. "Daddy Freeman, can I use your telephone? I'd like to call Beatrice and my friend Beth Eden. I'll pay you for the long-distance telephone call," I say. "Yes. Let me talk to Beatrice when you finish," he replies. Daddy Freeman starts talking to Winston as I make my way into the hallway to make my call.

When I dial the number and the telephone rings, someone picks up on the other end and says hello. I recognize the voice and say, "Beatrice, this is Ruby. How are you doing?" "Hello, Ruby!" she answers. "I'm just fine . . . and you?" "I'm fine, too. Is Beth Eden there?" Beatrice says, "Yes. She's right here."

Soon, there is another voice on the other end. "Hello, Ruby!" Beth Eden exclaims. "How are you?" "Beth Eden, I'm fine. I only have a few minutes to talk," I explain. "I want you to know Phillip and I are not married anymore. We do have a girl together. Her name is Joy Grace. Phillip and I divorced, and I married Eddie, who lives on the same street as Drum Mom. We have one girl, Kathleen, and I am expecting another baby in June."

"Girl, you're having babies after babies and are on your second marriage," she comments. "Yes, that's my life," I retort. We share a laugh. "I still don't own my beauty salon," I continue. "I'm still working in the same place. What about you and London?" Beth Eden replies, "I'm still here with Beatrice and still working with London. She owns two salons."

"Two salons! How did London do that?" I ask. "She made so much money from the first salon and was able to pay Marty back for the money he spent for her to get that salon," she explains. "The other money she made, she found a place to buy for a second salon. She has me managing the first salon, and she manages the new salon. We are so busy. The money is so good that it's hard to take a day off."

"That's wonderful. I'm proud of both of you. Is London still living with Marty?" I inquire. "No," she answers. "They went their separate ways after London paid back the money. London is also buying herself a house. She has a new boyfriend and he lives in her house.

London tells me Marty is sick and doesn't want her or anyone visiting him. Marty only calls and talks to Beatrice."

"Well, I'm working hard on getting my own house and salon," I say. "I hope it's real soon. Here where I live, it's hard for colored people to buy a home, and it's hard to own a business."

"Ruby, when you find you a house, work from your house," Beth Eden instructs. "Some of your customers will come to your home if it is nice. But you can't have children running around the house while you're working. Children have to know their place if you work at home." "Beth Eden, that's something to really think about!" I reply. "I should go. Daddy Freeman wants to talk to Beatrice. I'll talk to you later." When I am done talking, Daddy Freeman comes to the phone. Winston and I leave and go back home.

All night long, I think about what Beth Eden said to me: "Work from home."

*****

On Sunday, June 30, 1957, I give birth to another girl. Eddie and I name her Regina Morgan. Everything with this birth is the same as my experiences with Joy and Kathleen, except

- in our town, colored people are now called *Negros*.

- the Civil Rights Act of 1957 gives Negros voting rights.

- there are six babies born in the hospital on this day. Three are white babies in the white nursery, and three are Negro babies in the nursery in the basement.

- a white mother talks to the other white mothers in the hospital, saying, "You do not want the Negros breastfeeding your white baby. Negros in town are talking about being equal to white people and having the same rights as white people. Negros think they are going to vote and go to the same school with our white children. I will die before that happens! I don't think it's safe for our white babies to suck on a Negro breast." The white mothers feed their own babies.

When it is time, I leave the hospital and we take Regina home to Drum Mom's house. Drum Mom, Winston, Joy, and Kathleen are in the front room waiting for us. I sit on the couch and Eddie gives me the baby. I say, "Winston, Joy, and Kathleen, come and see the baby." I see that Winston is smiling and excited. Joy and Kathleen come and look at the baby; they start smiling at her. Winston stays where he is and says, "What is it, Momma, a boy or girl? Hurry up and tell us!" "Children," I slowly begin, "you have a baby sister, Regina." Winston looks at me and faints!

Chapter Twenty-two
THE MOVE

After Winston falls to the floor, Drum Mom says, "Eddie, pick that child up and bring him over here to me!" Eddie hurries, picks Winston up off the floor, and then lays him in Drum Mom's lap. I am holding Regina. With a scream, I say, "Drum Mom, is he breathing?! Is he alive?! Joy and Kathleen, go into the bedroom, so I can put this baby down on the couch! Go!"

The girls run out of the room, I put Regina down on the couch, and then I get up off the couch and move toward Drum Mom. Drum Mom is shaking and slapping Winston's face. By this time, I am crying. "Give me my son!" I exclaim. "No!" Drum Mom replies. "Ruby, run to the bathroom and get my smelling oil. Hurry!" I turn to run, but Eddie is right behind me, so I push him out of my way. He falls, and his upper body lands on the couch, just missing Regina. I bring the smelling oil to Drum Mom. She puts some smelling oil on her finger and puts it to his nose. I am screaming!

"Winston, wake up, wake up!" she yells. Then she hits his chest, and Winston grunts and wakes up. "Ruby, he's all right! Winston is all right!" she assures. She sits Winston up on her lap, and then we both start praising and thanking the Lord that Winston is all right! Suddenly, we stop and see Winston wiping the oil from his nose. "Drum Mom, why you hit me? That's the first time you ever hit me," Winston comments.

"Winston, get up off Drum Mom's lap," I direct him. "Walk to the kitchen and walk back here to the front room." Eddie gets up from where his body had plopped on the couch, and he comes and stands beside me. We watch Winston walk to the kitchen and back to the front room. "How's his walking?" Drum Mom asks. "He walks fine, like normal," I reply.

I then sit down on the couch and pick up Regina, saying, "Winston, you fainted and fell on the floor. You wouldn't wake up. Your Drum Mom hit your chest to wake you up. Now, walk over here to your momma." Winston walks over to me. "Now look at your new baby sister, Regina," I say. He looks at her for a long while; then he touches her face and smiles. Winston says, "Momma, I look a little like you, and Regina looks just like Daddy." Eddie smiles. "Winston, go in the back and play with your sisters. Let me know if you start hurting from the fall," I say.

After Winston leaves the room, I say, "Eddie, please get Regina and give her to Drum Mom so she can see her." Eddie takes Regina from my arms, gives her to Drum Mom, and comes and sits on the couch beside me. Drum Mom says, "Yes, Winston is right! She looks like you, Eddie! I believe this girl is going to be different than all the other children." "What do you mean by that?" I inquire.

"A girl who looks so much like her daddy will be very close to her daddy," she notes. "She'll have ways like her daddy. Just like you, Eddie, she'll be able to build and repair things. She'll take good care of herself, and if need be, she'll take care of herself *by* herself. Ruby, you won't be able to control this one!" I say, "Drum Mom, you and Daddy Freeman amaze me. The two of you can look at a new baby and tell what you think that baby will be like in life." "I am amazed at myself," Drum Mom says, almost braggingly. All of us laugh.

"Drum Mom," I begin, "I know my life has not been what you expected from me. I have a husband and four children living in your house. Eddie's trying very hard to find us a place to live. I've been saving our money so we can rent or buy a home. We make enough together to rent and have enough on a down payment for a house. Please continue to be patient with us. As soon as we find something, we will move from here into our own house." "I understand," she responds.

"I'd like to thank you for everything you do for us," Eddie interjects. "You're like a momma to me. My own parents don't treat me, my wife, and our children the way you do. I will always love you for that and for letting my family live here with you."

*****

Now, Winston is entering the second grade at the elementary school. He is seven years old. Joy is four, Kathleen is two, and Regina is three months old. And after three months, Regina is weaned from my breast. She likes drinking dairy milk better than nursing me. Since this is the case, I decide to go back to work at Miss Johnson's beauty salon.

On my first day back, I arrive and see new customers at the shop waiting to get their hair done. "Ruby, since none of your customers are here, you can start with Mrs. Coleman," Miss Johnson suggests. "She is the lady in the blue and yellow dress." "Yes, Miss Johnson," I reply.

I walk over to Mrs. Coleman and say, "Mrs. Coleman, my name is Ruby. May I fix your hair today?" "Yes, you surely can," she answers. I smile at her and say, "Please come and sit in my chair." I get started on the process.

When I am finished with her hair, she is thrilled at my work. "Ruby, I'll be back here for you to fix my hair in about a month," Mrs. Coleman says. "I look forward to seeing you again," I respond.

Miss Johnson and I continue to work all day, with only thirty minutes of break time. When we finish up and the last customer walks out of the salon, we each sit down in our own chair and rest. I think about what it will be like having my own salon with a lot of customers coming to my house, looking for me to fix their hair. I realize now that I don't have to rent a building to start my own business. I just need a home. Like Beth Eden suggested, I can work from my own home. If this is going to happen, Eddie and I must find us a house.

My thoughts get interrupted when Miss Johnson says, "Ruby, what a day! It's like this every day. More women are starting to work and need to spend money on the way they look at work. This means they are willing to come here, get their hair fixed, and pay us for it. My feet hurt from standing so much, but the service we provide is a beautiful thing. Let's get everything clean for tomorrow so we can get out of here and go home."

Eddie waits for me to finish cleaning up the salon so that we can walk home together. When we arrive at home, we get cleaned up, eat dinner, and then talk to and play with the children. Soon, we put the children to bed: Winston sleeps in the front room on the couch, while in the back bedroom, Regina sleeps in her baby bed and Joy and Kathleen sleep in the bed.

*****

On school days, Winston gets up early, takes his covers off the couch, folds them, and puts them in the closet in the toilet room. He puts on his clothes, eats breakfast, and walks to school. Meanwhile, Eddie and I get ready to walk to work. When Joy and Kathleen wake up, Joy makes up their bed; Drum Mom handles making up Regina's bed, then cooks and takes care of Joy, Kathleen, and Regina.

Eddie, my family, and I do the same things every day, except on Sundays and Mondays. On Sundays, Daddy Freeman takes Winston and Joy with him to church. If we are lucky, and Regina doesn't wake up, Eddie and I try to sleep in as long as we can. Mondays are Drum Mom's rest days. I wash clothes, do all the chores around the house, cook, and take care of Joy, Kathleen, and Regina. Eddie visits his parents. Tuesday starts our workweek, and our routine in life repeats itself.

*****

In January 1959, I get pregnant. At that time, Regina is eighteen months, Kathleen is three years old, Joy is five years old, and Winston is eight years old. I tell Eddie, Drum Mom, and Daddy Freeman the news. While Eddie is happy for us, Drum Mom and Daddy Freeman don't seem to be very happy about the news.

*****

In June of the same year, while Eddie and I are at work, Daddy Freeman walks over to Drum Mom's house to talk to her; he tells her that he wants to speak to Eddie and me when we get home. So, after we arrive home and eat dinner as a family, Drum Mom says, "Eddie and Ruby, Freeman is coming over tonight to talk to the two of you." "About what?" I inquire loudly. "Is he not happy about the baby I'm carrying?" "I'll leave it to Freeman to say what he has to say," she replies.

With those words, the children go to the back bedroom and play. The three of us make our way to the front room of the house and sit down. We are quiet as we wait for Daddy Freeman. He finally knocks on the door and says, "It's Freeman." "Come on in, Freeman," Drum Mom answers.

Daddy Freeman comes into the house, speaks to everyone, and then sits down on a chair. "Eddie and Ruby," he begins, "I've talked to Mr. Lacey, and he has a house for rent. His previous renters moved out of town. He owes me a favor and gave me first choice to find someone to rent from him. Do you want to rent his house?" "Yes, we do!" Eddie and I say in unison.

Daddy Freeman continues, "The house is a duplex on College Street. It has three bedrooms, a bathroom, a kitchen, and a living room. Since it is a duplex, there will be another family living next door."

"Eddie, it sounds like the house for us. I don't care if we have a family living next door," I say. "When can we move in?" Eddie asks. "Mr. Lacey has to clean the house first. He told me the house will be ready in July. That's about a month from now," Daddy Freeman explains.

Eddie and I get up from the couch and walk toward Daddy Freeman. I hug him and thank him for finding us a house. Eddie also thanks Daddy Freeman, shaking his hand. "Drum Mom, Daddy Freeman found us a house!" I exclaim.

"I'm so happy for you two," Drum Mom answers. "There aren't many homes left in this town screaming for someone to come and live in it. Eddie, this day is a good day for your family. Your own house! Ruby, don't do any pruning when you get in this house. Plant, just plant." Drum Mom turns to Freeman and says, "It was hard for me to keep my mouth shut! I had to bite on a lemon to keep from saying anything to them!" We all laugh joyfully.

*****

Ten days later, Mr. Lacey allows Eddie and me to go with him to visit the duplex. We walk inside and see that work is being done in preparation for us to move in. We have a nice-sized front room with two doors—with one door being the entrance door. When I walk to the door on the right and turn the door knob, I find that the door is locked.

Mr. Lacey sees my efforts and says, "I have a key to give you later that will unlock your doors. Always keep this door in the front room locked. If you unlock and open this door, you will face a locked door to your neighbor's kitchen. Remember, when your door and your neighbor's door are open, any one of you can walk in and out of the other home." Eddie and I nod our heads at Mr. Lacey, showing that we understand what he is saying.

Beyond the front room is a hallway. On the left side of the hallway, there are two bedrooms. On the right side of the hallway, I see a room with a toilet, a sink, and a closet. I walk into the room and say, "Oh my, Mr. Lacey! This toilet room has a real tub, so we can take a bath!" "Yes, Ruby!" Mr. Lacey responds. "I've updated this room for the two of you and the children. This room is now a bathroom instead of a toilet room."

Beside the bathroom is a large bedroom. The hallway from the front room leads straight to the kitchen, which has a stove, a sink, an icebox, and racks on which to store dishes and food. Then there is a door leading from the kitchen to the backyard. In the backyard, there are two large, sturdy trees with two long clotheslines between them.

"Mr. Lacey, this is a nice house. We thank you for letting us rent here. We promise to pay you on time and take good care of your property," Eddie comments. "You are welcome," Mr. Lacey replies. "I know you will take care of my property. Freeman gives me his word and says you two will do right by me!"

Eddie walks outside and leaves me alone in the house with Mr. Lacey. "Mr. Lacey, can you put a salon hair sink in the front bedroom?" I request. "I fix you wife's hair and I want to fix hair in our home." Mr. Lacey smiles and says, "I will do this for you only because of my wife and Freeman." I thank him and walk outside the house.

Eddie and I are very happy. We leave the duplex singing together with joy. At one point on our journey back home, we stop walking, hold hands, and say to each other, "We have a home! Our home!" When we arrive at Drum Mom's house, we tell her about our new home. She smiles; "Ruby, when you move into your new house, will you be bringing the children over here before you go to work?" she asks.

"Drum Mom, yes, for a while—until I can get one of the bedrooms set up for me to do hair in our home," I explain. "What! Do hair in our home? Ruby, when did you decide that you are going to do hair in our home?" Eddie asks. Drum Mom sits back in her chair and stares at me.

"Eddie, I decided this today after we left the house," I comment. "If I do hair from home, I'll be home with our children and have our meals ready. If I work from home, I won't have to pay for space to rent like I do at Miss Johnson's beauty salon. We can save that money. All the money we save will be ours to spend. I just have to figure out how to keep my customers coming to me and convince them to come to our home."

"Well, your plan sounds good. I just wish you had discussed this with me first before you decided!" Eddie says. "Don't you do anything else like this again! That house is my home, too! If you want to do anything in that house that will involve any part of me, both of us need to talk and decide what we'll do together." "Yes, Eddie, you are right. In the future, I'll always talk to you first," I reply. Drum Mom looks at me and leaves the room. I cuddle up under Eddie and remind him that we have our own home. After a while, we retire for the night.

The next morning, Eddie and I happily walk to our respective places of work. As usual, Miss Johnson and I are busy at the beauty salon. Amid the work, I write down information for all my customers, saying to them, "This will help me help you. I will know what type of hair you have. If you come here and say you want to look like Lena Horne, I can tell you what I can do to make it happen. If you want color in your hair, I'll have information on you to let you know if that color will work for you. This is what I learned in beauty school. I want to start practicing what I learned."

Lucille comes into the salon today, which is her regular appointment day. When she sits in my chair, I say, "We are moving into a house on College Street in July. I'm going to start doing hair in my beauty salon room in my house. I'll have to buy a hair sink, hair chair, and dryer."

"I'm going to Covington this week," Lucille comments. "Maybe I'll see Phillip and tell him what you need." "Lucille, I am married to Eddie," I say. "Phillip respects my marriage. He will not want to hear about what I need to start my own business. Leave him out of this matter. I'll find another way to buy what I need. It may take me a while, but it will happen." After our dialogue, we proceed with business as usual.

*****

In July, Mr. Lacey gives us a key to our new home. We pay him rent for two months so that Eddie and I know how much money we have left to spend on things we'll need.

Eddie and I have nice things for our first home. His parents do not help us or give us anything for our house, but my family helps us: Drum Mom gives us all the furniture from the girls' bedroom, bed sheets, towels, wash cloths, and some dishes, pots, and pans. Daddy Freeman buys us furniture for the front room. Our cousin John, who lives on Barbee Street, gives us a kitchen table and chairs, some forks, spoons, and knives from his restaurant in the "Hole." And Eddie and I buy two bunk beds and a chest of drawers for one of the bedrooms (on credit).

On moving day, two men come to Drum Mom's house to help us move. Daddy Freeman pays one man to use his car, and both men for working to get us into our house. Since I'm six months pregnant, my job is to tell the men what they need to do.

Finally, everything is packed and ready to go; Eddie and the two men load what they can into the car. We then get into the car (including the two men) and drive to our house. Once there, Eddie and the two men start unloading the car. Suddenly, from inside the house, I look out the front-room window and notice that a black truck has pulled up in front of our house. I look and see Fred driving the truck, and Lucille is on the passenger side, yelling out the window, "We got us a house!" They get out of the truck. "Hi, Lucille and Fred. I'm glad you've come to help us!" I say with a smile as they enter the house. "I can help you with those things we have in the back of our truck," Lucille comments.

Fred gets out of the truck and walks around to the back of it. Lucille walks over to Eddie and me, saying, "I heard Mrs. Williams is closing her beauty salon and selling some of her equipment. Fred and I talked to Mrs. Williams, and she gave me those things in the back of the truck. It's yours! Happy Homecoming!" One of the men then calls Eddie over to help him unload the car, so Eddie leaves our presence. I hug Lucille and say, "Thank you, my friend. Lucille, you're making me cry!"

While Lucille and I are still in the embrace, she says, "Don't shed no tears for me! Phillip bought all those things from Mrs. Williams and told me to go and pick them up. I talked to Fred, and he got a truck. We went to Mrs. Williams's salon. She told Fred the things she wants us to have from the salon. He and some men loaded the stuff in the back of the truck. Ruby, Fred doesn't know all the details, just the half-truth. He knows Mrs. Williams gave me these things because we don't have any money to buy them from her." I pull away from Lucille and stare at her. She stares back at me, turns her head, and yells, "Men, Lucille's here! We have a pregnant woman on board! Get to work! We don't have all day!"

Eddie walks in with the first load. I say, "These things belong in the front room." He puts them down on the floor and walks down the hallway. He then walks into the bedroom that is on the left, yelling, "Ruby, come in here and look!" I walk into the room.

"Why did Mr. Lacey put a hair sink in a bedroom? Is he crazy?" Eddie inquires angrily. "Eddie, he's not crazy," I say softly. "I asked Mr. Lacey to put this in here. This room is where I'm going to do hair." "Why do you have to take a bedroom away from the children to do hair?" Eddie asks. "We have four children and one on the way. Where will all of them sleep? In one bedroom? Why can't you wash hair in the kitchen?"

I then hear someone come through the door. "Mrs. Ruby, where do you want this to go?" the man asks. "Eddie, this is going to work out," I quickly comment. "You'll see. Let me go in the front room and tell the man where to put the things he brings in the house." After my explanation, I exit the room, leaving Eddie looking around the room.

"Eddie, Eddie, I need your help!" Fred yells out to Eddie. Eddie leaves the bedroom and helps Fred unload the truck. They bring a hair floor dryer into the house. I show them where I want to put the hair dryer. Next, they bring in two beauty chairs. They put the reclining chair in front of the hair sink, and the other chair by the window. Then they head back to the truck. Fred then brings in a tall table, and Eddie brings in a bar stool. "Eddie, can you put the bar stool down on the floor and move the chair away from the window?" I ask. Eddie proceeds to put the bar stool on the floor; he stares at me before he moves the chair.

"Fred, can you put the tall table next to the window?" I request. Fred puts the tall table by the window. Then he and Eddie put the hair chair in front of the table. I move the bar stool behind the chair and in front of the window, then they leave the room. When I look around at everything in the room, I start crying.

Lucille hears me crying and enters the room. "Ruby, are you all right?" she asks. "Lucille, I am better than all right. This is what I always wanted since I realized what I needed to do to be a success-ful hairdresser and have my own beauty salon. God and so many people helped me. People sacrificed everything they have to give to make this come true for me. Yes, for me! My own beauty salon! This is changing me from the inside out! I am going to be more grateful for things people do for me. I promise I will give back this kindness to others." Lucille smiles, kisses me on my cheek, and then leaves me alone in my beauty salon.

Soon, the men have unloaded everything from the car. All per-sons involved, including Fred and Lucille, go back to Drum Mom's house to pick up the rest of our things; I stay behind at our new home. During this trip, Eddie has the use of Fred's truck for moving the bed and other furniture. When they get everything out of Drum Mom's house, they haul it all to our house. The men then make a fi-nal trip to Daddy Freeman's house to pick up the front-room furniture, to Cousin John's restaurant for the table, chairs, and utensils, and to the furniture store downtown for the two bunk beds and chest of drawers.

While they make their final trips, Lucille and I stay at the house. Lucille works in the front, and I work in the kitchen in the back. When I hear someone knock on the door, I walk over to answer the door and see Mr. Lacey standing on the porch. "Hello, Mr. Lacey. Come in," I say, welcoming him.

"Hello, Ruby," he responds, walking into the house. "Ruby, I see you are busy moving into the house. I forgot to give you the key to that door that opens to your neighbor's door." He points to the front-room side door, then continues. "Remember to keep that door locked at all times so no one can come in here unless you let them in here." I take the key (that's on a small chain) from Mr. Lacey and say, "Thank you. I understand." He leaves. I walk down the hallway and see a small nail hanging high on the wall in the hallway. I place the key over the nail and go back to work in the kitchen.

Soon, Lucille and I hear the men pull up in the car and in the truck. "Ruby, I got this!" Lucille says confidently. "I know where you want to put the furniture. You can keep working in the kitchen and rest there, if you need to."

The men bring the kitchen table and chairs in first. They pick up the boxes off the kitchen floor and put them on the table. I then open the boxes and start putting things in place.

"Eddie, you and Fred follow me to the bedroom," Lucille says. They do as she has requested. Once in the bedroom, she says, "Bring the bunk beds into this bedroom and work on assembling them. When you get through with that, put one bunk bed on this wall and the other on that wall." Lucille leaves the bedroom, and Eddie and Fred get to work on the bunk beds.

Lucille walks into the front room and says, "The two of you bring all the other furniture and things into the front room." The men go back and forth to and from the car and truck until they finish unloading everything. I walk back and forth by the rooms to see what Lucille is having the men do with everything.

Finally, I hear Lucille say, "Everybody, that's it for tonight! You two men can go on home. Thanks for getting all this done today." I walk to the front room and see the two men walking out of the house. "Thank you so much for your help," I say to them. They turn around and nod their heads at me.

I close and lock the door after their departure. I then hear people behind me shut the bedroom doors and the bathroom door. I walk down the hallway and try to open the doors, but they're locked. "Lucille, stop!" I yell out. "You all stop playing with me and let me in these rooms!" When no one comes out of the rooms, I walk to the front room and yell, "Everybody! Report to the front room, now!"

Lucille, Fred, and Eddie open the once-shut doors and proceed to walk slowly to the front room. I look at each of them. When I look at Lucille, they all start laughing at me. I say, "Lucille, I'm going to—," but Lucille interrupts me, saying, "Look around the front room."

I look at Lucille and then look around the front room. "Lucille, this front room is beautiful!" I say. "Look, Eddie! Daddy Freeman picked out some beautiful furniture for this room. We have a black leather couch and two black chairs, a table with a vase of plastic red roses, and a floor television!"

"The couch folds out into a bed. This is a bed couch," Lucille notes. "Oh, my goodness, I think I'm going to cry!" I exclaim. "Wait. Before you start crying, you have to look at the bedrooms and the bathroom!" Lucille adds.

Lucille then takes my hand and walks me into the bathroom. She has placed blue towels on the wall hanger and blue rugs on the floor. The closet is full of bed sheets, more towels and face cloths, toilet paper, soda, and toothbrushes. We have plenty of soap with which to take a bath in the bath tub. There is also an empty basket for our dirty clothes. "This is beautiful!" I comment. "Where did these things come from?" "They came from your friends. I collected money from our friends to purchase these things for you and Eddie," Lucille replies. "I'll have to thank all of my friends," I note. "Lucille, let me know the names of my friends who gave you money. I need to thank every one of them."

We walk out of the bathroom. Lucille takes my hand again and walks me to the children's bedroom. I see two bunk beds with covers, white bed sheets for curtains, and a chest of drawers. "This is so beautiful! My children's room is beautiful! We have four beds: one for Winston—who will sleep on the bottom bed—one for Joy, one for Kathleen, and one for Regina. Beautiful, just beautiful!"

"Let's go to yours and Eddie's bedroom," Lucille then suggests, once again holding my hand and walking me to mine and Eddie's bedroom door. When she opens the door, my mouth opens wide. I find myself speechless. I see Dum Mom's bedroom furniture in the room. I see the baby crib beside our bed. After I stop and breathe slowly, I think I can finally say something.

"Eddie, look at our bedroom!" I yell. "The sheets and covers match the curtains! Look at that picture of us on the wall!" I start screaming and start twirling around and around in the room until I fall back onto the bed. After I fall on our bed, I start crying. Eddie comes and holds me tightly, saying, "Welcome home, Ruby. This is our new home." I hug Eddie as my tears fall onto his shoulders. I say, "Thank you, Eddie, for our new home. Lucille and Fred, thank you for making this one of the happiest days of my life. Two of my best friends help us make this day end in a great way."

"This day isn't quite over!" Lucille responds. "Fred, go to the truck and bring that package from the front seat in here." Fred leaves; he then brings back a large grocery bag. "Lucille, where do you want this to go?" he asks. "In the kitchen," she replies. "Ruby and Eddie, we need to go to the kitchen." Eddie and I get up from the bed and walk to the kitchen. "We need to stand around the table," she explains. We all do what Lucille says to do.

Lucille then pulls out a loaf of bread. "This day, we give you bread so you will always have food to feed your family," she says. Fred pulls out a jar from the grocery bag and says, "We have no wine because we can't buy wine, but we have a jar of moonshine!" We all laugh. After our round of laughter, Fred says, "Seriously! Pretend this jar of moonshine is wine! This day we give you wine, so you will never go thirsty."

Eddie and I hold each other and smile, basking in Fred and Lucille's kindness. Fred again reaches into the bag and pulls out four small glasses. He places them on the table and opens the jar of moonshine. He pours some of the moonshine into three glasses. He takes one glass, walks over to the sink faucet, and runs tap water into that glass; he hands me the glass of water. He gives Eddie and Lucille a glass each with some moonshine in it, and keeps a glass for himself. "Let us make a toast," he utters. We raise our glasses, and Eddie says, "I'm going to give this toast!" Fred says, "Yes, Eddie. Go ahead."

"God, thank You for this house," Eddie begins. "God, bless this house and everyone who lives here. Let this house be a house where You live. Grant us love and prosperity. If trouble comes our way, let us look to You for our help. Thank You for our friends, Fred and Lucille—for they have done us a mighty good deed. Remember them. Amen." We drink from our glasses. "This is the first time I've drank liquor," Eddie confesses. "I have to say, it tastes pretty good."

"Fred and I are leaving," Lucille announces. "There is some bologna in the grocery bag. You can have a bologna sandwich for breakfast, lunch, and dinner. In fact, there's enough bologna in that bag to eat for the rest of the week."

With a laugh, I say, "That's good. Thank you, Lucille. That will be enough bologna for us and for the children to eat tonight and tomorrow." Lucille says, "What children? You and Eddie are the only ones staying here for the weekend! Fred and I are going to pick up the children from your Drum Mom's house. I talked to your Drum Mom, and she's glad we're keeping the children for the weekend. I think she wants to know how she will do being in that house alone." Eddie and I smile at Lucille and Fred.

"So," Lucille continues, "we will pick them up and keep them until Tuesday morning. We'll take them back to your Drum Mom's house on Tuesday. That gives you and Eddie three days to break this house in before the children come to live here." We all laugh, then Eddie and I walk out with Fred and Lucille to see them off.

Eddie walks to the truck with Fred while I stand on the porch with Lucille. "Lucille, who gave money for you to buy these beautiful things for us?" I ask. "Phillip is your friend," Lucille whispers. "He says he also likes red roses and wants you to have them in your house. I tore off one red rose petal and glued it to the vase. Look at the vase again and you'll see it. I know what you found in the letters Phillip sent you. That's why I put the roses in the front room on top of the table. I didn't want what any other man likes to be placed in your bedroom with Eddie." I stare at Lucille.

"Come on and walk me to the truck," she says. "I have to pick up your children." I walk Lucille to the truck. Eddie and I watch as they drive away from us. Eddie then scoops me up and carries me into the house—into our bedroom. He puts me down on the bed and goes back to the front room to lock the door; then he returns. Eddie and I are finally alone—alone in our own home. We soon get ready for bed, and he holds me to his chest all night long.

The next morning, we are awakened to someone knocking at our front door. Eddie gets up from the bed and goes to see who is at the door. I hear him talking to someone, but I don't recognize the person's voice. Then I hear Eddie say, "Ruby, get up and come to the front room." I get out of bed, put on a robe, and walk to the front room.

"Ruby, these are the Mayses who live on the other side of the duplex," Eddie explains. "Hello. Please have a seat," I say. They sit on our brand-new couch, and I think to myself, "Eddie and I haven't even sat on that couch and here are these strangers, the first to sit down in our front room."

"We are the Mayses," the man says. "We live next door. My name is David. My wife is Geraldine. Our girl, Laura, is three years old. Our son, Thomas, is eight years old. We hear that you have children. Where are your children?"

"My name is Eddie Morgan," Eddie says, introducing himself. "This is my wife, Ruby. The children are with our friends. We have one boy, Winston, who is eight years old. Joy is five, Kathleen is three, and Regina is eighteen months. We are expecting another one in October."

"We have children the same age!" David responds with excitement. "We just stopped by to introduce ourselves, and my wife wanted to give you a bag of pecans and a bag of apples." Geraldine hands me the bag of pecans and apples, and I say, "Thank you very much."

"We're not going to waste any more of your time. We just came by to meet our neighbors. Since our children are the same age, we'll make sure to keep our side of the door locked so my children wouldn't try to come through the door. Geraldine and I work during the day. We just want to be friendly neighbors," David explains.

"We will be good neighbors, David. We'll keep our door locked too," Eddie assures them. "Ruby works at home. If you see our children doing wrong, let us know. Ruby will be at home working, and she can keep an eye on your children when they play outside. She's good at letting you know if she sees any of the children doing wrong."

When the Mays family stands up from the couch, David says, "It was nice meeting you." "I hope you enjoy the pecans and apples," Geraldine adds. "It's nice meeting all of you. I know we will enjoy eating the pecans and apples. Thank you again," I reply. Upon their leaving the house, Eddie locks the door behind them, and I carry the pecans and apples to the kitchen. Eddie and I go back to bed.

*****

On Tuesday, Daddy Freeman picks up Eddie and myself to drive us over to Drum Mom's house. When we arrive there, we spend time with Drum Mom, catching up on how she has been doing. She says, "I did fine staying alone in this house. The first night, I couldn't sleep. All night long, I think I heard every crack and every drop of water from the faucets hitting the sink. That's what kept me awake. The second and third nights, I slept all through the night. I guess I got used to the noise. I'm fine and will be fine here by myself. Eddie and Ruby, I have to come by and see your new house!" I say, "Yes, Drum Mom, you do. We'll get you over there as soon as we can."

When Eddie leaves to go visit with his parents, I continue to sit and talk with Drum Mom. "Ruby," she begins, "I am very proud of the new person you have become. I thought for years that you would continue to see out of unclear lenses—being blind in one eye and halfway seeing out of the other eye. I say this because I saw how unclear lenses made you an unwed mother, leave a good man, leave Winston with me to go off to beauty school, divorce, bring your husband to live in my house, and have all these children by different men. But now I see: your unclear lenses got you to this place—a place where you marry another good man, have smart and disciplined children, get your own house, and now have your own beauty salon. Even though you did things I would be afraid to do, you made it all happen and now your plate is full of blessings." After her spiel, Drum Mom hugs me, and I hug her back.

Meanwhile, when Eddie arrives at his parents' house, he goes inside and says, "Hello, Momma and Daddy. I need to say something. Ruby is your daughter-in-law, and our children are your grandchildren. I am your son! I don't understand why you couldn't help your son and his family move into their first house. Ruby's family and friends helped us. Because of the way you two act toward me and my family, we will not cause any troubles for you. I won't be bringing the children over here again. If you want to see them, you'll have to take the steps to make it happen. I love you both dearly—I just refuse to let my family be mistreated by you. When you go to church, I only ask that you just keep us in your prayers." After speaking his peace, Eddie leaves his parents' house and walks back to Drum Mom's house.

Soon, Fred and Lucille arrive at Drum Mom's house with our children. The kids run into the house and are happy to see their Drum Mom, their momma, and their daddy. Lucille and Fred then come into the house. "How were my children? Did they obey you?" I ask.

"Yes, they are very good children," Lucille answers. "I didn't have any problems with them. You have great children. Now as for me, I am worn out! I know motherhood is one of the best jobs a woman can have, but Lucille is only interviewing for that job. I am not working hard to get that job."

"Fred and I should leave. I must catch up on my sleep. We got the truck outside. Do you all need a ride back home?" Lucille inquires. "Yes, we need a ride home," Eddie and I say in unison.

Since we have a ride back to our house, we bid farewell to Drum Mom and leave her house with our family. We all get into the truck and Fred drives us home.

Chapter Twenty-three

WHAT NEXT?

Upon our arrival at our new home with our children, Winston, Joy, and Kathleen jump out of the back of the truck and run to the front door. "Momma, the door is locked. We can't get in," Winston observes. "Just wait a minute; we have to get out of the truck, too," I respond. Eddie gets Regina and holds her in his arms while I try to get out of the truck with my big belly. We thank Fred and Lucille for the ride home and for everything else they have done for us. Fred and Lucille then drive away.

I walk beside Eddie to the front door, which he then unlocks. As the children run into the house to the front room, we are not too far behind them. Their faces of excitement are noticeable as they look around in the house. We follow them to the bathroom. "Momma, we have a bathtub in here. This is going to be my favorite room!" Winston exclaims.

Next, we let them lead the way to the beauty salon room. "Momma, is this where you're going to fix hair?" Joy asks. "Yes, Joy," I reply. We then walk over to the children's room. They quickly claim their own bed and their own dresser drawer. After checking out their room, the children make their way to our bedroom; Joy comments on how pretty she thinks the room is. Then we proceed to walk to the kitchen. "Momma, you cook food in this room?" Kathleen inquires. I tell her yes. The kids walk to the back door and look at the backyard. Upon noticing the smiles on their faces, Eddie says, "This is your new home."

"There's one more room we didn't see," Winston acknowledges. "No, this is it, Winston," Eddie replies. "I saw a door in the front room. Joy, let's go and open that door," Winston says, taking off running with Joy in tow. We follow their lead, heading to the front room. Winston tries to open the door, but he can't because it is locked.

"There will be no running in this house!" I command. "That door is always locked. It opens to the house where another family lives. You are not allowed to unlock that door, and you can't go over to their house through this door. This house is called a duplex. Two families live in this one building. One family lives on one side, and another family, like us, lives on the other side. Stay away from that door! Do you understand?" "Yes, Momma," Winston and Joy respond in unison.

After touring the house with the children, we get settled in. The children sit at the kitchen table, and I prepare them some bologna sandwiches. Winston prays over the food and for our new home. I say to myself, "We have been truly blessed! This is their first meal at our new home—a bologna sandwich. My children look so happy!" After they finish eating, I say, "It's time to get ready for bed. Bath time."

Winston asks to take his bath first. When he finishes, I let his water drain out, and then run fresh water for the girls. Joy and Kathleen take their bath together. When Kathleen finishes, she dries herself, puts on her night clothes, and goes to bed. I stay in the bathroom with Joy. I put Regina in the bathtub with Joy and explain how to bathe her. Joy does a good job of this. Then when Joy finishes bathing Regina, I say, "Joy, stay in the tub with Regina until the water runs out. When the water runs out of the tub, I'll take Regina from you, so you can get out of the tub. I'll dry Regina, put her night clothes on, and put her to bed. You take care of yourself." Joy gets out of the tub and takes care of herself, and I get Regina dried off and clothed. Joy and Regina then go to bed. Once all the children are asleep, Eddie and I go to bed.

*****

After eating breakfast on the next morning, Eddie says, "Ruby, Winston and Joy start school in two months. I need to walk with Winston and show him the way to go to school. He'll be walking with Joy, and we need to know he can lead the way to school and back home."

"Eddie, you are absolutely right!" I say. "I haven't thought about school. When will you start?" "We'll start this morning before

I go to work," he answers. "Well, let me go and wake him up to get ready for his walk with his daddy!" I respond eagerly.

After I get Winston dressed and ready for the day, Eddie and Winston leave the house. When they leave, I look at the clock, and it reads seven o'clock in the morning. I watch as they walk up College Street. Then, when they make the right turn, they continue walking (still on College Street) until I can no longer see them. I then head back into the house.

Eddie and Winston walk past our church, Holy Gospel Missionary Baptist Church, then turn right onto Highway Nineteen heading to the overhead bridge. When they come to a stop, Eddie says, "Winston, when you walk to school, stop right here so you can cross the street. Look both ways for cars coming up and down the street. If you see a car coming, wait until there are no cars on the street so that you can walk to the other side. Do you understand?" "Yes, sir," Winston replies. "Since you understand, I'll let you lead me safely across the street," Eddie instructs.

Winston sees a lot of cars going up and down the street. Finally, when there are no more cars, he takes his daddy's hand and says, "Let's cross the street. Hurry up, Daddy." Winston then proceeds to lead Eddie safely across the street. "Good job, Winston," Eddie says, encouraging Winston. They continue walking.

They make their way onto the overhead bridge. Winston stops on the overhead bridge and asks, "Daddy, what's that down there?" "Down there are trees and a railroad track," Eddie answers. "The trains cross the railroad track. Do you get scared when you look at the railroad track and see how far down it is from the bridge?"

"No, Daddy. I'm not afraid of anything," Winston boasts. "That's good, because Joy may be afraid to walk across the bridge," Eddie explains. "Girls just get scared. If she gets scared, take her hand and walk real fast across the bridge. She will be all right once she crosses the bridge. Now, let's keep walking across this bridge."

After he and Winston cross the bridge, Eddie says, "We need to turn left on East End Street. Can you read that sign?" "Yes. It reads East End," Winston says. "So, what are you going to do at this point?" Eddie asks. "Turn left on East End Street," Winston replies. So, they turn left and continue walking until they are standing in front of the grocery store.

"Winston, that's the neighborhood grocery store," Eddie informs him. "You must pass this store to go to school and to come back home from school. This store will let you know you are going the right way. When you see the grocery store, walk past the store and keep walking on this same street, which is East End Street."

They continue walking until they get to Peach Street. "We are going to turn right on Peach Street. Can you read that street sign?" Eddie asks. "Yes," Winston answers. "It's Peach Street, and we need to turn right and cross the street." Winston then pauses, saying, "Wait, Daddy, here comes a car. We have to wait until there are no cars coming so we can cross the street." When Winston sees that the street is free of traffic, he takes Eddie's hand and they cross the street. They walk up Peach Street and arrive at the side door entrance of Johnson Elementary School.

They spend time walking around the school. Soon, Eddie says, "Now, Winston, walk me back home from this school. Remember, this time we are not walking to school—we are walking home."

Winston starts leading the way back home. He walks down Peach Street and then waits until it is safe to cross the street before he heads left on to East End Street. He takes Eddie up East End Street, passes the grocery store, turns right onto Highway Nineteen, crosses the overhead bridge, and then stops. He looks to see if there are cars going up or down the street. When it is safe, he takes Eddie's hand and they cross the street. They walk to College Street, turn left, walk past the church, turn left onto the same College Street, and proceed all the way home. When they make it to the house and walk in, Eddie looks at the clock.

"Ruby do you know what time we left?" Eddie inquires. "Seven," I reply. "It's nine thirty. That's two hours and thirty minutes going and coming. So, that's one hour and fifteen minutes one way."

"Did I do good, Daddy?" Winston asks. "Yes, you did, for your first time," Eddie responds. "What we learned today is that our walking time is too long. We need to get to school in less than an hour. That will put you there before school starts at eight o'clock. If we hadn't stopped to talk and stopped to walk around the school, I know for a fact you would have been at school on time. Tomorrow, when we leave the house, we won't stop on the bridge to talk and we won't take the time to walk around the school. Today, I left my watch here at the house. Tomorrow, I'll take my watch with me. I'll time us exactly when we leave the house and when we get to school. Then I'll time us when we leave the school and get back home. Son, I bet our time will be better tomorrow." Winston smiles and proceeds to walk into the kitchen.

Eddie then kisses me, saying, "Ruby, I got to go to work. Do you have any customers today?" "I only have two customers today. I know things will pick up once my customers know it is official that I'm working at home," I explain. Eddie nods, then I say, "Have a good day, Eddie!" After bidding him good-bye, he leaves for work.

Next, I wake up Joy, Kathleen, and Regina so they can eat breakfast with Winston before my first customer arrives. "After you finish eating, you all need to do your chores," I instruct them. "Winston, make your bed. You are expected to do this every day when you wake up. Joy, make your bed and Regina's bed. Show Kathleen how to make up her own bed. Winston, show Joy how you wash dishes.

"Also, Winston and Joy, I have customers coming here to get their hair done. Watch Kathleen and Regina and let me know if they don't mind you. You all better behave. If you don't behave, I'm going to stop doing hair and come back here and whip you until I'm tired. You'll be in your room and in the kitchen all day instead of watching the television shows. I have to work and make money for us to eat and live in this house."

Soon, my very first customer is knocking on the door. I stare at my children and say, "That's my customer, and you all better behave yourselves!"

I go to the door and let my customer into the house. My first customer is Lucille. She comes into the house and we hug each other. "It's so quiet in this house. Where are your children?" she asks. "They're here doing their chores," I answer. Lucille then goes through the house and speaks to and kisses all of them. When she kisses Winston, he wipes the kiss off his face. "Winston, you don't like me kissing you anymore?" Lucille asks. "No, Mrs. Lucille," he responds. "I don't like girls kissing me. The only girl I want to kiss me is my momma." Lucille and I laugh.

Lucille walks into my salon and says, "Lucille is here! I'm the first customer. The first to sit in the chair at the hair sink, the floor dryer, and the styling chair. After me, there will be no first. Come on, Ruby, and get started on this nappy head and cut my kitchen!" We laugh as she sits down in the styling chair. We continue to talk until I finish. Lucille looks in the mirror and begins bragging about how beautiful she looks.

She then reaches into her purse and pulls out money to pay me for my work. "Lucille, this one is on me!" I say. "You and Fred have been so good to Eddie and me that I wouldn't dare let you pay me. Put your money back in your purse."

"Ruby, your children still got to eat!" Lucille exclaims. "I told Fred you were going to fix my hair and not charge me anything. But Fred wouldn't have it that way. He gave me money to pay you for my hair. See, I know you! I know you very well! So, I put the money away Fred gave me for a rainy day. This money I have in my hand is from your friend. He knew you had to pay the first month's rent when you moved into your house and wanted to make sure Joy and the other children had enough food to eat."

Lucille hands me the money. I look at the bundle of one-dollar bills and then count the money. "Lucille, Phillip gave me fifty dollars!" I utter in shock. "I know how much it is!" Lucille retorts. "He gave me the money, and you know I had to count it for myself. Fred knows the places where I hide things. So, I did everything to keep him from finding out about this money. I put the money under my breast, in my socks, in my shoes, rolled and pinned it up in my hair, and I'm not telling you the other places I had to put your money. So, if the money smells, that's your problem."

We laugh, and then I say, "Lucille, Phillip really does care about me." "Phillip cares about *you!*" Lucille says, repeating my words. "Ruby, this is not just about you. Phillip cares about you, and he also cares about Eddie and the children. He sent one-dollar bills so it will look to Eddie like you fixed hair for this money. Phillip is going to step aside. He just wanted to help the children and wanted you to have a successful start to your new business. If you need him for anything else, you'll have to go directly to him. My job between you and Phillip is finished. Phillip's job is finished. Eddie is officially The Man!" After saying what she has to say, Lucille gets her things and leaves.

I put enough money in my apron pocket to buy groceries. As for the other money, I unscrew the knob on the rail post on my bed and put it in there. I then replace the knob onto the post and lock it tightly. I make sure the other three knobs are also tightly screwed on. I then go and check on the children; they are playing. Soon, I hear a knock at the door. "That's another customer," I inform the children. "You all behave. When Momma finishes, I'll make you a sandwich. I need to go to the store and buy you all a sweet treat for being so good."

My second customer has arrived, so I proceed to do her hair. She pays me seventy-five cents for this service. When she leaves, I go and check on the children, who are still playing. "I am through fixing hair for today," I say. "Come on and eat your bologna sandwich. After you eat, you can watch television." They start jumping up and down on the floor. When they finish eating, they go into the front room to watch television.

After they have watched television for an hour, I say, "Winston, go and bring Momma your little red wagon." Winston heads to the bedroom and then brings the wagon back to the front room. "It's nap time," I say. "Winston, turn the television off. I need everyone to go to bed and take a nap. Use the toilet before you get in bed. Joy, put Regina in bed with you. I'm going to the grocery store. All of you, stay in bed until I come back home. Only get out of bed if you smell smoke or if there is a fire. Do not go to the front door, the back door, or the other house to our neighbors." "Yes, Momma," Winston and Joy say in unison. I leave when they all go to sleep.

I take the little red wagon with me as I walk downtown to the grocery store. I buy groceries, put them in the wagon, and then start walking back home. I see Eddie standing outside the repair shop. He sees me and waits until I approach him. "Hello, Ruby. What you got in that red wagon?" he asks. "I got groceries!" I reply. "We're going to have a good meal tonight. No bologna sandwiches tonight!" "That's good. I'll be home as soon as I get off work," Eddie says.

After I part ways with Eddie, I walk on up Main Street and stop in front of the telephone company. I say to myself, "I need to go in there and ask for a telephone. How can I run my business at home if I don't have a telephone?" I park the little red wagon—containing my groceries—outside the telephone company. I walk into the store and sit in the back. I think to myself, "I'm here at a good time. There is only one white man at the clerk's desk and no other white people waiting in the lobby."

I wait my turn to go to the front desk. I look back through the front window and think, "Good! My little red wagon and groceries are still in front of the building." When the white man finishes at the desk, he sits down. Then a clerk asks, "Hey, girl! Do you want something?" I respond, "Yes, I want something." She signals me to come to the front desk. I walk past the white man who has just sit down in the chair.

When I get to the front desk, the white clerk asks, "What do you want?" "I'd like to sign up for a telephone," I explain. "Why do you need a telephone?" the white clerk then asks. "I need a telephone for my home," I reply. "What's your name, girl?" she asks. "My name is Mrs. Ruby Morgan," I say. She looks at me and says, "Sign here. I'll get the telephone. You'll get a bill every month. If you can't pay your monthly bill, we will come to your house and get your telephone."

I start reading the paper the clerk has given me. She notices me looking down at the paper. "Girl, can you write your name?" she asks. "Yes, I can write my name," I answer. "Well, what's taking you so long?" she inquires. "I'm reading this piece of paper before I sign it," I explain. "I just told you what's on that piece of paper!" she retorts. To these words, I respond, "Yes, you did, and you spoke so well about the statements on this piece of paper." She smiles at me; I grin at her. I then sign the sheet of paper and get my telephone.

I leave the front desk with my new telephone. I notice that the white man is no longer sitting in the lobby. I walk out the door, get my little red wagon with our groceries, and walk home.

When I arrive back at home, I find that the children are still sleeping. I put the telephone in my salon room, saying to myself, "Thank goodness Mr. Lacey put a telephone line in this room when he put in the hair sink." I plug the cord into the wall jack and then pick up the telephone from its base. I hear a dial tone coming from the telephone, so I dial Daddy Freeman's telephone number to the barber shop. The telephone rings and then Daddy Freeman answers, saying, "This is Freeman's Barber Shop. May I help you?" "Yes, you may help me, Daddy Freeman," I say. "Be happy for me! I have a telephone in my home!" Daddy Freeman says, "That's good, Ruby.

We're busy here. I'll be by later to see your new house. I'll talk to you later." I hang up after our brief conversation ends.

I then wheel the little red wagon into the kitchen and put away the groceries. "I know I bought two chickens! There's only one here!" I say to myself. "That white man stole one of my chickens! Well, God, if he needs to steal from me, he must need that chicken more than we need it. God help that man!"

I start cooking dinner. I fry a chicken and cook mashed potatoes, green beans, and cornbread. The children smell the chicken frying and soon wake up. When they come into the kitchen, I tell them to go into the front room and watch television, and they do as they are told. As I am finishing up with my cooking, Eddie walks through the door. "Somebody's cooking in this house, and it sure does smell good!" he comments. Eddie then speaks to the children, comes into the kitchen, and kisses me. "Eddie, are you hungry?" I ask. "I'm starving!" he replies. "Well, dinner is ready. "It's time to eat," I say. Then, yelling into the front room, I say, "Children, go in the bathroom and wash your hands so we can eat dinner."

When everyone is seated at the table, Eddie says grace and we eat. After dinner, I give the children a lollipop for being good today. When they finish eating their candy, I say, "Winston and Joy, clean the kitchen." They start pouting, so I say, "Pout all you want to. The longer you pout, the shorter time you'll have to watch television with the family if your attitude does not change. Don't come in the front room until this kitchen is clean!" Winston and Joy work fast so they can watch television with the family. They finally finish and join us in the front room. An hour later, I turn off the television so that the children can get ready for bed. When they are asleep in their beds, Eddie and I go to sleep.

*****

In the morning, Eddie gets up and wakes up Winston. Eddie puts on his watch. At seven in the morning, when they are dressed and ready for the day, they leave the house and start their walk to school. Eddie lets Winston lead the way. When they get to the overhead bridge, Winston stops and sees Daddy Freeman's car coming up the street. Winston waits. Then when Daddy Freeman gets to where Winston is standing, Winston smiles and waves at him. Daddy Freeman blows his horn and keeps on driving.

They cross the street, walk on the overhead bridge, and continue walking to school. When Eddie looks at his watch, he notices that it is 7:45. He says, "Winston, our time is excellent. We made it to school in forty-five minutes. That means you are a few minutes early and you will be at school on time. We'll wait till eight o'clock to start walking back home."

When it is eight o'clock, they start walking back home. They get back home in forty-five minutes and head into the house. "Ruby, Winston did it!" Eddie boasts. "He walked to school in forty-five minutes and walked back home in the same amount of time." "Winston, great job! Eddie, what's next?" I ask. "Tomorrow, Winston will walk with Joy to school. I'll walk behind them and see what they do," Eddie explains. "That's great, Eddie!" I reply. Eddie then gets some leftover chicken from the icebox and heads out to work.

I have three customers scheduled for today. In-between customers, I feed my children breakfast and lunch. I cook dinner when the last customer leaves and have it ready when Eddie comes home. Everything we do in the evening is routine.

*****

The next morning, Winston and Joy practice walking to school. Eddie walks a distance behind them. He notices that when they start walking on the overhead bridge, Joy stops and looks down. "Joy, come on," Winston urges. "We got to get to school." Joy says, "I'm scared."

"Hold my hand. We're going to run across the bridge. I want you to count the number of steps we have to take to get us off the bridge," Winston says, making a game out of it. Eddie sees Winston holding Joy's hand and they start running; he also hears Joy counting while they are running. Then, when they get off the bridge, they stop. Joy turns to Winston and then Eddie hears her say, "Twenty. It takes twenty steps to get off the bridge." They continue to walk, and Eddie continues to follow behind them.

When they arrive at school, Eddie shows up one minute later. "You two are at the school. It took you fifty minutes to get here," Eddie comments. "That's still early for you to make it to school on time. Joy, why were you counting when you were running on the bridge?" "Winston told me to count the number of steps it takes to get us off the bridge," Joy answers. "How many steps did it take?" Eddie asks. Joy says "twenty."

After waiting a few minutes, at eight o'clock, Eddie says, "It's time to walk back home. I'll be following you." Winston and Joy start walking. When they get to the overhead bridge, Winston holds Joy's hand. They run and Joy counts. Then, when they get off the bridge, Joy says, "Twenty. It takes twenty steps to get us off the bridge." When they arrive home, Winston says, "Momma, we're back home. Joy is with me. She's safe."

Eddie walks into the house and says, "Ruby, Winston and Joy did really good. They made it to school and back home in fifty minutes each way." "Winston and Joy, I'm so proud of you. Eddie, do they need to walk again in the morning?" I ask. "Yes, we need to walk one more time," Eddie confirms.

After Eddie eats breakfast, he leaves the house. During the day, I work in my salon and everyone gets their chores done. And when Eddie comes home from work, we go through the same evening routine before going to bed.

*****

The next morning, Winston, Joy, and Eddie walk to school and return home. "Ruby, Winston and Joy will be just fine walking to school and coming back home," Eddie says assuredly. I nod.

Then Eddie looks at the mail on the kitchen table and says, "Someone sent us a telephone book. We don't have a telephone; this must be for our neighbors." "Eddie that telephone book is ours. We have a telephone in the salon room," I inform him. Eddie looks at me and asks, "Ruby, when did this happen?" "Eddie, we need a telephone in this house. I'm pregnant. If you are not here and my water breaks, I need a way to get in touch with you or Daddy Freeman to come and get me and the children. If I can't get either of you, I can call the hospital. The telephone is in the salon so we won't be disturbed at night when we sleep," I explain. Eddie nods and then leaves to go to work.

*****

In September, Winston and Joy start school, and Kathleen and Regina are left at home with me. Every day (as is standard), I let them play and watch television in the front room so I can see them while I'm working. Then, after Winston and Joy come home from school, they do their homework on the kitchen table. When they both finish their homework, Winston gets Kathleen and Regina and takes them to the kitchen.

The children sit at the table. Winston teaches all of them what he has learned in school that day. Then he reviews his homework with everyone. After he is finished, Joy does the same thing. Winston looks over Joy's homework to make sure she has everything right and that everything is completed. Winston doesn't mind looking over her homework, and Joy does all her homework by herself. She always has the correct answer for each question or problem. She brings home all A's on her homework papers and on her test papers.

In turn, Joy looks over Winston's homework. If she sees that Winston has the wrong answer on his homework, she tells him the correct answer. Winston then erases his answer and writes the answer that Joy gives him. And when they are finished with their homework, they put it on my bed. I check their homework before going to bed. It is usually all done and correct, and I feel a sense of pride in my smart children.

*****

One evening in late September, as we are watching television, someone knocks at our front door. "Who is it?" Eddie inquires, having gotten up from the couch to go and investigate. "It's Freeman!" Daddy Freeman responds. Eddie opens the door and lets Daddy Freeman in the house.

The children are so happy to see Daddy Freeman. They run to him and start jumping up and down around him. "Hello, Daddy Freeman. Come on in and sit beside me," I say, greeting him. "I'm too pregnant to get up and greet you, but I'm glad you're here. You've finally come to see us."

"Yes, it took me a while to get over here," he replies. "I wanted to make sure you had settled down in your new house. Before I sit down, I want Eddie and the children to show me around the house." After Eddie and the kids give him a tour of our house, Daddy Freeman comes and sits beside me. We hug each other; Eddie then sits down on the chair across from the couch.

"Daddy Freeman, thank you for this furniture," I say graciously. "See, we are taking very good care of everything you gave us." "You are welcome," Daddy Freeman responds. "Everything in this house is so beautiful. You have a beautiful home. I see how you turned the bedroom into your own salon. That's a good business room. Your customers will enjoy coming here to your house."

"Can I get you something to eat or drink?" Eddie offers Daddy Freeman, who answers, "No, I'm fine." I chime in, saying, "Children, tell Daddy Freeman 'good night' and get ready for bed." They do as I say, leaving us alone with Daddy Freeman.

"Ruby, you look like you're going to have that baby any day now," he says, observing my state. "Yes, I do!" I respond with a laugh. "This pregnancy is different than the others. I haven't had any sickness with this child. It's funny! I think this one is going to come out singing! Every time I sing or play music on the radio, its feet kick my belly on the exact beats of the music. It's like the child is singing or dancing to the music. I should be in pain when the baby kicks me, but all I want to do is laugh, sing, or listen more to the music on the radio. When I stop singing or the music stops, the baby stops kicking me."

"Well, maybe that means this baby is going to be a musical genius," Daddy Freeman says. We laugh. "Eddie," Daddy Freeman continues, "a few days ago, I bought a new car because I just wanted to. I have an old one that's paid for and this new car I just bought. The old one is in good condition. I can't drive two cars. I know you can drive, and that you have a license to drive a car. Do you want my old car?"

Eddie is surprised to hear this. He looks at me, then looks back at Daddy Freeman and says, "Yes! I mean, I don't mind walking, but we can use a car. I can drive Ruby to the grocery store in the car instead of me having to go back and forth to buy groceries. Ruby is so pregnant that she can't walk to the grocery store with Winston's little red wagon. We can take the children riding and visit you and Drum Mom. Most of all, I'll be the one to drive my wife to the hospital to have this baby! What do you say, Ruby?" "Eddie, you've already said it all," I reply.

"Mr. Freeman, I'll pay you for the car," Eddie offers. "Eddie, did you hear me?" Daddy Freeman promptly interjects. "I asked, do you *want* the car, not do you want to *buy* the car. You said yes, so, I am going to give you the car. Can we agree on this matter?"

"Yes, we can agree. We thank you wholeheartedly," Eddie replies. "Here are the keys to your new car! I don't want to walk home; I need you to drive me home," Daddy Freeman explains. "Yes, sir. Ruby, I'll be right back," Eddie says.

I hug Daddy Freeman, saying, "Thank you so much for this blessing! You are so good to me and my family. Thank you!" After receiving our thanks, Daddy Freeman leaves the house, with Eddie in tow. I sit down on the couch, hear the car start, and listen to the engine as Eddie drives off with Daddy Freeman. I start crying, thinking about how blessed I am to have Daddy Freeman in my life.

Soon, Eddie returns home in our new car. After he comes into the house, I watch him pace back and forth, thanking God for all He has done and all He will do. Eddie starts to cry silently to himself. When I see him so full of emotion, I start crying again.

*****

Early on Wednesday morning, October 7, 1959, my water breaks. I rouse Eddie from his sleep, saying, "Eddie, wake the children up! Tell Winston and Joy to get Kathleen and Regina and go get in the car. Bring the suitcase from their room and take it to the car. It has their clothes in it. I'm having the baby!" Eddie wakes up the children, then they all rush to get into the car. When Eddie starts up the car, Winston says, "Daddy, where's Momma?"

Eddie turns the car off and runs back into the house. He helps me get out of the bed. "Wait a minute, Eddie!" I say, putting a halt to his urgency. "Get that radio off the table and put it in my suitcase." He proceeds to get the radio, put it in the suitcase, and walk me to the car.

Once everyone is situated in the car, Eddie starts driving to the hospital. "Eddie, don't go to the hospital!" I insist. "Turn around and take the children to Drum Mom's house. Knock on her door and tell her I'm having the baby!" Eddie turns the car around really fast. "Eddie, what are you trying to do to us? Kill us!" I exclaim. "You don't have to drive so fast. I believe we have some time before this baby comes."

Eddie continues to drive until we arrive at Drum Mom's house. He gets out of the car, walks up the steps of the porch over to the door, and starts knocking on it. I look at the children and softly say, "Your daddy left you all in the car. Winston and Joy, get everybody out and go stay with Drum Mom. You all know what to do at Drum Mom's house."

Eddie persistently knocks on the door and yells for Drum Mom to wake up and come to the door. Daddy Freeman hears the noise, wakes up, and rushes over to the house. When Daddy Freeman spots the children trying to get out of the car, he runs to the car and helps them. He then sees me in the front seat and asks, "Ruby, is it time?" "Yes, Daddy Freeman, it's time," I respond.

Drum Mom finally comes to the door, wearing a robe and a hair scarf on her head. When Daddy Freeman sees her, he starts laughing. "Daddy Freeman, what are you laughing at?" Winston asks. "I just remembered something. That's all," he comments.

"Freeman, bring those children here in the house!" Drum Mom retorts snappily. Upon her words, Daddy Freeman ushers the children into the house. When Eddie runs back to the car, Daddy Freeman yells, "Eddie, slow down! It's all right! Ruby's all right!" Eddie hops into the car, starts up the engine, and proceeds to drive at regular speed. And once the children are situated in the house, they go to bed. "If any one of us hears anything, make sure the other one knows what you hear," Daddy Freeman says to Drum Mom as he heads out the door and walks back home.

After Eddie and I arrive at the hospital, we head to the Negro side of the emergency room. When a bed becomes available and I am in it, Old Doc Jones comes by and examines me. "Ruby, this baby is coming, but not right now," he informs me. "You have some time before you'll deliver this one. Your husband can stay in the room with you. They'll call me when you're ready."

"Doc Jones, may I play my radio in here?" I ask. "Yes, that'll be fine, as long as you keep the volume low," he responds. He then leaves my bedside. "Eddie, get the radio out of the suitcase and turn the music on. I don't want to wait all day to have our baby. The baby will hear the music and want to come out of me," I explain.

Eddie pulls the radio out of my suitcase and turns the knob to a Christian music station. I'm not hurting, so I start singing the songs as they play on the radio. "Ruby, you're singing. Aren't you in pain?" Eddie asks. "No, I'm not in pain. I just feel like singing!" I exclaim.

Suddenly, as I sing, the baby starts kicking in my belly. The kicks are in rhythm with the beats of the Christian music. About an hour later, the baby's rhythmic kicks get stronger. "Go tell the nurse to get Doc Jones. My baby is getting ready to come out," I say.

Eddie soon comes back with Old Doc Jones. "Ruby, you are not ready to deliver that baby," Doc Jones says. "Doc Jones, yes, I am. Examine me! My baby is ready to come into this world," I say with insistence.

When Old Doc Jones examines me, he says, "You *are* ready to deliver this baby! Nurse, get Ruby to the delivery room, right now!" Old Doc Jones leaves in a hurry, and the nurses come running into the room. Eddie kisses me and holds my hand until we get to the door of the delivery room for Negroes. "Ruby, I love you. Everything is going to be fine," Eddie professes. "Eddie, go to the Negroes' waiting room and the doctor will talk to you later," the nurses say, instructing him. They push me through the door—leaving Eddie standing there—and wheel me to the room to prepare me for my delivery.

Old Doc Jones comes into the delivery room. "Ruby, you are wide awake," he comments. "Yes, I am, and I am ready to have my baby," I reply. "Okay, let me tell you when I'm ready," he says.

He moves to the foot of the bed, waits for about a minute, and then says, "Ruby, I'm ready. Push hard." I give one hard push. "That push was great!" Old Doc Jones says, encouraging me. "The head and shoulders came out with that push. Ruby, push one more time." When I push, the rest of the baby's body slides out.

"Wow, I've never seen anything like this," Old Doc Jones says in awe. "Ruby, your baby is here. You have another girl. This child is just a kicking and moving her fingers everywhere. The nurse will get her cleaned up and bring her to you later. How do you feel?" "I feel fine," I reply. Old Doc Jones says, "I'll go and give the news to your husband. He can see you and the baby in the basement."

The nurses proceed to clean me up and then take me to my room in the basement. I am the only patient in the room. I get up off the delivery bed and walk and get into my hospital bed. I don't feel tired; I'm not hurting, and I am ready to get my baby and go home. Carrying this baby was easy, and having this baby was easy. I think to myself, "This child is going to be special. She likes music! She hears the music and moves to the beat of the music. Look at me! I'm starting to think and talk like Drum Mom and Daddy Freeman. I really have no clue who she will be or what she will do."

When Eddie walks into the room, we talk and wait to see our baby girl. The conditions in the hospital are the same as when I gave birth to Joy. And now, here I am with my fifth child; the circumstances in the hospital are the same, only having changed in the last two years since Regina was born. Nowadays, white women don't want Negro women breastfeeding their white babies. "Eddie, this girl and Regina will be close sisters, because they have both come into a world that is changing for the Negros," I say.

The nurse brings our baby girl into the room and gives her to me. The nurse then turns around and leaves, and Eddie and I look at the baby. "She is so beautiful! I can't tell who she looks like," Eddie comments. I look at her and agree that she is beautiful. She has all her body parts; she smiles a lot; she doesn't look like my other children. "Oh, no! She looks white! I don't want to think about her color anymore! I just want to hold my special baby," I think to myself.

"Eddie, look at her again," I request. "She looks like my momma and me. Look at her hands; her hands are younger, but they look like my hands. She smiles like me. She likes the same music I like." "I didn't know your momma, but you're right, Ruby. Now that you say so, she does look a little bit like you," Eddie says in agreement.

After we observe our new daughter, Eddie stays with the baby and me for a while and then leaves before nighttime arrives. He drives to Drum Mom's house and sees Daddy Freeman talking to the children. "Ruby is walking and doing fine. We have a baby girl!" Eddie announces to everyone in the house.

After hearing this news, Winston stands up from the floor, puts his hands on his head, and says, "Another girl! I guess I'll always be the only boy in this family. Why are you and Momma doing this to me?"

"Nobody here is doing anything to you. It's the Lord's doing," Drum Mom notes. "Now, do you want to question what the Lord does?" "Not at all, Drum Mom," Winston responds. "I'll pick up the children when Ruby comes home," Eddie says. "Okay, we're doing fine," Drum Mom assures. "Just take care of Ruby and the baby girl. Eddie, does she have a name?" "Not yet," Eddie answers.

The next day after work, Eddie comes to the hospital. The baby is with me when he comes into the room. "The other children and your Drum Mom are fine. How are you and the baby doing?" Eddie asks. "We are doing fine," I respond. "What did Winston say when you told him he has another sister?"

"He was fine with it," Eddie replies. "He's used to having a bunch of girls in the family." "Eddie, I'm ready to go home, but they won't let me leave the hospital," I complain. "Ruby, the doctor and nurses know what they're doing. Do as they say. We need to give this girl a name," Eddie comments.

"Eddie, her name is Ruth Morgan," I say. "Ruth is a Bible name. She is going to be a loving child who will never leave the one she loves. Wherever we go, she will go. Our God will be her God!" "I like the name Ruth! Let me hold my Ruth," Eddie says with authority.

*****

After seven days, Eddie comes to pick up Ruth and me, and we leave the hospital and go home. When we arrive at home, Ruth and I get comfortable in bed, and I start to reflect on the fact that Ruth is my first child who will have totally grown up in our own home.

After Ruth and I get settled in bed, Eddie leaves—and soon he brings the children and Drum Mom back to the house. The children come to my bedroom and look at their new sister. I tell them that their new sister's name is Ruth. After Drum Mom checks out the house, she finally comes to my bedroom. "How are you doing, Ruby?" she asks. "Drum Mom, I am just fine. Thank you for keeping the children. Here is Ruth. Sit down so you can hold her," I say.

Drum Mom sits down on the bed and holds Ruth. "Ruth is a beautiful name," she comments. "She's beautiful, like all your children. I can't tell who she looks like in the family."

I laugh at Drum Mom's words, saying, "She looks like me!" "Yes, I can see that now," Drum Mom says reservedly. She then looks up and stares at me. "I cooked and brought plenty of food for everybody to eat. Will you need anything else?" she asks. "No, cooked food is good. Thank you," I reply. "Winston and Joy will help around the house. Joy will be quite helpful; she'll try to take care of me and Ruth, so I can get back on my feet. Somehow, Joy knows what needs to be done around here and she makes it happen."

"If you don't need nothing else," Drum Mom begins, "I'm going to tell Eddie to take me back home." "Okay. Eddie will keep checking on you for me," I relay. Drum Mom nods her head and leaves with Eddie.

*****

In four weeks, I am back on my feet and working in my salon. I now have more customers coming to my home to get their hair done. I stay on the grind, stopping my work only when Ruth needs to be fed or I need to cook dinner. And though I'm making more money than when I first started working from home, I'm not making as much as I did when I worked at Miss Johnson's beauty salon.

*****

Toward the end of 1960, I get pregnant again. Then on Tuesday, May 23, 1961, it takes me seven hours to deliver another baby girl. (I now have one son and five girls.) This delivery is hard on my body. "Ruby, you should let this girl be your last child," Old Doc Jones suggests. "I don't think your body can handle any more children."

Eddie and I name our new daughter Joan Morgan. She is beautiful and charming—with a gorgeous smile—and she is aware of everything around her. She looks smart; she also looks exactly like Eddie's mother.

*****

Shortly after Joan comes into the world, Kathleen starts the first grade. She is five years old and will be six in December; Winston is eleven; Joy will be nine in November; Regina is four; and Ruth is one going on two.

Our home is now full of children. Winston sleeps in the front room on the black leather, pull-out couch. And all the girls sleep in the same room. "We have too many people living in this small house. We need to try and find a larger house," Eddie comments. "Eddie, we don't need to find a house—we need to *buy* a house!" I say with gusto. We know what we must do.

Since deciding on purchasing our own home, Eddie and I work hard and save our money to buy a house. When we find a nice lot, we truly believe that we can build a house on this lot. We get our thoughts together and go and talk to Drum Mom and Daddy Freeman about our dream.

When we have that discussion with them, Daddy Freeman tells us exactly what we must do to own a home. Eddie and I then decide to work together to devise a plan based on Daddy Freeman's advice.

Amid our discussion, Drum Mom seems excited about our plans. But, she keeps glancing over at me. Finally, she asks, "Ruby, are you pregnant?"

*****

I am suddenly awakened out of my vivid recollections of my mother's story at what had been and would be one of many pivotal junctures in her life. I come to my senses enough to realize that I am in the midst of the homegoing of our loved one. As the service gets under way, I can't help but think that in my memories of her life story, there is so much of it that had yet to unfold.

CPSIA information can be obtained
at www.ICGtesting.com
Printed in the USA
LVHW04s2328150618
580542LV00010B/39/P